I0736967

This is dedicated to everyone who dreamed of marrying a charming and powerful fae prince.

While secretly hoping he'd rail you against a bathroom wall until you screamed his name.

On repeat.

CONTENT WARNING

This is a dark paranormal romance and contains some darker themes, including graphic sex, some violence, and the kidnapping of a child (no death). If you'd like any further details, please email me at jaymineve@gmail.com

STAY UP TO DATE

The best way to stay up to date with the Shadow Beast Shifters world and all new releases, is to join my Facebook group here:
www.facebook.com/groups/jayminevenerdherd
We share lots of book releases, fun posts, sexy dudes, and generally it's a happy place to exist.

CHAPTER ONE

SAMANTHA

It was cruel that the sun shone brightly today, when everything would change for me.

Today, when there were no more obstacles to block the dark path my future was treading along.

"Are you ready?" the female shifter who had been tending to my dress and veil asked.

I didn't know her name. She was new, with bright orange hair. This color was unusual in shifters, but Clarity's alpha, Lorenze Patche, had been collecting *any and all* shifters who reminded him of Mera and adding them to the pack.

His obsession with the woman who managed to snag the Shadow Beast was at its peak, but if he'd spent any real time with Mera, he'd have known all these new recruits were pale shadows—*ironically*—of the shifter who was one of my true friends.

Or maybe former friend, since I'd fucked up in a way that possibly couldn't be undone.

"No, I'm not fucking ready," I finally said, and my attendant jerked away. Her brown eyes widened enough that my reflection was briefly seen. *White.* I was dressed in a sleek white dress, off the shoulder and fitted all the way to my heel-clad feet. My dark hair was pulled up, the red undertones standing out against the white veil.

Just as the alpha wanted.

Bastard.

Today I would mate his youngest son, the alpha in waiting: Grant.

Grant was a pathetic beast, but it was hard to hate someone who was just a puppet, living under the control of his father and older brother for most of his life. When the oldest Patche offspring died a few years ago, Grant was suddenly in line for alpha, about to be mated to a complete stranger.

He overcompensated these days, acting all extra-asshole, but he was a damn boy. He was twenty-two years old to my thirty. Our mating was wrong on so many levels, not the least was the fact that his brother had been my true mate, and Alpha Lorenze was trying to replicate something that could no longer be.

Fuck, I wanted to destroy that bastard, but he held the last precious thing in my world, and I couldn't lose her too.

"Is there anything I can do to help your nerves?" the female asked, misinterpreting my *No, I'm not ready* from before.

"I just need some time alone," I murmured, refusing to look her way again.

She left in a hurry, and I remained in the small white tent that had been erected for the ceremony. The mating was to be held in the forests off to the side of one section of mountain, on this perfect summer day. If I'd been truly mating a shifter I loved, it would be one of the happiest days of my life.

Instead, I was a prisoner.

And my time for a miracle had run out.

CHAPTER TWO

LEN

The trumpets rarely sounded in Faerie, and when they did, it usually meant some cataclysmic event was on the horizon. I spent only half my time on my world of birth these days, and I wished that today I'd chosen to visit the Library of Knowledge and my family there.

However, I was due to see my mother, so I'd made the journey back to Faerie earlier than expected. Just in time for the trumpets.

"I thought I'd find you here."

Her voice was soft and melodic, and a history spanning over a thousand years flashed before my eyes. My mother had a way about her, that was for sure.

Turning from the weeping wanderer plant, I smiled as Glendriel, queen of the Silver Lands, entered my garden. One of the few who had permission to move beyond the gates, she appeared as if by magic, her long dress sparkling in the bright lights that shone down from the crystals above. Her hair glistened just as brightly, silver and sweeping near her ankles.

"Mother," I said softly, falling into the less formal greeting. I might be centuries old, but my mother was my leader and elder, and she would always have my love and respect. "What are you doing here? I was on my way to the Silver Lands. I just needed to check in on my—"

"Children?" she interrupted with a lilting laugh. "I'm a plant grandmama and I'm not even upset about it."

Her energy flowed with her words, power slapping against my skin. Those who were not used to being around her often reacted to her mere presence, but it was comforting to me. My father was taken from us when I was much younger, and since then the two of us had maintained the strength of the Silver Lands. Our royal house had been claimed in battle, and since then we had held on to it through blood and power.

We would not let it fall. Not while there was still life in our veins.

"Are you here because of the trumpets?" I asked, giving the wanderer plant one last pat. It stole some of my energy, but I didn't reprimand it. All of my plants held a little piece of my power; it was what bonded us. Thankfully, I had plenty of power to share.

"The trumpets are one part," she said with a graceful shrug, "but the larger is the need to see my favorite son." I was her only child, which in no way belittled those words.

I wasn't surprised that she'd known the trumpets would sound before they actually did. My mother was one of the most powerful Fae still alive. For this, the Silver Lands were respected and feared. Despite the losses, there were many blessings too.

"How do you want to travel to the Capital?" I asked her. She held out a hand, and a chuckle escaped me. "Of course, would there be any other way except to go in style?"

The queen smiled before her happiness faded a touch. The silver in her eyes grew brighter, as if she were channeling more power. "Unfortunately, on this day we must make haste. There's an urgency in the call, and I am worried that missing the meeting would be a grave mistake."

Some of my mirth dried up. Very little in this world—or any of the worlds—scared my mother. And she wasn't scared today either, but there was concern in her ancient eyes. Which in and of itself concerned me.

"Let's go, then," I said, taking the hand she still held before me.

The beam of light she called from the gems that littered the sky of Faerie was bright enough to blind any who looked upon the glow for too long. Used to this mode of transportation, I closed my eyes as she swept us away.

Our trip to the Capital took only a few minutes, the energy in those sacred silver gems powerful enough that, if necessary, they could move worlds. When the tingles across my skin faded and my mother released me, I opened my eyes to find that we were in the center of the Capital, right before Parliament House, where all the royal leaders converged to make decisions that impacted Faerie as a whole.

This world was made up of moving lands, moving houses, and magical rock masses. There were only a few solid and stable sections of territory, and the Capital was one of them. Massive, spanning for thousands of miles in all directions, it was made from a chunk of quartz, with minimal magical properties, outside of its many *cords* that anchored it to whatever made up the center of Faerie. It was what we referred to as *the Deep,* an area that no fae could enter and survive. At least none still walking this world, so we only had myth and legend to guide us as to what lay below.

The Great Queen had been the last to travel along the cords, and only she knew what was in the Deep, but her line was long gone, vanished just before my time, and for some reason even those older than me could not remember anything about her.

A spell or power did not want the Great Queen found, and for that Faerie was weakened.

Mother moved first toward the Parliament House, a large domed building, littered with a multitude of crystals across the highest points. The energy gathered from these crystals powered the building itself, which was a hive of activity today.

Most of the time only a few generals and some princes and princesses used it for research and training purposes. But during the trumpets, which were still blaring across the land, all the VIPs showed up. Fae scurried across the vast expanse of white tiles surrounding the main structures, some moving toward their leaders while others entered the building.

"Come, let's enter," my mother said, snapping into her role as queen. A beam of purple *reven crystals* appeared across her forehead, forming a crown. I could make the same crown appear, via a small, embedded crystal near my temple. The reven stone powered our energy and identified our houses to those who passed. "Are the generals and council inside?" I asked.

"Almost there," she said quickly. "I need to secure our zone before they arrive though."

It's our duty to ensure the safety of our fae. Her most repeated life lessons as a royal, and a truth set in stone: *If you are in my inner circle, I will protect you with all I have.*

There weren't many who called that circle home, but

enough that I was on alert for threats in the Solaris System, the Library of Knowledge, and strangely enough, Earth.

The pull I felt toward a planet with inhabitants that were infantile compared to Faerie was... odd. But it was there nonetheless, and maybe one day soon I'd have time to explore the pull further.

Mother was halfway across the white tiles, so I picked up my pace to stay with her. The massive doors at the front were the first line of defense against unauthorized entry. Two purple beams, originating from four-foot reven gems attached to the side of the doors, scanned every fae who stepped up. The barrier parted only when identity was confirmed.

When it was our turn, there was a brief flash, a small tug at my power, and then we were welcomed inside. Easy as always for those from the Silver Lands, helped in part by the fact that the security stones were gifted from our kingdom by the king before Glendriel. A truth that pissed off many of the other royal houses over the years, but no one had large enough gems of power to switch out the revens, so our jewels remained.

On the inside, Parliament House's front foyer was less busy. The open space was sparsely decorated with gem mats, charged from the panes of glass above that allowed the jewels in the sky to shine down. This was where fae could rest and recoup their energy.

We didn't linger in the foyer, even as I nodded to a few friends and acquaintances. In my many years as a prince of the Silver Lands, I knew all the other royals and fae of importance. We were near eternal and did not have offspring easily. These days, it seemed we could only reproduce after a loss. Mother often wondered if it was the fate of my father that allowed them to conceive and birth a child before he was killed.

Mysteries of life we'd never know.

Through the foyer, we entered the first of the massive

stadium-style courtrooms. The center stage was circular, and surrounding it was the ten sections for each royal family. Once, many millennia ago, the Great Queen resided in the center stage, but now it was for the reigning monarchs. Mother would sit here, and I'd take my place in the front row of the Silver Lands.

But first she spent her time perusing the area to discern any magical attacks. This was done using *gafal* gems—small ocher pieces that crumbled away in her hands as she sprinkled them about. If anything untoward was in the area, it would flash bright red. She also used her energy, and I did the same, sending it out from my body to sweep along the courtroom.

Nothing negative was detected. The room was clean and sterile, the rows of black padded chairs showing no sign of wear or dirt.

"We're secure," Mother said with a nod. She turned as someone called out, "Queen Glendriel."

It was King Nathaniel of the *Golden Greats*, a collection of four hundred moving lands which sat to the east of Silver Lands.

"Do you know why the trumpets were sounded?" he asked as he hurried forward, his second in line behind him. Jonah was not his child—the king had no offspring—but was a trusted family friend.

Mother shook her head. "I was informed that there would be a call, but so far we're in the dark about the reason behind this."

Before Nathaniel could say anything else, Mother turned to me. "Can you ensure the safety of those arriving, Len?"

"Of course," I said with a nod. Nathaniel was an ally, so there was no risk to leaving Mother with him.

As I strode from the room, my power hummed inside my veins, so much stronger when I spent extended time in Faerie.

Everything was exactly as I wanted, my life moving along a path that I could not be unhappy about, with the only dark mark to my existence a lack of mate.

For decades, my walks had not led to any sign of a true mate, and I was at the end of my hope.

The next was my last chance, then I would settle into an eternity alone.

Duty first, even if it broke a piece of my soul that belonged to another.

Such was life.

CHAPTER THREE

LEN

Outside, more fae had arrived. The crowds were gathering thick and fast, and I was surprised to see even the most reticent of royal houses had many members arriving around the front entrance.

Those from the Metallic Meadows usually never bothered to show up for meetings, even when the trumpets sounded. They were the scoundrels of our kind, the renegades who lived outside of the few very basic rules that governed Faerie and the magic here. It was rumored they were the ones to drive the Great Queen from Faerie.

Drive... or destroy. I'd heard both stories, and having met their "leader" I was going with the latter. King Fredrick had been a royal prince of another long-fallen line of Faerie, the last of his kind who'd rallied all those unhappy in their own royal houses to rebel and live free. Which would have been all well and good if they didn't decide to take out the other royal families in this bid for freedom.

The war had been huge, resulting in possibly the greatest loss of fae in our history, and despite it having ended almost a thousand years ago, no one here had forgotten. Hence why those from Metallic Meadows were rarely welcomed at events. Fredrick might technically be a prince with a seat on the council, but that didn't offer him acceptance.

"Len," Fredrick said as he crossed nearby, his near seven-foot frame giving him a height advantage over almost everyone. He was a giant for the fae, and I'd long wondered if there was some ogre or another demi-fae in his lineage.

"Fredrick," I returned. "Didn't expect to see you here."

His slow smile had me palming the stones lining the sides of my jacket. My movement was subtle enough that he shouldn't notice, but it would give me the split-second power advantage if I needed it.

"Wouldn't have missed this particular meeting for anything in the multi-worlds," he replied in his smooth tones. Bastard's presence was fucking unsettling. I always felt like I needed a shower after standing near him.

"What do you know about this calling?" I pushed, since he clearly knew more than he was letting on.

That fucking smile grew. "Just that it will change everything."

Before I could ask anything else, or punch his smug face, he waved to the rest of the Metallic Meadows council and they were off. None of them spoke or made eye contact as they hurried past. For a "free" royal house, there was very little evidence of it.

Fredrick had grown too accustomed to his power. If you couldn't handle it, power in its absolute would corrupt absolutely.

Once the Metallic Meadows were inside, I focused on finding everyone from the Silver Lands. At this point they were scattered about, so I sent out a small pulse of power to call them over. As they crossed toward me, I scanned the area for dangers, but it appeared that almost everyone here was focused on finding their royal lines.

That, and discussing the reasons for the trumpets, which were finally dying off in the land of Faerie. Fredrick, piece of shit that he was, knew what this was about.

Unease settled in my chest, and not because I was afraid of him. In a one-on-one fight I'd destroy him, but he never played by the rules. Clearly, he had some grand plan if he'd initiated a worldwide call. I'd just have to remain on high alert; awareness was half the battle.

"Prince Len."

The call distracted me as I turned to our third-in-command. General Terese was a statuesque female with shoulder-length blond hair, bright blue eyes, and a smartass mouth. She had a mind for battle, and often beat me at strategy games. My mother had long wanted a romantic match between the two of us, but there was nothing but respect and friendship there. Maybe after my last walk I'd feel differently.

"Terese," I said with a smile, relaxing. *Just a touch.* The first time my brothers—Shadow, Reece, Alistair, Galleli, and Lucien—visited me in Faerie, they were shocked by the formal way I carried myself. It was why when I was off this world, I gave into my deeper nature to joke and relax. The duality of my personality felt almost natural now, as I effortlessly fell into whatever one worked for the situation. Both were my true self, and both were comfortable.

"Do we know why the trumpets sounded?" Terese asked as other members of our court gathered with us.

I shook my head. "No word yet, but there was a disturbing

comment from Fredrick, so as always, let's remain on high alert." Turning my gaze across the three dozen silver members gathered, I raised my voice. "Are you all wearing the full range of gems?"

The council didn't always fight, since we had an army as well, but Mother insisted everyone learn the basics of combat and using our gems as weapons. Training I completely agreed with.

"Aye," they all called.

I wasn't surprised. I'd trained with most of them and would trust them at my back in battle.

We made our way to join the lines entering Parliament House, and once inside, we wasted no time moving straight to the courtroom. It was no longer empty, with many of the ten royal lines having filled their seats.

The *Golden Greats*, under King Nathaniel, were all seated. King Fredrick was on stage now too, while the rest of his house sat without expression in their section for *Metallic Meadows*. Beside the Metallic Meadows were the members of *Copper Straits*, also formed in the eastern lands of Faerie where minerals and crystals were prevalent. Their queen, Gemma, was seated next to Mother, the pair in a lively discussion. They were old friends and allies.

Next to Copper Straits sat the *Mist Dwellers*, who existed on vast cloud-like structures that ferried them about. Their queen was Hatina, and she was dressed in her usual white attire, with her red hair the only pop of color. She was in conversation with King Julien of the Ranges, a series of weather-beaten territories to the west.

The last four territories were: Zone of Darkness, with King Fernando, a land of very little light and inhabitants with cat-like appearance and senses; the Coral Cove, with beaches that rivaled the most amazing ones created by Angel in the

Honor Meadows, led by Queen Wenda; the Great Wilds, which was the area most of my garden florae had been procured from, with Queen Sabatha, who was another of Mother's best friends; and finally Ochre Sands, with a Desert Lands' vibe, led by the eccentric King Petre. He was not on the stage yet, but I could see him conversing with members of his council.

As the last of the fae entered and the courtroom doors were sealed, the final bellow of the trumpets faded and it was time to get to business. Unease settled in my chest, deepening from what Fredrick had initiated earlier. Faerie had been going through some turmoil lately, small squabbles between royal lines, and it felt like a simmering of energy was coating all of us.

A simmering filled with negative intentions, which to my best knowledge, always preceded a larger scale battle. Maybe even a war.

When I took my seat in the front row, Mother pulled her attention from Gemma and Sabatha long enough to give me an approving nod. After losing my father at such a young age, I appreciated the relationship I had with her—she was one of the few beings in this world that I would die for in an instant. Even if such a concept pissed her off to no end.

Parents should never bury their children, Len, she'd tell me on the regular, and while I agreed, it wouldn't change my actions should my time come to make that sacrifice.

A blanket of power coated the room as the energy of the courtroom settled. The ten royals stood in a curved line around the circular stage, and those of us in the seats shifted forward on high alert. Only the ones who initiated the trumpets knew what this meeting was about, so there was a sense of anticipation in the air as we all waited for the announcement.

A deep rumble of magic preceded the blast across the room. *King Petre of the Ochre Sands calls for an abolishment of the*

Great Queen's line, and a new supreme ruler to be chosen from among the ten royal houses.

There was a moment of silence as this announcement sank in, and then one by one all the kings and queen sat, except Petre and Fredrick.

"I stand as the second to his decree," Fredrick said with his trademark fucking smirk. I'd bet my left nut that he was the one who'd set this shit in motion, but knowing how little he was respected, had opted to act as a "second."

"It has been over a thousand years since the last sighting of the Great Line," Petre added, more somber than Fredrick as he turned to address all ten houses. "We're weakening without someone to enter the Deep and touch the origin of Faerie energy. If we don't act now, we'll cease to exist in the next few thousand years."

Part of what he said was true, but the consequences of severing the Great Line was completely unknown. Logic said that maybe it was only this remaining connection to the Great Queen that kept Faerie functioning at all, and that by destroying what remained, we too would be destroyed.

"We will cast a vote to decide if the Great Leader is to be replaced," Fredrick boomed again. "And if so, we propose a leadership trial to determine which line will step up and receive the ultimate power."

As if it were that easy.

One didn't just win a trial and turn into the sort of fae able to enter the Deep.

These two assholes were proposing to mess with magic that none of us understood, and I had to hope that reason would prevail among the other houses, or we'd all be doomed.

CHAPTER FOUR

SAMANTHA

Alpha Lorenze's energy filled the room a beat before he entered himself. He was here to escort me down the path, and while I knew this was my duty, I didn't move.

I'd been mentally preparing myself over the last few years, pushing away friends and shutting my emotions down, all so I could deal with this fucking moment. And yet... my feet wouldn't move. Instead, I was overwhelmed with an urge to kill the alpha. Unfortunately, he was the only being with information I needed, so I could do nothing.

I'd spent a lot of time over the past year beating myself up for not talking with Mera.

Maybe she would have been able to help, but I didn't trust the Shadow Beast not to just decide this was too big of a problem before wiping us from existence.

I didn't trust male shifters period, and he was the fucking god of them.

"You better be making your peace with your life," Alpha Lorenze spat from behind me. Clarity's alpha was always growling, spitting, or rumbling. The stupid asshole never just spoke in a normal tone. Trying *too* hard to sound alpha was the weakest move of all.

"There's no peace," I murmured, giving my reflection one last look before turning to face him. "But I will not back out. You know that. You've kept me dangling here until your son was of age to be mated after his first shift. I know what my duty is, but once it's done and you have your heir, you better keep your side of the bargain or I'll rip your fucking head off and dance in the blood."

My words were smooth, matter-of-factly. The alpha knew how I felt about him, so he didn't even blink at the threat. It wasn't the first I'd made toward him and wouldn't be the last.

"First pup you produce, then you can have the mongrel. That's the terms of our agreement. I want a powerful heir, and you're the best chance for that."

I shook my head with a sad sigh. "I was his brother's mate, not his. I had to exist here watching him start a life with another while you refused to let me leave. What makes you think it'll work any better with Grant—?"

His slap rocked my head back. My wolf roared up in my chest, snarling and raging to tear through this bastard, but somehow I managed to hold on to her before she forced our shift and destroyed the white dress.

"I waited for my fucking son to pull his head out of his ass," Lorenze snarled. "I even released you from the pack in the hopes he would see what he was missing, and when he didn't I killed him." He had, the psychopath. "Grant is the same blood.

The same. So the same mate will work. Now get your ass out there, and don't forget to smile."

My lips parted as the corners curved up, and he blinked. No doubt it wasn't a nice smile, and he appeared a touch nervous as he backed away. I had no idea what he'd just seen in my face, but my eyes were burning as fury pulsed within me. The skin on my cheeks and neck was on fire, partly from the slap and partly from my wolf pushing forward.

I stepped from the tent onto the red carpet that lined the path toward where the pack had gathered. I could see them all below, and the rest of the scene was nothing short of magical—no expense had been spared for the alpha to be. The backdrop was lined in flowers and candles, lighting up the shadows cast by the forest, and to an outsider it would be the perfect romantic setting for a wedding. For me, it was akin to walking to the gallows.

No friendly faces turned my way. The pack used to think I was staying to keep them safe, since initially I'd negotiated their safety when I'd negotiated for everything else, but that had changed when the alpha's insanity grew. I'd had to focus all of my attention in one area, which meant the pack went back to being the punching bag of an insane alpha.

If I could have saved them, I would have, but there was a being more vulnerable than all of them who needed me more.

Grant waited at the end of the red carpet alone. This might be a weird mashup of a human and shifter mating ceremonies, but they'd drawn the line at bridesmaids and groomsmen. Probably because I had no friends to fill those positions.

Two beautiful, laughing faces crossed my mind; my heart ached for Mera and Simone. We could have been true friends; I knew that as certainly as I knew that this was the worst day of my life. But, again, I couldn't dwell on what might have been. I had to focus on what I could control now, and now... it was time to get mated.

Grant didn't look any happier than me as I closed the distance between us. I was thankful my legs didn't tremble as I stopped beside him, and we both faced Alpha Lorenze. There wasn't a noise from the crowd behind, and it appeared that even the wildlife was in hiding, because the clearing was deadly silent until...

"We are gathered here today..." the alpha boomed—I swear this megalomaniac bastard wanted to be human with the ways he was emulating their ceremonies today. "...to celebrate the strong mating of my son, future-alpha of Clarity pack, Grant Patche, with his true mate, Samantha."

The lies spilled so effortlessly from his lips.

My wolf raged at the falsehood of this bond, but I had her locked down hard enough that all she could do was cut her claws into the palms of my hands hanging uselessly at my side. I welcomed the pain so I could feel something other than sorrow. A quick glance down told me that the sides of my dress were spattered with red. It felt fitting that the purity of the white was already tainted. Just like this mate bond.

The alpha continued for a few minutes, speaking in raised roars about the strength of this pack, the alpha in this bloodline, and the brilliance of his future offspring.

"The Shadow Beast will cower before us on the day the next generation is born. We will command him," he finished with a growl. His son and the rest of the pack howled, while I remained silent.

Command the Shadow Beast. He truly had lost all rational thought and reasoning. There was only one being who could possibly, on occasion, *when she really worked for it*, command that demon of darkness. And it sure as fuck wasn't this pathetic alpha who couldn't even protect his own pack from his lack of sanity.

When the howls died off, there was a cold change in the air, icy winds whipping around us in a sudden frenzy. I wasn't the only one to glance up in time to see the sun's strength fade under a sudden cover of clouds. *What in the...?* No natural storm could blow up that quickly.

The alpha didn't care, his determination to mate us today his sole focus. "The next step, in the full moon tonight, is for my son's first shift and the consummation of this bond." He had to shout over the rumbling of the dark, ominous clouds. The winds picked up too, until leaves were flying around us. "Today, you will mark each other, and combine our bloodlines."

I could barely hear him, but Grant was already moving, facing me with a determined look on his face. His first shift was tonight, hence the need for the ceremony today, but he had enough power to already partially shift his jaw to mark me on the shoulder. An ancient act between mates, which was in general no longer practiced.

The alpha wanted the bite and our later consummation in human *and* wolf form to take place in front of the entire pack. Old fucking pervert that he was. But I just had to get through this shit to save the most vulnerable little girl. I had to give myself up to the pain and shame, let it go, and move on with my life as best I could, knowing that Tabitha was safe.

One heir. That's all I was obligated to provide, and then I was taking off for a new life.

"Shift, bitch," the alpha commanded me.

The storm picked up its intensity, as a few chairs went flying past. The clearing was now so thick with forest debris I could hardly see the pack, but nothing was deterring Alpha Lorenze today.

When I tried to draw on my wolf, who'd been hovering

under the surface of my skin all day, she refused to rise. *Please,* I begged, *he will kill her. You know he will, and she's our pup. We can't let that happen. We are strong enough to withstand what she cannot.*

My wolf was wild and untamed. She had been since I was very young, when I shifted long before my twenty-second birthday. I'd never told anyone, pretending my first shift was the solstice after I turned the age of shifter adulthood. The abnormalities in my life had never been broadcast and I wasn't about to start now. I just had to hope my beast would bend for Tabitha.

The change started slowly, surging up from deep in my gut, bringing with it the icy energy that I associated with my wolf spirit. If I hadn't known we were dark-furred with auburn undertones like my hair, I'd have expected she would be white, to match the ice in her veins.

The bones in my jaw finally cracked as wolfish features formed, including the sharper canines required for this part of the ceremony.

"Now!" Alpha Lorenze screamed.

Grant leaned over toward me, prepared to make first mark as was the alpha-to-be's right. Somehow, I didn't flinch away. Somehow, I didn't slash my claws across his throat to rip his head from his shoulders. Just as I felt the first scrape and break of skin on my shoulder, the storm around us died in an instant, and Grant stopped moving.

Blinking, I looked between Lorenze and Grant, wondering what the fuck was happening.

They were both frozen, mouths partly open, Grant's face still partially shifted. Sending my wolf back inside, her icy energy faded as I turned to take in the mess that was the rest of the pack and wedding zone. Only a couple of chairs and members hadn't been blown away, and they too were frozen on the spot.

Who in the worlds had the power to stop a...?

I didn't even finish that thought before it hit me suddenly. There was only one being who could do this. *The Shadow Beast.*

The Shadow Beast whose name had been invoked by the alpha right before the storm started.

Had he called him just in time to stop this ceremony from happening? And if so, where was he and would he have Mera with him?

I knew one thing for certain this time: Mera would not rest until she got the truth from me.

One way or another.

I just had to hope that the truth didn't cost the most important being in the worlds to me.

My daughter.

CHAPTER FIVE

SAMANTHA

As I walked back along the red carpet, my wolf was calmer in my chest, and I had the sense she thought we'd gotten a reprieve from our fate. I didn't have the heart to remind her it was no doubt temporary. Our fate was set in stone, and it was my own damn fault for allowing myself to fall apart all those years ago and to hand my heart to someone to be used against me.

A heart that, ironically, I hadn't even known I'd lost until recently.

The eerie calm remained as I continued up the red path, all the way back to the tent. The pair stepped out of the shadows a moment later, taller than was natural, more beautiful than should be possible, and... with a baby strapped to the fucking Shadow Beast god's chest.

Simone had told me Mera was in labor, but damn, seeing the truth of it was a whole other thing.

At some point I'd ground to a halt, and it was Mera who closed the last few steps and raced down the path to me. "Sam!" she cried, her voice filled with the sort of power I hadn't felt the last time I'd been in her presence. It wasn't the only change either. Her ombre red hair was more luminescent, the green in her hazel eyes piercing, and her skin faintly glowed as if so much energy pulsed inside of her that it couldn't be contained.

"Mera?" I said hesitantly, unsure why she was even here. "Did you hear about the mating?"

Tiny flames flickered to life in her eyes, and if I'd been in a different mood I might have even reacted to that. "I did *not* hear about the mating," she growled, sounding like she was barely holding on to her fury. "Because my so-called friend has been ghosting me for years. Fucking years. I don't even know why we're here now, outside of the fact that Simone thinks you deserve one last chance."

She crossed her arms, and I swallowed hard. Flickers of pain tried to push through the numbness, but I couldn't let them out. If they got out, all the rest would too. "I'm sorry," I said listlessly. "I was trying to deal with the shit in my life, and I just couldn't... I couldn't care about anyone else. I only have so much energy to give, and it's been fucking spent up."

Her face softened minutely. Shadow moved in to stand at her side, one of his massive hands pressed to the back of the baby carrier. "Congratulations," I said softly, my heart aching for everything I'd lost in my fuck-ups. "She's beautiful."

She was more than beautiful, with thick curls of red falling down her face, and the same shadowy glowing skin as Shadow. She looked to be about eight months old, but it was hard to tell behind the protective hands of her father. Changing the subject because I couldn't do the baby thing right now, I asked quickly, "If you didn't hear about the mating, what are you doing here?"

The Fates weren't about saving me these days, so there was some other reason.

"Your alpha invoked my name," Shadow rumbled, his tone prominent in the unnaturally quietened land. "Mera worries about you, so I keep an eye on this pack. When my name was spoken, I knew we needed to return here."

Mera wasn't looking directly at me, and it was clear that I'd hurt her even more than I thought. That harsh truth cut through some of the numbness in my chest and I took a step closer. A rumble escaped from Shadow, but he didn't stop me. No doubt he knew his mate was an uber badass and could take me out with a mere thought if she wanted to.

"I'm so sorry, Mera," I told her softly. "I'm a terrible friend."

"The worst," she sniffed with a growl. "The. Fucking. Worst."

I nodded hard. "You're right. You're totally right as always. I wanted to tell you the truth, but I'm..." I shot a quick look toward the scariest dude in the room. "I'm worried about how certain *shadowy beings* might react. I must protect someone who can't protect themselves."

This got their full attention. Gazes locked on me, one set of eyes concerned and the other with flames raging. "I can find out very easily," Shadow warned me, chest rumbling harder. "It's not good for your health to hide information from me."

Mera reached out and put her hand on his arm. "Babe, if we read between her not-so-subtle lines, this is kind of the reason Sam has been avoiding us. Maybe tone it back."

He rumbled again before shaking his head. "I don't tone, you know that, Sunshine." She shot him a small smile and soft eyes, and he let out a huff. "But I might have time for a stroll with our baby girl. Give you two a few minutes to chat."

Shadow might think he didn't tone... but for his Sunshine he went close.

There was no place he was out of earshot though, so I proceeded as if Shadow was at my side listening. "I truly am sorry, Mera. You and Simone are shifters I could see myself being best friends with forever. Growing old together—" I paused. "Wait, do you age?"

She shook her head. "Nope. Neither does Simone, but that's her story to tell. Back to yours."

She was impatient, and as predicted, I could no longer hide the truth from her. Not when she was face to face with me.

"You know how I told you that before I shifted I dated a moon-loving, crystal-wearing, gorgeous man who marked me with his vision of a wolf." I pressed my hand to my tattoo, the memories still not clear, outside of those few moments I'd managed to recall.

Mera nodded. "Yes, I remember. The tattoo caught my attention because it's super lifelike, and because it was not a normal shifter wolf, but more like..." She trailed off and I blinked at her, waiting for the rest of the thought.

"More like what?" I finally prompted.

"Simone's new wolf," she whispered. "Holy fuck. It's just like Simone's new hybrid form, and... it must be connected. Shadow said that we're all connected, which is why I have not... *will not...* give up on you."

Simone's hybrid wolf form? I'd clearly missed a lot in my prison of Clarity pack and shutting out the rest of the world.

Mera shook her head at the confused expression I was shooting her way. "We'll deal with that later. Let's get back to your story before Shadow gets antsy."

I glanced back down the path again. "How much longer can he keep holding Clarity pack in stasis?"

Mera laughed, relaxing. "He could hold them forever. Don't worry about that."

Fair enough. "So, anyway, the crystal-loving dude," I continued. "The weird part about my relationship with him is that I could only ever remember those few facts. At the time I thought it was because I was away from the pack, my wolf angsty about being alone. Or maybe it was due to the fact that he was human, or at least I thought he was human…"

Mera was nodding, her expression encouraging.

"Turns out, I was pregnant."

She went so still she could have been mistaken for a Clarity pack statue. "Pregnant? To a human?"

I shrugged and coughed out a weird sound. "The baby is not human, and timing suggests it was crystal guy, but I can't actually remember anything else from that time. I don't even remember being pregnant. Apparently, I stumbled into Clarity when I was pregnant and in the fog of memory loss, shifted here, and found out my mate was the alpha's son. They didn't take kindly to me being knocked up, so they took the baby from me. The only reason she wasn't killed was to be used as a bargaining tool. They hid her from me until I tried to escape into your old pack."

Mera's mouth was so wide open now I could see down her damn throat. "You never knew about your baby until Alpha Lorenze called you back?"

I shook my head. "I don't remember any of it. Being pregnant, giving birth, shifting and finding my true mate. Anything that was connected to that part of my history and the child is a blank space in my head. Completely blank."

The pain of knowing what I'd missed was all I had from that time.

"Why did they let you leave in the first place, if they had the baby to keep you there?"

I swallowed hard, trying to find words. "The alpha's son rebelled and rejected me. He didn't want used goods. The alpha released me in an attempt to force his son's hand. It didn't work, and after the alpha killed him, the contingency plan was initiated. I was yanked back in and forced to exist here until the second son was of mating age."

Mera's arms were around me so fast that I almost shoved her away as a reflex. It was only as the warmth of her energy surrounded me that I relaxed. It had been so long since I was hugged like this, full-bodily, and I couldn't contain the sob that rose up in my chest. This was why I'd avoided seeing her or Simone. Why I'd avoided close relationships. I could not afford to hope or wish or want for a life that was out of reach.

"Why didn't you tell me?" Mera choked out against my shoulder. "We would have helped you save your child. No mom should have to miss out on those days with their baby."

Fuck. She really wanted to break me.

When she pulled back, she stared into my eyes hard enough to see my brain. No idea what she was searching for, but if she thought she could pry memories free like that, she was welcomed to try. The gods knew I'd already tried everything.

"We are going to fix this," she said with all the confidence of her goddess-like powers. "You should have known that Shadow would smite that fucking alpha in a heartbeat. Why did you waste all this time trying to deal with him and sacrifice yourself?"

I swallowed hard. "At first it was to keep the pack safe, but when he finally allowed me a decent amount of time with my daughter, I discovered that she's sick. He's the only one who knows exactly what and how to stop this illness from taking over her system. I can't kill him, despite my desperate need to, and I can't even keep the pack safe any longer, since all my focus is on Tabitha."

"Tabitha," Mera breathed. "A new bestie for Aurora."

Gods, that painted a perfect picture. "She's my little angel, but there's something seriously wrong with her, Meers, and I can't fix her without his fucking help."

Mera's forehead crinkled as she pondered this. "If this happened before you were twenty-two, then she should be like... ten, right?"

I pressed my lips so hard together that they ached. "She should, but she's still a baby. I've known about her for a few years now, and in that time she's aged so slowly it's a barely noticeable change."

Mera's concerned expression grew. "Are you sure she's your child?"

My nod was rough. "Yes. Her energy is mine, I knew it the first moment I touched her. Even if some of her energy is foreign."

Tabitha was only half shifter. The other half, I'd guessed at, but I didn't know for sure.

"Foreign?" Mera repeated.

I nodded again. "Yeah, the mixing of two genetic lines is making her sick and stopping her from aging. If she doesn't have whatever Alpha Dickhead holds for her health, she starts to fade completely. So, I'm stuck doing his bidding. One heir for his pathetic son and I get Tabby back with instructions on how to keep her alive."

Mera shook her head, face creasing in sad lines. "Girl, you know that Shadow can read minds, right? At least he can read shifter minds. We could have stripped that information and all the rest from Lorenze in a heartbeat."

If she'd have stabbed me with a knife, I would have been in less pain.

"I... I never—" I had to clear my throat. "I never knew that. Alpha Lorenze doesn't allow information like that in our pack, and I never had the chance to know the end of your story."

I mentally beat myself up for a few minutes, while Mera looked on in sympathy. Which somehow made it worse. Should have expected I'd made a stupid as fuck move like that.

A sigh escaped. "I think I was scared for Shadow to know about Tabby in case her mix of genetics was not sustainable. That he would choose to destroy her rather than release whatever she is into the world. I just... I couldn't handle that. It was better to sacrifice time and freedom in the hope that eventually I could have my child and the secret to her health from Alpha Lorenze."

"I wouldn't allow him to destroy her!" Mera said in a rush. "Not that I even think he would. He doesn't interfere with free will much, and gods know Aurora is scary and powerful already. There's nothing your daughter could bring to this world that ours wouldn't try and one-up."

"I should have expected it," I said softly. "That after having a child of your own, you'd understand my desperate need to keep her alive."

Mera snatched my hand up and squeezed it tight. "I understand better than you think, and I don't care what Shadow says, we're saving your girl."

For the first time in years, a flutter of hope took flight in my heart. A hope I prayed wasn't the final stitch in the fabric of my undoing.

CHAPTER SIX

SAMANTHA

Mera left me to race after Shadow. I took the opportunity to tear off the lacy bottom of my dress so it was no longer dragging on the ground. The veil was next. I ripped it free along with the millions of pins until my hair fell in curls down my back. I allowed myself a moment to breathe deeply and let the wild in my soul free.

My wolf rose and howled, the icy power flowing through my veins as some of the weight that had been resting on our soul lifted. It sucked to know that if I'd just opened up to my friends, I might have avoided the last couple of years of turmoil, but there was no going back.

I shouldn't be too surprised; I'd been conditioned to shoulder my own burdens. No one had ever stepped in and taken any of life's stresses from me, so it was true to character that I'd decided to handle this situation without outside help.

And yet, somehow, help had still arrived. Right when I needed it.

Fuck. Maybe the Fates didn't hate me completely. I'd been sent a fiery angel and her shadowy mate at the final hour. *Please let this be a new path forward for Tabitha and me.*

A minute later Mera and Shadow were back, and the look on Shadow's face reminded me why I'd been hesitant to tell them this secret.

Celebrated too quickly.

Dread swelled in small increments within me, and if I'd had anything in my stomach I would have vomited. "Why are you angry?" I finally asked, too tired and stressed to care that I was questioning the Shadow Beast. "I will fight you to keep my daughter alive. I don't even care if you can smite me with a mere thought."

He regarded me closely, like he'd never really seen me before. The icy energy rose as my wolf lifted her head and faced her creator. "You are no ordinary shifter," Shadow said, and there was thankfully no fury in his clinical tone. "What is your heritage?"

I shook my head. "You know as much as I do. My parents must have thrown me away at birth. I spent years in random packs until I ended up in Clarity."

I had never mentioned to any that I could shift long before my twenty-second birthday, and I wasn't about to start today. I needed Shadow to trust and help me, not be more suspicious of my genetics.

"I could search your mind?" Shadow offered, and I was already shaking my head.

"Too many have claimed ownership of me, my mind, and my body. For now I'd like to keep my thoughts to myself. The priority is finding my daughter. Can we do that?"

There I went again, demanding shit of the Shadow Beast,

but just the knowledge that I might be able to find and help my daughter had impatience slamming against my soul until it felt like my wolf was about to burst through my skin. Every part of me felt out of control.

Mera grasped my hand once more. "Shadow is not angry with you or Tabby," she said to me. "He's just beating himself up that once again alphas he created are tapping into their megalomaniac side and hurting the shifters they should be protecting."

Flames shot up around the Shadow Beast, and it didn't escape my notice that his daughter popped her little hand out and started to play with the fire. A small giggle followed, and I was starting to see what Mera meant about her powerful child.

"You can fix the alphas," I told the flaming beast. "They just need checks and balances. Until now they've been the ultimate power, and we haven't even had any shifter wars to keep them in line. Time to step in and remind them who the supreme god is and what happens if they break the fucking rules."

Shadow's flames grew larger, and the shadowy façade of his beast washed over his features before he got himself under control. "Don't worry, once we deal with your alpha, then I will deal with all of them."

Good. It would be nice to know that not just my pack but all packs would finally be safer. What happened to Mera and me wasn't an isolated incident. I knew—*from rumors*—that Shadow and his friends had been dealing with a lot of end-of-world shit, so it was understandable that they'd been busy. But, when it was quiet, he also needed to deal with the race of beings he created here.

Mera wrapped her arm through mine, the pulse of her power against my skin warm and familiar, with a touch of new strength that bordered on uncomfortable. We followed Shadow as he led the way to Alpha Lorenze.

Everyone was still frozen in place. "Are they aware of what's happening?" I asked, looking at the statue-like shifters.

"No," Shadow said shortly. "At the moment, it's as if they're all asleep standing. But the alpha is about to find out what occurs when you piss me off."

Bastard deserved that and more.

When we reached the bottom of the red carpet, Shadow didn't hesitate to slam his fist into the alpha's face. It was odd to see, since the frozen form didn't move, but I couldn't help but wince at what looked to be many crushed bones.

At first, I thought he'd just been hitting him for fun, but then I realized it was Shadow's way of touching the shifter so he could sift through memories and thoughts. A swelling of power had my wolf reacting, and we almost howled again, but this time I managed to keep her locked down. Years of training were coming in handy, even if it did annoy my beast to no end.

"Can you read his thoughts?" Mera asked in a low voice.

Shadow shot her a look of disbelief, and I had to chuckle. They were funny together. I hadn't expected that.

"His mind is a fucking mess," Shadow said with a huff. "I'm wading through some depraved shit to get to anything of substance."

"Always here to help," Mera said with a wink in my direction. "But, seriously, take your time, love. It's all good."

A puff of flames and steam surrounded her briefly as he sent fiery power her way, but she just waved it off. Thankfully, since her arm was still through mine, she kept me from being fried. I couldn't wave off fire like these two.

"He's got your daughter held in a pack safe house in the forest," Shadow murmured, his gaze shifting off into the distance as he probed the alpha's mind. "She'd been there the entire time, hidden in plain sight. There's usually about eight guards around her. He's scared of you, Sam."

That look of uneasiness the alpha had given me earlier today hadn't been the first, but his hold over me was strong enough that I'd never made a move against him. "I'd have tried to kill him many times over the past couple of years if he wasn't in control of my daughter's health. My rage—" I cleared my throat "—my wolf's rage was enough that I think we would have succeeded."

"You can have the opportunity today, if you'd like," Shadow said with a shrug. "His mind tells me that he's beyond saving. Mera's choice is generally to strip their wolves and make them human, but I support death as well."

Mera hugged my arm a little tighter. "I think living as a human is a huge punishment, one that can go on for years, while killing them is so quick. You know?"

I examined her face, seeing the duality of personalities there. Part of Mera remained the shifter with empathy for others, while the goddess side was more vengeful. I wasn't sure which path I'd take with the alpha; my only focus for the moment was on Tabitha.

"I don't know what I'll do," I said. "I really just want to get to the safe house."

"I'm starting to think this bastard's mind is a mess for a reason," Shadow said suddenly. "I never searched the other alpha's mind before I torched him, but I wish now I'd taken the time. This doesn't feel natural. It has a tinge of manipulation from another source."

Mera released me to take a step forward. "Do you think someone is targeting shifters to get to you? Could this be more mental manipulation like Dani was so fond of?"

I expected Shadow to laugh that off. I knew that the packs

weren't always handled well, but Lorenze and Mera's old alpha were the only ones I'd heard of being true psychopaths.

"We will find out soon enough," Shadow told her. "The world appears to be giving us a small break at the moment. No life-or-death situat—"

"Whoa!" Mera all but shouted. "You can't just put that out into the universe. Holy shit, Shadow. You're going to bring the damn apocalypse down on our heads."

This time he did laugh, a low husky sound that sent tingles down my spine. "The universe belongs to me. I'm not worried about what comes next."

Mera didn't look so convinced. "I'll be sure to say *I told you so* when the time arises," she said, wrinkling her nose.

Shadow's expression lightened, but he didn't speak again, spending the next few minutes probing into the stationary alpha's mind. "Okay, Tabitha is easy enough to find," he said, "but the only reference to her health is a bunch of stones that he appears to put under her bedding at night. They're recharging her energy from what I can tell."

That was it? Stones were keeping her alive.

Questions spilled from me. "What sort of stones? Can we just take the ones he has? What is it that stops her from aging and being healthy? The alpha told me that if he didn't administer his cure, she'd start to weaken and lose life force. I assumed it was some sort of potion or elixir."

I'd had years to go over every possibility. Stones hadn't even made the list.

Had it been that simple all along? Once again, I'd screwed up and lost time with my precious daughter. Time I could never get back, but I could change it from today.

Today we would be free.

CHAPTER SEVEN

SAMANTHA

Shadow released his hold on the alpha's head but didn't allow him to move again. The stasis energy remained strong. "The stones are unknown to me," he said. He didn't sound happy about it. "I won't be able to deduce anything until we see them. They feel powerful through his memories. Apparently, they appeared when the child was born, underneath you as you gave birth, and he's used them ever since to keep her healthy."

Healthy was an overstatement, considering she was still a baby ten years after birth, but at least she was alive. Alive I could work with. "It frustrates me to no end that I can't remember," I bit out.

Shadow's concern grew as he examined me. "The alpha should not have been able to manipulate your mind like that. What happened to you is beyond a shifter's capabilities."

I'd also long suspected that, but without my memories it was impossible to know what truly happened to me.

"Let's go find her," Mera said impatiently. "I think Sam has waited long enough to have her daughter safely in her possession. We can deal with the other shit later, including the mind manipulations."

I straightened and wiped my hands against the tattered remains of my wedding dress. Was this really the moment I was going to have Tabitha in my life permanently?

Would my heart actually explode at the emotion of it.

"It's fucked up," I whispered through a ragged throat. "But part of me is grateful that I've only known about Tabby for the past few years. I would have lost what remains of my sanity if I'd had to keep handing her back to that bastard for any longer than that." A selfish thought, since my child had existed without her mother for years. Even the small time I had with her now had allowed a bond to develop. A bond that should have happened years earlier, but I had to be honest—more years of this would have broken me completely.

Shadow, oddly, was the one to move closer, reaching out as if to touch my mind. By instinct, I shied away, aware of what his touch could do.

"I could search your memories," he told me. "Ensure that what you've been told is what happened at the time of her birth." He jerked his head toward the alpha, disgust marring his perfect features. "I'm struggling to see the truth through the confusion in this one's mind."

"Not yet," I said with sharp jerk of my head. "The past isn't as important to me as the future. Not after almost losing my freedom today."

"Of course," Shadow said simply, before he turned away. In typical godlike fashion, he didn't wait for any of us before he strolled along the path toward the main shifter camp. Mera and

I followed silently, and even though her arm was no longer tucked through mine, there was comfort in our closeness.

Some of the hurt feelings had faded. Mera finally understood why I'd acted the way I did, and it seemed that she was letting go of her anger over it. Personally, I still had a lot of growing up and repenting for my actions, but everything could wait until I had Tabby with me.

Tabby, and the stones that were apparently keeping her energy flowing.

Alpha Lorenze had allowed me to see what happened when he refused her "health elixir" as he called it, and the sight of her grey skin and listless body had terrified me to the point that I'd never questioned that bastard again. Risking my daughter was an absolute hard limit for me, and I never stepped close to the line after that day.

The alpha knew my weakness and he'd leveraged it just like any good dictator would. With my uber-independence and refusal to ask for help, I'd been prime pickings for his plan for the perfect heir—

"Stop blaming yourself," Mera said shortly as we continued along the path.

Turning my head, I shot her a wry grin. "Can you read minds too?" I asked with a humorless laugh.

"I was just guessing based on your expression," Mera said, "but I can read thoughts." She said this so casually, as if she wasn't admitting to some crazy ass power. "With Shadow's help," she continued. "I'll probably be able to do it on my own soon, but I'm learning these powers at a stupidly slow rate. Not cool."

This time my laugh was more genuine. It was a small relief to know she wasn't in my head; it was a fucking mess in there. "You're going to live forever. Don't stress on not knowing everything now."

She shrugged "After what we've just learned, it wasn't hard to guess that you were beating yourself up. I would have done the same. But if I've learned anything, it's that blaming yourself for being a normal person and screwing up isn't helpful. Acknowledge, learn, and grow from the mistakes. If you continue to be your own worst enemy, you'll never rise and claim your future."

Rise and claim your future. Five simple words, nothing prophetic or even groundbreaking, but it lit a small fire in my gut. For too many years I'd been allowing life and all its bullshit to happen to me. Accepting situations I never should have accepted. Even my memory loss...

Shadow had offered to try and lift it and I'd knocked him back out of fear and exhaustion. But if I kept this shit up, I'd be the same fearful and broken shifter in the next ten or twenty years. I might live longer than a human, but my time was still finite.

"You're right," I said quickly, shaking my head as if I could clear years of cloudiness and neglect. "I need to change the narrative. Change my fucking attitude. And find the damn future my daughter and I deserve. I've been playing the victim for too long, but it has to end."

Mera shot me a proud smile. "Girl, you have the brightest future ahead of you. I might not be fully psychic. Or even a tiny bit psychic. But I know that what I say is truth. I've lived it, and I've seen it with my own eyes. Angel is the brightest fucking light since claiming her true future, Simone too. Both of them took risks and got hurt, but now... they couldn't be happier. You will do the same."

Shadow, who had clearly been listening in, called back to us, "All of those that Mera considers pack have a greater destiny than they would have ever thought." He didn't turn, his broad shoulders visible a dozen yards in front, but his voice was as clear as if he stood beside us. "But only if you fight for it. The path to light will not come easily. But if you want it hard enough, you'll make it in the end."

"I want it," I said without hesitation. "I will find this light you speak of, and maybe then my daughter will thrive too."

These days I fought for two, which was more than enough motivation.

We reached the main section of village where the houses were scattered amongst the trees. Shadow picked up the pace, and my heart already felt lighter just knowing we were heading for Tabitha.

He turned off from the path, following a trail more suitable for when we were in shifted form. He used his powers to clear the debris. At this point I was moving as fast as I could without actually climbing onto Shadow's back. We were so close. So fucking close to being done with Clarity and its bullshit. So close to having my daughter in my arms.

When we were deep in the forest, the air chilled off slightly as we rose in elevation. I didn't recognize the terrain. I'd been in Clarity for a long time but I'd never explored this area.

Or so I thought, until we reached a small cabin. This was Alpha Lorenze's private dwelling, and I'd snuck up here once using a different path to search for Tabitha. She hadn't been inside. There was literally no sign of a baby at all, and I'd bailed before I got caught.

"She's not here," I called to Shadow, pain spilling into my words. "I've searched this cabin before."

"She's here," he shot back.

Mera placed her hand on my shoulder and squeezed gently. "Shadow won't let you down," she said soothingly. "Trust in him. In us."

Trust. If I'd done that from the start, I could have saved so much pain.

A new narrative.

I was ready and this was the first step.

"I trust in you," I breathed. "Keep reminding me to open my mind and eyes. It might take a while, and I might need your grace more than once, but I'm going to keep working at it."

"You have all the fucking grace," she said fiercely. "Not a worry, my friend."

The tear escaped before I could stop it, but thankfully Mera didn't notice. Or if she did, she didn't make a deal about it, and that was just one more thing to be grateful for.

Shadow reached the cabin first and disappeared inside. "What if there's guards in there still?" I said, worry in my tone as I picked up the pace. "He's holding Aurora, and the alpha was a straight-up megalomaniac. He could have left any multitude of traps inside."

Mera snorted out a laugh. "Girl, if there's something in there that could challenge Shadow, we're all fucked. It'll be fine."

Right. *Gods.* I had to remember they were not like the rest of us.

When we made it inside the building, it was exactly as I remembered. A very sparse home, with only one brown lounge, a small round dining table, and nothing else. The fire wasn't lit today, giving it a cold and abandoned feeling. I knew this wasn't the alpha's main residence, but one he escaped to. It would have been the perfect place to stash Tabitha, but I'd searched every nook last time.

We paused in the kitchen, and I looked around the sparse space. "Where did Shadow go?" I asked Mera, not seeing his presence either.

"His energy is below us," she replied softly, leaning over to run her hands across the roughly hewn planks of wood on the floor. "My asshole of a mate clearly thinks I need to figure out how to get down there myself."

Despite my internal panic and drive to get to Tabitha, I had to suppress a smile at the relationship between Mera and Shadow. They were clearly destined soul mates—anyone with sense would know that, but that didn't mean it was always smooth sailing. They were still testing each other, and I liked to see it. The challenges kept their life interesting, but they knew at the end of the day they were a team. They had each other's back no matter what.

I never expected a relationship was in the cards for me. Not any longer.

But if it ever was, I wanted this sort of love.

An imperfectly perfect one.

CHAPTER EIGHT

SAMANTHA

Mera figured it out in about two minutes, finding the small groove that released a trap door. It had been very cleverly disguised. I'd never have found it without help—without her amazing extra senses. She lifted it all the way back to reveal wooden stairs leading down into darkness.

My heart squeezed so tight in my chest that I coughed to try and relieve the pressure.

Mera's head jerked up to meet my gaze. "You okay?"

"No," I choked out, as anger added an extra layer to my voice. No, not anger, pure rage. "He's been keeping my fucking daughter in a hole in the ground. No wonder she's failed to thrive. That bastard. Remind me to kill him before we leave."

Not just kill but destroy. He had to cease to exist in this world and the afterlife, and I had the sense Shadow would know how to undo that waste of alpha genetics. Mera told me to trust in them. To rely on them.

In this situation, I would be.

Mera let me descend first, and by the time I reached the level below my fury had red tinting my vision.

"Here," Shadow called, appearing in the low light filtering in from a few gaps in the wooden walls. He held a small bundle in his hands, and I let out a cry as I raced forward.

"Tabby!" Sobs broke from me in loud gasping sounds. My chest was crushing in on itself; I couldn't breathe. Not even when Shadow placed her in my arms and she lifted her head just enough so that I could see her violet eyes. "Baby, baby girl, baby." I just clutched her and cried, until a scream wrenched from me. It was dragged up from my soul, followed by a howl as my beast roared to life.

For so many minutes I clutched at my reason for existence, just holding her until I found the will to stop howling and just breathe. Lifting my head from where I'd had it tucked down near her frail body, I used my shoulder to wipe away tears so I could see her clearly.

"Mommy has you," I whispered, examining her.

A gasp escaped me when she reached out and pressed her hand to my face. It was the first time I'd seen her move her limbs so independently rather than lying like a complete newborn. Her white-blond hair even looked a little longer, and her skin—a shimmery silver—looked healthier than usual. She was full of life for once.

"In his mind," Shadow said softly, watching me with flames in his eyes, "the alpha indicated that he drained her before she visited with you, so you'd always worry he was the only one keeping her alive."

The rage that had simmered down briefly returned in a blast.

"He will pay for everything," I said shortly. "For her suffering. My own is one thing, but hurt my child and I will make sure you regret it forever."

Shadow nodded, not having a single issue with that statement.

Mera, who'd been standing off to the side, caught my attention when she moved closer. "She's perfection," she breathed, sounding choked up as if she'd been crying with me. She wrapped an arm around us. "We're going to figure this out, Sam. We'll right the wrongs done to you and Tabby."

With her free hand, she reached out and brushed some of Tabitha's curls back before she slid her finger across the tips of her ears. Across the obvious sign that my daughter was only half shifter. It was this feature that had prevented me from asking for help, in the worry Shadow might choose to destroy her unknown genetics.

"She's fae," Shadow said simply. He didn't sound surprised, and I had to guess that the moment he held her in his arms he knew the truth. The very slight curve to the top of her ears an indication of her heritage. "But her energy is almost muted. I don't feel much from her."

"I guessed she was fae," I said truthfully. "But I never knew for sure. Are there other races with pointed ears?"

"Yes, there are," he told me. "But when you add in her need for crystals, her true heritage becomes obvious."

"Why can't we sense her energy?" Mera asked, brushing her hand down Tabitha's cheek. "It's almost like she's a dead spot of power."

"I feel her," I said quickly. "That's how I knew for sure she was my daughter. But no one else appears to have the same connection."

Mera shot me a sad smile. "Girl, she looks just like you.

Gorgeous. Like a baby model. I have no doubt she's your child, but it is curious about her energy."

Small flames flickered around Shadow. "I'm not sure if it's the fact that she'd been deprived of what she needs for growth and development, or something in her genetics. We need to return to the library and research. Len will also be helpful in this situation."

I knew who Len was from my time in the library, but weirdly I couldn't picture him in my mind. I just knew he was Shadow's fae brother. "What if they try to take her from me?" I managed to say, still working on trusting them. "I remember that the fae don't have children easily. She could be highly valued."

Shadow had always been my first concern, but the fae themselves was number two. Somewhere out there, Tabitha had a fae father, and in the Library of Knowledge there were enough visitors from Faerie that word could get around.

"Not going to happen," Mera burst out before Shadow could reply. "Not a fucking chance."

"Sunshine is correct," Shadow confirmed. "The fae would never attack the library, so you'll both be safe there. We do need some outside help, though. Consider allowing Len in on the situation. He's a great and trusted source of information."

If I trusted in Shadow and Mera, then it stood to reason that I might have to trust in their friends too.

"The fae are very long-lived," he continued, "but if Tabitha is ten, she should be more aged than she is. I'm not up to date with their younglings, due to the lack of them born in the last many decades, so any help will go a long way."

Hence the worry that Tabitha might be desirable in their world, but hopefully that worry was already put to rest. "If there's no risk from Len, then I'd gratefully accept his help."

"Let's get back to the library," Mera said. "I'm done with this fucking town."

Drawing Tabitha closer, I breathed deeply, enjoying that the continuous, low-lying panic I felt without her was easing. Her delicate, flowery scent filled my senses, and I savored this small moment with her.

"Fuck, this hurts my heart," Mera said from beside me. "I'm going to kill that alpha now."

A rumble from Shadow followed, and I lifted my head to find he'd taken Mera into his arms, stroking a thumb across her cheek. "This is Samantha's kill, Sunshine. You know that."

Mera pouted, her gaze lingering on her own beautiful daughter, still strapped to her mate's chest. A daughter who was watching her parents closely with those ancient gold eyes. "Fine. But she better choose right."

Her lips twitched and I couldn't help but chuckle. Despite wanting to kill the bastard a few minutes ago, I'd calmed enough to want his suffering to go on longer. "Can we just leave him frozen in the middle of the path for a few weeks? Even better if he's somewhat aware of what's happening but can't move."

Shadow's smile was darkly sinister, and it sent a tingle down my spine. "I can make that happen. Then, when we're done figuring out your mystery, we can return here for you to make a final decision on punishment."

Perfect. My focus now was all Tabitha. After my memories were returned and her growth and health were back on track, I'd deal with the alpha.

"Let's get out of here, then," Mera said. She started for the stairs, before pausing and doubling back. I was wondering what she was doing until she returned a second later clutching what looked like a purple plank.

"The crystal bed," she explained, and I could have kicked

myself for forgetting. Just having Tabitha in my arms had wiped out all other thought.

"Thank you. Fuck. We need that until we figure out what else is missing from her life to help her thrive." There had to be something, I refused to believe she couldn't develop and live for many years after this.

We left the basement, making our way up to the cabin and back into the forest. Tabitha was pressed close to my chest, still moving her hands about, touching my face all the time. Paying attention to her energy, since I was the only one who could feel it, I was ready to react the moment I felt any weakness and place her on the crystal mat that Mera carried.

For now, thankfully, she was strong.

"You'll never go back to a dingy basement," I whispered as we powered through the forest. "You'll have the same light I'm searching for, Tabby. The same bright future. I love you so much." My throat grew too tight to speak, so I just mentally whispered all the positive affirmations for us both. Tabitha made some sweet cooing sounds against me, and by the time we reached the main part of town I felt calm and happy.

And ready for the next steps in our future.

As we passed some of the frozen shifters, Shadow waved his hand, freeing them from his spell. The few nearby shook their heads and looked around in confusion until they noticed the seven-foot god in their midst. Most of them fell to their knees, while a few continued to just blink in confusion. Shadow wasted no time addressing them. "You're getting a second chance as a pack," he boomed as his energy exploded around the town. "Alpha Lorenze will be removed from power today, and now you can rebuild. I'll be back to check what you've done with this chance. If I find you've been wasting your gifts as shifters, I will strip every single one of you of your beast, and you'll live out the remainder of your existence as a human. Do not disappoint me again."

From where I stood, a few shifters were visibly crying. I felt bad for them. We'd all been victims to the alpha, but I also understood Shadow's strong stance on this. Clarity had let our alpha go too far without fighting back, and that wasn't the shifter way. Now they had to prove they were worthy of their beasts.

"Is Alpha Lorenze dead?" Jewel, a small blond shifter asked. She was one of the newer recruits to our pack, and I'd heard her try multiple times to get out, but the alpha never let them go once they were snared in his web. I'd had to jump through so much shit to get out the first time, and he'd only let that happen because of his contingency plan to get me back. When the time was right.

"Not dead," Shadow told her. "He's frozen and will remain so for the time being. He's also aware of what's going on around him, so feel free to give him a small taste of whatever he's put you through over the past years."

Permission to torture granted. That bastard would finally reap what he'd sown.

I always said that what you put out into the world came back on you, and he was about to find out how bad that could be.

The few shifters closest to us rose, their expressions clearing of fear and sorrow, to be replaced with determination and... hope.

"You're saying he will not break through and punish us?" someone else asked Shadow. I couldn't see who through the gathering crowd, but it was a masculine voice.

"I'm holding him in stasis," Shadow replied shortly. "He will not break free."

Shadow turned then, done dealing with Clarity, and Mera

went to follow, but I remained a few seconds longer, mostly because Grant was wobbling his way along the path, expression confused as he rubbed a hand over his face. "Samantha?" he said slowly. "What the hell is happening? Did we finish our mating?"

His eyes dropped lower to the child in my arms, and when he lifted his gaze to meet mine again, I didn't let my expression soften. Grant had stood aside and let his father make these decisions to force a mating. I mean, sure, his father was insane, and had murdered his brother, so I understood his reluctance to speak up, but in truth he'd never tried to fight at all. It had just been easier for him to just go along with it all.

"You're the alpha now," I said, letting some of my energy leak into those words. "Don't let this fucking pack down like your father has. Because we'll be back."

"We will!" Mera added with force. "Last chance for Clarity."

No one argued. They could hear the resolution in her tone. If they screwed up this chance, Clarity would cease to exist.

For good.

CHAPTER NINE

SAMANTHA

Walking away from Clarity pack with Tabitha in my arms felt like a dream. My head grew fuzzy as adrenaline died off, and I hoped to fuck I didn't pass out at some point. Mera never left my side, and I tried not to spiral into kicking myself once more for pushing this friendship away. I had to leave the past behind and focus on the future.

The trip into the white hallway that led from Earth to the library passed in a blur, and I wasn't imagining the concerned looks being shot my way by both Mera and Shadow.

"You've got this," she whispered to me.

I had to swallow a few times, before I had enough moisture in my mouth to speak. "It's just surreal. Today was my doom, and somehow I was saved. When does that happen? It's too good to be true, and I wonder if it's just the prequel to losing Tabby for good."

Speaking my true fear out loud allowed me to breathe more freely.

"Between the dozen or so gods and powerful creatures I know," Mera said fiercely, "that won't happen. Someone will have a solution. There's always a fucking solution."

Her passion awoke some of my own fire, cutting through the fuzziness of my brain. "Yes, shit, yes. You're right. It's just been a really fucked-up few years, but it's turning. I have to believe that."

"Damn right," Mera said. "I'm going to cliché quote from a book, but this is the first day of the rest of your life. Past is dead. This is our future."

Cliché or not, it was exactly what I needed to hear.

The white hallway ended as we entered the Library of Knowledge. I'd forgotten how awe-inspiring this room was. Looking like a cross between an ancient cathedral and the library of my dreams, it held millions of books from across the many worlds.

As we entered, I couldn't help but flash back to the first time I saw it. It had been as broken and lost as I felt, and now it was brimming with energy, the massive ceilings carved with scenes of battle and life. The hundreds of shelves spanned across the space, guarding knowledge and doorways to multiple worlds.

This was almost its own little galaxy, and I could only hope my own redemption story was as beautiful as this library's.

"Home," Mera breathed, tilting her head back as she smiled. "Fuck Earth and all of its bullshit."

Shadow let out a low chuckle, his amusement lightening the atmosphere even further. "Now you know why I left the shifters to their own devices. That world is out of alignment. It drains my energy."

Mera didn't argue, but I could see the wheels turning in her mind. Probably trying to figure out what the issue with Earth—and the alphas—really was. And more importantly, how they could rectify it at some point in the future.

She shook it off a beat later and focused on me. "Let's deal with the memory blocks in your mind," she said. "There's no moving forward until that's resolved."

Hugging Tabitha closer to me, I pushed down my instinct to refuse. A quick glance at the library ceiling reminded me that I couldn't rebuild without breaking a few walls first. "Okay," I said with a nod.

The fear didn't go anywhere, but I was facing it.

"Aurora needs to be changed and fed," Shadow said shortly, moving once more. "And I'll find Gaster to help with the memories."

Mera nodded at the retreating back of her mate. "Okay, yes. We can meet back here soon." She turned to me. "Gaster will be good to have as a backup. Shadow is powerful, but his energy is a bit like a steam train. Sometimes he goes hard and fast and breaks his surroundings." Her lips twitched as she met my gaze. "I don't want him to break you."

A surprise smile crossed my lips too. "You know... me either."

Her laughter was light as she stepped closer to run a hand across Tabitha's hair again. She continued to hold the crystal mat in her free hand, and despite how weighty it looked Mera showed no sign of fatigue. "I still can't feel her energy," she said. "Does she need her mat?"

"Her energy is solid," I replied, shifting her away from my chest so I could see her violet eyes. "In fact, she feels stronger than I've ever felt when I was with her. Shadow was right, that fucking alpha was deliberately weakening her so I'd assume she was frail and needed his *miracle cure*."

My anger flickered strongly to life once more. I hoped that bastard was suffering in Clarity.

"Come on," Mera told me. "You'll want privacy for this next step. Let's head into the lair."

The lair. Shadow's private dominion. I hadn't been allowed past the entrance last time, and no lie, I was curious about what lay on the other side.

As we walked through the library, Mera was greeted, bowed to, and waved at a hundred times. Every being, from all walks of world, knew exactly who was in their presence, and she was treated like the queen she was. "Far cry from Torma pack," I said, my chest warming at what I was experiencing. "You're owning your glory, girl, and I'm so fucking proud of you."

Mera's glow would have blinded a human. "It took me a long time to realize that I had worth. Shadow built me up, but I took it from there, and even now, I continue to grow."

"You were always a fighter," I reminded her. "You refused to deal with Torma. You tried to make it better. I'm the one who needs to step up and find some worth."

My hand was engulfed in her free one. "You're a fucking warrior. From here on out, there's no more talk of weakness. Most would not have survived what you did, and we will walk the path of queens together."

This moment cemented something I'd always believed but hadn't experienced: the true mate to your soul might actually be one of your girl friends.

"Thank you," I whispered. "I will find the path, I promise."

Mera didn't have an ounce of doubt on her face, and I strived to mimic that level of confidence as we continued to stroll through the library. When we finally reached the swirling portal, Mera stepped through and pulled me with her. A weird wash of energy surrounded us before we emerged into another library.

"Holy shit." I blinked a few times to ensure I was seeing clearly. The light was low, almost as if everything were lit by firelight, warm and comforting. "How many libraries do you have? I mean, not that you could have too many or anything, but damn..."

"Right?" Mera said with a happy sigh, spinning on the spot as if taking in the vibe of the place. "Books just make me so happy. The scent. The feel. The look of them lined up in chronological order to complete a series." The genuine happiness on her face was cute as heck.

"It's where dreams are made," I agreed. "I've had to lose myself in books so much over the last few years. It feels like I've read literally every fantasy and romance that's been written."

Mera leapt toward me, face bright as her eyes grew super wide. "Holy shit, girl. I cannot wait until Simone gets back from Valdor. I'm telling you, there's an entire world of fiction you haven't discovered yet. We are starting a fucking book club."

Future. Hope. The oddest concepts, and yet I was feeling it more than I could remember in a long time. Just the thought of being around for a book club... with a true pack... and Tabitha healthy and alive... I wanted for nothing else.

"I'm totally in," I said. "That's the sort of girls' night I dreamed about."

"It's gonna happen." Her determination told me that it would, no matter what the future held for us. "But first, let's get your memories back."

She led me toward a lounge area, where there was an actual roaring fireplace, surrounded by a bunch of very comfortable-looking couches. "Sit," she said. "Shadow will be here in a moment."

I didn't question how she knew that; it was no doubt a part of their bond.

As I sat, I laid Tabby along my thighs, keeping a hold on her sides. She wiggled against me gently, and I loved to see her freedom of movement. It was a true gift to even have time to examine her, from her shimmery skin and blond curls to her eyes, which were truly mesmerizing. It almost looked like slivers of crystal were embedded in the rich amethyst color. Even dressed in the threadbare grey jumpsuit, she shone like a jewel.

"There's no hiding that she's otherworldly," Mera said as she peered over my shoulder. She placed the crystal mat beside me on the couch, before reaching for a throw that was draped over the end of the same chair. "Let's give her some time to recharge."

It was a good idea, and despite my sorrow at letting her go so soon, I didn't hesitate to lift and move her closer. "Yes, let's do it."

Mera draped the throw across the smooth purple surface, and as I gently placed Tabitha down I leaned in and pressed my lips to her cheek. Breathing in that floral scent which I had no reference for, I choked down some sobs. "I have loved you for a thousand lives," I breathed against her soft skin. "I will never let you go again."

A muffled sob joined in with mine, and I turned to see Mera with her hand pressed against her mouth, tears leaking from the corner of her eyes. "You're killin' me, Smalls," she sobbed. "I don't even cry. Stupid baby hormones."

"I love you too, Mera," I said suddenly.

Fuck, okay, that was probably a weird thing to say to

someone I'd only known briefly, but it was true. I'd known from our first meeting that she was a soul-sister, and... I'd missed her.

Her tears slowed as she stared, wide-eyed. She recovered near instantly from her shock, as she leaned over to throw her arms around me. "I love you too, Sam! I've missed and worried about you so much. I couldn't be fucking happier that you're here with us now."

My eyes closed briefly as I absorbed the warmth in both her hug and her words. I'd been alone a lot of my life, but that wasn't the case any longer. Friends and my daughter. We just had to figure out how to get Tabitha back to full health, unlock my memories, and then I could daydream about having a true pack.

It was all I wanted, and I was going to ensure that it happened.

No matter the consequences.

CHAPTER TEN

SAMANTHA

Just as Tabitha relaxed onto her crystal mat, Shadow appeared beside Mera. I mean, I was sure he walked into the room, but the dude existed in shadows, and it was as if he just appeared from nowhere.

Tabby didn't react, even as she stared up at the giant beast. "Her eyes are brighter," Mera said. "The color is stronger."

Everything about her was stronger, especially her energy. Which I was still the only one to be able to feel.

"Are you ready?" Shadow asked. Aurora was in his arms now, removed from her carrier, and when Mera held out her hands for the little girl, the beast placed her right into them.

"Hello, my sweet, A," Mera cooed, and there was no mistaking how much Aurora adored her mother. Her baby face went soft as she reached out and pressed both hands to her mom's face. "You're hungry," Mera said suddenly.

"She communicates with you?" I asked, shaking my head. "How old is she?"

"She's a few months old," Mera replied with a smile, and I was surprised because the child appeared much older. "She sends me emotions through touch, or if she feels like it, from across the room. Just brief senses of what she needs."

"That must make parenting easier," I laughed.

"If she didn't keep vanishing to visit her friends, it would be really fantastic," Mera added with her own laugh. "She's always jetting off to Damon, Angel and Reece's little one. They're giving us immortals wrinkles."

Shadow huffed. "You're perfect, Sunshine."

It was her turn to soften. She looked at her mate the way Aurora looked at her parents, with the sort of unconditional love that would destroy worlds. The pair remained locked in a moment together, but then they got back to business.

The business of releasing memories.

Mera kissed her daughter on the head and leaned down to place her just off to the side of Tabitha's crystal bed. "Can you wait a few minutes for boob?" she asked the infant.

Aurora let out a low gurgle and smiled at the same time. Mera must have taken that for a yes, because she didn't pick her up again. All three of us watched them, waiting to see what would happen if they touched.

Only they never did.

Aurora, who was an inch or so smaller than Tabitha, just remained where she was, happily waving her hands in the air. Tabby was no different, and surprisingly, after a few minutes, she too started to wave her hands in the air, strong and sure.

"She just learned from her," Mera breathed. "Holy shit. Maybe the fae young need other babies around them to grow and develop?"

Shadow shook his head. "It can't be that. Fae don't have many children," he reminded her.

"There will be a book in the fae section," Mera said, jumping to her feet. "Are you okay here while I run and check it out? I know Len will be a great source, but he's not here yet, and I don't want to wait."

I desperately wanted to say no. I needed her support during this memorial retrieval. Not only because her mate was a scary beast, but for many other reasons.

What if my past was better left hidden?

I didn't say a word though. Tabitha was my top priority and finding out anything about fae children could only help with her health.

"We'll be fine," Shadow said. "Gaster has finished his task and is entering the room as we speak. He'll ensure that this is done as painlessly and safely as possible for Samantha."

"Two of my current favorite words," I drawled. "Also, alive. That's one that we need to put on repeat. Keep Sam alive. Keep Sam alive."

Mera waved me off. "Most of us have died once or twice. We come back stronger, so don't stress on that. I'll stroll into the underworld and retrieve you if I have to."

"You won't," Shadow growled. "You will leave the underworld to me. We've already been looking into it for Alistair. If there's a way, we'll figure it out."

Mera's face held so much optimism. "Yes, we'll figure it out, mate. Now I'm going to research."

She leaned down and kissed her daughter super quick. "Mommy will be back soon," she told her, and the child reached up and pressed her hands to her cheeks again. Mera all but melted at whatever passed between them. As she straightened, Shadow was at her side, and she climbed him like a fucking tree.

The heat that sprang to life the moment their lips met was near volcanic, and I sent a rueful smile down to the baby girls. "You two find a love like that one day, you hear me? Never settle for less."

Aurora waved her arms harder, and I was about to touch her when there was a rumble from the beast behind me. Figuring that was a warning, I kept my hands to myself and instead brushed a finger along Tabitha's cheek. Aurora suddenly reached out and grabbed my daughter's hand, wrapping her tiny one tightly around it.

I was still touching Tabby too, and in that moment I was sent a burst of warmth. There was no real context to the warmth, except for me to know that Aurora was happy. She was loved and safe. Tabitha would be too, as soon as I could remember my truth.

The past might be scary... dark... filled with horror. I had no idea what I would find, but I did know that remembering her conception and birth was important to ensuring she grew and developed to her full potential. Anything else, I could and would deal with as it came to light.

A weird sound escaped Tabby, and I was about to call out to the Shadow Beast in case Aurora's power was clashing with Tabitha's, but then my little girl smiled. A proper, beautiful, gummy smile. Two teeth popped into existence a beat later, a pair on the bottom, which most certainly hadn't been there two seconds before.

"Holy shit," I gasped.

Mera and Shadow were half over the couch now. "I think Aurora just gave Tabby teeth," I managed to say around my shock.

"Holy shit," Mera echoed. "How is that possible?"

"It's power," Shadow said without hesitation, always confident in his knowledge. "Tabitha has been deprived of the energy and power she needed to develop. What sort of power I don't know, but maybe we should leave these two here for a little while together. Aurora often has the answers."

Mera was nodding while I remained in hopeful shock. Shadow's theory made a lot of sense, and already it appeared that Tabitha was more alert.

"This research is so important," Mera burst out. "I'll be back soon!"

She took off, and Shadow's gaze never left her until she was gone from sight. When he turned back to face me after that, I could see a darkness descending over his expression. He'd gone from scary, sexy god, to scary, super fucking scary god. "Let's get on with the memory retrieval," he rumbled.

I was nodding like a good girl, because *damn*, when he commanded, it would be done.

Gaster thankfully appeared a moment later, which relieved some of the tension. And some of my panic. I'd been here when he broke Mera's memory block, and I trusted him with this process. "Miss Samantha," he said, a huge smile lighting his face. "It's so good to see you again. I know our Mera had been worried sick."

Despite his appearance, which was that of a demi-fae goblin, he had the demeanor of a fancy butler in a six-star hotel. *Wait! Demi-fae!*

"Gaster," I all but shouted. "It's so good to see you. Can you please tell me if my daughter is fae?"

He blinked once slowly, and then again, before his gaze dropped to Tabitha on her crystal bed. He hadn't felt her, just as the rest of them couldn't. "Impossible," he breathed, leaning in closer. "A shifter and a fae cannot make a child. Two fae can barely make a child."

"Impossible happens around here a lot lately," Shadow replied drily. "There's something with Mera's pack of friends that causes the norm to fuck up. Best we don't assume anything."

Gaster recovered from his shock quickly, before he looked my way. "Do you mind if I touch her?"

I shook my head. "Please. She's ten years old but hasn't aged almost at all. We need to know more about her genetics and how to get her healthy."

Gaster reached out and touched Tabitha, and as he did Shadow leaned over and gently removed Aurora's hold from my daughter. "Best not to muddle her energy," he said softly.

"She doesn't feel fae," Gaster mused as he looked her over. "But then again, she also doesn't feel like a shifter. It might be that she needs more energy to build her own up, and until that happens, she'll be this dead spot for those of us trying to reach her power."

Pain threatened to engulf me again, but I pushed it down. "All I ever have is more questions. Maybe breaking through my memory block is step one to figuring it out."

Gaster nodded, removing his touch from Tabitha. "Yes, let's get started. We must move away from the young ones. I don't know what explosion might result this time."

Images from the spell he used on Mera flashed across my mind, and I knew he was right.

"They'll be safe," Shadow said. "You can trust in me to keep the children safe even if it costs my life."

I believed every word he said.

"Thank you," I whispered, and maybe for the first time I didn't completely fear the beast.

After that, everything moved quickly. I lay on the floor in a wide space, and Gaster quickly traced a complex-looking circle around me, before placing some gems around the perimeter of it. "This will help me keep the energy contained," he said conversationally, his relaxed manner somewhat comforting.

When he was ready, he initiated the circle and I felt the energy close over the top of me. Almost immediately, Gaster started to chant, an icy bite of energy hitting my skin. It was sharp, cutting as it drove into my head, probing through the blocks that existed deep in my mind.

"This is not a spell like Mera's." Gaster's voice was strained. "But it's magic of some kind. More ancient than I've encountered before." He paused for a beat. "And it's fae in origin."

Our theory of Tabby's heritage was growing more plausible by the minute.

"I'm going to have to increase my power," he warned me.

"Do it," I grit out, ready to take my life back. "Go as far as you need—short of actually killing me." The fear of my unknown memories had faded under the need to have more information to help Tabitha. With no one able to read her, my memories might be all we had.

There was another pause from the goblin. "I'm sorry in advance for what I'm about to do."

Oh. *Fuck.*

The next cut was deeper, and I couldn't prevent a whimper from escaping. "I'm going to need your power, Shadow," Gaster bellowed. "This is ancient and deeply ingrained."

Ancient? Why would my memories be suppressed by ancient energy?

The pain increased again, and as Shadow's fire burned through the sharp cut of Gaster's power, the scream I'd been containing burst free. I'd been doing so well keeping it inside, but now that my skin was being flayed from my body—at least, that's how it felt—there was no more brave face. "You've got this, Sam," Shadow rumbled.

Easy for that fucker to say.

The next scream was louder, and I sobbed through my

pain, my wolf rising to shoot her own icy energy around, almost as if we were scrambling to find a tether to hold on to.

Shadow was saying something else, the tone vibrating through my body, but I couldn't really "hear" in my current state. Though I was fairly sure that somewhere in his rumble were the words: I'm not sure she'll survive."

Great. Just fucking great.

CHAPTER ELEVEN

SAMANTHA

Part of me wanted to pass out, but I also refused to on the chance my body decided to check out of this life. If I let myself fall into the darkness, maybe I wouldn't be able to hold on as strongly—and I had to stay here for my daughter. No fucking way was I giving up one more second of time with her.

Shadow and Gaster were no longer visible to me. A sheen of white surrounded my body, and at some point I must have thrown up on myself; the scent of vomit permeated the air.

There was just so much pain. And burning. And screams.

When I'd almost exhausted my strength to hold on to consciousness, darkness hovering at the edge of my vision, I felt a brush of icy energy against my senses. It felt like my wolf, but a million times stronger. It washed across the pain, and my chest heaved as I sucked in air.

For the first time since this started, I was able to fill my lungs fully, and the urge to vomit again faded. I had no idea what or who was helping me, but I was beyond grateful for the mild reprieve.

Shadow's voice cut through my cage, and I could make out his words clearly this time. "Len is here."

Len was here? The fae friend who might be able to help with Tabitha? I was sure I'd met him before, or at least been in the same room, but I couldn't recall anything about him. Was it his power that felt like an icy balm over my pain? Almost as if he'd inserted a barrier between me and Gaster's hacking into my brain.

Speaking of...

"I cannot break her block," the goblin said. "It would break her mind. We should wait for Len to physically arrive, since he's apparently sent his energy through first."

First. So it was his power protecting me from the pain. But why?

"Agreed."

Shadow and Gaster withdrew their energy, and with it the ice faded. My chest grew tighter at the loss, and I tried not to mourn what wasn't mine to keep. *Len.* The name continued to swirl in my mind, but I couldn't place the face that went with it.

Even without a face, I'd know his energy and power anywhere now—the sanity I'd clung to in a sea of pain.

As more lucidity returned, I managed to pull myself up into a sitting position, grimacing at the sight of my clothing. The vomit-strewn wedding dress was now destroyed beyond repair. I couldn't think of a better outcome for the outfit.

Just as Gaster moved forward, looking as if he was about to help me up, a blast of icy air cut through the room, dulling the heat from the fireplace. My pulse spiked in the same instant the power wrapped around me, just as it had when I was near dying.

"Gaster," Shadow said in a rumble of his own fiery power. "Get out of here. I'm not sure what's happening with Len, but I need you to protect the library."

The goblin was gone before I could blink, as a possible danger in his library drove him to new speed.

"Is Len dangerous?" I asked, still not quite able to get to my feet. My limbs were taking their sweet-ass time coming back on board, my shifter healing slower than usual. Or maybe the damage was just greater than I'd suspected.

"Yes," Shadow replied. "But generally not to us. Something has triggered his fury."

He shot me a long, dragging sort of look, like I'd been the one to piss off the powerful fae. Deciding it was best not to mention the soothing energy that had saved me before, I just crossed my arms and eyeballed the beast back. I might be on the floor in a vulnerable position, but that big bastard wasn't going to intimidate me again.

This was his damn friend on the way, and it had nothing to do with me.

Right? *Right.*

Shadow's gaze was pulled from me as the energy grew stronger, and as he shifted his position in front of the couch, guarding the babies, he also created a glimmering energy shield around them. How powerful was this fae that *the fucking Shadow Beast* was taking precautions against him?

A blast of cold shocked me, as small particles of ice appeared in the air around us. "Will the girls be safe?" I called, my legs refusing to hold my weight.

"I will protect them with my life," Shadow reminded me, and I once again decided to trust in him.

"What do you need me to do?" I said, wobbling around like

a newborn pup. The toll the spell had taken on my body was debilitating. It was really the last thing I needed when some super-powered fae was busting the library down.

"Just stay still and quiet," Shadow murmured. "Let me deal with him."

"Are you actually worried?"

A smoky laugh was his only response, and it did somewhat calm my panic.

Len was one of his brothers, and whatever was causing the upset in his power, surely it wasn't directed at Shadow. *Or me.* There had to be a reasonable explanation.

"Brace yourself," Shadow warned a second before the light grew so bright in the room that I was blinded. Deciding that I had to do something, I half stumbled, and half dragged myself closer to the couch, determined to get between Len and the babies. Shadow's shield was amazing, but I had to do my part as well. As a mother, I stood between my child and danger. *Always.*

Alpha Lorenze had taken that from me for too long. It would never happen again.

Unable to see my daughter, I could thankfully feel her energy, and it drew me in her direction. Everyone else might think she was a dead spot, but to me she was a beacon so much brighter than even the light saturating this room. When I hit the couch, Shadow's rumble rocked the room. The floor shook beneath me, and I would have fallen on my face if the cushions weren't there to prop me up.

"Brother," Shadow rumbled harder. "We are beyond blood, you know that, but you better have a fucking good explanation for bringing this sort of power into my library. Around my daughter and mate."

There was a brief pause, and then a raging snarl as a deep,

lyrical tone unfurled around us. "You hurt what's mine. Brother or not, you had to know this was coming."

Len's beautiful voice vibrated through me, starting from the top of my head to settle as a deep burning heat in my center, burning in a vastly different way to the pain from Gaster before.

Branding. Claiming.

In mere seconds, I'd been broken down and rebuilt.

And something told me my life would never be the same again.

CHAPTER TWELVE

SAMANTHA

"What do you think I have that's yours?" Shadow rumbled, a blast of fire cutting through the ice. Two elemental beings were about to go to war, and I really didn't want to be this close to the explosion.

Len paused, the silence heavy. "I felt her pain. Who do you hide from me?"

Her pain...

I didn't question if it was about me. I knew it was because he'd been in my mind, soothing the burn with his power.

"Brother..." Shadow's voice was nothing more than a whisper of death. "You need to calm down—"

He didn't even get a chance to finish before there was an explosion of pure, unfiltered energy. I'd never felt anything like it before, and as I threw myself forward over the top of the shield that covered the girls, I wondered if this was the last moment I'd have to hold Tabitha.

Even if Len didn't smash through the shield, Shadow's retaliation would be swift and unforgiving. The library would end up in tatters, and there was no way to know what collateral damage would result.

To my surprise, though, when the energy faded, the light and iced air did as well, and everything became crystal clear. Shadow had not moved, and it appeared that he was frozen to the spot. Standing behind him, a crystal in either hand, was a silvery being. He was concealed in shadows that hid most of his features from me.

I stood slowly, legs shaking. "What did you do to Shadow?" I asked in a breathless rush.

The silver form didn't move. "It will not hold him for long," Len said. "But he had to learn that nothing... not a brother... father... or my own mother will stand between me and what's mine."

Mine. Fuck, that word was destructive, and just a tiny bit enticing. The tugging sensation low in my gut became more consistent, dragging me toward this godlike creature.

"Who are you?" I knew it was Len, but that was a name. I needed something more.

"Len, prince of the Silver Lands," he replied instantly.

Len, who was of course a prince, had enough power to freeze the Shadow Beast in place.

Finding strength, I moved more between the silver figure and the babies, noticing from the corner of my eye that Shadow was twitching.

"I took him by surprise," Len said, following my line of sight.

We both knew that he hadn't. Shadow had been standing

there ready for him, so either the beast let him strike first, or this fae was some sort of superpower all on his own.

"Who are you truly?" I called, keeping a close eye on him, "Len, prince of the Silver Lands? How are you so powerful?"

He moved closer, and the icy shadows that had been surrounding him faded.

A gasp slipped from between my lips. *Holy gods above.*

The urge to rub my eyes was strong, since I had to be hallucinating.

Len was perfection.

Carved from those very gods, he stood a foot or more taller than me, his broad shoulders encased in a long silvery coat that moved about his body despite the lack of breeze in here. His face was sharp lines, hard curves, with full lips that were surprisingly masculine.

Piercing silver eyes locked on me, and even knowing that I had met Len before in the library, there was not one familiar feature on his breathtakingly beautiful face.

"Who are you?" he shot back. "A siren?"

I shook my head hard. "No—No. I'm Samantha of the Clarity shifters."

"Shifter..." he echoed, blinking in clear confusion, and for the first time since his presence could be felt in the lair, he appeared to relax. Both in energy and appearance.

He ran a hand through his short silver hair, sending it up in attractive tousles atop his head. There was literally not one unappealing part to this male, and at the same time not one part that wasn't otherworldly. He was filled with magic and energy, all of which was sliding over my skin and deep into my essence. *WHAT WAS ACTUALLY HAPPENING HERE?*

I was grateful when Mera chose that moment to burst into the library and all but tumble into our midst. This was also the moment Shadow exploded free from the spell that'd been holding him, lunging for Len. Mera, who put the scene together in a heartbeat, let out a shout and dove between the two of them. "NO!" she bellowed, fire bursting to life across her hands and arms. "Shadow, no!" Her hand landed on her mate, somehow stopping a bulldozer from taking out everything in this room.

Len hadn't moved a muscle, not even when Shadow raged toward him. All the while his gaze remained firmly locked on my face, sending my internal temperature from freezing to boiling in the same minute. I needed a breather from the intensity of his gaze, but there was nothing that could force me to look away.

Until... A cry split the air, and I jerked my head toward the couch.

Mera, who was at my side just as fast as she jumped between the raging males, let out a "what the fuck" as we stared at our girls.

They were sitting together on the couch.

Sitting. On. The. Couch.

The glow of Tabitha's skin was near blinding, and it didn't escape my notice that again she looked older.

"Did Aurora do that?" Mera asked, her hand grasping mine as if she needed support. As she turned to me, she must have noticed the tattered state of my dress, not to mention the liberal amount of vomit covering me. Before I could explain, the fire of her energy surrounded me, and when I looked down again I was clean and clothed in a simple white shirt and jeans.

"Thank you," I whispered.

She just grinned. "I've been practicing some new tricks."

She certainly had.

"Now, back to my question." She turned toward the babies once more. "Did Aurora help Tabitha sit on her own?"

It was possible, but I had an inkling it was someone else.

"Aurora looks older too," Shadow said huskily, his beast still riding him. "Since Len entered the room."

Hence the reason for my inkling. This wasn't about Aurora or Tabitha's power.

It was about Len's.

Len who was fae and part of the world I was terrified would steal my daughter from me. Shadow had promised that wouldn't happen, but apparently no one controlled the powerful fae in the room.

Turning, I found him standing mere inches away. "What in the hell—?" My words choked off as he took another step closer, until we were almost touching.

"You all have a lot of explaining to do," he said softly, with a feral undertone.

Mera turned then and made a move to touch Len, but Shadow snatched her up in his arms before she could make contact. In a beat, he'd hauled her away behind him, making sure he stood closest to Len.

Mera's snarl was loud. "Holy fucking fuck. I know you didn't just do that, mate."

Shadow let out a smoky huff. "Len just froze me on the spot, Sunshine," he growled. "He's ancient, out of control, and gunning for blood. This is not the fae you know and love."

"Yes it fucking is!" Mera insisted. "Besides, if I can handle your ancient ass, I can handle his."

The look on Shadow's face would have been comical if we weren't in this situation—he was desperately searching for what to say to keep his mate safely behind him, all the while knowing he'd already lost the battle.

For a beat, I swore that Len's lips twitched. "I would never harm Mera or your child," the fae bit out, no other sign of humor. "You can handle my energy, so I wasn't worried about using it against you."

This logic appeared to calm Shadow, and I found myself relaxing as some of the tension faded. Reaching back for Tabitha, I pulled her up into my arms, noticing how much more solid she felt against me. She was still tiny but clearly growing. A flicker of hope surged in my chest.

Len tilted his head, eyeing the tiny child in my arms. "This is my daughter, Tabitha," I said softly. "We believe she's part fae." There was no point in lying to him, especially when we needed his help.

His expression didn't shift, but the chill in the air grew a little more prominent. "She's definitely fae," he bit out, pushing even closer.

Tilting my head back, I realized how badly I'd underestimated his height. He was a fucking giant, and as I stared at the soft, silvery glow of his skin, I was struck by a sense of familiarity. Not because I could remember him, but because…

Tabitha held her arms out then as if she'd just come to the same realization as I did.

"She looks like Len," Mera whispered, no longer behind her mate. "What the hell is happening, Shadow? How is this possible?"

Len's hand came up slowly, as if he didn't want to spook me. He brushed a hand across the soft curls of Tabby's head, so gently that it was almost an art. His grace was second to none.

"I feel her energy," he said slowly. Only the second to be able to do that. "She's mine."

Those words echoed through my head as our gazes met.

One of my greatest fears had come to pass.

Tabitha's father had found us.

And he was a fucking prince of Faerie.

CHAPTER THIRTEEN

SAMANTHA

Sanity kicked in, along with all the mother instincts to protect my daughter. Holding her tighter, I spun away from Len, and all but jumped over the couch to keep distance between us.

"She's mine," I growled as my wolf reared her head. "I've waited years to be free of my pack, able to hold her whenever I want. I will kill anyone who tries to take that from me."

As I huffed and continued to back away, Tabby finally lowered her arms, tilting her head up to look at me. "Sorry, baby," I whispered. "I have to protect you. We don't know his intentions."

Len watched me but didn't move closer. He allowed me the illusion of safety, and I felt marginally better about it.

When he tilted his head in a similar manner to Tabitha, I wondered how I hadn't seen their similarities almost instantly.

No wonder he had felt familiar, he was clearly someone I knew very well in the past. "You cannot give her everything she needs," he said softly, gaze locked on me the way a predator watches their prey. "She's fae, and if you say you've waited years, it's clear she hasn't thrived on Earth. I can help you figure it out."

My gaze darted to Mera, silently asking her if she found any answers. "No helpful books on raising their young," she said sadly. "They're all magically updated, and it appears that young are rare as anything these days."

Len crossed his arms, the gesture accentuating the breadth of his shoulders in the silver duster jacket. He didn't say anything further, allowing me to come to the only logical conclusion from this information: I needed him to help save my daughter.

"Promise that you won't take her from me?" I managed to rasp around the lump in my throat. "Swear it on whatever is the most important thing in your world."

Len nodded. "You have my word, sworn here before Shadow and Mera, that I will do everything in my considerable power to ensure that you remain her primary custodian. Faerie children need their parents, their mother. And while this isn't going to be an easy journey, I believe we will find our way through."

"Why not easy?" His words didn't fill me with confidence.

Len's answer was sharp and succinct. "Because there has never been a half-fae born before. Tabitha is one of a kind."

Shadow let out a rumbling growl. "Samantha has a memory block. This is what we were trying to lift when you threw your temper tantrum."

A burst of laughter escaped Mera, remaining even as her mate shot her a dark look. "No, no, sorry. I just... karma is fun."

Shadow huffed. "I don't throw temper tantrums, Sunshine. I command and everyone fucking obeys."

Mera's lips were pressed hard together as if that would stop the next snort of laughter.

Shadow shook his head, ignoring his spluttering mate. "The block is from an ancient fae magic. It could not be lifted, even using the combined strength of Gaster and myself. Hopefully, you will have more of an idea."

Aurora chose that moment to lift herself up from the couch, into the air, and sail across to her father's arms. Shadow visibly calmed the moment she settled against him.

Mera's laughter faded as her expression shifted from amused to... well, definitely not amused. Her mate acting all "daddy like" had hunger sliding across her features, and I really couldn't blame her. The beast holding that child like she was the most precious thing in the world was a vibe.

My gaze returned to Len since I couldn't apparently look away from him for more than a few moments. "Do you remember me?" I asked, since we were discussing the memory block.

"No," he said shortly. "Whatever is blocking your memories has affected mine as well. It's almost as if we've been glamoured. Spelled by Faerie magic."

Glamoured. That sounded scary and very mystical. But seriously, to affect Len it had to be the most powerful of Faerie magic. Before I could hyperventilate, he shifted course. "You feel the connection between us now that we're together, right?"

Straight to the fucking point.

"I do," I replied, equally as honest. "I just don't understand any of this. When did we meet up? Why can't I remember anything about you?"

Mera stopped eye-fucking her mate for a moment to turn to

me. "So, you don't even remember meeting Len in the library, years after you would have had the block on your memories?"

I shook my head. "Nothing. And yet I remember the library clear as anything."

"I don't remember meeting her in the library either," Len confessed. "But I do have a theory about what happened years ago when we must have first met. It could explain why all our memories together were tainted."

That grabbed my attention. "What's your theory?"

Those silver eyes flicked down to land on my daughter, before returning to my face. "You're not ready to know. And if I'm wrong, I could lead you down a path of disappointment. For now, we must remain close enough to each other not to trigger the memory loss again. The only way to do that is if we return to Faerie. To my kingdom. From there, I will be able to figure out the rest."

Of course he had a kingdom. Why wouldn't he? He was a prince after all.

The thought of leaving for Faerie with Tabitha was terrifying on an entirely new level. Len had said he'd do everything in his power to ensure she remained with me, but I knew that at times shit would be out of his power. That was just how life worked.

But, again, I had no other option.

Mera made her way to my side, hugging me close. "You can trust Len," she murmured near my ear. "He's a good one. I know he'll figure out how to lift the spell on you guys and ensure Tabitha thrives."

"I know, but I'm still scared." No point hiding it. Every being here could probably hear the racing of my pulse.

"We will visit you," Mera promised, hugging me one more time. "You won't be alone for too long." Her head turned to find Shadow. "Right? We can visit?"

"We can," Shadow told her. "I've been wanting to get you back into the realm."

Mera's temperature must have risen twenty degrees in that moment. She smiled. "I'll bet you have."

There was a backstory there, one I wasn't privy to, but that didn't matter. What mattered was their offer to visit. For the first time I had a true pack, and their strength fueled my own. "Yes. Okay. I'm ready to go to Faerie and find the answers."

"Tomorrow," Mera cut in. "Today, I have all my family and pack in one place. We must take this chance to celebrate."

Len looked like he was about to refuse, even going as far as opening his mouth, but Mera cut him off. "Don't fucking argue with me, Len. One damn night is not going to ruin your plans."

His expression softened as he met her stare. "You're correct. Plus, I do need to fill you all in on what's transpired in Faerie recently."

This got Shadow's attention. The beast stepped closer. "This is what you got called back for?"

Len nodded, and I had to marvel at the lack of tension between them. it was almost as if their fight never happened. In Clarity, they'd still be trying to destroy each other, but in true family style, these powerful males had already forgiven and forgotten.

Glancing down at Tabitha, I found her smiling and staring up at me. "We're going to be okay, baby," I told her, keeping my voice low as I pressed my lips to her cheek and breathed her scent in. "I just know it."

The future was uncertain, but that didn't mean there wasn't hope.

As long as Tabby was healthy, I'd deal with the rest. Even if it was a sexy as fuck fae prince who was apparently my baby daddy. Stranger things had happened. Right?

Yeah, probably not.

Len and Shadow started to discuss something to do with Faerie, and as they moved away from us, Mera spun toward me. "Holy shit, Sam!" she breathed, her eyes wide as she bounced. "What just happened? How did it just happen? You banged Len? I just..." She fanned her face and practiced some deep breathing exercises.

A strangled laugh of disbelief escaped me. "I don't know how this happened, but the only conclusion I can come to is that he's the crystal-loving hippie," I whispered back. "Which is literally all I can remember, along with the tattoo."

Pressing my hand against the wolf on my side, I tried to bring up memories of that time, but there was only blank space. "Len does all the supernatural tattoos," Mera added, like she was ticking off pieces of the puzzle. "And his power is enhanced by crystals."

It made sense, and yet there was so much we still didn't know. "Why would our memories be affected like this?" I wondered. "I mean, to the extent that I don't remember having a child, or my time with Len?"

After meeting the fae in the flesh, there was literally zero chance I would ever have forgotten him by natural means. I mean, he was the most devastatingly gorgeous supernatural I'd ever seen.

"We'll figure it out," Mera said determined. "You and Len are part of our family. Tabitha is one of our babies. We won't rest until this damn mystery is solved."

Something in her tone froze in my chest. "Len and I aren't star-crossed lovers about to fall into each other's arms and declare our undying love," I whispered in a rush. "I mean, whatever happened between us was so unnatural it caused a ten-year memory loss for us both."

Mera didn't look convinced. "I've lost my memory before too. It's masking the truth, but it can never erase it. I think we're going to find out your true self very soon, Samantha Rowland. Trust me on this, you're about to get a fucking glow-up to rival mine. And I can't wait."

I wanted to argue again, but a part of me refused to say the words.

Maybe I was finally stepping into my true path.

A path that had been hidden by whatever entity stole my memories, but now that I was aware, I would fight until I found my truth.

CHAPTER FOURTEEN

LEN

Shadow and I moved away from Mera and Samantha to repair the final broken bonds between us. And while I was looking his way, my focus was definitely on someone else. "I'm sorry, brother," Shadow said first, surprising me. He was a lot of things, but quick to apologize was not one of them. Especially when I'd initiated the attack. "If I knew that Samantha and Tabitha had anything to do with you, I would never have stood in the way."

Reaching out, I clasped a hand on his shoulder. "No, that was on me. Instinct took over." I shook my head at the mindless state I'd been in. Was still in, if I was being honest, as a barely contained beast raged within me. "I'd have destroyed the world to get to her." Another shake of my head. "It was a true mate calling. But why and how the fuck is this even possible?"

Shadow's expression darkened. "A true mate calling? What

is it about today that brought the call to life, and... do you still feel it now?"

I didn't. The beast raged higher.

"There's a need," I admitted, thinking of the pull toward her smooth, dusky skin, long dark hair, and plump pink lips. "But it's not the strength of a true mate bond any longer."

Almost as if there was a block in the way once more.

For now, all I felt was the call of an incredibly beautiful and desirable woman.

There was a pause as Shadow considered my words. "You felt the call when we were attempting to break the memory block. Now that she's fully blocked once more, it's not a surprise that the intensity of the pull toward her has faded. But how did she end up with your child? When did this happen and how were none of us aware?"

They were complex questions, since Tabitha should have been an impossibility. But then again, our pack was built on impossibilities. *Tabitha*. The name rolled around my mind, swirling and bouncing from thought to thought, and I couldn't stop the deep ache that settled in my chest.

Daughter. I had a daughter I didn't know about until this moment, and I still hadn't even held her. The fear in her mother's eyes when I'd moved closer had stopped me, but eventually I would know what it felt like to hold my young. A long-forgotten dream I'd all but given up on.

"I have no idea, but I'm going to find out," I rumbled as the raging beast of my power slammed against the cage once more. "This memory loss we're both facing is energy and magic based. Someone or something did this to us, and I intend to find all the answers."

Death awaited any who kept me from my child—except for her intriguing mother. I'd have to be careful about how I approached this situation. I didn't know the full story of

Samantha's history with Tabitha, but I'd already seen enough. She was wary of fae and desperate to keep her child with her, and I had to assume she had very good reasons for that.

For now, Samantha had to understand that unless Tabitha returned to Faerie, she would remain underdeveloped and weakened. Once she gained strength, she could leave if she had a strong fae with her to balance her energy. And eventually she'd learn to balance her own.

"Her alpha kept Tabitha from her," Shadow said. My gaze snapped from him to Samantha, who was calmly chatting to Mera. "He hid your daughter and forced Samantha to promise herself to his son in exchange for getting her back. He pretended he was the only one who knew how to keep Tabby healthy, since he had her crystal mat."

My rage grew as icicles danced in the air around us. "He's dead, correct?"

Shadow paused. "Not yet. But he remains locked in stasis, and I feel hits against his energy as the pack takes out their frustration on him."

That calmed some of my ire. "I see why she's so protective of Tabitha. Her fear was palpable when I arrived in the room. I thought it was something to do with you, but I see now that it was me."

"Yes," Shadow confirmed. "She didn't tell us about Tabitha for many years because she knew of my connection to you and yours to Faerie. She was afraid that Tabby would be destroyed as some sort of hybrid monster, or taken from her to your world. You're going to have to tread very carefully with her."

He was reiterating what I already knew, and I wondered if this might not be my greatest challenge.

"What is happening in Faerie?" Shadow asked abruptly, changing the subject. "Does it concern Solaris System safety? Or is it internal?"

There was no straightforward answer to such a complex situation. "It is internal," I started, "but there's a possibility it could seep out into the worlds, depending on the outcome."

Shadow nodded, as if he were expecting such an answer. "Tell us more at dinner, when everyone is present. It sounds like there might be a need for a new group project to keep our pack safe."

With such a strong pack behind me, Fredrick of the Metallic Meadows would have to watch his back if he thought he was going to claim the throne as the new Great Ruler. The fight for now was to keep the Great Queen's line from being severed altogether, but if we lost that battle, then I would ensure Queen Glendriel held the spot as ultimate ruler.

Another reason I needed Samantha and Tabitha in Faerie, so I could deal with both soul-changing events that were taking place at this time in history.

Like I'd called her with that thought, Samantha and Mera crossed over to us, just as Shadow asked, "Does it concern you that I couldn't break the mind block?"

With one eye on the shifter and another on my brother, I let out a deep breath. "Yes and no," I admitted. "You're not fae, and if this is ancient magic from my kind, it might only be broken through other fae magics. On the other hand, you're a superpower, so it's always going to be a worry when you fail at any magical task."

Shadow nodded, his gaze moving to Mera. "I went at maybe seventy percent, knowing my mate would have broken me into little pieces if I'd permanently hurt her friend."

I would have broken him into little fucking pieces. "Mera would never hurt you," I said, forcing myself to remain calm. She adored Shadow, and what they shared was everything I could have hoped for him. A true, unconditional mate bond.

The sort of bond I'd taken my mate walks to find but had never happened for me.

Except maybe it had, and some fucker had messed with our minds, stealing precious time from us. Clearly Samantha and Tabitha were the reason I'd been feeling a call to Earth. They held the answers, and I had to hope we had time to uncover them all.

"Are we ready for dinner?" Mera asked as she settled in beside Shadow, bouncing Aurora in her arms. Their child, with her ancient golden eyes, was the future of our pack. All the young were. I had to marvel that Tabitha would be part of such a strong pack.

A pack that only grew stronger by the day.

Samantha held our daughter gently, looking upon her constantly, as if checking she was okay. She often leaned in and brushed her lips across the top of her silvery-blond hair, and down on her cheeks, cherishing the child as if she were the most important thing in her world.

If I hadn't already been destroyed by the revelations here today, I was now.

"I'm ready for *after* dinner," Shadow answered Mera's question from before. "So, let's get the food part over with."

Mera paused, her eyes widening as her own *appetite* took over before she got herself under control. "After dinner, mate," I heard her murmur. "I'll hold you to that."

Shadow smiled. It was fucking disconcerting to see that big bastard so happy. I should be used to it by now, but there had been decades of him barely showing emotions, and it would take a long time to adjust to this new version.

The gods help us all if anything ever happened to Mera or Aurora.

Shadow and I exited first, a habit to check that there was no danger before the others emerged into the Library of Knowledge. The females could handle themselves just fine, but it was our jobs to stand between them and danger. Not the other way around.

No matter how often Mera argued with us, we stood firm in our resolve. This didn't weaken them in any way, and if anything, it showed how important and strong they really were. Queens who deserved to be sacrificed for. They also needed to live for their children, and the future of the world.

I would never shirk in my duty to protect those who deserved it.

Not while there was breath in my body and magic in my veins.

CHAPTER
FIFTEEN

SAMANTHA

The dining area was full when we entered, most of the tables taken up by those who utilized the Library of Knowledge from the worlds of the Solaris System. But there was always one table that remained free. The Shadow Beast's table.

Only, today it had some occupants. A familiar shifter popped up from one of the chairs, and my chest squeezed tightly at the sight of her beautiful face. With her blue-black hair streaming behind her, Simone sprinted for me. "Sam," she cried, throwing her arms around me. "I can't believe you're here!"

She was squeezing me tight when she appeared to notice the baby in my arms. Her hug gentled immediately, and I let myself sag against her. Simone and Mera felt like old friends, the sort where you could go years and not see each other, but when you were back together it was home.

When she pulled away, her hands still on my arms, she looked me over. I did the same, noticing subtle changes in her that spoke of a power glow-up, just like Mera had.

"Friend, you must tell me everything that has happened to you since we last spoke." I shook my head, taking in her ethereal glow. She'd always been beautiful, with her tanned skin and dark eyes, but now she burned brighter. A literal glow infused her essence, and it wasn't a natural shifter evolution. It was more.

A tall and blond, not to mention hot-as-hell and vaguely familiar dude, slid in behind her, and when he flashed fangs I knew this was Lucien. Simone tilted her head back, her glow increasing as she shot him a smile. "I ended up in Valdor, the vampire world. And the masters forced me to enter a damn *find a mate* contest." She turned back toward me, words spilling out faster as she continued. "Turned out I did find a true mate, and it was this fucking guy, coming out of nowhere to claim me like the master vampire he is. I also happened to die a touch and come back as some sort of lycan shifter hybrid."

The tattoo on my side flashed in my mind, and I understood what Mera had told me about that tattoo predicting the future in some ways. "You look amazing," I told her. "Strong and so perfectly sure of yourself. I can feel your new confidence." From previous conversations, I'd learned that Simone's parents hadn't been the most caring, and when Mera ended up in this world she'd felt so alone.

That clearly wasn't the case any longer.

Lucien wrapped a possessive hand around the back of his mate's neck, and Simone's expression was one of pure bliss as she turned back to meet his gaze. "I feel stronger," she admitted. When she finally dragged her eyes from Lucien, she returned to me. "And you have a baby. How do you have a baby, friend?"

A small laugh escaped me; it was a little hard to believe. "This is my daughter, Tabitha." A brief pause. "I have a lot to explain, and since half the story I don't even know, it's going to be odd, but with Len's help I'll do my best to fill you in."

Simone and Lucien both shifted their gaze to Len, who had been standing like a quiet, lethal shadow just behind me. Yeah, I knew exactly where he was at all times, that icy energy familiar as it beat at my own.

Their brows furrowed as they examined the silver fae. "Len?" Lucien drawled. "What does this have to do with you, brother?"

Before he said a word, wind burst through the room, dry and scented with creosote plant. Everyone was distracted as Angel and Reece strolled along the path between tables, and I examined the child snuggled in the badass angel's arms. A little boy, who appeared to be about six months older than Aurora, if his size was any indication. This had to be Damon.

The others smiled and relaxed at the sight of the newcomers. "This pack has grown and prospered in ways I could never had predicted," Lucien said, with a glint in his eye. He pulled Simone even closer, until she was nestled back against his chest, and as he leaned down to press his lips to her throat, I caught a glimpse of fangs. It didn't bother me though. There was nothing scary in his demeanor, and instinctively I knew he'd die before harming his mate.

All the males in this group showed the same alpha, protective characteristics. A far cry from the "true mate" I'd been presented with in the pack. Both Patche brothers had been weak and pathetic, and now that I was free of their father's control, I'd never settle for a bonding like that again.

When Angel and Reece reached us, I found myself staring into her pink-hued eyes, feeling as inadequate as I had the last time we met. Angel was strong and capable in ways I'd never be; she was my secret woman crush. Not that there was anything "woman" about this mystical being.

"Who is this beautiful little girl," she cooed when she leaned down toward Tabby.

"This is Tabitha," I said softly. "My daughter."

"And mine," Len added drily, finally admitting the *insane* truth to the rest of his family.

Everyone in the vicinity went silent. The only faces not shocked were Mera's and Shadow's, who were already seated at the table.

Reece finally broke the silence. "Yeah, okay. We all need to get our asses in chairs, because this is a story I have to know."

He wasn't the only one.

No one spoke again as we were ushered toward the table, and I was grateful when Len took the seat across from us. His energy right at my side would have been too distracting, or so I thought until I realized that now I got to stare at his even more distractingly perfect face without any barriers.

Fuck.

It wasn't just his face, but also his broad shoulders spilling over the sides of the chair as he attempted to fit his extra-large frame into the small space. I mean, it wasn't hard to understand how I'd fallen into bed with him, and whatever attraction had sprung up between us was still well in effect today. My mouth was dry, and other parts of me were not, and... damn.

Resisting the urge to fan my face or possibly wipe at drool, I forced myself to look toward Mera. "Since we have a lot to chat about," she said, "let's all get comfortable, and we'll order food after."

On cue, a faceless, odd-looking robotic server hurried over.

It was followed by a few others, each holding what looked like a highchair without legs. It took me a minute to figure out how they worked, as they clipped them on to the side of the table. One ended up between me and Simone. One between Mera and Shadow, and the final between Angel and Reece.

The others slipped their children into the chair, not bothering to buckle the strap. "They can zap themselves in and out of existence," Mera explained when she caught me staring. "No point trying to trap these little powerhouses."

Angel laughed and didn't disagree.

With some reluctance, I looked down at Tabitha, not ready to let her go yet, but knowing that she needed to keep progressing. Developing. She'd already achieved so much today, and it would be good to see if she could sit in the chair like all the other babies. Forward movement was the only way, even if my heart ached at the newborn stage I'd missed out on, being all but done.

I could feel Len's icy silver gaze, but once again he made no move to add in any parenting tips. He remained relaxed in his chair, but I'd been around enough predators to know that it was all a façade. He'd be up and at my side in a heartbeat if needed. Biding his time didn't take away from how deadly he was. That demonstration in the lair before had been all I'd need to never *ever* underestimate Len of the Silver Lands.

Tabitha didn't cry or seem upset when I settled her into the chair with its small tray. She just waved her arms, made some cooing sounds, and looked around with her purple gaze.

"She's absolutely stunning," Angel said, shaking her head. "It has been so long since I saw a fae young." She shifted her body toward Len. "How is this even possible? Of all the races, the fae have the least compatible genetics with others."

"Even with other fae," Len added without inflection. "We

barely produce young these days, so there's something deeper going on with this little one. Whatever happened between Sam and me, it's got a backstory that we need to discover."

None of them looked less confused, and since Len and I had about twenty percent of the story between us—much of which was still guessed—that confusion was not going anywhere.

"I'll start," I said quickly, knowing it would be easier if everyone was on the same page. "Apparently, ten years ago I was pregnant and gave birth to Tabitha before I passed out and the alpha stole my child away. When I awoke, I had no memory of anything to do with Tabitha, and instead believed the story that I'd been in an accident and was recovering." Thinking back on the time after I woke, there were signs of what had happened to me, but who would believe they'd been pregnant and given birth and not remembered any of it? It was easier to accept the lie.

"The alpha took my child because he recognized her heritage as that of only half shifter. He thought he could use her power when she was older. He never intended to give her back, or even inform me of her existence."

"Really hope they're kicking that fucker in the balls," Mera piped up with, before letting out a huff.

"They are," Shadow said with a slow smile. "He's suffering."

That appeared to calm his fiery mate as she nodded a few times. "Good."

"When did he decide to use the child to control you?" Len asked softly, and if the sudden chill in the air was any indication, he was barely holding on.

"When I shifted before them for the first time and the alpha's son recognized me as his true mate. He rejected me near instantly, which I was grateful for, even if at the time it felt rough. When I finally got free of the pack, the alpha told his son about the baby and how they could use it to bring me back and control me forever, and the son refused. Alpha Lorenze destroyed him that day, and decided his second son was the one who would mate with me. He wanted my connection to Torma and Mera. To the Shadow Beast."

My gaze drifted across to where they were watching me. "You two are famous amongst the packs now. Everyone wants a connection to Shadow. No matter how many times I explained that I'm just as terrified of the beast as the rest of them, they thought I was the key."

Shadow smiled, as if pleased by this, but there was fire burning deep in his eyes.

I continued, grateful that no one had interrupted. "Alpha Lorenze brought me back to the pack after that, told me my history, and the moment I felt Tabitha's energy I knew the truth. He kept her close enough that I didn't forget her again, and I did everything in my power to get her back. The only reason I'm not mated and popping out shifter pups now is his son was too young and hadn't shifted yet. But today... today was the day, and somehow Shadow and Mera showed up at the right moment to give me and Tabby a chance at a real life."

Simone reached out behind Tabitha's chair and grasped my arm. "Why didn't you tell us?" she rasped, her eyes glassy as she swallowed hard. "You lost years of time with your daughter. Years being part of this pack. We could have prevented so much heartache."

Swallowing roughly myself, I shook my head. "I didn't know that Shadow could read minds. The alpha told me only he knew how to keep Tabitha alive, and I mean... look at her. She's ten years old and barely looks six months. Most people can't feel her energy, but I can. And at times she was so weak. Which I now know the alpha did deliberately. That bastard."

Len let out a growl, and fuck if everyone didn't still at the sound. "Fae children require massive influxes of energy in their early years," he rumbled, voice scary deep. "The crystal mat would have kept her alive, but she couldn't thrive. Not on Earth, with its lack of power."

Panic choked me for a second before I swallowed it down. "Is it too late now to help her?" I managed to ask.

"No," he said immediately, as if knowing I was about to burst at the seams. "You can think of it as her being in stasis, but as you can see, already in a world of strong magic and power, she's blooming. Once we're back in Faerie, it will only be days before she's much bigger than Aurora and Damon. There's no fast tracking her growth—she will not look ten for quite a long time, but she will still develop just as she always would have. No permanent damage."

Relief had me sagging into my chair. "Thank the gods."

This was the point that the servers returned for us to order. I just went with a sandwich; not sure my stomach could handle anything heavier.

Angel, who had clearly been processing everything in that ancient brain of hers, was the first to speak after the servers left. "The fact that you don't remember anything from being with Len, or the pregnancy and birth, leads me to believe the spell over you has something to do with the ancient faerie magic that controls true mate bonds."

True mate bonds. It had been such a negative phrase for me over the last few years, but Angel was talking about fae bonds. Not shifters. I knew next to nothing about the world of Faerie. Hell, it hadn't been that long ago that I was completely unaware of *any world* outside of Earth.

Were their bonds different to shifters?

"Fae go on magical walks to find their mates," Len said, answering the confusion on my face. "We're put into a trance-like state, infused with the fertility energy, and when we leave we're drawn to our mates. We can find them anywhere across Faerie, or I guess technically, across the worlds."

"Not that it's ever happened between worlds," Shadow added. "Fae stick with fae. It's a known fact."

Len nodded. "This is true. Our magics and energy are generally not compatible with other races. And as far back in history that I know, there's never been a true mate pairing from outside of Faerie."

"How do the walks work?" Mera asked, before I could delve into what he'd just said.

Len answered her, even as his gaze remained on me, taking in my reaction to everything. "When we go into the trance, we don't remember anything that happens during that time. It's only when we return and wake, if we found our true mate, they will be there with you and the memories return. If you didn't find your mate, you will wake alone and with no memories. Until your mate is found, the walks remain a mystery."

I was just about fucking done with these mystical bonds that appeared to remove free will.

Len's eyes narrowed and I realized in my shock that I must have blurted that out. "There's still free will," he told me. "Anyone with a mate can choose to reject them. As you and Mera know, it's not even that rare, but most of the time those of us who have walked this world for millennia understand that your true mate is the only being who will truly complete you."

I'd insulted him, and that hadn't been my intention. But after everything I'd been put through from my true mate and his family, the bitterness was somewhat ingrained.

Or maybe there was a touch of unhappiness from another factor...

"If we don't remember, that must mean we aren't true mates, right?" I'd drawn the logical conclusion, and it fucking bothered me. Even though the fae and I were strangers.

Yeah, I might have lost my damn mind.

CHAPTER SIXTEEN

SAMANTHA

Everyone remained silent after my last statement.

A statement that hadn't given any indication if I was happy or not by the fact that we weren't mates. Maybe because I didn't even know how I truly felt about it. Today had already been the longest, strangest day in existence. My emotions and thoughts were messy, and it'd take days—and probably therapy—to truly figure out my feelings on this whole Len situation.

"I don't think we can assume that yet," Angel said suddenly. "Firstly, the spell could be masking a lot. And secondly, if you can produce a child, there must be a deeper bond. Not to mention some fae in Samantha's heritage."

"I was thinking the same," Mera piped up. "I mean, the first time I saw her I thought she was more gorgeous than any shifter had the right to be. She held a little *extra*."

As the others around the table started to nod, I didn't do my normal and argue. It wasn't that I thought I was ugly. I knew I was reasonably attractive, but so were most shifters. The *extra* they spoke of had been imbued in us through the Shadow Beast. I didn't see how I had *extra* extra but arguing about it just felt redundant.

"How do we find out exactly what's causing the memory loss?" I asked, pushing us back toward the important stuff. "How can we solve the mystery that has surrounded the entire situation with Len? I mean, my life has always been riddled with weird happenings, but this is definitely the weirdest."

"Always?" Len responded so quickly I almost jumped. "What weird happenings?"

My next words were raspier as my throat tightened. "I shifted before my twenty-second birthday." This was the first time I'd ever admitted it out loud. "I actually can't remember when I first shifted, but I was young. I never had parents around to ask, so I was just a wild shifter pup until I fell into packs."

Mera leaned so far forward she was all but draped over the table. "You told me that you were with the hippie crystal lover before your first shift."

I shot her a rueful smile. "Yeah, sorry, I spent so much of my life covering up my differences that it was second nature to stick with the lie."

No one looked upset by my fabricated story, and I had to assume that in their long lives most of them had been part of a ruse once or twice.

"Shifting as a pup is unheard of," Shadow rumbled as he sank back into his chair, his eyes unfocused. "For my *rules* to be overrode, there has to be some sort of mixed genetics."

Mixed genetics for me as well? If only I knew who my true family was, that would have made this entire search easier. "I can't help with that," I said with a shake of my head. "My parents are nonexistent. It's quite possible my first shift was after the trauma of losing them or whatever happened."

"Can I touch you?"

My head jerked toward Len, his deep, smooth tones filling my mind. "Touch me?" I echoed, giving myself a moment to recover.

He nodded. "It's the best way for me to feel the energy and blocks on your memories. It sounds like they might go back much further than ten years. Touching Tabitha might help as well."

Despite the request, he made no move closer. If anything, he'd clearly been going out of his way to keep his distance and allow me time to come to terms with who he was, and the path we must traverse next. For that, and the sake of answers, I was willing to take a chance on him.

"Yes," I said with a decisive nod. "Yes, I would appreciate it if you touched us to see what you can read."

And maybe a *teeny* tiny part of me was curious how his touch would feel. Icy like his power? Or heated like the liquid silver swirling in his eyes?

Len stood as the food arrived, pausing while the dishes and trays were placed before us. When the robots left, he let out a deep breath. "It can wait until after you build up some strength." He retook his seat as I wondered how fucking ragged I looked. I'd blame it on this shitty day and the need for a shower, even with Mera's energy conjuring us some fresh clothes and removing my vomit stench.

My meal was placed before me, and I noted that Len only had what looked like berries and watermelon, or their fae equivalents since they were a little different to Earth's version. "Would you mind if I gave Tabitha some?" he asked, noticing my stare. "I'm curious to see if she's drawn to fae foods."

I almost said no, since she'd only just learned to hold herself upright. But, considering she was also no ordinary child and strengthening her was the ultimate goal, it felt stupid to refuse. Surely Len would know if it was dangerous for a fae to eat so young. "We consume these dishes from birth," he added when my silence extended a moment too long for politeness. "She will not be harmed."

The *from birth* comment made me wonder if there was a whole range of reasons our daughter hadn't thrived, even outside of the fact that she hadn't been in Faerie.

Our. I'd just referred to her in my head as *our,* and it terrified me that already this joining felt natural. Len was a fairy tale I couldn't afford to fall into.

Nodding like a Bobblehead, I forced myself to focus. "Yes! Yes. Let's see if she wants any."

Len spent a few seconds preparing the fruit, cutting it into strips and making sure nothing was a choking hazard, then he leaned forward and placed a small plate on the tray. I'd never fed my daughter before, not from the breast or bottle, both of which I understood were greatly bonding. I'd missed so much, but I wouldn't let that stop me from being here for everything else.

Taking my eyes briefly from Tabitha, I noticed that Mera and Shadow had placed a few pieces of fruit before Aurora. Angel and Reece did the same with their boy. Despite their young ages, these children were clearly ready for extra nourishment to help with their astronomical growth. Aurora and Damon all but dove for their food, small hands grabbing up the mash and cubed fruits, eating with more skill than I'd expected. Tabby, on the other hand, was unsure. This was a huge first for her. She prodded the closest berry with her right hand.

"Go on, baby," I said, leaning down to her level. "Just take a little taste."

I picked up a piece of fruit, but before I could put it in my mouth, Mera shouted, "Noooo!"

My hand froze as I stared wide-eyed at her. "What?"

She was shaking her head fast. "You can't eat food from Faerie. It's designed to trap you in their world."

Len laughed, the sound a deep bass, and it drew my full attention. "That only happens when you're *in* Faerie, and only for those too weak to resist. Samantha should have no worries."

Mera relaxed, sinking into her chair and retrieving her cutlery that she'd all but thrown across the table. Fairly sure Reece was wiping mashed potato off his chest, but he never said anything as he continued eating.

"Okay, good," Mera sighed. "I just wanted to check."

She went back to eating, and I lifted the red melon once more. As it touched my lips, a literal burst of flavor almost knocked me from my chair. "Holy shit," I murmured, looking down at the fruit. It was as if the best watermelon in existence had been infused with the sugary sweetness of lemonade. A second taste had my eyes all but rolling in the back of my head, and I had to physically stop myself from stealing the rest of my daughter's food.

"Does all food in Faerie taste this good?" I asked with a shake of my head.

Len was watching me with his usual intensity. "To the fae it does. We have stronger senses than a lot of other races, though all of them enjoy our food."

A strangled laugh escaped me. "Despite your previous assessment, there's nothing fae in my energy or power," I warned him. It was best to put that out there before any hopes were raised.

He opened his mouth to reply, and at the same time Tabitha let out a small coo and grabbed a strip of the melon.

With amazing dexterity, she lifted it easily and put it straight into her mouth, biting down with her two new front teeth.

Len's attention shifted from me to her, watching with that same unwavering stare. Tabitha made a happy sound, her eyes lighting up as the purple swirled. Swirled, just like the silver of her father's eyes. Now that they were close, it wasn't just that he could feel her energy that told me she was Len's, but it was clear that the purple of her eyes was all but a darker shade of the silver in his.

Their faces were even similar, with those proud and perfect planes. A prince and princess of Faerie.

She finished her fruit in seconds, before reaching for more. With each bite and swallow, her skin glowed brighter, her eyes grew clearer, and she started to babble to the extent I could almost make out words.

"Samantha," Len said softly, drawing my attention from Tabitha. I wasn't the only one watching her closely. The rest of the table had locked in on her new changes. "You need to eat also. Your energy is too low."

He saw too much, and his concern twisted my insides in a way I didn't want to examine, so I chose to focus on the sandwich. Lifting it and taking a bite, I found the flavor almost bland after the fruit of Faerie. Strange, since it was fresh bread, warm chicken, and a tangy dressing that should have completely satisfied me. Still, it was food and I needed to finish it.

After eating half the meal, I felt some of my own strength return, and I had to admit Len was right. I wasn't glowing like Tabitha, but I had been weak. I'd allowed myself to grow weak, which pissed me off to no end.

But I was finally free to grow and prosper, to take the next step along my path, which might be into Faerie. All I could hope was that in Faerie, I'd find the answers to the many questions that had plagued me over the past few years.

Once I had my answers, I'd never be weak again.

That was a promise.

CHAPTER SEVENTEEN

SAMANTHA

When we'd eaten, and the details about Tabitha, Len, and me were out in the open, it was time for the pack to deal with some other concerns.

"Tell us what's happening in Faerie?" Shadow asked, a glass of amber liquid in his hand, which he absentmindedly swirled as he faced Len.

Len wasn't eating any of the food he'd ordered—it seemed it was there simply to feed Tabitha. A fact that warmed my heart like the stupid sap I was.

"King Petre of the Ochre Sands and King Fredrick of the Metallic Meadows, two royal lands in Faerie, have called for the abolishment of the Great Queen's line." His words were clipped.

This statement shocked some of the others around the table, especially Angel, Reece, and Shadow, who leaned forward. Mera and Simone appeared to be just as confused as I was.

"They want to hand off the ultimate power and call the bloodline gone?" Angel asked, her face paler than it had been a second ago. "Through what means?"

Len lifted his own glass of amber liquid that had appeared in front of him courtesy of the server. Even from across the table, I could smell plum and the magical equivalent of alcohol. "They will have to sever the Great Queen's cord that leads to the Deep. To the origin of Faerie," he said. "It will take all the royal houses to achieve such a feat, and I can't say if everyone will survive the blowback of power."

"Has that line ever been severed before?" Angel asked. "I don't ever recall it happening."

Lucien shook his head, his gaze meeting mine. "It hasn't. We've only ever had one Great Queen."

The silence felt heavier after that.

Shadow took a drink. "If they sever the line, there'll be an imbalance of power. A black hole that would eventually consume Faerie and possibly the rest of the worlds. What's the plan to counter this?"

Len's jaw tightened, adding harder lines to his impressive features. "They will appoint a new Great Leader. The severed line will be attached to one of the royal houses, allowing them the same rights and power as the Great Queen. They'll be Faerie's new ultimate leader, able to touch the Origin."

Mera pushed herself forward. "What's the Origin?"

Len expression lightened. "It's the source of creation. Theoretically, all worlds have an Origin, a foundation of power that began life as we know it. Generally, it's not accessible for the average inhabitant of the worlds, but the Great Queen could touch ours. From this, she gave us extra crystals and strength..."

"Until she disappeared," Shadow added. "And then Faerie has weakened."

Len nodded. "Correct." He dropped his glass with a thud. "We cannot allow that power to fall into the hands of either Fredrick or Petre. Neither are worthy, nor would they be able to handle such strength. If the trials come to pass, I must compete so that my mother and the Silver Lands control the power."

His mother. The queen of the Silver Lands, and... Tabitha's grandmother.

Shadow was on his feet now, towering over us, darkness sliding briefly across his skin before it slipped away. "We'll be there to ensure that you have every advantage to succeed here. And if you don't, and there's a war, you know we'll have your back. We cannot allow this energy to fall into hands that would misuse it. Everything must remain in balance, or the Solaris System will implode and the rest of the worlds will be destroyed."

Grim expressions surrounded me, and I wasn't surprised. A cloying pressure pushed against my body, and I found my gaze lingering on my daughter, who was still munching on melon. Part of me wanted to shield her ears from such worry, but another knew that it was because of their presence here, these three tiny supernaturals, that we would fight until our last breaths to ensure that the power didn't fall into hands it shouldn't.

"Is it safe for Sam and Tabby to travel to Faerie if there might be some sort of fallout from the severing of the lines?" Mera asked, looking down at Len.

Simone jumped in as well. "Yes, we only just got them back in our lives. We need to protect them from all this supernatural bullshit for a while."

Their love was overwhelming, especially when I'd been

such a shitty friend lately. Seeing their loyalty was definitely a motivator to do better though. To be worthy of this pack.

"Samantha and Tabitha must return," Len said simply. "Tabby needs to boost her power, and now that the stasis is broken, it needs to happen sooner rather than later. Even more importantly, Samantha and I need to unravel the aspects of our memory loss and how this entire series of events came to be, considering she's a shifter."

A dark thought that had been hovering deep down for a while burst from me before I could stop it: "Are you disappointed that Tabitha's mom is a shifter?"

His silver gaze crashed into mine, the color darkening to resemble a stormy midnight grey. "You have given me the greatest gift a fae or male could ask for," Len said seriously. "A gift that I will protect with my life. You're both my family, and there's not an ounce of disappointment. Only joy."

My heart slammed in my chest so hard it was painful. I'd been utterly unprepared for that response, unprepared for the truth that despite my shifter genetics he wanted us in his life. *Family*. My daughter would have the family I'd never had.

"When do we leave?" I whispered, throat tight.

"Now," Len said, standing, his silver cloak sweeping out from his body. A second before, he'd been warm and open, now he was back to the mysterious and devilish god-like creature. Truth be told, I liked both sides of him.

Standing as well, I reached down and freed my daughter from the chair, pulling her close against my chest. Only to be hit with another heart wrenching shock when she wrapped her arms around my neck, holding on with strength. As my breath caught, I closed my eyes to absorb a near perfect moment.

"She's growing stronger already," Len said, sounding closer.

Pulling away from Tabitha, I saw him beside us, and despite my agreement to allow him to touch us, he kept enough distance that we wouldn't accidentally brush together. I wondered if he'd forgotten his decision to probe the spell until he said, "I've decided to wait until we reach Faerie to explore the memory loss. There we'll be at our strongest, surrounded by my gems and the power of the Silver Lands." His decision made perfect sense, and I was both disappointed and relieved to have our inevitable touch delayed.

Simone, Mera, and Angel got to their feet and moved closer. "As soon as you know what's happening with the great line, we'll join you in Faerie," Simone said. She tilted her head back to find Lucien. "We can do that, right? Go into Faerie."

He nodded, a slight smile lifting his lips. Simone's face brightened as she spun back to me. "Yes! Just stay safe, friend, until we get there." She hugged me hard.

Feeling overwhelmed once more, I tried not to cry. "I'm blessed to have friends like you all," I said roughly. "Tabby is going to have a true family. A true pack. It's a gift."

"You're both going to have a true family!" Mera said fiercely as she threw her arms around me. "We're here for you now, and we'll make sure that you get your happily ever after too. Just like in our favorite paranormal romance novels."

Mera was a huge reader. Simone was as well, always sending me recommendations. I'd never replied, but I'd secretly read and loved every single one. It felt almost like a bond between the three of us, and I was ready for more.

"See you all in Faerie," I said as we parted ways. "And thank you." *For everything.*

They all murmured goodbyes, then I found myself walking side by side with Len, heading toward the unknown of Faerie.

There was no way for me to comprehend how many ways my life was about to change, but I was determined that no matter what, I'd never look back at my old life.

That was done. Time for a new path.

CHAPTER
EIGHTEEN

SAMANTHA

When we left the dining room, the main library was quieter than it had been before. I had no idea what time zone it was here, or maybe it was its own time zone, but the light had faded through the windows that lined the room.

"I meant what I said before," Len's tone was rough. "You and Tabitha have a family. I'm your family."

There was a sense of claiming in that statement, and I tried to stop my pulse from racing away. *He's being a good father. It means nothing more than that.*

"Thank you," I managed to say without letting all my emotions escape. "It's hard for me to believe that a day I'd consider to be one of my darkest has turned into one of the best." I'd probably jinxed myself saying that out loud, because if I knew my paranormal romance stories, this was the moment it all went to shit.

"Tell me more about today," he said. "I know some of what transpired, but I need to know everything."

Dark memories sprang to life, bitterness lacing my tone. "Today was my mating slash wedding day to Grant, the alpha's second son." A glance at Len revealed no visible emotion on his face. Quickly, I detailed the rest of what happened, from Shadow and Mera showing up, to us finding Tabitha, and finishing up with the moment he burst into the library. "I would have done anything to save Tabby," I said as we approached a shiny white door embossed with flowers and thorns that I assumed was Faerie's.

Len paused, letting out a deep breath. "I'm going to kill every fucking one of them," he said softly. It was almost scarier than when he rumbled. "You don't need to ever fear their control or influence in your life again. For they have ceased to exist."

I'm going to kill every fucking one of them. The deep smooth rumble of those words would live rent free in my mind forever. Len was destroying me in ways I'd never expected. I'd been prepared to fear the fae and Faerie, but he... he was changing everything.

Sparks raced across my skin to settle deep as an ache in my center. It wasn't difficult to figure out why I'd fell into bed with him. Not difficult at all.

"I appreciate that," I said. "At the moment, Alpha Lorenze is frozen, a veritable punching bag for the pack he mistreated. His son is free though, and I still haven't decided if he is a victim in all of this as well, or someone who was just too weak and pathetic to fight back. I'm giving him a chance to prove whether he's worthy of living or not."

Len shook his head but didn't say anything further. Instead, he stepped forward to press his hand against the door. The white lit up briefly, music drifting out to wrap around us, tugging against my chest, tempting me to step closer.

I almost let it take me in. I enjoyed the sensation of my will fading under the stronger power, until I remembered that I'd very nearly lost my freedoms today. I wasn't about to surrender them a second time. Shaking my head, I stepped back, and the music's pull faded.

"Good girl," Len murmured. He said it so low I wondered if I was supposed to hear it.

Good girl. Fuck, that deep rumble slipped down my body, and if the damp heat between my legs was any indication, the fae might have just unlocked a new kink.

Tabitha distracted me when she let out a low musical sound, very similar to that coming from the world of Faerie. She leaned out of my arms, and I only just managed to keep her from flying away. "She tried to jump." I gasped as my fingers flexed against her tiny body. "She's trying to get through the doorway."

"A very good sign," Len told me. He pressed his hand against the door once more, the brightness increasing until it opened. This was the point the nerves really kicked in. I'd understood the concept of going to Faerie, and in my mind it was akin to stepping into the Library of Knowledge—weird and magical, and hopefully a journey I could handle.

For Tabitha, I could handle a lot. But that didn't mean there weren't nerves.

As I stepped forward to follow Len, his arm swept around both of us, and I gasped at the contact. There was no bare skin, his coat and my clothing a barrier between us, but somehow it burned into my soul, branding me with his touch.

Len leaned down closer to my ear. "I need to guide you

through the doorway," he said. "It's easier if you don't fight me."

"No worries," I got out breathlessly. "Lead the way." *Sir.*

It was a silent add-on, and I didn't stop to examine this sudden need I had to release myself into his control. Hadn't I just gotten out of a damn situation where I'd lost my free will. Suddenly I wanted to just serve myself up to the first sexy fae that crossed my path.

Someone fucking help me.

Faerie was thankfully a huge distraction, and I strained to see my first glimpse of the world through the bright entryway. Eventually the white under my feet started to shift, as the land darkened to a green that was so deep it was a mix of emerald and black.

Len released his hold on me. A chill wrapped around me as he moved away, and since it wasn't cold here, I had to assume that was all to do with the fae prince. Even Tabitha let out a low mournful cry, as if she'd been enjoying the closeness of her father and his power.

That makes two of us, baby.

As the last of the light faded from view, I found another gasp slipping from between my lips. It was hard to distract from the sexy fae, but the garden before me was doing a pretty good job of it.

Gates surrounded what looked like a magical garden, with plants behind the gates, towering well above the tops of us. Flowers and vines, so many varieties that were not native to any place I'd seen.

I warily eyed the two huge plants on either side of the gate, with their dozen or more razor-sharp teeth, as they kept a watch over the entrance.

"They won't hurt you while I'm here," Len said, reaching out to open the gate.

As we stepped through, he ran his hands over both plants, giving them almost loving pats.

"This is yours?" I asked as I pushed forward, following in his path.

"Nothing in Faerie truly belongs to us," he said simply. "We claim friendship with our land, and in some ways choose where we reside, but nothing is owned by me. I have tended this patch of land since I was young, some thousand or so years ago, and in that time a true oasis has formed. We are symbiotic, with my power entangled here to help this garden thrive. In return, it offers me comfort and solace. Along with protection."

It only took a few minutes of being in the garden to see the truth in what he was saying. There was a wild and ancient feel to the flourishing plants, flowers, and trees that filled every space, outside of the paths that wound between them. The tops of some trees I couldn't even see, hidden by the flowers that towered above me. Their bright heads twisted and turned in the breeze, seemingly moving with the energy of the air.

Maybe it was the glory of the garden, but it took me a beat to register what Len had just freaking said. "Wait," I spun and faced him, clutching Tabitha closer. "Did you say... *thousand or so years*? You're... old. What the hell!" At most he looked to be in his late twenties to early thirties.

Len laughed, a rich sound that had more of the plants freakily moving toward him. "We're a long-lived race," he said. "Near eternal, and very hard to kill, but it can be done."

"Is that part of the reason why you struggle to have young?" I wondered, the thought occurring to me.

"Yes, but apparently it wasn't always this way. The last few hundred years has our new births almost nonexistent." He glanced at the child in my arms. "Until Tabitha."

She was special in more ways than one.

"Let's hope our memories hold the key to why Faerie has

been weakening," I said with a decisive nod. "It'll be good to have a means to help this world."

It was a stretch, but there had to be a deeper reason behind everything.

"We should head to the Silver Lands," Len said after standing in the tranquility of his garden for a few more minutes. "It'll get dark soon."

"There's a sun here?" I asked, not able to see where the light came from through the trees.

"Yes, we have one semi-weak sun," Len said. "We also have five moons and a lot of crystals embedded high in the crust of our world. They all give us energy and light, rejuvenating the energy of the fae. We live in a symbiotic relationship too."

"I like that," I said softly, surprised by how relaxed and at home I felt here. "This world feels calmer. Less chaotic than Earth." It might have been a stupid thing to say, considering I'd seen less than two percent of Faerie, but the vibe felt right.

"You both look stronger," Len noted, those silver eyes locked on me. "It makes sense for you to be here. With me."

It did make sense, and that freaked me out a touch. I wasn't used to life feeling *right* or *calm* or *perfect*. In this moment, I had all three.

"So, does everyone in the Solaris System speak English?" I asked, changing the subject to another question that had plagued me since my first time in the library. "Your accent is almost a cross between British and American, which is weird, right?"

His lips twitched like I was amusing him. "English is what Shadow speaks, and he made sure to introduce it through the worlds. I've also learned how to blend into cultures, and this accent is the most natural for me."

Shadow introduced English to the worlds. Okay, yeah, that

was never in any of my history classes. I knew who to believe though: the beings who literally lived through history.

"Are you ready to leave now?" Len asked.

"Yep," I said quickly, smiling as Tabitha waved her arms. We started to move, and she shifted forward in my grip, telling me she wanted to go to him.

This time, I finally felt comfortable allowing that.

"Len," I called since he was a few steps ahead. He turned back, the plants framing him on either side. Lifting our daughter out toward him, I smiled. "She wants to go to you."

The little girl waved her arms once more, and I noted how healthy her skin looked. She glowed in the soft light of Faerie. *Just like her father.*

Len's eyes met mine briefly, before his gaze dropped to Tabitha, and I swore it was fear that creased his features before they smoothed out once more. "Are you sure?" he asked.

Tabitha waved her hands harder toward him. "I'm sure," I said decisively. "She deserves to have both her parents in her life. To have the family you've promised. As scary as it is, I don't own her, and cannot just keep her all to myself."

Len's expression softened, and even as he reached out for our daughter, he was looking at me. "You've already lost too much time with her, and I never questioned your need to keep her close. If anything, I admire the ferocity and protectiveness you hold toward her. It's all I would ask for in the mother of my child. All I would ask for you."

Slayed. Actually slayed.

"Thank you," I whispered, thanking him for so much more than just those words. "You gave me space when I was a mess and desperately clinging to sanity, but now it's time for you to hold your child."

"I've dreamed of this forever," he admitted, shaking his

head as he brushed a hand over Tabitha's hair. "It's hard to believe that we're finally here."

Nearly impossible. This was a second chance, forgotten romance story, with the added bonus of a secret baby. Only nothing was that simple or clear-cut in this world, but I couldn't bring myself to care. My daughter had her father, and she hadn't been taken from me. As long as that remained, whatever else happened, would be fine by me.

CHAPTER NINETEEN

SAMANTHA

It had been quiet in the garden since we entered, with only the very slight swish of plants moving against each other as a background noise. When Len reached out and wrapped his hands around Tabitha's tiny waist, shifting her from my arms, everything just got *quieter*.

Calm, even.

There was no explosion of energy or power as the two touched. Tabitha didn't suddenly grow into a ten-year-old, or anything too extraordinary. There was just a moment where the world appeared to hold its breath as father and daughter stared into each other's eyes.

A weird ache shot through my ovaries as my body went all goo-goo over this daddy and daughter moment. Their first real moment together. It held me mesmerized as I watched them, so eerily similar in their magic and beauty.

Len leaned in and whispered a stream of words that weren't English before he switched back. "Little one," he breathed, "you are a miracle."

Tabby didn't squirm, she just reached up and placed her hand on his face, and the pair remained locked together. Fuck, it was true that in a perfect moment, time stood still.

Should have known it was too good to last.

A crash echoed around us, repeating a beat later, like a near deafening siren. Len reacted immediately, handing Tabitha to me as he swung himself around, putting his body between us and the front gates. He was now clutching large grey crystals in both hands, and I had no idea where they'd come from.

He was large enough that I couldn't see much around him, but whatever had caused the alarm had not ceased, as the sirens continued to sound. Inching forward, I attempted to ignore the buzz of Len's energy against mine. "What's happening?" I whispered. "Are we in danger? Should I shift?"

My beast was useful in many situations, including a resistance to magics.

"You don't need to shift," he replied shortly. "They shouldn't be able to enter, and if they do manage to find a way inside, I will rip them to pieces before they get close to you or Tabitha."

I trusted in what he was saying, but I also wasn't interested in playing the damsel in distress, waiting for her knight to save her. It was my least favorite trope in the books I read, because I couldn't relate. To me, the best couples fought side by side. Sure, most of the time they had differing strengths and weaknesses, but there was a balance.

The balance was important.

With that in mind, I called up the extra senses of my beast, which allowed me to see the fae waiting on the other side of the gates.

"Should we just ask what they want?" I said to Len, wondering if he was extra paranoid because of Tabitha and my presence.

He pulled his gaze from the gates, turning to me. "They're guards from the Metallic Meadows. They're summoning me for a reason, and I'm reminding them that I don't bow to their command."

Great. A fae power play.

This was one of those times where he had the strengths needed for the situation, since I had no clue of Faerie politics. Relaxing, I let them do their thing while I spent my time brushing Tabitha's hair back, and occasionally tickling her little face.

When Len finally moved, he strode off toward the entrance, and I followed. As we reached the closed gates, I saw that the other fae—the guards—had backed away, their heads lowered in a respectful pose. Len had won the power play this time.

"Why are you here?" The *don't fuck with me* in his tone was strong.

The closest guard spoke, without lifting his head. "King Fredrick needs all the leaders back at the Capital, so we can have the final vote on severing the line."

I was standing close enough to Len that I felt him stiffen. It wasn't obvious on his face or in his demeanor, but he was pissed about this command. "How long do we have to appear?"

"Three days," the same guard said. "Attendance non-negotiable."

"Noted."

Len turned his back on them, and I watched as they straightened and left without another word. The moment they were out of sight, the alarm shut off, and I relaxed once more. "Is this meeting going to be an issue for us?" I asked.

"No issue," he said, as he opened the gates, and we stepped outside of his garden. "It just means hurrying in our plan to lift the glamour impacting our memories. We have three days until the vote, and we need to make them count."

Despite knowing the pain that awaited, I was more than ready to be free of this glamour.

As we moved farther from the garden, I blinked at what I was seeing. "Are we on a floating island?" I asked, tilting my head as I attempted to take the scenery in. I hadn't noticed until now, since we'd all but landed at the front gate and went straight into the garden, but from this angle I could see a clear drop-off from the grass around us.

Len, who was relaxed once more, held his hands out for Tabitha again. I handed her across without hesitation.

"It's not floating exactly," he said, pulling her close to his chest, "as this land is anchored. But much of Faerie consists of lands that move around within their territories. There's nothing below most of them, except the Capital, which is the source of our cords and anchors to the Origin."

"The Origin that the Great Queen could access?" I confirmed.

He nodded. "Yep, that's the one. Now, let's head home. I don't like how close those Metallic Meadow guards got to you and Tabitha."

"You don't have to protect us," I reminded him. "We're capable. I've been taking care of myself for my entire life."

Yeah, sure, a very short, finite life compared to Len's, but that in and of itself spoke of my capabilities. Shifters and humans died easily, and I was still alive. Still fighting.

Len shook his head, a chuckle escaping those perfect lips. "As long as there is life in my veins, I will defend what is mine. We have our strengths, and I do not diminish yours. Pick your battles, little Storm." He paused, reaching out as if to touch my face before he refrained. "For there are some you'll never win against me."

The nickname fell so effortlessly from his lips that it almost distracted me from the fact that he'd used *mine* again. And I'd liked it just as much. So much for being a strong, independent shifter.

"Storm?" I questioned, forcing myself to ignore the rest.

A smile quirked his lips up. "It's a rare occurrence in Faerie, but when the great storms happen, they sweep in and change everything. The power grid, the feel in the air, even the ancient plants of my garden. It's rare and powerful, and filled with so much beauty." The intensity of his gaze was almost my undoing. "They remind me of you."

Storm. I repeated it in my mind, and it felt familiar somehow. "Did we use nicknames when we knew each other before?" I wondered suddenly, and he stilled as if that thought hadn't occurred to him.

"That word hovers in my mind when I think of you," he finally said. "So... maybe we did."

A name also hovered in my mind when I thought of Len. It'd been there since he burst into Shadow's library, and the urge to use it was growing stronger. Maybe there was some merit to us having used these names when we were together before.

Len began to walk, carrying Tabitha as he moved closer to the edge of the land. As he walked, he went into tour guide mode. "Sixty percent of Faerie is inhabited by the ten royal houses. We all claim territories, which is where we strengthen ourselves using the gems and crystals from those moving lands. Thirty percent are the demi-fae, who govern themselves separately, and the final ten percent makes up the stationary lands, like my garden here. It's in what we call a no territory zone, even if this garden repels all but me and those I allow in. Many of my plants are prized and used for spells, which gives me an advantage in negotiations."

"It's an amazing garden," I said, turning for one final glance. "Impressively so."

He nodded. "Thank you. Now, we need to leave. Time is of the essence, so we should head to the Silver Lands to work on the glamour." He paused. "And introduce Tabby to her grandmother."

Grandmother. *Shit.* "As in, the queen of the Silver Lands?" I asked breathlessly.

His laugh was easy. "Yes, but she's not as scary as the title implies." He tilted his head briefly. "Well, I mean, that's not totally accurate. She is scary and powerful, but not to her family. She will adore Tabitha. She's the miracle that none of us ever expected."

If that wasn't the truth. Even for me, as a shifter who generally had young easily, she was still a miracle. "Okay, so how do we get there?"

He stared out into the abyss beyond this land, clouds hovering on the horizon. "The crystals above allow us to travel between lands, providing we're powerful enough to wield them without getting fried."

"Are you powerful enough, Winter?" I joked, the *other* name feeling okay to say after his nickname revelation. Winter was a word that encompassed Len for me, stemming from my fascination with the way his eyes turned icy when he filled the room with winter energy.

His lips moved, a brief twitch. "We're about to find out."

His hand wrapped around mine, touching me so casually, as sparks of power shot between us. A blast of bright purple light surrounded us, and as the energy raced across my skin, a whoosh filled my hearing, and we were sucked up into whatever lay above.

Holy shit. I was in a world of trouble, and this was the most excitement I'd had in years.

Bring it on.

CHAPTER TWENTY

SAMANTHA

"Winter!" I choked out as we arrived at our destination, clearly deciding to overuse the nickname now that I could.

"Winter is your nickname for me?" he asked, a flicker of emotion darkening in his as the skin across his forehead tightened.

"It's been on my mind too," I said in a rush, before adding, "Does it bother you?" I focused on the fae, ready and willing to stop using the name if it upset him.

I mean, nicknames were cute for me, but maybe it was an insult to a Faerie prince. Maybe I'd only ever *thought* of him as Winter and never used it out loud.

To my relief, he shook his head. "Not at all, I've just never had anyone give me a true nickname. Do you have any memories of why you called me *Winter*?"

Tabitha leaned forward and wrapped her arms around his neck, as if she were offering comfort. Len's eyes darkened, until they were silvery winter storms.

"I don't remember, but I know the reason. Before and now, it would still be the same," I managed to say without revealing my emotional state. "When you're feeling strongly about something, the ice in your silver eyes swirls and rages, and it's mesmerizing. Just like the wintery power you spill. When it hits my skin, it's... nice."

Nice was a vast, *vast* understatement of how it felt, but I'd already made a fool of myself. No need to let the fae prince know that already in our short time together, I'd started to develop quite strong feelings toward him.

Len's expression as he watched me closely stirred strong feelings inside, so I quickly changed the subject. "This is your kingdom," I said, taking my first look around. "Is that a crystal bridge?"

We stood just a few paces away from the purple bridge, which curved and twinkled in the low light of their sun.

"The *gateway*," he told me. "It's the bridge between the royal holdings and the rest of the Silver Lands."

Looking beyond it, I could see houses and buildings spanning out for... well, ever. There was no visible end in sight of the floating, connected, silver and purple structures, many of them joined by crystal bridges and walkways.

A floating silver city.

"Everyone has their own home that they design," Len continued. "We don't own anything, but we do borrow for our time in this realm. The bridges are made of reven, our sacred stone. Its protection prevents other royal houses from trespassing without permission."

"Am I about to get zapped?" I asked, only half joking as I looked around at the multitude of "amethyst-like" reven stones.

"I have given you permission," Len said. "You have all the rights of a royal in the Silver Lands. A fact I will ensure is spread within the next day or two."

Whoa. Rights of a royal? That was... a lot. "I don't need special treatment," I told him in a rush. "Just don't zap me. That's all I ask."

He shook his head. "You're my family. You get the royal treatment. No debate."

Sometimes the prince in him was very apparent.

I decided not to argue further, since there were sure to be more important battles between us in the future. Instead, I focused on my many pressing questions. "What exactly do the fae do with their lives?" I asked as Len started to move toward the royal territory. "I don't imagine you have painters or vets and such here? You don't require the same careers as shifters or humans, which makes sense, but what do you do?"

He paused briefly, tilting his head. "What is this need that you have on Earth to *do*? Why did you create a society that never allows its people to just *be*. What is it you're striving for?"

A small snort of disbelief escaped me. "Uh, usually money. Most of us enjoy food and a roof over our head, and even with the packs keeping us *safe* so to speak, that doesn't come without a price."

Len considered it for another second, and I had never felt the vast differences between us so strongly as I did right now. "Faerie has rules," he murmured. "We have ways that all contribute to our energy and upkeep of the territories. But in general day to day, most pursue their areas of interest. Some head to the solid lands and dig for stones. Some examine the power grid and try to find ways to improve what we have. Others are scholars, studying the past and predicting the future. And there are a few that tend to fields of food which is shared freely. If a fae is born, on those rare occasions they are welcomed into their royal lands with a home and comfort and food. The rest they figure out as they explore their interests. There's always at least one fae who shows an interest in an area of need."

Sounded fake, but okay. "What about trash?" I burst out. "Surely there's not a fae who loves collecting other people's shit?" Literal and figuratively in this instance.

Len's smile grew. "We don't really generate a lot of trash, so to speak. But whatever waste is left from our lifestyle, we deal with ourselves. It's our creation, after all, right?"

For some stupid reason I felt offended, and like I had to step in for Earth. Even if what he was saying sounded like the sort of evolved civilization we should strive to be.

"This is not a slight on your kind," Len said suddenly, and fuck if this asshole couldn't read my mind. "We do not judge how others live. What works for us isn't designed to work for anyone else. It's just the way of Faerie, and since we are billions of years more ancient than Earth, it makes sense that we would have evolved and developed a different way of life."

My brain was still grumbling like a cranky old man with hooligan kids on his front lawn, but I let it go because I could tell he really wasn't judging Earth. In this instance, different didn't mean anything other than different.

"Okay, that's fair," I finally said. "And I'm looking forward to seeing more of the inner workings of Faerie."

"I'll show you anything you want to see," he promised, and those words dripped down my body and into my gut, making it swirl as I fought the urge to breathe heavier.

Thankfully, before I embarrassed myself by moaning, we reached the huge gates at the entrance to Len's home. It didn't escape my notice that they were a larger, grander version of the ones at his garden. They too opened before he touched them, and I found myself holding my breath as I passed through the threshold. I could feel the power swirling, almost as if it were draping over my skin, holding me still for a moment and then finally releasing me.

"Sorry about the scanning," he said. "I didn't think you'd feel anything, but your eyes narrowed. They do that when you're uncomfortable."

Damn his observations. "It felt almost like walking through a web that wasn't quite ready to let me go."

His gaze lifted from mine to examine the gates, which were silently closing behind us. "Only fae feel the energy. We definitely need to get to the bottom of what your mind is hiding from us."

"Yours too," I reminded him.

Len didn't argue, giving a slow nod. Almost a bow. "Mine too."

My throat was tight, so I turned away and attempted to get myself together. This fae was wreaking havoc on my composure and internal stability. Part of me wished that he'd step away so I could breathe freely, while another part knew that already I craved his presence.

The juxtaposition of my feelings right now was boggling my mind.

And my soul.

Len ended up being the distraction I needed, odd considering he was what I needed a distraction from, but as he fell into tour guide, I found myself relaxing.

"This is the main royal courtyard," he said as we walked forward. "We use it for large banquets, celebrations, and morning energy renewals under the sky crystals."

The courtyard was huge and round with light stone pavers lining the floors. Pillars, looking very sentinel like, surrounded the circular boundary. There was no ceiling, just the pillars and some crisscrossing structures high up. As we moved closer, I could see the pillars had carvings across them, depicting what looked like fae performing various tasks from meditation, to painting, to eating in large groups. At the peak of each pillar was a reven stone.

"You use those stones to recharge too?" I asked, scanning the twenty-foot-high structures. "And you also consume food?"

"Some do," he replied. "Some exist just on stone energy. Our young require extra sustenance, but once you reach a certain age, you have the choice."

He chuckled suddenly, and I realized I'd screwed my face up. Relaxing all the muscles, especially those wrinkling my nose, I forced out a strangled laugh. "I just cannot imagine living without food. I've been forced to a few times, and it was the absolute worst."

He was no longer laughing. "Who withheld food from you?"

The question sounded innocent, but his eyes were swirls of darkness as he met and held my gaze. "My dead true mate," I breathed.

Len's expression hardened. "It pains me that fucker is already dead and I cannot kill him."

When he made statements like that, I really, *really* wished that I had my memories and could explore this connection between us. Since none of that was possible, all I had was a racing pulse and damp panties.

Needing a second to pull myself together, I paused near a pillar. Just as I was about to follow, a tingling sensation caressed the back of my neck, and I turned to find a fae nearby, watching me. Light, aqua colored eyes met mine, and I found myself examining him just as closely.

Not as tall as Len, he was still a head above me, with broad shoulders and ashy blond hair that touched the bottom of his ears. Expression amused, he straightened and tilted his head, gaze running along my body. "You don't belong here," he said in a smooth tone as his gaze returned to my face.

"I'm with Len," I said quickly.

He quirked a brow as he straightened. I noticed he was wearing an ornate silver breastplate, looking like a warrior. Was he part of this land's armed guard?

"Len?" he queried, as if he'd heard wrong. Or shit, maybe it was always Prince Len here and I'd just made a major fuck up. Before I could correct myself, Len wandered back into view, Tabitha waving her arms around as she bathed in the crystals' light.

"Eyes off her, Tyrin," Len drawled. "Or I'll take great pleasure in removing them." He sounded casual, but only a fool would think he was joking.

Not that the threat deterred *Tyrin*, who stepped closer to me. He had a similar icy wash of power to Len, just less intense. "Aw, come on, brother," Tyrin said. "You leave your gorgeous woman standing out here in the open. Seems you want me to step in."

I waited for Len to correct him about *your woman*, but he did no such thing.

"Brother?" I queried, unsure if it was literal, or more how Shadow and the others used the term. Brothers of choice, not blood.

"Oldest friend," Len said shortly, giving me the answer I needed. "Though he might be relieved of that duty if he doesn't back away from you."

It was a warning. And damn if that possessive timbre to his tone didn't have me feeling a little hot under the collar. Tyrin's grin was huge, but as he pulled his gaze from me to face Len, he finally noticed Tabitha. His smile faded near instantly as he stilled, mouth half open, hands listless at his side.

"How is this possible?" he finally said in a near whisper. "A child? A royal child has been born."

As if that had been an official announcement, the gems above us burst into life. Purple filled the air, and as the power surrounded us Tabitha started to cry. The first, real baby cry I'd ever heard from her, and it terrified my heart.

Was bringing her here a mistake? Maybe her half-fae side was not strong enough to withstand the energy?

CHAPTER
TWENTY-ONE

SAMANTHA

I moved faster than should be possible, like the human women who somehow lift cars off their children in times of panic and fear. In this second, I felt like I could lift this damn world to get to my daughter.

"Enough!" Len bellowed, and the lights ceased their glow. At this point I was all but pressed into him, wrapping my hands around Tabitha to examine her.

"Is she okay?" I cried, not seeing anything wrong. She had stopped crying the moment the lights faded, and was once again waving her hands, looking as content as anything.

Len captured my flailing hands. He held them both, his palm large enough to contain them. "She's fine. Tyrin's burst of energy triggered the crystals into reacting. They shine brighter for royals, but I usually stop them before they flare when I approach. The energy would have felt odd for Tabitha, stirring up her fae side. She only reacted in shock."

Tyrin, who was still standing, blinking, stunned, shook his head. "I apologize. It was not my intentions, but brother, you must tell us how this happened!" Without waiting for an answer, he reached out and extracted one of my hands from Len, kissing it gently. "Mother of fae children. You are a gift from the gods."

Len's chest rumbled, which I only knew because I was semi-plastered to him still. As I removed myself from both of them, I wondered if my face was as red as the heat in my body suggested.

"Last. Fucking. Warning," Len bit out. "Don't test me."

"She's exquisite," Tyrin said with a smile, but made no attempt to touch me again. "You cannot expect me to ignore such a precious gem."

"I can and I do," was the reply.

Tyrin held both hands up, his shit-eating smile returning once more. "Okay, so how about you tell me why there's a shifter and a half-fae child here. Spill or I'll fight for their honor."

He produced a sword from somewhere, and I subconsciously found myself stepping between him and Tabitha. For all of three seconds before I was whirled behind the prince.

Tabby was in my arms in the next second, and I was once again witnessing all the fury that Len could bring. Meanwhile, Tyrin was still grinning, the sword relaxing in his hand, before it vanished just as quickly. "Come on, Len. You know I'd never strike at you. I just wanted to see how far the beast had come from its cage. Quite far by the looks."

From what I could see, the silver prince relaxed, but a buzz of his energy remained across my skin. "Word of warning," Len said, feral in his tone. "Until we sort out whatever sorcery has caused me to lose time with my child, and leave Tabitha and Samantha undefended, it's best that no one comes too close to either of them."

I'd be lying to myself if I didn't admit to a tinge of disappointment that his protectiveness might just be about the mystery. It wouldn't surprise me to find my feelings were deeper. He was a fae prince after all, and I was just a shifter.

"They have my protection too," Tyrin stated, standing taller again. "My sword is yours. You know that. I will stand between all harm and your family."

Len reached out and Tyrin met him halfway. They clasped hands, or more like forearms, in a handshake of sorts. "I will let you know everything as soon as we have answers," Len told him. "For now, can you advise the others that Fredrick is sending his guards out to ensure everyone is at a meeting three days from now. They're readying to sever the Great Queen's line faster than anticipated."

In a blink, the relaxed Tyrin was gone, replaced by a fearsome warrior. It was a similar transformation to that of Len when he iced out, and it was both fascinating and terrifying to witness. These fae lulled you into a false sense of calm and security before they brought forth their beast and ripped you in two. And so quickly, that I wouldn't be surprised if you were still smiling as you died, not even realizing what happened.

Not a race of beings to be underestimated.

"I will inform the queen," Tyrin said. "Then we will call on our allies to form a strong front when we stand against them in three days"

Len nodded. "Thank you."

Tyrin nodded decisively, before turning to me. "My lady, you take care, and we'll catch up soon."

Len smacked him hard across the back of the head, and Tyrin just howled with laughter. He went from jokester to scary bastard so effortlessly that I was impressed. He wandered off then and I focused on Len. "He's an interesting character," I said, hugging Tabitha closer, enjoying her in my arms once more.

He nodded. "Tyrin and I have been through a lot. Almost as much as I've been through with my other brothers. I've been lucky to find such a strong family unit."

"You have," I acknowledged immediately. "As a shifter, all I've ever wanted is a strong pack, and it's the same hope I have for Tabitha."

Len's stare was intense. "You both have a family now, no matter what the suppressed memories reveal to us."

In one sentence he hit on a fear that I hadn't even consciously allowed myself to acknowledge. The fear that when we figured out our secrets, and the reasons for the Faerie glamour, that it might destroy this fragile family unit we'd been building. Len's words were reassuring, but at the same time there was no true way to predict what we'd discover and how it would impact us all.

"We should continue," Len said softly, distracting me right when I needed it. "You look drained. It's been a long day and I want to get you settled and rested before we attempt to break the glamour."

As if he'd gave me permission to feel it, every iota of exhaustion crashed into me, and I held Tabitha a little tighter, to ensure I didn't drop her. "I am rather tired," I admitted, forcing myself to straighten. Len had this way about him that allowed me to express weaknesses without making me feel weak for them.

Before I could say another word, he leaned down and wrapped his arms around me, lifting me wedding-style. Tabitha let out a low squeal, clearly excited by the chance to ride in both her parents' arms, but I was freaking the fuck out. "Put us down!" I demanded. "I can fucking walk."

Just when I thought he would allow me my weakness without making me feel weak.

The arrogant bastard straight up ignored me, striding forward with the same ease and grace of his normal walk, and I was too scared to fight his hold in case Tabitha got hurt or dropped in the process. My mouth worked perfectly fine though. "Seriously. I'm not kidding. I don't need to be carried. I'm only here so you can bond with your daughter and help with my fucking memory loss, not to be carried around like a baby."

He didn't slow, stepping us onto a particular large reven bridge. On the other side I caught sight of a giant mansion—Len's home no doubt—but there was no time to examine it outside of noting that it was dark, with slate and stone accents. Not a lot of silver details for a silver prince.

"Put me down, you fucking asshole!" I snapped again.

His hold tightened and he moved faster. "Anyone ever tell you that you have a dirty mouth," he smirked. "Tabitha's first word is going to be fuck, just like Aurora's."

He wasn't wrong, and I knew I should try to curb the language around my daughter, but seriously. "This is kidnapping, Winter!"

Heat caressed me briefly, and I wondered if it was a reaction to the nickname.

"Are you sure you consider this kidnapping?" he asked softly.

I had to swallow hard to speak around the lump in my throat. In truth, it probably couldn't be considered kidnapping when one: you weren't a kid, and two: you kinda wanted to be 'napped by them. Which sounded so much dirtier than intended.

Unable to fight back, I just held my daughter, who was apparently still enjoying the ride if her little smile was any indication, and fumed internally. This fae bulldozed through my composure and knocked down my barriers—barriers that were in place for a damn good reason.

I'd already near lost myself to someone more powerful than me this week, and I had no intentions of doing it again, no matter how appealing the second *someone* was.

Len continued toward the large dwelling and I noted there were no gates or barriers. No doubt no one risked his wrath by trespassing on his territory. When we reached the front door, it did the usual and opened without his touch. There was a reason he was arrogant. Confident. *Powerful as fuck.* Whatever you wanted to call it.

Inside, the space was light and airy, without any of the darker aspects of the exterior styling. High ceilings, and a set of stairs in the center of white marble floors, indicated that there was at least another level above.

"You'll have your own area," Len assured me as he strode toward the stairs and ascended like he wasn't carrying an extra hundred and fifty pounds of shifter and child. Bastard wasn't even breathing heavily—*Wait, was he breathing at all?*

"I'd appreciate my own space, thank you," I replied stiffly.

"When you're done resting, there'll be a royal dinner to attend," he continued. "You must be introduced to the court. That way, everyone is aware of your status and will give you the support befitting your position. After, we'll work on the memories."

"Royal dinner?" I shot back. "Last minute addition?"

He just shot me a slow smile, and I shook my head. I'd worry about the dinner later. First came rest. Maybe after a nap I wouldn't care that I'd be meeting the Silver Land's royal court in jeans and plain shirt. I mean, it wasn't as if they'd expect anything more from a shifter, so I might as well live up to it.

"Where have you gone?" Len asked, startling me from my thoughts.

Focusing again, I noticed that we'd arrived in a bedroom. A gorgeous bedroom, in a shade of green that was a lighter version of my eye color. The room was dominated by a large bed, with bedding in varying shades of green, silver, and gold. There wasn't much else in here, outside of a set of double doors that appeared to lead to a balcony, and another door through which I caught a glimpse of a white bathroom.

"Sam," Len said, "are you okay?"

Shit, right. I hadn't answered his question from before.

"Yes. Yes, I'm totally fine. I was just mentally laughing about showing up to your royal dinner in my jeans—making my usual bad impression on the world."

At the bed, Len lowered me gently to my feet. My legs were weaker than expected, so I mostly sat on the side of the bed, keeping Tabitha in my lap. The fae prince crouched down so he was near eye level with me, his expression bleeding sincerity. "Leave that worry to me. For now, get some rest. I won't go far in case we trigger the glamour and lose this time as well, but I can give you privacy. I'll return later with food."

He always thought of everything, and I still had no idea how to deal with being cared for. "Thanks," I said, a yawn cutting me off as my true exhaustion hit once more.

I owed Len a hell of a lot already, and it scared me to know how deep into his world I was falling. Even the demanding part of his personality was growing on me.

Secretly, deep down, it was probably the part I liked the most.

CHAPTER TWENTY-TWO

SAMANTHA

When Len left, I was alone with Tabby. It was the first time I'd ever been alone with my daughter, and I was nervous as fuck.

Angling our bodies so we were lying in the middle of the bed, we rolled to face each other and our gazes met. "So," I said with a low laugh as she stared at me with those luminescent purple eyes, "apologies in advance for anything I screw up. I'm kind of new at this, but I can promise that I'll always do everything in my power to be the best momma ever. To not let you down. To keep you safe and ensure your happiness. You're the greatest part of my life, and I don't want to fail you again."

She smiled and cooed, and I found myself grinning harder. "Your little toothies are bigger already," I told her, marveling at how strong and healthy she appeared. Len hadn't even brought her crystal mat with him, because in this world she didn't need it.

Tabitha reached out and I extended a finger so she could wrap her tiny hands around it. She went to sleep like that, just holding on to me like I was the comfort she needed—and no lie, I watched her sleep for what felt like hours, tears streaming down my face as my heart tried to carve itself from my chest. This little angel owned it anyway; might as well give it to her.

Eventually I had to get up and use the bathroom, so after securing pillows all around her, I washed up and removed my jeans, prepared to sleep for a few hours. If I were to get through everything heading my way, I needed to be significantly less exhausted.

Hopefully, if Len figured out clothes for the dinner, he'd also find one or two sets of everyday wear. Not to mention a toothbrush would really come in handy right about now. Hairbrush too.

Out of the bathroom, I snuggled in next to Tabby—who hadn't moved an inch—and let the exhaustion drag me under. With it, though, for the first time was happiness. No matter what happened, today had been better than I could have hoped for.

The longest day of my life had started as the worst, but the ending... definitely the best.

NOTHING WOKE ME. No sound or touch, but I felt him in the room. With exhaustion still clouding my mind, I blinked my eyes open, catching a glimpse of Len. He was sitting in a chair near the bed, watching over us. My stomach clenched tightly at the look on his face, and I wondered what had held him captive in our room, keeping an eye on us as we slept.

His actions could have felt creepy, but he'd sat far enough away that the vibe was more *protective*.

Glancing down, I realized the weight across my chest was Tabitha. She'd moved onto me in her sleep, and somehow looked bigger again, her waves of hair longer as they drifted around her precious face.

"She moves toward you in her sleep," Len told me as he remained motionless. "I know you've been worried that you missed the chance for a true bond with her, but I can assure you, she already adores her mama."

Sliding my hand up and across her back, I held her protectively. "She destroys me with her presence," I admitted. My voice broke as another tear escaped. Not like I hadn't shed plenty as I watched her earlier. "And I have no damned idea how to be a mother, but I'm determined to learn and grow into one that she'll be proud of."

Len's voice was rough. "I have no idea how to be a father either, but I already know she's blessed enough to have two parents who care enough to worry they aren't good enough. With that, we'll always strive to be better for her. To make the world better for her."

There was a catch in his tone with that last line. Lifting my head to see him clearly, I said, "You're worried about what's going to happen at this meeting in three days."

He stood, and as he moved closer I noticed that he'd shed his coat and was wearing more casual clothing: a plain black shirt, well-fitted across his broad shoulders. The material descended into black pants, encasing long legs.

Len in black was almost too much for this shifter.

He sat on the edge of the bed. "It does worry me," he said, "because I sense that they're going to follow through with the severing of the line, no matter what the decision of the royal council is. Fredrick doesn't like to be told no, and he abhors rules."

He ran a hand through his silver hair, leaving it tousled in the most delicious way. "He's one of the few fae that rushes into plans. Generally, since we're very long lived, we don't feel the same urgency as other races."

"How long since the Great Queen was here in Faerie?" I asked.

He paused, his lips twitching. "At least a thousand years. So, yeah, I guess it's not a rush. But it feels like we're being pushed when the last meeting was only a couple of days ago."

"You should trust your instincts on this," I told him. "If your gut is saying that something is off with this Fredrick, it probably is. I say, go in expecting the worst, and then you'll be prepared to deal with it." Tabitha shifted on me, and I patted her back a few times. "If it turns out that he's not up to anything, then all that happens is you're overprepared. It's a win-win."

Len nodded. "Very wise. I will be on high alert for this meeting." His expression softened. "Have you rested enough? Would you like some food?"

My stomach made a rumbling sound, and I tried to remind it we'd eaten in the Library of Knowledge only a few hours ago. Maybe all the travel between worlds burned calories. "I could eat," I admitted.

He pulled himself to stand and I forced my mouth to close. Drooling was not appropriate with a baby on my chest. But damn, I'd never been so acutely aware of another person before. There was no explanation for it, outside of a true mate connection. I'd had a shifter mate, but Mera and Shadow told us that we could have more than one mate. Especially if there was a mix of genetics, and evidence was pointing to me being part fae, somehow.

"I'll return shortly with food," Len said.

When he left, I was able to focus and extricate myself from underneath Tabitha. She stirred briefly, but then I patted her back for a moment and she settled. When I entered the bathroom this time, I blinked at the multitude of changes. The previously empty white shelves that lined either side of the mirror were full of toiletries.

How in the gods? How had Len done this?

Opening more drawers, I found makeup and hair care essentials. I honestly had no idea how he'd procured all of this without leaving the house—to prevent the glamour triggering and stealing our memories once more—but he'd figured out a way.

This fae prince was disarming me, and I wanted to hate it, but it was impossible. Not when every part of me was filled with lust, want, need, confusion, and breathless anticipation of what he'd do next.

Not wanting to leave Tabby alone for too long, I quickly brushed my teeth and fixed up my hair. I was wearing my shirt and underwear still, so I pulled on the jeans I'd left in here earlier, and when I returned to the room, Len was also back.

He'd brought a table with him this time and it was set with a large array of food dishes. He gestured toward one of the two chairs, and I moved slower, working to keep my composure. He held my chair out for me, and as I sat Len helped me scoot forward.

When he was sitting opposite me, I didn't even glance at the food.

My entire focus was on the fae prince.

On the questions burning inside me.

"So... the bathroom products, the food, and all this talk of family," I said bluntly. "Are you seducing me?"

Because it's fucking working.

He flashed me that breathtaking smile, his silvery skin and hair standing out against the darker backdrop of his clothing. "Why? Are you seduced?"

There he went again, reading my mind. He needed to be taught a lesson. "Not even remotely," I shot back, the biggest liar in the room.

His expression didn't falter. If anything, his smile grew. "Guess I'll have to try harder, then."

Holy beast of the shifter gods.

I was fucked. So completely and totally fucked.

CHAPTER TWENTY-THREE

SAMANTHA

Needing a distraction, I finally checked out the food. The scents wafting from the dishes were mouthwatering, and I had no idea where to start. Reaching out, I grabbed a glass of what looked like water, hoping to fix up my dry mouth situation first.

"It has a slight lemon flavor," Len warned me, and I didn't bother to tell him lemon water was my favorite. The first sip burst across my tongue, light and with a citrus hit. It was so thirst-quenching that I found myself gulping down the entire glass.

As I placed it back on the table, a small, slightly hysterical laugh escaped. "Will I be trapped here now? I'm consuming food in Faerie." He'd said I wouldn't be affected, but maybe I wasn't as strong as he believed.

Len lifted a small jug to refill my water. "Would it be terrible if you remained in Faerie?" he asked.

"No," I admitted, claiming my glass once more. "But I'm not okay with losing my free will. If I choose to stay forever, then that's a different story, but I won't be forced."

He nodded as if he understood. "As I said in the library, you're too strong of mind to be taken in by the glittery trappings of this world. Mera was strong enough to resist as well, but at the time, Shadow used whatever means he had to scare her into compliance."

A snort escaped me. "Poor Shadow. He had no idea what he was getting himself into."

Len joined my laughter. "He would have it no other way. If you'd met him before his Sunshine, you would understand how truly blessed he is now. Blessed and very aware of it."

That thought sat nicely with me. I wanted nothing more than for my friends to have a true, *adoring*, slightly-scared-of-them mate. "Mera feels the same," I said, knowing that for sure. "She fought through the most powerful memory block to find Shadow again. It's a worry that we haven't been able to do the same."

"It's a very different situation," he replied immediately. "Mera and Shadow had already formed a bond. A true bond. No magic can compete with that. We were glamoured before a bond could form, and until the spell is broken, there's no knowing our true status."

"We weren't called together after you found me during your mate walk," I reminded him.

His expression didn't change. "Two magics have interfered here, and I will figure out the why and how. It doesn't mean there's not a bond, it just means it's being strangled by Faerie glamour."

"What about the fact that I'm not fae?" A second reminder. Even if I had a sliver of fae in me somewhere, it wasn't like his pure blood. "No fae has ever bonded with a shifter."

"I don't care."

It took me a beat to truly comprehend this, and when I did my insecurities reared their ugly head. "You might not today, but there's probably a reason you're only compatible with your own kind. Outside of being with me because we have a child together, did you think about the fact that I'm going to die in a hundred to two hundred years? A mere blip in your life."

The room grew darker and colder as his energy swirled. "Samantha..."

One word. It sounded like a warning.

"That's my name," I shot back.

He moved faster than I could track, kneeling beside me, our gazes even. The blast of icy energy slapped me in the face, but it wasn't painful, just mildly uncomfortable.

"I'm only going to say this one time," he murmured, in those smooth but feral tones he did so well. "No part of me is here with you because we have a child. She's the perfect miraculous bonus to this equation, but a child is never enough to make a true mate bond. Furthermore, you will not be dying in two hundred years, or any years. I have magics and knowledge to keep you alive, and that's exactly what I'll do. End of fucking story."

He stood suddenly, and I choked on my next breath, equilibrium completely fucked when I was this close to him.

"I promise," he continued, "to not allow your insecurities to break us before we have a chance. I might have only just found you, Sam, but I'm already certain about one thing: you are mine."

Mine. *Mine, mine, mine, mine.*

The word rocketed through my head, and if it had been

said by Grant or his alpha dick of a father, I'd have vomited on the floor. But it had come from the most perfect fae prince.

Here I went, living my own personal fairy tale again.

"Did you hear me, Storm?" he growled, apparently needing an answer.

"Yes," I said softly.

Len's lips tilted up. "Good. Now eat some of the food, and then get dressed for the event. You've got two hours. I placed a selection of dresses in that room over there."

As he pointed toward a smaller door I hadn't noticed earlier, Tabitha stirred on the bed and let out a low murmur. "Ma, ma, ma, ma."

My world tilted on its axis. Had she just...? Did she just...? *Did she call me mama?*

The heat behind my eyes reached inferno level as I all but dove across the bed to reach her. "Baby girl," I cooed, sliding my hands under her, scooping her up into my arms. "Baby, mommy loves you so much."

Tiny arms wrapped around my neck, and I couldn't help the sob that escaped. This was what I'd fought and suffered for. Suffering that meant nothing now that I had her here with me like this.

"Faerie energy is strengthening her faster than I expected," Len said, and I looked over her head to see his face. His expression was heated and emotional, the silver in his eyes swirling harder. "She's strong and resilient, like her mom."

"And her father," I whispered. "She will be formidable."

Len nodded. "No doubt." He moved closer, holding his hands out. "While you eat and dress, I'll change and feed her, if that's okay with you?"

I felt no unease by his suggestion. "It's fine with me, as long as Tabby is happy to leave."

As if she'd understood, she wiggled against my hold, and I

gently sat her down on the bed. She was on her butt facing me, but then she turned herself around and started to *crawl* toward Len. Holy shit, her development was hard to believe, and I couldn't be freaking happier.

"Looks like we have our answer," I said with a smile so big it felt like it was breaking my face.

Len reached down and lifted Tabitha into his arms. As he lifted her, she placed both hands against his cheeks and pressed her face closer. "See you soon, Storm," he told me with a wink.

"You got it, Winter," I shot back, trying not to go stupid over how nice it felt to have a nickname with someone. It was rather pathetic that there'd been no other close relationships in my life to warrant such a thing.

When Len left with Tabitha, I wasted no time sampling the food. Maybe it was my hunger, but honestly, I could have lived in some of these dishes. Fruit, stir-fried meats, and a range of vegetables. I didn't know what any of the ingredients were called, but it didn't matter.

It was all delicious.

When my stomach was groaning and I felt a deep sense of satisfaction, I dragged myself from the food and headed toward the closet. If I chose a dress first, then I'd know the style of hair and makeup needed to pull it off.

When I entered the surprisingly large wardrobe, I drew to a sudden halt. There was row after row of clothing. *How in the shifter packs...?* I'd been expecting maybe like three dresses and some shoes, not a freaking department store. It was so much more than I needed or deserved, but again, arguing with Len about it felt a little ungrateful, so I decided to just thank him profusely, and find the perfect dress for tonight.

Maybe, just for once, I could enjoy the moment and not wait for the axe to fall.

Even better, maybe this time, there was no axe.
A girl could dream.

CHAPTER TWENTY-FOUR

SAMANTHA

I wasted ten minutes just racing through the room, running my hands over the clothes and picking up every pair of shoes. Len had thought of everything, from casual to formal, matching underwear, and even swimwear. I had no idea where they swam in this world of floating lands, but I hoped I'd be here long enough to find out.

Not knowing how formal the dinner was tonight, I ended up choosing a simple black dress, strapless and corseted at the back. It was dressed up with lace details along the skirt, which was shorter in the front and longer down the back, skating across the floor as I walked.

After hanging the dress on the bathroom door, I hurried to the mirror, dressed in a strapless bra and matching black panties. Pulling open all the drawers, I had fun using the full range of beauty products provided, including kohl on my eyes, mascara to lengthen my lashes, and a pop of pink on both cheeks. I also darkened my lips to a ruby red for another color break in the black ensemble.

The red brought out the red tones in my hair, and when I slipped into the dress, holding the corset against my chest, I was satisfied with how I looked. I'd left a slight curl to my long, dark hair, and the makeup made my eyes wider and greener. The black of the dress had my skin looking bronzer, giving me a glow-up that I hadn't seen for years.

This polished mask was going to come in handy when I was fed to the royals tonight. I had no idea what to expect, but if this was anything like the books I read, it could end up a bloodbath. The outsider trying to steal the prince was a tale as old as time.

His mother would probably have me hanged at dawn.

"Sam," Len called from the bedroom.

"In here," I replied, leaving the bathroom. "Could you help me lace up the corset at the back."

I'd been looking at my feet, trying to walk awkwardly in heels while holding the front of the dress, so I missed his initial reaction. It wasn't until the silence extended and I lifted my gaze briefly, that I noticed the stunned look he wore. Tabitha was in his arms, but he appeared to have forgotten she was there as he watched me.

Heat slid into my gut at the hunger in his gaze. Len was no shifter, but he held some alpha characteristics, which had my beast lifting her head. She'd been quiet since we went to Faerie, and I hoped to have a chance to run her soon. It wasn't a necessity though, since the ability to keep her contained was another one of my shifter quirks. Maybe there was a chance that Len might consider running with me. A little predator and prey moment. The thought of such primal play was enough to have my legs weak, while my panties had officially drowned.

Slick heat filled my center as I moved closer to Len, noticing that he wore a dark suit. It fitted his tall frame flawlessly, the silver shirt a perfect contrast.

He looked like a god.

"You look *fucking stunning*," he rumbled.

"As do you," I breathed. "Thank you for the clothes and toiletries. It's so much more than I ever expected, and I'm grateful."

He relaxed, the predator fading from his gaze as he gently placed Tabby in the center of the bed. Her clothes were changed too, but before I could catch more than a flash of purple, he was standing right before me, blocking my view of anything else. Even with heels adding four or five inches to my height, I still had to crane my neck to meet his gaze. "You needed help with your dress?" he said softly.

My dress? What was he talking about?

The only help I needed was a fae prince tearing it from my body.

"The corset?" he prompted, a twinkle in his eyes.

Ohhhh, right.

"Yes, please," I managed to say without embarrassing myself further.

Turning to give him my back, smooth strokes caressed my skin as he moved the dress into place. He took his time, tugging at each strap of the lace, pulling it tight against my body, and with each pull I felt a corresponding one in my gut. Followed by a flutter in my damn pussy.

This fae was our destruction.

A beautiful destruction.

"You don't need to thank me," Len said after a few deliciously tortuous moments of strapping me into my dress. He leaned down, breath brushing across my bare shoulder as his mouth caressed the edge of my ear. "You've already given me everything."

My stomach was swirling—my head too—as I fought for composure.

Another scrape of his skin against mine, tingling energy and ice between us as he added, "I'm going to enjoy unstrapping you later," he murmured, and I had to squeeze my thighs together.

"Awfully presumptuous of you, Winter," I managed breathlessly.

"Hopeful," he replied, before he released me from his hold. "Are you ready to go?"

I was ready to come, if that throbbing ache in my center was any indication.

"Yep, sure. All ready."

Somehow, I pushed down my arousal, taking a few deep breaths before I turned. Len picked Tabitha up once more, and I could see her full outfit. She wore a purple dress, with a matching coverup over her diaper.

"You got clothes for Tabby too?" I asked, teetering forward on my heels to see her better. "And new diapers?"

Len chuckled. "No, not a diaper. You've probably noticed that she hasn't needed any such item up until now."

"I did, but thought it was to do with her lack of development."

He shook his head. "As I said earlier, we don't really create waste. Fae use every part of what we consume."

Okay, sure. That made sense, but also, "There's a toilet in the bathroom."

I'd used it already, and it worked just like back home.

Len nodded. "Yes, there are multiple bathrooms in my house. They're here for when my family from other worlds visit."

Ah, right. That made sense. "It's looking less likely that I'm fae," I said with a sad shrug. "I use the bathroom. I need to eat. I'm not following the characteristics."

"That's not necessarily true," he said quickly. "We won't know the truth until we lift the glamour. And either way, it doesn't matter to me."

He said it so matter of fact, leaving no doubt to the truth of it. "Let's head out," he said. "Tabitha ate already, but she might want more from the party."

My new excitement at her development washed away all other thoughts. "I couldn't be happier that she's eating and growing so well."

He nodded. "She also bathed in the crystals' energy." He paused. "And she called me *Dada*." There was a ring of pride in his tone. "Who knew such a tiny being could own my heart so thoroughly."

I understood completely. "We're blessed."

He reached out and brushed a hand across my cheek. The unexpected touch had butterflies dancing in my stomach. "You changed my life in a split second. I will owe you for eternity."

I'd take eternity with him.

"You owe me nothing," I managed to say. "We're in this together."

A concept that finally felt real.

It was time to leave after that, as Len led us from the bedroom and into the hall before we ventured back down the stairs to the entry way. Nerves kicked in as we exited. This was like the first day in a new pack but a million times worse. Shifters, at least, I understood. I knew the rules. Faerie and fae were a whole other ballgame, and I was walking into this event with no knowledge or skills to help me fit in.

Except for the Silver Lands prince at my side.

Hopefully, that was all I'd need for the royals to at worst ignore me, and at best be polite.

Len led me back across the bridge to his house and we headed toward the courtyard. I could hear the chatter of voices before any fae came into view, and when we stepped past the first pillars I choked down more nerves. There were at least a hundred gorgeous, glamourous, supernatural beings in the space, dressed in long gowns and suits.

Just as I was practicing some deep breathing exercises, a familiar blond fae popped up in front of us. "Lady, you have destroyed my heart and my—"

Len let out a low rumble. "If you value your life, Tyrin, you won't finish that sentence."

Tyrin held both hands up, looking almost as godlike as his best friend in a tailored black suit. He wore a long silver duster jacket, as did many of the fae males around us, adding to their otherworldly façade. But tonight Len was minus his jacket. He didn't need it to be otherworldly.

"Everyone is curious about why you called this last-minute event," Tyrin said conversationally, lifting a drink from a nearby tray and taking a sip. The contents were a very pale pink, visible through the crystal sides. "You should hurry and put them out of their misery. No one will get drunk until you do, and I need a night to forget my woes."

Len slapped a hand on his shoulder and I saw the brief squeeze. "It'll be okay, brother. No matter what happens, we'll ensure your happiness. The walk to find a mate isn't infallible, as we've just discovered. There's always hope."

I didn't know Tyrin's story, and I didn't understand Faerie culture regarding this "mate walk," but I did recognize and empathize with his loneliness. I especially loved the way Len offered his friend comfort and assurance. A sign of true brotherhood. Well, that, and the constant ribbing.

Len handed Tabitha to me. "Hold her for me, little Storm. I'm going to do our introduction and ensure you are treated as a princess in the Silver Lands."

Wait, what? That wasn't at all what I wanted. I was willing to take the introduction to his court so I'd remain safe—mostly for Tabitha's sake—but I wasn't a princess. Introducing me as one was a surefire way to piss everyone here off. It hadn't escaped my notice that we'd already drawn attention upon arrival, and even with Tyrin's distraction, the vibe was more than curiosity.

"Winter!" I called after the stubborn fae, but he was already striding into the crowd. *Fuck.*

A low chuckle had me turning with exasperation to Tyrin. "Give up, gorgeous," he said sipping his drink again. "Len is a powerhouse when it comes to protecting what's his. You no longer walk your battles alone, and for that you should thank the gods."

That gave me a moment's pause. "I'm not a princess though. I'm not even fae."

Tyrin leaned in closer, and I could smell the scent of his drink. It had a strong whiskey vibe, despite the pink color. "You are whatever the hell you want to be. Don't let genetics dictate your happiness. Don't let anything dictate it. You walk in there, head held high, and you show them why the fates chose you for their prince. Princesses might be born, but queens are made. So yes, you're right. You're no princess... you're a damn queen."

Well, okay, then. "I see why you two are best friends," I managed to say.

His lips landed briefly on my cheek, and then he was striding away. "Remember my words, Samantha. You're a queen."

As he disappeared into the crowd, I tried to ignore the additional curious faces that had turned my way. It seemed they'd finally noticed the tiny fae in my arms.

Gasps rang out around us, along with the whispers.

"A fae child!"

"How is this possible?"

"Len held that child. I thought I was dreaming."

It went on and on, and normally this would be my cue to get the hell out of here, but I was still channeling my inner queen. Tyrin was right. I was done allowing others to dictate my status in life any longer.

Fuck that, and the alpha it rode in on.

Striding forward, I headed for the prince. Len was about to announce my presence to his land, and I would be by his side. Living in the shadows was for the shifter god. Not for me.

Not any longer.

And one day very soon I wouldn't need pep talks to remind me of my worth. I'd just feel it.

No one should ever accept the bottom of the barrel; we all had strengths beyond what we believed. We just had to be brave enough to take that first step.

Queen energy, here I come.

CHAPTER
TWENTY-FIVE

SAMANTHA

My bravado held out long enough for me to weave through the crowds, ignoring all the stares, until I caught sight of Len's silver hair. His height was an advantage in more ways than one.

As I got closer, I noticed he was leaning down, chatting intensely with another fae. Their face and outfit were obscured, and from my current angle it looked almost as if he was pressing his lips to their cheek.

I ground to a brief halt, before shaking my head and pushing forward once more. Len owed me nothing. I had to remember that all we shared was a daughter and missing memories. He might not have found a mate on his walks, but that didn't mean he wasn't dating or betrothed to another fae. After all, on Earth, arranged marriages were the norm for royals.

As painful as it was, I had to remember that I was here for Tabitha and to unlock my memories. Sure, it had felt as if we were building toward something deeper, but maybe that had all been in my head. He called me family, which could encompass a multitude of different scenarios, many of which did not include romance.

A fact I would have to accept, no matter how much it pained me.

When I found the strength to look for him again, he had finished with the other fae and was now up on a small round platform. "I have an announcement," he called. As his deep voice rumbled across the space, everyone quietened. "Thank you all for gathering at such short notice."

"Always up for a party," Tyrin shouted back, and the atmosphere was relaxed as lilting chuckles rang out.

Len shook his head at him. "We are well aware, Warrior," he called, before growing more serious. "However, this is a moment that I have been waiting for my entire life. A moment to introduce you all to two very special beings. I want to induct them into the Silver Lands, I want your fealty and protection toward them, and I hope that all of you can understand my joy in this moment."

Somehow, he knew exactly where I was, as he turned and held a hand out. Lights brightened around Tabitha and me, and I found my feet somewhat frozen to the ground.

Queens are created. Len was my family.

This would all work out okay if I just trusted in the process.

As I moved forward, the train of my dress fanned out behind me, and I never took my eyes off the enigmatic prince, who still held out a hand to me. Taking it without hesitation, I sucked in a deep breath as he used his strength to lift us up with him. The area was small, so as he positioned me before him, my back ended up pressed against his front. Against every hard line, and just like that, it was very difficult to remember all the ways "family" could be non-sexual.

"This is Samantha," Len said as hundreds of curious eyes locked on us. The faces I could see were all beautiful, with skin tones ranging from white to brown and black, with a few that looked pink and purple as well. There was no mistaking their otherness, and that *extra* Mera had referred to.

"Samantha is a shifter from Earth, and my chosen fae princess." There he went with the princess thing again. Surely, he couldn't be betrothed to another when he spoke in this way. "And this is Tabitha," he continued. "Our daughter."

The gasps were near deafening, as the reality of Len having a child hit the crowd. Tabitha waved her hands in front of her. "Tabitha, a princess of the Silver Lands." Len's joy and pride was evident in his tone.

"Praise the Great Queen!"

This call rang out from someone nearby, and I turned as a stunning female with silver hair tumbling down her back stepped forward. She had her hands pressed to her mouth, silver eyes wide and shimmery as if she was trying not to cry. As she pushed through the crowd, the fae bowed their heads, and I knew that I was about to meet Len's mother, queen of the Silver Lands.

"Do you all swear fealty to Samantha and Tabitha, through your fealty to me?" Len called, drawing my attention back to the crowd. There was no pause as a rush of *"ayes"* rang out through the room. And it did surprise me to look around and see not a single angry or confused expression.

"Do you accept them as part of the Silver Lands royal court? As one of us!"

"Aye!"

All that was left was the queen, still striding forward, as

more of her fae lowered their heads to her. Len moved his attention her way. "Mother," he said with a smile. "Do you accept your heir? The princess of the Silver Lands?"

She was close enough now that I could see how silver and stunning she was, just like her son. Her dress glittered with spun gold and silver elements, and on her head was a crown, dotted with reven stones.

She stopped in front of the stage and I knew I was supposed to bow or curtsey or something, but when I tried to move, Len's hand snaked around my stomach, holding me in place against him.

"Tabitha," the queen breathed. She held her hands out and I fought the urge to spin and hide my daughter. This had been in my nightmares for a long time, losing her to whatever race she shared DNA with. But Len had told me to trust him. He told me he wouldn't let them take our daughter, and he'd held to his word so far.

I would continue to place my faith in him.

The queen's face softened. "I understand your fear, Samantha, but I promise I just want to hold my granddaughter. I would never take a child from her mother. Not for any reason."

Her statement bolstered the feeling that I was making the right choice in trusting them all. With a smile, I loosened my hold on my daughter. Tabitha appeared to consider the beautiful, and eternally young, queen for a beat, before she held her hands out and cooed.

The queen's eyes went very glassy. "I've waited thousands of years for this," she choked out, her silken tones a little ragged. When she accepted the child into her arms, cheers rang across the room.

A new sense of joviality fell over the courtyard. Drinks were shared once more, and everyone went back to what they were doing before Len's announcement. To my surprise, the fae didn't press forward to crowd around the queen and Tabitha, seeming to understand that they needed a moment to meet and bond with each other. Just seeing the two of them together had butterflies dancing inside me once more. I'd have my own butterfly sanctuary in there if this kept up.

Icy energy caressed the side of my neck as Len leaned down into me. "You did good, Storm."

My chest heaved as I took in my first proper lungful of air. "Quietly shitting myself. Which is super inconvenient when there's no bathrooms outside of your house."

His chuckle was warm. "I've got you. No matter what you need, you only have to ask."

"Still seducing me, I see."

"Always."

Always.

Thankfully, the queen distracted us by lifting her head and addressing me directly. "Samantha, it is so nice to know you. But please, tell us, how did this happen? How did we not know?"

Fantastic questions, and I had zero answers to give her.

Len stepped off the stage then, before reaching out and sweeping me off as well. "We don't know, Mother," he said. "Our memories of the time we were together have been wiped. Faerie glamour is keeping us in the dark—all we have is Tabitha's energy, which is part of us both. Sam doesn't even remember being pregnant or giving birth."

The queen didn't visibly react. Her comment before about waiting thousands of years indicated that she was well versed at patience and hiding emotions. "Mystery or not, there's no denying her legacy here," she finally said. "And if we figure out who did this to you both, they will wish they never crossed the Silver Lands."

She went back then to examining Tabby, the pair locking eyes for so long I wondered if it was a staring contest. Everyone knows that if staring reaches a certain amount of time, it turns into a contest. I didn't make the rules.

"She's perfection," the queen said.

"Thank you," I replied quietly. "And thank you for not hating on her differences... for just accepting her as the miracle she is."

The queen let loose a low chuckle, filled with sadness and probably many other emotions, that I, a being thousands of years younger, could never understand. "If you live long enough, you learn that in the end the only thing that matters is love and loyalty. I don't care that she's half shifter. I don't care if she's only one millionth fae. All I care is that she's in our lives to love. The rest is irrelevant and changes nothing about my level of joy in this moment."

I shook my head. "I honestly never saw this event going as it has. I expected rejection and anger since that's what I'm used to." Len reached out and took my hand, shocking me with his touch and comfort. "I'm very grateful that Len is the father of my child." I faced him fully. "You gave me the gift of family, and I honestly don't think I can ever thank you."

"We're never going to be even," he said, releasing my hand so he could caress my cheek, his thumb brushing down the curve of my jaw. "I will owe you for eternity for our daughter."

No lie, I forgot everyone else in the room, even that his mother was standing two feet away with my daughter in her arms. All I could see was Len, and I was desperate for his kiss.

"Ma, Ma, Ma, Ma."

Tabitha broke the moment, and I shook my head and took a step back. It had been so easy for me to forget that not ten minutes ago I'd seen him kissing someone. *Maybe kissing someone.* But the point was, we needed to clarify exactly what was happening here between us before I went any further. Not just for my sake, but for Tabitha's.

I wasn't in the position for a fun romp with a fae prince only to see dust on the pillow in the morning. My time for that was done. This shifter needed all or nothing.

Queen energy, as it were.

CHAPTER
TWENTY-SIX

SAMANTHA

"Do you mind if I take Tabitha around and introduce her to a few fae?" the queen asked me. "I won't remove her from your line of sight."

Despite calling my name before, Tabby appeared content in her grandmother's arms, and I wanted the two to bond. "No worries at all. Thanks for checking first."

She nodded, before turning toward the closest group of fae, who let out a boisterous cheer when the child entered their midst. "You really do celebrate your young," I said, smiling at the happiness in the air. This was a nice atmosphere for Tabby to be in, and this night couldn't have gone any better if I'd written it myself in a story.

I mean, outside of Len's possible love interest. Which I was going to bring up very soon.

"They're the greatest gifts we have," he said. "In Faerie,

power is there for the taking, eternal life available to those who want it, and gems fill our coffers. But children are rare and precious."

Nodding, I turned away from the queen, giving her son all my attention. "I didn't understand the absolute truth of that until Tabitha came into my life." I paused, deciding now was as good a time as ever for my other questions. "Alright, I have two questions."

Len relaxed against the nearby pillar, smiling down at me. "Hit me."

Depending on his answers, he might get his wish.

"What's your mother's name?"

Calling her "the queen" all the time was getting a little old.

"Glendriel," he said, that smile remaining in place.

Queen Glendriel. Regal and befitting a queen of Faerie.

"Okay, great. And who were you kissing just before you stood on the platform?"

The smile wavered but it didn't fall. "Are you jealous, little Storm?"

Fucking hell.

Lie or the truth?

"Yes." The truth it was. "But more than that, I don't want to invest in something when the other party isn't as equally invested."

Len straightened, his expression serious. "You are the only female in my life. Romantically. From the moment I felt your energy, heard your call for help, I've been lost to all others."

He looked like he was about to continue, but I didn't need anything else. I'd seen something innocent, and he'd cleared it up. This almost felt like a grown-up relationship, and I was so here for it.

"Thank you for being honest with me," I told him, relaxing.

"I just didn't want to keep wondering and considering worst case scenarios. Asking was the easiest option."

Len leaned down so our faces were closer together. "I have no secrets from you, Sam. Never be afraid to ask me questions. We have lifetimes to learn about each other, and I personally can't fucking wait."

My lips tilted of their own accord. "And you think I have a dirty mouth."

His eyes turned to my favorite winter storms. "You have no idea."

Yeah, I was going to need a demonstration of that, because his expression was promising me *all* kinds of goodness.

"Now that your questions are out of the way," Len said, still close enough that his icy power was coating my bare skin, "I think it's time for us to attempt to unlock our memories. Mother will keep Tabby safe. It's probably better she's not in the house anyway, just in case there's any energy blowback."

Whoa! Was I ready for that? Leaving Tabitha here, in a room of virtual strangers, in the land of Faerie, went against every grain of my being. But, as I took a second to consider his proposal, I had to admit that he'd made some decent points. After Shadow almost killed me trying to lift the block, I knew there was a risk of energy explosion, which was a risk to Tabitha.

"Swear to me that my daughter will be returned to me as soon as we are done," I said, my tone brittle. Blind trust was reserved for those without my history. "Give me your word."

"I give you my word, vow, and promise," he said without anger or hesitation. "Tabitha will be safe with my mother and returned to you the moment we're done."

Once again, my instincts told me I could trust him. And his mother.

"Okay," I nodded, "but I want to say goodbye and explain what we're doing, so she doesn't think she's being abandoned."

Len nodded. "I'll bring her to you. Wait here."

He hurried off to Glendriel, and feeling a little parched I stumbled over to a nearby table of crystal glasses. Choosing one with clear liquid, I was anticipating the citrusy water again, but when a sweet fizz of blackberry hit my tongue, I paused. "Whoa."

Taking another tentative sip, I almost moaned as the sweet and tart flavor coated my tongue. It was so damn good, and by the time Len returned with Tabitha in his arms, tracking me down at the refreshments area, I'd finished the entire glass. Looking between me and the empty crystal, his lips tilted in a crooked grin. "You're going to regret that one tomorrow, Sam."

Blinking slowly, I smiled broadly at him. "You're very beautiful," I said.

His grin grew, even as he shook his head. "You are beautiful, sweetheart. And I've got your baby so you can say goodbye."

This was probably the point I figured out I was a tiny bit tipsy. Not enough to really impair my judgement, but enough to loosen my tongue.

Tabitha went eagerly into my arms, and I hugged her close, breathing in her delicate and floral scent. "I love you so much," I gushed. "Mommy and Daddy are just going to see if we can lift the Faerie glamour. Are you okay staying with Granny Queen for a little while?"

Len snorted. "Granny Queen. She's going to love that one."

Ignoring him, I focused on Tabitha, who shot me a toothy smile. "Yes, Mamamama."

I couldn't help myself, leaning in and kissing her little cheeks over and over. "You are so clever, baby girl. We're so proud of you."

It hurt me to know she'd been suffering all those years on Earth. Weak, not getting the sustenance she needed. No matter how much Len reassured me she'd existed in a stasis, to see her so vibrant and healthy now broke me into pieces. There was no level of pain I could inflict on Alpha Lorenze that could make up for what he took from her. From us.

As soon as my memories were unlocked, I would go back and deal with him. For good.

Returning Tabitha to Len, he bowed his head to me before moving through the crowd once more to hand her to the queen. I followed, since there was no point waiting behind this time. "We will all guard her with our lives," Glendriel assured me when I got closer. "Call if you need any energy assistance."

Len nodded. "I have some ideas to try first, but if that fails, I'll ask for help."

Tabitha waved at us, and I blew her a kiss, all the while ignoring the ache in my chest at walking away from her.

"She'll be fine," Len assured me, his arm sweeping in behind my back as he guided me toward his house.

"I know," I said. "If I thought she wouldn't be, I'd never leave her with your mother. Queen or not." Yeah, loose tongue was definitely in the cards, but Len showed no sign of being offended.

Curious fae watched us leave, but none commented or even attempted to stop the prince as we marched through. When we reached his bridge, he slowed his stride, and I enjoyed the quiet.

"You called me Daddy," he said suddenly, and there was a rumble in his tone that had me sliding to a halt.

If he asked tomorrow, I was going to blame my next state-ment on the wine. "You're definitely daddy material."

His intensity grew. "I'll take that as a compliment. But more than that, I'm honored by your inclusion of me toward

Tabitha. It means everything, and I didn't want the moment to pass without acknowledging it." He stepped closer, his thumb brushing over my lip once more, and I was starting to think he had a small obsession with my mouth. "You slay me."

"Fuck," I breathed.

His lips twitched as his eyes darkened. "Always such a way with words."

"That's me," I choked out. "A true wordsmith. Shame I'm more of a reader than a writer, because the worlds are really missing out on the amazing prose hidden in my brain."

The twitch turned into a slow smile that wrecked my insides; they churned and burned, the need nearly sending me to my knees. What was in that fucking drink? And was I regretting it... or did I want more?

His chest rumbled, and I found my hands resting against the broad planes. *Wait. Hands, what the hell are you doing?*

Len reached up and wrapped both of his across mine, trapping me against him. "I find myself fighting the instinct to murder any who have touched you," he said, leaning in to murmur the words. "It's not a normal fae reaction. We're possessive, yes, but also reasonable. I have zero fucking reason when it comes to you."

I'd seen that in Shadow's lair, and maybe this was still the fae booze talking, but I couldn't believe I'd had doubts about him before. That had been a stupid moment of insecurity. Len was a grown-ass fae, and if he wanted to be with another, he would be. Dude was thousands of years old. He'd had all the time to choose, and all signs indicated he was choosing me.

"*My reason* toward you," I whispered back, "appears to be a little faulty these days too." Leaning forward, the need to taste Len was a driving force. But before I could fall into his mouth—well, more like chest due to our height difference—he wrapped his arm around me and got us walking once more, across the bridge and into his house.

The tremble in my limbs remained as we entered the front door, and this time instead of going up the stairs, Len led me to the right, opening a nondescript white door. Lights brightened as we walked inside—without him hitting a switch of course—and when I saw the contents I wanted to run around hugging every shelf.

"Wow," I gushed, "another library. I feel like I've died and gone to book heaven being around you band of merry bastards." Mera called them something like that, and while I couldn't remember the exact saying, I loved the concept.

Walking toward the closest of the shelves, I noted that the room was much smaller than Shadow's—this was more of a huge study—but had the same dark wooden shelves lining the walls.

"I've always had an area specifically for books," Len said, following me deeper into the room. "Shadow and I first grew a friendship in battle, but we deepened it through a mutual love of knowledge, information, and stories."

"Books make me happy," I said with a small, contented sigh. Running my hands across the spines, I briefly wished one of my skills included absorbing stories via touch. I'd never have enough time to read all the ones I wanted. "When I open a book, it feels like opening a treasure chest. You never know what you'll uncover. An adventure without even having to leave your house."

Len nodded. "You won't have to worry about living your adventures through books any longer. I'll take you on as many as you want."

"And there you go seducing me again," I replied, trying to keep the breathiness I was feeling from my voice. "I'd love to do both. Read and live adventures. Eventually."

"You will."

A statement. No hesitation. Len was confident that we would deal with the glamour, deal with Faerie, and find this life of adventure.

It was everything I'd wished for. Not just for me, but for Tabitha.

"We should get started," Len said, more serious. "This room is magically enforced to contain the energy of some powerful books and crystals. It's the strongest room in the house, and should work as a safehold to attempt a memory retrieval."

My hand stilled on the spine I was touching. "I'm nervous," I admitted. "The pain when Shadow…" Gods, the pain. It had been so bad that I'd called a fae from another world to me, which was still hard to believe.

Len reached me in two strides, hands wrapping around my biceps as he held me firmly. "I promise to do whatever it takes to keep you safe, but pain is often part of the journey. If it becomes too much, if you reach breaking point, all you have to do is tell me. We will find another way."

"I'm pretty tough," I said, hoping to convince the both of us. "I can take it. I need these memories back, so short of literally breaking my brain, I want you to push all the way."

Worry creased his brow as he released a long breath. "Full disclosure, I've attempted to break the glamour on my own brain without any success. As I try, the power slips away, and I'm led back to you. This started with you, and I can only hope if we figure out your block, mine will release as well."

"Okay, that makes sense," I said with a rapid series of nods. "So, what do we do first?"

"Change," he told me. "Get comfortable. I will set everything up to protect you."

He released me, leaving an icy burn where he'd touched.

"You'll need to unlace me," I reminded him, hoping for more of that ice across my bare skin.

Comfortable clothes were going to include an underwear change. I'd been aroused so much tonight; at this point my panties were nothing more than a damp fucking rag.

Before I could act on my current need, Len finished loosening the back of my corset and I focused on catching the dress before it fell. "Return quickly," he said in a low rumble. "We don't want to waste time."

Actually, I wanted to waste time. All the fucking time. My addled, horny, semi-drunk brain could think of nothing better than wasting *time* with the fae prince. I mean, what if we learned shit in the past that ruined everything for us? That destroyed this fragile but beautiful relationship we were building? What if the dream turned into a nightmare?

I might never have the chance again to be half naked with this sexy man, and I wasn't wasting it. Nope.

The wine had spoken. We were taking a chance tonight.

Turning in a somewhat graceful motion, I took Len by surprise when I stepped right into him. Tilting my head back, I let my hair fall down my back as I moistened my lips. His gaze followed the motion, and before he could say anything I pushed myself up and wrapped my arms around his neck for enough leverage to finally, *fucking finally*, slam my mouth against his.

I was kissing the fae prince and I had zero regrets.

CHAPTER TWENTY-SEVEN

SAMANTHA

The moment my lips touched his, mint with a hint of caramel sweetness filled my senses, and I was lost. Completely and totally lost.

My sudden decision to throw caution to the wind clearly surprised Len. It took him a second to recover, but when he did he returned the kiss with enough force that I wondered if he'd been wanting to do this as badly as I had. From almost from the first moment he stormed into the Shadow Beast's lair.

His lips parted, and mine followed as he demanded entry to my mouth. His tongue was dominant, and I had this sneaking suspicion that he liked to control in the bedroom. *Sign me up, Prince. I'm here to obey all commands.* Especially if there was an orgasm at the end of it.

"Sam," he rumbled against my lips, "I know you didn't drink enough to lose reason, so what...?"

With reluctance, I pulled away, already regretting the distance between us. "We have no idea what our memories hold," I admitted, breathing deeply to try and fill my aching lungs. "What if the past changes everything? What if we lose the relationship we've been building here. Our daughter has the sort of family and love I prayed for, and I don't want to fuck it up."

His long fingers wrapped around my chin, capturing my face. Gently, he forced my head back so our gazes locked. Winter sprang up in his eyes, which were swirling faster than ever. "There's no fucking this up," he said bluntly, with his usual confidence. "I won't let that happen. The past is gone, and it will not destroy the future, but we do need to understand it to move forward. For our sakes, and for Tabitha."

I knew he was right. I knew it with every iota of my confused brain. Releasing a long sigh, I nodded once. "Yeah, you're probably right."

Len's lips twitched, before his smile broke through, and I fought the urge to fan my face. This guy was devastating up close, and now that I'd tasted him I was settling into a new addiction: kissing a fae prince.

His smile grew, and I found a similar one crossing my face, almost as if I'd caught his happiness. There was something enticing in knowing you weren't facing the darkness alone. Normally, whatever came from the past would have to be dealt with by me. Just me. But Len was in my corner, and he'd promised that he would fight to keep the darkness from taking us.

No being: human, shifter, fae, beast or other, was designed to walk the worlds alone. In one way or another, we were all pack creatures, and it was a nice feeling to have Len in mine.

His smile faded, the storm settling in his eyes, even if they remained a darker grey. "Your kiss gave me an idea," he said softly. "Of why Shadow struggled to lift the glamour. Brute strength might not be the way to break the bonds it has on us. What if it needs to be unraveled in the same way it began?"

"The same way?" I repeated.

He nodded, gaze drifting away from my face as he appeared to run the idea further through his mind. "What if it's sex that will facilitate the breaking of the glamour. Sex is clearly how our relationship started—it might even be part of the glamour—so there's a circularity in using it to restore what was lost."

My heart pounded hard in my chest, because even though that statement wasn't the passion-filled moments I'd expected, the energy flowing between us did feel passionate. "It makes sense," I said, body thrumming with anticipation. "And you already know I'm willing." I'd all but thrown myself at him moments earlier.

Len's head dipped low and pressed a kiss to my cheek, brushing his lips closer and capturing mine. "There's no part of me not willing, Storm. I've been wanting to taste you… every part of you, since the moment I was called into the beast's lair. Fair warning though, I am a touch controlling in the bedroom." I'd already called that. "Nothing crazy, but I have moments where I need compliance. Are you up for that?"

My breath was audible in the quiet of the room. "I'm not sure how much dominance my wolf will accept, but I'm willing to try."

His thumb was on my lip, swiping across the spot he'd just kissed, and as he brushed the moisture, my legs weakened as damp heat throbbed in my center. "Try is all I ask, and this is your last chance to walk away." The intensity in his gaze held me captive. "There are other options to try to break the glamour."

"Can't walk," I managed to choke out. "And even if I could, I wouldn't."

It was no fucking lie. My legs were jelly, the heels barely keeping me stable. In fact, I was fairly sure the only reason I was standing was the grip I had on Len's jacket, my fingers wrapped in the silky material.

A low rumble started in his chest. It was so animalistic that I fought the urge to climb that fae like a damn tree. "Tonight you can command me," I whispered.

His eyes flared. "Kiss me."

There was no hesitation as I lifted myself higher, pushing closer until my body was firmly against his. Len remained still, not touching as he watched me closely. When my lips pressed to his, he allowed me point three of a second to steer the direction of the kiss, then those rumbles from his chest spilled from his lips and filled the room.

His hands slid up my sides and buried in the long strands of my hair, tightening as he opened his mouth and deepened the kiss. Loosening my hold on his jacket, I attempted to run my hands down his body, but his energy wrapped around me, halting the touch.

"You come first," he warned. "No touching until I have my fill of you. Until you scream."

Holy gods.

The trembling in my body increased as my pussy throbbed. It had been a long time since I had sex—actually, the last time was with him—and I was fairly sure with Len's skills I'd be screaming before he even finished this kiss.

"Undress," he commanded as he released me, stepping back to watch.

The dress top was already sagging and loose from where he'd unstrapped me, so I easily slid it down my waist, wiggling to free myself of it completely. As the material fell to the floor around me, Len's energy flared, and that was when my wolf pushed forward. I'd expected she wouldn't be into his commanding attitude, but for some reason there was no antagonism in her power. If anything, she also wanted a piece of Len.

As wolfish energy filled the space, Len's eyes grew hooded. "Down, pup," he commanded. "She's mine for tonight."

I waited for the pushback from my wolf, but she just let out a low whimper that filled my head, and... well, fuck, sank back inside.

Looked like we were both ready to be commanded by this Faerie prince.

When her energy faded, Len's gaze dragged across my skin as tension coiled deeper in my gut. My skin felt like it was on fire under his look, and I almost moaned just from that.

"Undress, Storm," he said, smooth tones wrapping around me.

Shit, right. I was still standing there in underwear and heels.

The bra went first, aching and heavy breasts falling into their natural position. I'd had a baby, and even with shifter genetics they sat differently than they did in my early twenties, but I liked their curve. I also liked the flare of Len's energy as he watched me.

Hooking my thumbs into the thong panties, I shimmied them down my legs until they pooled at my feet. As I stepped out of them, my heels made a soft thud on the floor.

"Heels?" I asked.

"Leave them," Len said.

When he moved, I could have sworn the oxygen was expelled from the room. I struggled to fill my lungs. There was something about being naked and vulnerable while he was fully dressed that had my heart racing, but not in fear.

Turned out that maybe... just maybe, this was a kink I was

into. I was about ready to fall at the fae's feet and give myself over to him. As he moved closer, the throb in my clit picked up pace to a steady flicker, which had me desperate to press my fingers against it. But at the same time, I enjoyed the anticipation of what Len would do next.

Instinct told me that he would not leave me wanting.

In any way.

CHAPTER TWENTY-EIGHT

SAMANTHA

"Y ou are the most beautiful fucking creature I've ever seen," Len rumbled, shaking his head. "You are more than shifter and fae. I don't know what the *more* is, but there's no other in the worlds like you."

His words... the compliments, coated my skin, sending goose bumps across the surface, as my nipples pebbled hard. That throb between my thighs increased, along with a buildup of energy in my gut that grew stronger with each second. His hand traced across the tattoo on my right side. "I marked you with a wild wolf?"

"I believe so," I whispered back, voice husky. "When we were together."

As he touched the lycanthropic beast, the colors and patterns started to swirl and move against his energy. "Definitely of magical origins," he said. "I have given my brothers similar tattoos, but I don't remember this one."

His touch grew firmer, as if he were stroking the beast and me all in one slide, and I fought down the groan. The anticipation of the moment he allowed me to fall apart had me fucking panting.

Len's hand was replaced by his mouth as he leaned forward and started at the junction of my neck and collarbone, before slowly exploring lower and lower. My heels gave me enough height that he wasn't bent completely in half, but as he moved down my chest I knew it was going to get more difficult for him.

As he gripped my tits, kneading and caressing, they ached and throbbed like my clit. How in all the fucks could he do this to my body with nothing more than a touch? If I had to guess, I'd say he was unraveling me at my core. Here was hoping he rebuilt me even better.

"You taste..." His breath slid across my skin. "...familiar but also not. I need those memories released."

I felt the same, and even though a part of me still worried it would all be destroyed, that was future Sam's problem. Releasing the memories would give me more of Len, and I was ready for it all.

As his mouth enveloped my nipple, I almost stumbled, but the firm grip he had on my hips kept me stable. The swipe of his tongue across the hard tip sent a sharp throb through my pussy, and I jerked involuntarily. Len's chuckle was dark against my skin.

The next swipe of his tongue included some teeth as he took my other nipple into his mouth. The brief pain was enough to have my hips jerking again; his hands tightened, his strength keeping me from moving. I almost came from the nipple stimulation—and his firm hold against my skin—but somehow I managed to bite my lip hard enough to hold off the orgasm. Blood filled my mouth but I didn't care, too lost in what was happening to my body.

Len lowered himself until he was on his knees before me. This was the part I loved about his control. He wasn't using it to force me to pleasure him, as Alpha Lorenze or Grant would have done. Nope, he was using it so he could pleasure me and draw it out as he saw fit.

He'd seemed worried by his need to mildly command me in the bedroom, but if it was mostly centered around bringing me to orgasm, I was all in.

Len pressed his lips to my stomach, which wasn't perfectly flat, but he apparently didn't care as he looked up at me. "You carried my child. I'm going to worship you until you understand what a goddess you are. I will tell you when you can move, okay, Storm?"

Another command. Another throb between my legs.

All I could do was nod, and it appeared that was answer enough as he lowered himself, his tongue sliding across the seam of my pussy as he tasted me for the first time. I'd been wet for what felt like hours, but at this point the damp heat near coated my inner thighs.

As he tasted me again, Len groaned and then he whispered, so low I wasn't even sure I was meant to hear it, "You're about to be my undoing."

All other thoughts were lost as his tongue swiped from the bottom of my pussy to the top. My hips jerked against his face as I clenched my hands at my side, wanting to touch him so badly but unable in the thrall of his command. I'd be a fucking idiot if I did anything at this point to halt his talented tongue.

He sucked my clit into his mouth and like with my nipple there was a strike of pain as his teeth closed; all it did was increase the swirls in my gut. Sparks raced across my skin, like all nerve endings were lighting up, and I was going to come. There was no stopping it at this point.

Of course, this fucker knew exactly when I was about to explode, and right when the scream lingered on my lips and I tipped over the edge, he slowed his assault.

A strangled sob escaped. "Not yet, sweet Sam," he murmured, pulling back so I could see as his tongue swiped across his lips, devouring the last of my arousal on his face. "I'm not done yet."

Fuck the gods.

Would I survive this? Did I even care?

Len leaned in again, fingers sliding inside me to match the swirl of his tongue, and I couldn't stop my hips from rocking. Nothing in this world would be able to stop that rocking.

The orgasm was there again, cries spilling from my lips in mews, until he eased back again. "Len," I panted. "The fuck, dude?"

The laugh against my skin sent my clit into throb overdrive. "Trust me, Sam. Just trust me."

My groan was loud, but I decided that I did trust him. And even though this was shattering me, it was in the best ways, so I'd just enjoy the ride.

Len mouth-fucked me over and over with his tongue and fingers, curling those long digits up to stroke across my g-spot, all but rendering me mindless. Each time when I was about to release, he would slow his pace, changing tactics.

As I neared the edge of what I could handle, my body so fucking worked up that there wasn't a part of me which didn't ache and spark and throb, Len's power wrapped around me. I was lifted and gently lowered to the ground.

"Ride my face, Sam," he commanded, and when his mouth landed on my pussy once more, he didn't stop, allowing all that build-up to finally slide into the next stage.

My body trembled, my legs so violently that I could see them shaking as I wrapped them around his head, thrusting against his mouth as he'd ordered. "I'm going to explode," I screamed, the magic within me swirling in a way I'd never felt. "Len, I can't stop it."

"Come, Storm." His growl was muffled against my body. "Your magic is about to rip free."

This was the point I understood that there was a reason for all the edge play. Len had been pushing me to where every part of my body was filled with arousal and power and need. He was pushing me to this point.

My screams ripped through the air as a detonation of power collided with an influx of pleasure. Light filled the room, so bright I had to close my eyes. The edging created an orgasm that nearly stole my soul, and I forgot everything other than my pleasure. When I came, it exploded from me in a mess of liquid that had me worried for a second I'd peed myself. Until I realized it was cum.

Fuck me dead.

The orgasm was so intense I was almost embarrassed, but Len's response destroyed that instinct before it could even take root. He growled again, his mouth on me as he ate down every fucking drop of my pleasure. The fae prince devoured me until I was completely spent, a wrung-out mess sprawled on the ground. The bright light that had come from *somewhere... me...* faded as I came back to myself, having just experienced an out-of-body moment via fae tongue.

As my mind swirled with unspent emotions, and this incredible feeling of completeness, there was also a flicker of a scene. A memory. Filtering through the light that was still inside my head. "Len," I cried, "My memories!"

He lifted his head, stormy eyes locked on my face. "You remembered us?"

I realized in my euphoric excitement I hadn't made myself clear. "No," I said quickly. "Not everything. I just had a vision of you tangled around me in bed. A single screenshot, but it had to be from our time before."

He pulled himself higher, crawling over the top of me. He was still clothed, and I ached to strip them from him. "I don't remember yet," he said softly, before he dropped lower and pressed his lips to mine.

I'd never tasted myself on another before, and I wasn't sure if I'd feel grossed out, but instead it heightened my arousal. Len's tongue swept inside as he kissed me like I was his last breath, reminding me that we were making new memories tonight.

No matter what the past revealed, one thing was for sure: I wasn't wasting one second of my time with the fae prince.

Not for anything.

CHAPTER TWENTY-NINE

SAMANTHA

The kiss continued, building tension low in my gut, and I enjoyed that Len took his time. There was no rushing the foreplay, and with each taste of his lips I found myself panting and on the edge once more. "Can you get naked now?" I asked huskily when he eventually lifted his head.

His smile was slow, burning into me. "I don't trust my control around you. For once in my long life, it's hard to resist."

"Please don't resist," I said seriously. "Just don't."

I reached out for his jacket, and he didn't protest when I pushed the sleeves from his shoulders. He helped by lifting himself up on each arm so I could strip his jacket and shirt free from his upper body. When his top half was bare, I took a moment to really stare.

And drool.

I'd expected Len to have a sporty, lean and toned body. He was so tall and wore clothes so elegantly that I never imagined he would be super buff.

Only he was—broad shouldered and well-muscled. He had clearly defined lines beneath his pecs and down his abdominals. So. Many. Abdominals.

Lifting my left hand, I traced across some swirling silver and purple tattoos on his chest. "You tattooed yourself too," I guessed.

"I did," he replied, his powerful arms on either side of my head as he held himself up, giving me a chance to explore his skin. "They're ancient Faerie symbols. Power, life, longevity..." There was a slight pause. "...and love."

"Are you going to command me again?" I asked. His domination had been mild. He appeared more concerned with ensuring my pleasure came before his, but now we were ready for the next part.

His chuckle was low, sending shivers across my body. "I can release control now. I needed it before so that your pleasure came first, but now we will find it together. In that moment, I will attempt to lift the Faerie glamour."

My orgasm had given me a glimpse of the past. Now I wholeheartedly believed Len was on the right track to destroy the full block.

"Definitely a much nicer experience than what Shadow tried," I said with a laugh.

Len didn't laugh with me, and I figured it might have something to do with me mentioning another male when we were all but naked and about to have sex. Even if that other male was his family and happily mated.

"Shadow will never give you what I can," he said, with no arrogance.

"I don't want Shadow," I said firmly. "Not now. Not ever."

There was only one who could control and command me as Len had.

Pushing myself higher, I reached down and hooked my fingers in the band of his pants, working at the button. Len didn't fight as I released the clasp, easing the material down as far as I could reach, stifling my groan as the thick head of his cock made an appearance. Slightly darker than his skin, I ran my thumb across the hardness.

For a moment, all train of thought vanished, where I forgot I was getting him naked. Instead, I reached out and wrapped my fingers as far around the tip as I could manage. Silken heat caressed my senses, and a small panting groan fell from my lips.

Len lifted himself, leaning back so he was in a kneeling position before me, pants unbuttoned, cock jutting up toward his bellybutton. As I rose with him, I reached for his pants once more, only to gasp when they disappeared under my touch. Blinking down at his complete nakedness, I lifted my gaze to his face. "You could have just vanished our clothes at any time?" I gasped again.

He hands wrapped around my waist, yanking me forward so our bare skin was pressed together. "Of course," he said, "but where's the fun in that?"

Gracefully, he dropped back onto his ass so I was straddling him. Before I could reply to his *Where's the fun in that?* his mouth pressed to mine, initiating another soul-stealing kiss. This fae loved to kiss, and I was *here for it.*

Settling in against him, the hard press of his cock had me reaching down to stroke it the best I could between us. All the while the kiss never skipped a beat. Sliding against his body, the slick heat of my pussy coated us both, and I moaned softly. "Fuck me, Len. Right fucking now."

Yeah, I was demanding when I was horny.

That animalistic rumble entered his chest once more, and I

cried out as he lifted me like I weighed nothing before he positioned himself below me and thrust up. Despite my previous orgasm, he was too large for an easy entry, but there was more pleasure than pain, which heightened my arousal.

That initial stretch and burn had me panting like a wolf in heat, my head falling back as the most intense pulse filled me. My arousal leaked from around his cock, lubricating as he lifted me and thrust up again. It took multiple thrusts for him to have me fully seated on him, and when I felt that sense of completeness, I started to rock, riding him like my life depended on it.

He controlled from the bottom, hands firm on my hips as he moved me, but the pace and angle were really working for me so there was no need to fight it. "Eyes on me, Storm," he ordered, and like fucking magic my head snapped forward until I was locked in his wintery gaze.

"Len," I cried in a mumble, my entire body throbbing as the light burned around us again. This time it spilled from me before the orgasm hit. "I'm already close."

"Nope," he whispered with a wicked grin. "You don't come until I say. I've got you, baby. We will fall together and break this fucking spell."

The spell. The glamour. The reason we were here.

He buried his cock until it slammed against the farthest reaches of my pussy, and I lost coherent thought as a scream ripped from my throat. "So... so... d—deep," I choked out, words almost beyond me.

"I've got you," he repeated.

Tingles raced through my center until my legs were trembling almost as much as the last time. I was teetering on the edge, but Len wasn't ready for us to come yet. He switched his position, shifting me onto my back so I landed on the soft rug. Somehow, he kept his cock buried deep as he bent my legs at the knees before pushing them firmly to either side of me.

Thankfully, I was flexible enough to handle the position as he spread me as wide as I could so he had all the access to pull all the way out and thrust deep inside. With each thrust, a small gasping scream escaped from my lips, my control completely released to him.

The pressure building in my pussy would have been a worry, but I knew from the last time that this was the impending orgasm. "Samantha," he growled, "your eyes aren't on me."

I hadn't even realized I'd closed my eyes in pleasure, and the moment they shot open the brightest light near blinded me.

This time the light wasn't just from me. White and purple mixed together, creating a shimmery veil that surrounded us. When Len lowered his head to kiss me, I heard him say, "Ready, little Storm?"

I was so fucking ready. "Please." Yeah, I was begging, but if I didn't get the command to come soon, I was going to die.

Our glow increased, and as his tongue swiped across my lips, Len let out a rumbling groan. "Come, Sam. Scream my fucking name."

Yes, sir. The edge I'd been teetering on crumbled like it had never been there, and all I could do was hold on and scream his name as requested. The intensity of my orgasm had darkness dancing across my vision, and when I came back to myself, I must have asked him if I peed myself. There was a slow laugh and he said, "That's not pee."

Shifter gods. I mean, last time had been a lot, but that was... the entire lower half of our bodies were sticky with our combined pleasure.

When the last of the orgasm was wrung from us, Len slowed his movements, and I let out a long breath. Images flickered on the edge of my mind, and I knew that the memories were there, just in reach. "It worked," I said with a huff. "We broke the glamour—"

I never got to finish that sentence before a sharp pain cut into my chest.

So sharp that I couldn't speak.

Or breathe.

Or move.

It was a death blow. I knew that with all my being, and it hadn't come from Len.

An outside source had found me the moment the spell was broken, and it was too late to stop the darkness from taking over.

Dragging me from this world.

CHAPTER THIRTY

LEN

When Samantha collapsed in my arms, the rationality I'd cultivated for centuries vanished. The civility I wore as a cloak over the monster inside was destroyed, and as my roar filled the room, glass shattered around us.

A sliver of control remained, as I ensured she was safe from my rage. All the while I desperately ran the scenarios of *What the fuck just happened?* and *How do I save her?* through my mind. All I knew was that this did not come from sex or breaking of the memory block. It had been an outside attack, but there was no way anyone should have been able to infiltrate my royal land.

Our bodies remained joined even as she collapsed, and it was only the pulse of her power through every place we touched that told me she was still able to be saved.

But I had to get supplies.

I had a fuck-ton of energy inside me, more than the usual fae, but in this case I couldn't take any chances. I'd have one shot, and I had to throw everything at it.

Gathering Samantha into my arms, she felt way too fucking frail, and I scanned her quickly to try and discern the specific attack. She was barely breathing, her skin paler than it should be, while her heart stuttered in clear arrhythmia.

As I moved across the room, glass bit into my feet but didn't break the skin. Reaching my main shelf, I used my power to rip off the door, shifting Samantha in my arms so I could reach for the four stones I needed—two silver and two red *brafeta stones*, used in healing rituals.

Moving to one of the only spots not littered with glass, I placed Samantha down gently, before all four stones went around her, one in each corner of her body. As the last red crystal clicked into place near her right foot, I sent energy into the first, activating it. It then signaled to the others, until a rectangular dome of white light surrounded Sam.

A protective shield.

Roars ripped from my chest as I lost contact with her, but putting her into stasis was the only way to hold off death. "You can't fucking have her," I snarled to the unseen entity. "I will keep her from your clutches, and if you dare to try me I'll march into the underworld and destroy every fucking part of it to get her back. She's not yours."

She was mine. I would kill any who tried to take her from me.

Maybe it was my imagination, but the heavy cloak that had been coating this room since she was hurt eased a touch. Even Death knew that I was dead fucking serious. Pun intended.

Pulling myself to my feet, I called up my silver energy to cloak me in my usual outfit, including my jacket. The stones contained in it might come in handy as I tracked these fuckers down.

Sending out a message to Mother, I sensed she was already on her way. A fact that would have concerned me if I wasn't half out of my mind.

As I waited, I probed across the Silver Lands to see if there were any disturbances, before sending my scope out farther into the rest of Faerie.

There was nothing. No indication of what had happened. Not even a spark of energy that spoke of someone dabbling in power that they shouldn't.

When Mother's energy entered my house, I lifted Sam using my power. The stones protected her from touch, even mine, but I could keep her close in this way. The sparks of energy from the brafeta stones were opaque, so no one could see what precious cargo lay within.

"Len!" There was a frantic note in Mother's voice, and the sense of dread streaking down my spine heightened. I hurried out—with Sam floating behind me—to meet her in the front hall. She raced in, arms waving in my direction, face fallen and distressed. *Empty* waving arms. "Where's Tabitha!" I roared, beyond respect and reason.

A beat later, a much smaller brafeta box of light entered the space.

Fuck.

No! Not my baby too!

"She cried out and collapsed," the queen sobbed, her face streaked in silver tears, power leaking from her. "I didn't know what to do but try and keep her alive until I could determine who attacked." We'd taken the same action, and in doing so had slowed the march of death. But until we figured out who attacked, we were only delaying the inevitable.

"Oh, Great Queen," my mother cried, peering past me for

the first time. "Samantha too?"

Her gaze returned to me, and as the tears dried on her cheeks it was as if we both had the same realization.

"It's their bloodline," I said, as she whispered, "Their bloodline."

I nodded. "Yes, and it happened here in Faerie. An attack from another fae."

Like the ancient, powerful being she was, Mother drew her rage, fear, and pain deep inside, before straightening. Her crown appeared across her head a beat later. "I will call an immediate gathering of the royal houses." Her crown glowed brightly as power channeled around her. "Whoever did this is going to wish they'd chosen a different family to hurt. They will pay with their eternal souls."

She reached out and grasped my hand briefly, squeezing and offering comfort. "Just hold on to our girls, Len. Bring them to the Capital. I will do the rest." She released Tabitha to me as well and was gone in the next second.

Almost immediately, the gong of the trumpets echoed through my house and out into the Silver Lands. It would be sounding across Faerie, and with that I moved from my home, bringing the two precious light-encased beings with me.

Two beings that were the key to my existence.

With rage driving me faster, we reached the edge of the Silver Lands in a heartbeat, and I called on the stones embedded in the sky. I had enough of my own energy to power our journey to the Capital myself, but it was best to save it, in case it was needed to destroy whoever did this.

When the power of the reven stones wrapped around us, I felt Tyrin join me in my rage. He didn't ask what happened— he didn't have to. After a thousand years of friendship, he knew exactly what I battled, and like a true brother stood silently at my back.

We'd been through so much, and no matter what happened, he would fight by my side. Tyrin would have fit in well with my other brothers in the library, but he was tied to this world and had no plans to leave.

A concept I understood, even if I didn't feel the same way.

As the Capital came into sight, I slammed onto the main platform with a crash. So much energy rode along with me that I made more of an entrance than usual with Samantha and Tabitha floating in on either side.

Tyrin landed a second later, and behind him the rest of the Silver Land's warriors. General Terese moved to my side, none of her usual humor visible. She wore the face of a warrior. The others fanned out around us in a show of strength and support. Most of them probably had no idea what had happened, but they were loyal to a fault, and if needed would be there to fight and protect.

When we reached the door to Parliament House, the stones reacted to Samantha and Tabitha, blocking them from entrance, which I overruled with a flick of my hand.

There were gasps from some of the other royal houses who'd witnessed my act, but I didn't turn to acknowledge them. It wasn't general knowledge that I had power beyond most fae, thanks in part to strong Faerie genetics, but also my association with Shadow.

They'd lose their minds if they knew I was held to almost none of the normal rules that governed Faerie—not that I'd ever taken advantage of it. In my old age, it wasn't power I craved, so I kept the peace for the greater good.

But now that cloak of civility was gone.

For all intents and purposes, I was a final and true death, tracking down whoever hurt my family.

I'd be the last being they ever saw.

CHAPTER
THIRTY-ONE

SAMANTHA

Darkness took me deep.

So deep that for a fraction of time I believed this was my true end.

Len's rage surrounded me as I slipped through the cracks of this reality. My last thoughts were of Tabitha and the enigmatic fae prince, the two beings who'd captured and held my heart.

That fatal strike to my chest was nothing compared to the pain of losing them. Nothing.

Just as my final lucidity faded, there was another sharp tug at my center, but this time it wasn't a blow. It was a halting, as an energy dragged me back and then wrapped around me, as if suspending my body in time. With this power cocoon, some clarity returned, and I grew aware of what was happening outside myself.

Len stopped me from dying.

He'd called his mother.

Tabitha...

No! My Tabitha!

She'd been affected by whatever had happened to me, but at least it appeared they'd halted her from death too. We were not completely out of danger—whatever tried to kill us was still actively tugging away at our life force—but there was a chance to save us.

While there's life, there's hope.

My body jolted a moment later when we left the Silver Lands, until we landed in a new place filled with a lot of fae energy. Len raged ahead, keeping us with him, and I could feel Tyrin at his back, rage infusing his energy too.

In my state of stasis, not dead but also not quite alive, I was able to examine the extensive bonds that existed between Len and Tyrin. Not just between them, but also the rest of the silver army. I was filled with a sense of family.

They were fighting for us. For Tabitha and me.

When we tried to enter a huge building, my cage halted briefly, until Len disabled the security. The inside felt open, buzzing with energy, and as a half-dead shifter I wondered how I was feeling so much of Faerie. Some of my memories of Len might have returned, but there was still nothing to indicate I had any fae in my heritage.

When we moved into a cavernous room, I was halted again, but this time it was the gentle sway of Len's energy slowing us all. We remained stationary here, and I sensed that this was where we'd find out what had happened. We'd find out who I needed to kill for daring to try to destroy my daughter. If we hadn't been with Len and his mother at the time... it was terrifying to even finish that thought.

"Bring them here." Len's voice was a rage of energy, filled

with dark malevolence. Crashing sounded around us, and I wondered if he'd upended all the nearby furniture.

A beat later, there was a bang as doors slammed open. "What in all of crystal law is going on here?" an unfamiliar male shouted. "You will be brought before the counc—"

Whatever the male Fae had been about to say was cut off mid-sentence. Len hadn't moved from my side, but I felt Tyrin's power near the newcomer, and I had the sense that it had been his hand around a throat that ceased words.

Len finally moved, as did Tabitha and me since we were bound to the prince. "What did you do, Fredrick?" he asked, in a softly menacing voice. "What have you set in motion?"

Fredrick mumbled, words hard with a hand around his throat. "I set into motion exactly what I said I would," he finally choked out. "The severing of the Great Queen's power cord. Her line is dead."

The silence that extended around the massive room was heavy. *The Great Queen's line is dead.*

"You had no fucking right," Len said, still in that same wrathful, scary ass tone. "There was no vote, why would you move forward—" He paused, as if the truth had hit him suddenly. "You felt her. You felt when Samantha broke through the glamour, and you knew there was at least one descendant of the queen alive."

Wait, what?

Fredrick's choking increased, and since Len had moved at the same time, he was clearly the one hurting the other fae now. "You failed," Len snarled. "Samantha and Tabitha live, which means the line can be restored. Which is lucky for you since your current action could damn Faerie and all of us to death."

"What do you base that statement on?" This was from a different fae, a more feminine tone.

Len took a moment to answer, as if working out the finer

details. "I don't know everything, but when the line was severed, Samantha and Tabitha, my mate and daughter, were both struck down. That could only have happened if they were descendants of the Great Queen. I found them both on Earth, so clearly that was where the queen hid."

Mate. It was almost worth dying to hear that word from Len. For the first time in my existence, I was ready to claim a true mate. I just had to *not* die first.

The room erupted in noise at Len's revelation, a mix of shouts and cries as they tried to discuss everything in one go.

"Focus!" This shout was louder, and it came from Glendriel. "How do we restore their line? How do we save them and Faerie?"

"I have no fucking idea," Len rumbled. "Is there any alive who knows?"

There was a pause, and that same female who'd asked a question earlier said, "There's no way unless you venture into the Great Deep and reconnect the queen's line to the Origin. The original source of Faerie creation." The room felt hotter, as if she were channeling power too. "Which is why we would never have voted to sever the line. Without a connection to the Origin, all of Faerie might fall."

Glendriel's voice was hoarse. "Take him into custody until we decide what to do."

Fredrick laughed, a stupid bad guy cliche of a laugh. Len, who must have still been holding him captive, released a burst of power that locked the other fae in what felt like magical restraints. "I vote for his death," he spit out. "As soon as we figure out how to save my family."

Despite being all but dead, locked in stasis, and surely beyond tears, there was a damp heat on my cheeks. *Mate. Family.* My bucket of life was overflowing. Ironically, since I'd moved all that much closer to death.

"We need to head down into the Deep," Tyrin said, the first to answer. "I'm at your side, brother. We should leave immediately."

Len let out a deep breath. "We don't have the skills to survive the journey, but there might be some who do. We're going to need outside help. Godlike powers."

No need for two guesses of who he was going to ask.

His mom's energy moved closer. "Do whatever you need to save them," she said.

Noise picked up in the room again, and I felt Len's full attention focused on me. The burn of his power infused into my light filled cage as he pressed closer. "Love, I need our pack's help, and I can't take you from Faerie, since this is where the stones will be strongest. But know that the glamour is broken, at least for me, and I will never forget you."

He turned to his mother and murmured something I missed, before coming back to me.

"Keep fighting to stay here," he commanded. "I will never let death have you. You are mine, Storm. You hear me? Fucking. Mine."

Gods save me from possessive fae. Or not. *Yeah, definitely not.*

I'm going nowhere, Winter! I sent that out to him, desperately hoping he would hear.

Just knowing he was going to bring our pack here had a sense of calm and hope infusing me. Of all the truths in the world, there was one I knew for sure: we were stronger together.

All of us in the Shadow Beast's world.

In his pack.

We'd found each other for a reason, and together we would figure out how to save Tabitha.

This was her chance at a true life and family. I refused to let it be stolen away.

Even if, in the end, it cost me my life.

For my daughter, it was a sacrifice I was willing to make.

CHAPTER
THIRTY-TWO

LEN

Leaving Samantha and Tabitha in the care of my mother, when they were existing between life and death, was what I would test all *difficult* moments in my life against. I'd have rather carved out a vital organ to leave behind, but I also knew that they were safer in Faerie, and I could move faster without trying to keep them with me.

In truth, I needed to move faster than I ever had before and return to my second home, the Library of Knowledge. Then find my pack and hope that once I explained the dangers of the Deep Origin of Faerie, they'd still agree to help me.

They might be the only hope we had. Their unique blend of powers should allow them to survive the fires of the Deep. Not just fire, but there were rumors of frost, water, and creatures. There was a reason that no one went down there, despite the many riches and gems that existed in the depths.

"Give me her energy, son," Mother said in a gentle voice. Of the fae here, she was the only one who knew how close I was to losing my shit completely.

"Keep them safe. Please." The words were strangled, but I got them out.

"I will guard them with my life," she promised me. "They're my family too, and you know I'd go to the depths of the underworld for my family."

I had no doubt that she would. I'd seen it in my youth when any threatened the Silver Lands, especially the royal family. "Thank you," I told her, tapping my hand against my chest.

When I removed my hand, I sent with it the connection I had to Samantha and Tabitha, passing them across to the queen. My chest ached as I caressed their shimmery cages one last time, before I spun and took off. I couldn't look back or I'd never be able to leave, and I had to ensure that their lives were saved.

Fredrick, the stupid fuck that he was, got in my way as I was racing from the courtroom. Before he even opened his fucking mouth, I swung my fist and slammed it as hard as I could into his face. He dropped to his knees, a garbled cry squeaking out from his shattered jaw. The look in his eyes indicated I'd taken him completely by surprise. He was used to being the largest fae around, but I was a close second, and my power destroyed his.

"Keep him fucking detained until I return," I roared over my shoulder as I continued from the room. I had no time to deal with Fredrick this day, but I would soon.

For now, my only focus was on saving Samantha and Tabitha.

When I exited the building, I reached the edge of the land and called the gems down, needing their boost of energy for extra speed. It was also on my mind to conserve my own power, as I'd need every iota of it in The Deep of Faerie.

It was really too much of me to ask my family to help with this, but they were the only ones who might survive it. There was also the small issue of that line being cut in Faerie, possibly destroying our world, and in a ricocheting effect, the rest of the worlds. For that reason alone, I had to tell them.

Once I reached my garden, I was able to call up a doorway to the library. Racing through, I burst into the familiar room, the scent of power and books surrounding me. No fae lingered in our section, which wasn't a surprise, since they'd have responded to the trumpets initiated by my mother.

Pushing out into the main thoroughfare, I found Shadow's energy immediately. He was in the dining hall with Mera and Aurora.

Aurora.

I ground to a halt, my heart slamming against my fucking chest as I wrestled with my next actions. In my blind panic over Sam and Tabby, I'd forgotten that my family also had young to care for—to raise into a powerful new generation of supernaturals.

This was too much to ask of them.

To either leave their babies behind, or take them and risk the dangers down there.

I would have to figure out another way. Maybe there was still a fae alive with knowledge of the Great Queen, one not impacted by the lack of memory we all had of her.

If I asked the right questions, there might be answers out there.

As I was turning to return to Faerie, a burst of fire surrounded me. My energy didn't react defensively since I knew exactly who it was from.

The flames were no true threat me.

I stepped forward, through the wall of fire, and it vanished before I felt any burn.

"Brother," Shadow said gruffly, crossing his arms as he stared me down. He was alone. "Leaving so soon?"

Bastard always knew what was happening in his library. He'd have felt my barely contained rage the second I entered his dominion. "I can't ask this of you, Shadow," I said with a shake of my head. "In my fury, I forgot that you have young to protect. Just as I do now."

As Shadow moved closer, more of his energy rose to surround us both. "Len, need I remind you that your problems are my problems. Samantha is pack too. A part of my Sunshine's family." He looked behind me, as if double checking I was alone. "And since she's not with you, and I have felt a similar rage to yours before, I can only assume she's the reason you need help."

Some days his intelligence was a huge advantage, and other days... fucking annoying.

He wouldn't let me leave though. I knew that as well as I knew myself.

"Len..." One final warning, from a beast about to lose his shit.

"They severed the Great Line," I rumbled, my fury pushing up once more. "Samantha is somehow connected to the Great Queen, and when we attempted to lift the Faerie glamour on us both, Fredrick felt her energy." Rumbles spilled from my chest. "He was monitoring the energy, pushing to get the line severed, and when he felt her, he decided to just go right the fuck ahead without any permission."

"Samantha is born of the Great Queen's line?" Shadow said, brow furrowing as he attempted to piece it all together.

"Yes." I knew this for sure, even with all the information I was still missing. "When the line was severed, both Sam and

Tabby collapsed with a death blow. My mother and I managed to put them into stasis, to halt the pull of the next life, but we've only delayed the inevitable."

Mera, who'd reached us now, popped out from behind Shadow, her face ashen as she swallowed hard. "Are you kidding me, Len? A death blow? Where the fuck are Sam and Tabby now?"

Looking away from Shadow, I somehow managed to soften my tone: "They're in Faerie with my mother. The Silver Queen. She's keeping them safe while I try and figure out a plan to save them."

"You need our help?" Mera said again, anger spiking her tone. "Whatever you need, you fucking have it. You, Sam, and Tabby are pack, and we will destroy whatever and whomever we need to get them back."

Shadow nodded as he finally uncrossed his arms. "Always, brother. What's the plan?"

Before he even finished speaking, I shook my head and backed away. "It's too much risk for you and your family. Too much risk for Aurora. I won't ask it of you."

Shadow attempted to wrap his energy around me, to keep me from moving, but I was too strong for him to hold. "Tell us the risk," he said when I extricated myself easily. "We're not children. Allow us the right to choose."

A long breath escaped me. My family always chose to fight together. The moment I told them, they'd be in. "The only chance we have is to venture into the deepest parts of Faerie, where the original power exists. The origin of our world. This is where we'll attempt to repair the line that was severed."

"Fuck," Shadow growled.

I nodded once. *Fuck* was accurate.

"What is in the Origin?" Mera asked.

Shadow was the one to reply. "Pure power," he said, "and a

series of obstacles that are said to be unpassable for any not from the Great Queen's line." He paused and looked at me. "I never knew she had children."

I shrugged. "No one knows shit about her, but it was likely to have happened once she disappeared from Faerie. Sam could be the last of a long line of her descendants, or maybe there's more out there."

All of whom were now dead if they hadn't had someone powerful enough to hold them to their world.

"I have original power," Mera said suddenly. "Shadow does as well. Along with Angel and Reece. Fuck, most of us have an origin power of some description. We're the perfect ones to attempt to go down there."

She had just expressed the exact reason I'd been racing here in the first place.

"It's not Faerie origin power, though," I reminded her. "There's a more than fair chance we will all be destroyed the second we descend into the Deep. It's too much to ask when you have your own children to protect."

That gave Mera a moment's pause. "I wouldn't take Aurora down there, not when she's so young, but if we find someone we trust to watch her, we could go with you."

"No," Shadow snapped. "I will go with him, and you will stay with our daughter. She needs her mother."

Mera's return growl rocked some of the shelves nearby. "We're stronger together, Shadow. You know we are. But I accept that one of us must stay with Aurora."

Shadowshine. They were stronger together, but the risk was still there, and Mera knew it.

"Excuse me," a low raspy voice interrupted. "I couldn't help but overhear. If you need someone to protect our young Aurora with their life and multitude of power, I am happy to take that role."

Shadow and Mera turned to face Gaster, who stood in his usual calmness. This was the demi-fae who guarded the Library of Knowledge. Shadow's right-hand man. He was powerful and ancient; I knew that from even the small information he'd released to me over the years.

"Mera needs to stay," Shadow rumbled again.

Gaster stepped closer. "I'm from an ancient line of goblins," he started slowly. "I've lived through many wars and stood in the presence of the great line. The fae who severed that line has no idea what he's done. It's not just the Silver Prince who stands to lose, but all of us. You must go and fix what has been broken, for if you don't, the worlds will be thrown out of balance. To the point that I fear everything might be destroyed."

My worry of the rippling effect this might have in the great multiverse had just been confirmed.

"You remember the Great Queen?" I asked him.

He nodded once. "Aye. When she disappeared, it was almost as if a glamour washed across Faerie. None could remember her. But I was already working in the library, and it protected me from the effects. I have no idea where she ran to, but if your Samantha was on Earth, it stands to reason the queen set up her new life there, hidden in a near magicless world."

"And the rest forgot her," I mused.

Another nod. "Aye. At least the finer details."

Mera turned to Shadow. "I'm not going to say I told you so, but this might actually be your damn fault, Beast." He snorted, crossing his arms as she continued. "But if there's a chance the worlds will end, we both need to go. Our strength together is the only way to ensure that there's a future for our daughter. We both knew that one day we'd be facing an end-of-worlds event. It's written in the stars. One by one, these worlds need to be saved to save all the Solaris System. It's Faerie's time today, and we will go with Len."

Shadow wanted to argue. I knew my brother well enough to see the storm brewing behind his flame-filled eyes, but he couldn't argue with Mera's logic. "Gaster," he rumbled, turning to the demi-fae. "I'm going to recall Midnight and Inky from the Shadow Realm, and together you three will utilize every part of the library's energy to keep Aurora and Damon safe." He turned to me now. "I've already sent this message to Angel and Reece, Lucien and Simone, and Galleli. They should be here momentarily."

Gaster held his hands out, and I watched closely to see if Shadow would finally allow another to hold his beloved child. Mera lifted Aurora a little higher, before kissing her on both cheeks. "I love you, my precious miracle," she whispered, a few tears brushing her cheeks. "Mommy and Daddy have to go and fight for your safety, but I promise, we'll do everything in our power to return to you. Stay strong, sweet baby."

She buried her face against the little girl, and Shadow enclosed them both in his arms, blocking from view his last words and moment with them. When they finally untangled, the others were streaming into the library, just in time to see Shadow hand Aurora to Gaster.

The demi-fae took her with calm and steady hands, amidst the gasps and shock as the others circled around us. "This can't be fucking good," Reece rumbled, as the scent of desert whipped up around us. "The worlds are ending, aren't they?"

"Only explanation for that possessive bastard to share his child," Lucien added, reaching out to draw Simone into his arms.

This wasn't our first Faerie storm, and they knew exactly what to expect when Shadow called.

Wasting no time, I explained everything again, including Gaster's new information about the worlds and the balance.

"You will have one chance to repair the line, and it'll only be possible because you hold members of the Great Queen's line in your grasp," Gaster added when I finished.

"Sam and Tabby have to go to the Deep?" I asked.

He nodded. "Yes, but only one of them is needed. They're the only ones who can touch the final strand and repair the damage. We just have to hope they have enough of the power in their diluted bloodline."

"If they don't have enough power?" I asked, wishing we had the time to pry all information from Gaster before we left.

His rugged features fell, thin lips even thinner. "It will be all over for everyone. Including those from the Great Line."

Darkness danced across us, and for once, not all the shadows came from the beast of this library. Again, we found ourselves in a fight to save the worlds, and I had so much to lose.

I had everything to lose.

CHAPTER THIRTY-THREE

SAMANTHA

Queen Glendriel took us away from the mass of fae, situating us in a corner. The female with the authoritative voice joined her a moment later. "The alignment is off," she said without preamble. "It didn't happen immediately, but now that I know the line is severed, I can feel a fracturing of other fae power. Have you noticed it too?"

Glendriel's tone was clipped. "Yes. One line was severed, but it's not the only power bleeding from our world."

The other female huffed. "This is why we didn't agree in the last meeting. None of us truly knew the consequences of severing the line. It's never been done before."

Consequences. Like all the Great Queen's descendants suddenly dropping dead. I wondered if there were more of us out there, lives cut short all through the selfish actions of a power hungry fae.

Descended from the Great Queen of Faerie. I mean, it was near unbelievable, considering I was not only a shifter, but an outcast one with no real family. It might explain though, why I'd always had a few extra quirks as a shifter. And it definitely explained how I'd managed to produce a child with Len.

Glendriel and the other female fae were soon joined by more voices, all of them worried, discussing the sudden weakness in their power stones. "It's the balance," one male declared. "I feel the balance shifting. What have they done?"

More discussing back and forth, but I found most of it going over my head as the fuzzy darkness hovering at the edge of my mind grew closer... reminding me that I was existing in a state between life and death. This was not the time to grow complacent; I'd promise Len I'd fight to stay here. Even greater than that, I had to fight for Tabitha.

For the first time since I was struck down, I focused not on what was happening outside my cocoon, but more on my own internal power. Maybe I could use my inner strength to fight the darkness trying to take me.

My first attempt at drawing my power up to coat my skin failed miserably, but I didn't let that worry me. I had all the time in the world right now and one singular focus.

The darkness continued to try to invade, and the more I internally examined it, the more I was sure that it seeped from the place I used to hold light. Was that where my connection to Faerie and the Great Queen's line used to exist? And if so, how did I counter it now that the line was damaged?

Desperately needing to find strength, I calmed my mind, and instead of running from that darkness, I hovered close by, trying to feel if any of my old power remained. It took some time, but as I grew calmer again, I finally picked up some slivers of light, and the sort of wild energy that I associated with my wolf.

Hoping I wasn't making a huge mistake, I pushed even closer to the dark entity, sending my power down to find those slivers of light and shifter energy. Wrapping around those fractured pieces, I pulled at them, slowly, lifting piece by piece through the darkness. As soon as I attempted to speed up the process, the darkness swelled, and I found myself weakening; my lifeforce flickered dangerously. As soon as I backed off, though, the energy settled once more, and I could resume my search for the light.

Slow and steady won the race, and eventually I had enough light shifter energy to form a small barrier between my lifeforce and that darkness swirling inside me. As the fragile barrier settled in place, I knew that if I could just keep reinforcing it against the darkness, I could exist for a short time until they figured out how to repair the Great Line.

If they can repair the line.

There's been no mention of what would happen if the line wasn't repaired soon, but I sensed that it wouldn't be good for Tabitha or me. My shifter side could only hold off the fae darkness for so long—one could not lose half of themselves and remain alive.

I had no idea how much time passed while I was figuring out how to form that barrier, but it felt like seconds after I did, Len returned. The moment his energy caressed mine, that barrier of light grew a little stronger, and I wondered if maybe parts of that light I'd been drawing up was our fractured bond.

A bond that had formed for a second before the line was cut.

I had some memories now of our time on Earth, but it was still one small part of the whole. Until I could repair my connection to Faerie, I couldn't repair my one to Len.

Strong supernatural energy joined him a moment later, the fiery power of Shadow and Mera, along with the biblical rush of Angel, feeling like a breath of new life. At her side was a hot burst of desert that only Reece could bring. Lucien's power was more subtle but filled with life essence. Simone held the wild power of a shifter, with a primal source of life, similar to her mate. Then there was Galleli. I only knew of the transcendent from my last time and Mera, but his power felt like being hit in the face with a bolt of lightning.

All of them packed a punch, which was very obvious through my current means of *seeing* those around me. *Seeing my family.* For the first time I found myself praying to the universe that we made it through this. We deserved more family moments and celebrations. Not to mention a true pack for my daughter to grow up in.

I'd accept nothing less.

When Len reached my side, the burn of his power washed over me, and once again my barrier grew stronger, as if the two of us together could channel greater power than when we were apart.

Whatever outside force had interfered in our bond, it wasn't strong enough to keep us apart forever. I didn't know the answers yet, but I would figure it out. As soon as my life was restored.

"She feels stronger," Len said distracting me. "Our bond has started to form, and I can feel her energy wrapping around mine."

Glendriel answered him. "She's been drawing up her shifter energy, and it's allowing her to fight the dark pull of death."

"Can she be released from the stones now?" Shadow asked suddenly.

Glendriel was slower to reply this time. "Why would you want to release her? She's still in mortal danger."

Len ran his hand over my cage, and I swore to the gods that I felt his touch on my skin. Burning. Renewing. "We need her to venture into the Origin with us and restore the line. Only one from the Great Queen's line can make the final repair."

There was a flare of energy from Glendriel. Subtle, but she was surprised by this new knowledge. "I believe that she can be released for a short time. You cannot grow complacent though. Reinforce that barrier as much as possible, because the darkness is still drawing her into its clutches."

There was no lie in her statement. It still churned below my barrier, but I was confident I could hold it off long enough. Especially if I was with Len.

"What about Tabitha?" Mera asked.

"Tabby is so young, and weakened from her time out of Faerie," the queen said, voice quieter. "It's best to leave her in stasis."

Weakened. That one word sent shivers of dread down my spine.

"In that case," Len continued, "she must stay here with you. The rest of us will enter the Deep and hopefully restore the line before the darkness takes either of them."

"We should wake Sam now," Mera said shortly. "We have no time to waste up here. If the worlds are in trouble, then best we move our asses."

After a slightly pause, "The worlds are in trouble?" Glendriel asked. "Is it the imbalance we've been feeling?"

"Yes," Len replied. "These worlds are connected in ways we don't even understand, and by taking away a line of origin the balance is thrown off. I felt nothing when it first happened, but already in this short time it's more than noticeable. I have no doubt that if we don't repair the line, all the worlds will fall."

Hushed whispers and gasps erupted from the fae in the room.

"Best we get moving then," Reece growled. "I won't tolerate any risk to my family or our young."

"Same," Lucien agreed. "I've just found my soul, and I will not allow anything to stand between us and our future happiness."

The true mates were all intertwined, their energies the perfect match for the other.

Each of them would die or kill for their mate, and I already felt that way about Len.

We had to survive this next part of our journey.

There was no other option.

CHAPTER THIRTY-FOUR

SAMANTHA

Waking me from the stasis took only seconds. Len withdrew the stones' energy, and whatever had been holding me was released. His strong arms wrapped around me as I collapsed into them, and on this side, in the land of consciousness, pain hit me hard.

A whimper escaped, and I had to briefly close my eyes to reinforce my barrier from the darkness trying to drag me into the next world. The world of the dead.

Not yet, I whispered in my head. *It's not my time yet.*

I still had too much shit to do.

"Storm," Len murmured, the minty scent of his breath washing over me. I forced my eyes open, needing to see him. "Winter," I whispered back.

The heat of his power traced across my body, and I glanced down to see that I was no longer naked from our sex session. It was somewhat ironic that at the time I'd wondered if he was going to orgasm me to death, only to almost die at the end of one. The timing was less than desirable, that was for sure.

I could definitely use a little less of that irony *thank you very much.*

"You dressed me?" I rasped. He'd covered me in jeans and white shirt, simple, but with material lighter and silkier than I'd ever felt on Earth. "Thank you."

He pressed his lips to my cheek, tendrils of his power sliding inside to buff up more of my barrier. "I take care of what's mine," he said, with a hint of a smile. My body reacted in a way that suggested it had forgotten we were actively dying. Apparently, there was no moment in time I wouldn't be into this sexy fae prince.

Mera pushed forward and hugged me hard, uncaring that Len was wrapped around me as well. "You are not allowed to almost die," she said, with a low growl at the end. "I don't even care if it was in the middle of sex. That's no excuse."

I opened my mouth, before slamming it shut again as I shook my head in shock. "How the hell did you know?"

Her responding grin was huge. "I'm an expert in *just fucked hair* and you're sporting it in spades."

Shadow snorted. "Maybe it's *I almost died hair*. Did you even consider that, Sunshine?"

Mera paused, looking closer at me. "Nope. I've been fucked and *almost died* quite close together, and there's a distinct difference in the final hairdo."

There was some laughter around us, and even the fae abandoned their stoic expressions to smile. Mera had that way about her, breaking the tension in times of stress. It was a nice facet to her personality. "To be fair," I said, my voice a little stronger. "In this situation the hair is from both. So..."

She shrugged before nodding. "True."

Len lifted me up to my feet, continuing to keep a hold on me as my legs found their strength. "Were you aware of anything in stasis?"

I nodded. "I heard everything. We need to go into the Deep to save the worlds and restore the line."

"We do," he confirmed. "It's going to be dangerous, but you are from the Great Queen's line, and should be able to handle whatever comes your way."

I waved a hand over my chest. "I've always had this light near my shifter side," I said quickly. "Now I finally understand why. It was my connection to the Great Line and Faerie." My voice broke before I cleared my throat. "Now, though, it's all darkness. The only reason I can be out of the stasis is due to my shifter side forming a barrier. But it's weak, so we have to hurry."

"I'll share my energy with you," Len promised. "And when the line's repaired, your light will return."

His confidence fueled my own, and I was sure that we'd succeed. Not just for our daughter, but for all the worlds.

"I'll keep Tabitha safe," Glendriel promised, moving closer from where she'd been in the middle of the platform. A small bundle of light followed her. "The Silver Lands, along with our greatest allies, will protect her with the full force of our royal houses."

My heart swelled with warmth, and more of the darkness receded—it didn't like the power of love and happiness. Walking on unsteady legs, I reached Tabitha's cocoon. Running my hands a few inches above the surface—the closest I could get—I sent all my love into my daughter.

"Mommy loves you, little one," I whispered. "We're going to repair what was broken. Stay safe and keep fighting until we return."

Len joined me a beat later. "Daddy is here too," he said,

which sent an additional surge of warmth into my chest. "We will not fail, sweet one. You keep holding on."

His hand landed over mine on the crystal case, and we just breathed for a moment, hearts aching. But there was no more time to spend here. We had to move on to the task of saving the worlds.

"How do we get to the Deep?" Shadow asked, his form growing larger as he readied himself for this battle. Flames filled his eyes, and he looked very beast god. Mera, at his side, had flames dancing in her long red hair. The ombre colors shifted faster, and I loved how strong and powerful she looked. All our pack was rocking their badass power, filling the room with energy that actually made the fae appear quite weak. Even the ancient royal ones.

"Thank you," I said to them all. "I know you risk a lot... everything... by being here, and I don't know how I'll ever repay you."

We don't work like that.

Galleli's voice had me jumping. I was the only one. *We save the worlds together and no one ever owes anyone. This is family. Pack. Our treasora.*

They were destroying me but there was no time to cry. We had worlds to save.

"To answer Shadow's question," Len said, "we can reach the Deep from this land. It's what exists below the Capital. We will just need to follow the beams of light that connect below, and after that I have no idea. Since the Great Queen vanished, there's been no one that entered and returned alive."

Ominous, but it wasn't as if we were unaware of this fact.

"Sounds like we're about to be the first," Lucien called with a whoop. "Let's fucking do it."

We pushed closer, and I was grateful that with Len's power adding to mine, the pain was minimal, and I could move more freely. As we headed toward the exit, the fae shifted in unison, forming lines on either side of us, and then one by one they bowed their heads.

My breath caught in my chest, the air rattling around for a beat before I managed to exhale deeply. "What are they doing?" I whispered to Len, who was on my left.

"Honoring us," he murmured back. "We're risking a lot to try and save their world. A world that's in danger thanks to Fredrick's general love of power and disregard for rules."

"Fredrick," I said, my voice hardening. His actions almost cost me everything, including my daughter. Bastard would get what was coming to him.

"He will face the royal trial when we return," Len assured me. "For now, they're keeping him contained while they search out who else was involved."

There was no time today to punish him, and the council had better make the right decision when it came to the trial. Darkness swirled as my anger took over, and I forced myself to take a couple of deep breaths. As if he'd felt that shift inside me, Len reached out and captured my hand, lacing his fingers through mine to infuse more of his power into my being.

The darkness calmed almost instantly. "Thank you," I said, feeling more grateful than ever to not be alone.

Len didn't release me then as expected. Instead his grip remained firm as we exited the building. Shadow continued at the front of his pack, leading us toward the edge of this land. Like with the garden, there was a sharp drop-off, with the sky spanning out beyond us, and I almost stopped moving as awe took me aback.

It felt as if we were standing on the edge of a solar system, endless sky spread around us. It wasn't dark, but it also wasn't bright like morning. I'd call it twilight with a touch of early dawn as visible lights twinkled in various colors above us.

"The crystals and gems from the royal houses are particularly dense here," Len said, noticing as I tilted my head back to take it all in. "They help to power our lands and the world."

"It's incredible," Simone said with a shake of her head, which was craned back like mine. Mera was in a similar position. The only ones not wearing looks of shock and awe were Angel and the guys. They'd all clearly been here before.

"I saw this world from Shadow's house," Mera said softly, "but there's something about standing out in the open like this, with what feels like a damn universe whizzing around you... I'm not sure I'll ever get used to it."

"You will," Shadow said with a growl. "You're going to live forever, as per my damn wishes, and in that time you'll see every facet of the universes. You'll see the worlds so often that eventually you'll be well used to it."

"Mera will live forever," Angel agreed. "As will the rest of us, and we'll never stop exploring."

This was the sort of pep talk we needed before heading into a life and death situation.

Len, hand still wrapped around mine, led us toward the edge of the platform. It was here that he released me, and I tried not to mourn the loss of his energy sending tingles across my skin. When he leaned out, most of us did the same.

"Well, fuck," Simone said. "I'd have never thought to look out over the edge."

Beams of light were connected to the underside of the platform, dropping down farther than we could see from where we stood. Hundreds, if not thousands of them, all in a range of colors. Colors very similar to the gems that littered the sky above.

"How do we use them to take us into the Deep?" I asked.

"We just grab hold," Len replied, leaning more of himself over the edge, his hand wrapping around a purple beam. "Use the beam as your anchor and guide. Our gravity here is lighter, so you're not going to plummet like you would in other worlds. It'll be a slow fall."

I hadn't noticed the gravity thing at all, which was odd. Almost as if my body had adjusted the moment we arrived... Maybe I had more fae in me than expected.

Leaning over with Len, I was about to grab onto a turquoise line near his, when he shifted his strand closer to me. "You'll fall with me," he said simply. "Together."

I couldn't look away from his gaze. The truth was, I was falling *for* him.

Again.

My fragmented memories told me I'd been fully in love with this caring, enigmatic, powerful fae prince the last time. Kind of felt like I'd never *not* been in love with him.

Who knew love was as scary as taking a plunge into the Origin of Faerie.

On the precipice of doing both, I could confirm.

Completely terrifying.

CHAPTER THIRTY-FIVE

SAMANTHA

Before I had time to freak out, Len sent us both over the side. My stomach shot up into my throat for a beat, but then our fall slowed, just as he'd said it would. His hand remained over mine as we clutched the warmly vibrating line of power, leading us into the Deep.

Our pack fell with us, and I wasn't surprised to see that Shadow and Mera were on the same line. Simone and Lucien as well. Angel had her own line, but she was right beside Reece. Galleli was farthest out, his line a gleaming silver that reflected off the shine of his bronze breastplate.

No one said a word, and I wasn't sure about the others, but I was working to reinforce my barrier inside, and mentally preparing myself for what was to come.

The fall lasted at least an hour. My arm was aching by the

time we reached the end of the cords of power. "Brace your-self," Len called. "I have no idea what we're landing in."

A splash of red came into view just as Shadow bellowed, "Don't let go of your cord. Remain above the ground."

Len's free hand went under my ass as he jerked me into his body, his energy wrapping around us so we didn't land on the red. From this angle, I could see that the end of the line was a few feet above the ground, and we were a few feet above the end.

The light down here was darker than it had been above, the faint red all that was really visible. It was only due to the light from the cords of power that I could even see my pack. Shadow and Mera fixed that little issue when flames surrounded them, like our own personal lanterns. As their flames grew, we could see the ground much clearer—a rich red with lighter red swirls flowing through it, sparking at points.

"Will it zap us?" Simone asked, leaning out to look closer. Lucien tightened his hold on her, pulling her back into his arms.

"It's designed to drain our power," Shadow said. "If we'd landed, our energy would be sapped, weakening us for the rest of the journey."

"How do we move across it, then?" Lucien asked, fangs flashing in the light of the flames. "Bee and I recently fed and are at our strongest, but I don't want to sacrifice that energy before we make it into the worst of this place."

"It will get much worse," Len confirmed. "Don't use your energy to try and move yet. It'll also drain you."

We were stuck between a rock and the Deep of Faerie, apparently. Drop to the ground and be drained. Use our power to move onto another part and be drained. But hanging here wasn't getting us anywhere, so we had to make a choice.

Reece craned his head, looking left and then right. "What if we use these cords of power?" he said finally, returning his gaze to us. "To swing across as much of this red land as we can. That would be the lowest use of energy, from what I can tell."

There were a ton of lines around us, spanning off to the left and right.

Len nodded. "That's my thoughts as well. I think there's a call of stronger power to the right."

No one argued, trusting that the fae prince knew what he was talking about. I should be able to feel the same energy, but I was more focused internally. Keeping that barrier in place for as long as needed was my highest priority.

"We should move now," Angel said quickly. "It's draining us just existing here."

Great. This fucking land was already living up to its reputation.

"Reach for the next strand," Len said to me, nodding toward the closest red one. "I'll keep you from falling."

I didn't hesitate, thankful that my arms were no longer as pained as they had been. Len had given me a small reprieve when he'd held my weight against him. Wrapping my hand around the cord, I swung across. "If I had access to my power, would I have been able to walk over this red land without issue?" I asked as I swung.

Len was right behind me, pointing out the next cord—a blue one—to grab onto. "I have no idea. My understanding of it was that the Great Queen just bypassed all the securities, heading straight for the center of power."

"Considering how old she was, and how long she's been missing from Faerie," I huffed out, swinging to the next cord, "it stands to reason that I might only have a small slice of her power."

I could be a fiftieth descendent or something.

"No way to know until the glamour is fully released," Len

added from behind me, not sounding at all out of breath. "I lifted parts of it, but not all. Not for you anyway."

He made that sound like he remembered everything. "You remember us?" I confirmed.

"I do," he replied. "I remember our time together, and I know we're true mates."

He dropped that statement so casually, and I was fucking thrilled that he felt the same connection. I'd already figured we could be, but having it confirmed was a new kind of wonderful.

"Why don't I remember?" I asked. "It doesn't make sense that all your memories are back and mine aren't."

We managed to cross five more cords before he answered. "I believe that whatever the Great Queen did to disappear spelled her entire line to keep them from their heritage. She no doubt believed she was protecting you all, but this glamour is interfering with the true mate call. It sparked across me too, but now that it's broken, I won't be glamoured again. You, on the other hand, have probably been spelled since before birth."

He left the rest unsaid, but it was clear that sort of glamour was going to be much harder to break.

"It's why you never felt your fae side," Angel added, from where she was a few strands in front of us. There was no hiding a conversation with beings of exceptional hearing. "That's the part of you locked down with fae energy."

Breathing deeply, the ache back in my arms, I thought it all through. "So, the glamour I've been under since birth collided with the true mate energy of Len's walk, and the result was the sort of memory loss that cost us years of time with our daughter?"

"Yes."

This came from more than one of my friends.

"You're both lucky you didn't explode," Shadow added

helpfully. "The collision of two ancient and powerful energies is a recipe for disaster."

I might never find out why the Great Queen did what she did, or understand the life she lived, but I really hoped we could figure out how to repair the damage she'd caused. Otherwise, there was no future for my family. Or the worlds.

Conversation died off as we continued to swing through the air, the red floor remaining below, while darkness surrounded us. When we reached the last row of cords, which had to indicate the end of the land above, the nine of us hung there, staring out into what appeared to be endless darkness.

"Fuck," Angel said, the curse odd in her regal tone. "We now must make the decision we were avoiding. Drop to the ground, which will drain all of us, or rely on one of us to use our powers to ferry the others to safety. And by one of us, I'm referring to me and my wings."

I have wings as well, Galleli said, and again, I was the only one to flinch, but thankfully not drop from the cord.

"I also have wings," Mera piped up.

Shadow beasted out briefly. "Not a fucking chance," he growled.

Reece added his own growl. "I'm not comfortable with Angel ferrying us all," he said.

"We have no other option," Angel shot back. "But before we risk heading into the darkness with extra weight, I'm going to fly myself first to ensure this is the right direction."

Before Reece could protest again, her gorgeous angel wings popped out of her back and she flapped them strongly, heading out to hover in the shadows beyond the cords. Almost instantly, she was difficult to see.

The scent of storms and sand rose around us. "Mate, you need to get your ass back here," Reece demanded. "You don't have thousands of layers of power at your control any longer."

"I don't," she agreed, and I wondered what that story was. Not that I'd dare ask when we had much more pressing shit to deal with. "But I have my bond with you, and the new layers we're building. I will not falter."

In the dull light, Reece's face could have been carved from stone. His entire body too as he seemed to be fighting the instinct to leap from his cord and wrestle his mate to safety. Angel didn't say anything else, allowing him to come to his own conclusion.

"Go," he finally bit out, "but you better come back, Lale. In one damn piece."

"Always, love," she smiled sweetly. "You can't get rid of me that easily."

Her wings flapped harder, and to the sound of her mate's grumbles she disappeared into the darkness. Reece's energy flared, the bite of sand harsh against my skin. Which was an odd sensation, since there was no actual sand in the vicinity.

"You hanging in there okay?" Len asked. As I turned his way, the cord swinging slowly, a brief smile tilted up his lip. It added some warmth to my energy, which in turn bolstered my barrier.

I attempted to laugh it off. "Just a little fatigued. Trying not to embarrass myself by being the first to fall in this crew of god-like creatures."

Concern replaced his smile. "You're expending more energy than you realize in keeping that darkness at bay. I'm helping a tiny amount, but the bulk is you. You amaze me with your continued strength, little Storm. Even if the Fates did choose you as my mate, I'd have made the same choice among the trillions of beings in the worlds."

And just like that, I could have swung through these fucking cords for another ten years. Yeah, I wanted to be a strong independent female, but I completely believed I could be that and more with the support of a true mate.

"I would choose you, too," I said softly. "Every fucking day. The Fates did well."

He leaned in to kiss me, but before our lips met, the sound of flapping had all of us turning toward the abyss, ready to see Angel.

"Soon, mate," Len murmured from behind me, the brush of his power like lightning across my skin. "Nothing will stand between us and cementing this bond."

I believed him, especially if we could repair the line and figure out how to break the final strands of glamour over me.

Then, finally, we'd have a chance at true happiness.

CHAPTER THIRTY-SIX

SAMANTHA

The feeling of sand against our skin faded as Angel returned clearly unharmed, her wings strong and sure as she closed the distance. "Mate," Reece growled. "What took you so fucking long?"

It didn't matter how badass you were, these alpha males worried the moment their ladies were out of sight. Exactly how it should be.

"I was less than ten minutes," she shot back with a smile, hovering effortlessly before us. "I only went as far as the next land, which looks safe to approach. I should be able to easily ferry everyone across."

Mera's fiery wings expanded and she took off just out of Shadow's reach to hover near Angel. "I can help," she said.

At the same time, Shadow rumbled, "Get your fucking ass back here, Sunshine."

"I can help!" she repeated with more force. "We don't have time to fuck around, beast. If we don't save this damn line, the worlds will fall, and not even you could keep me safe."

His face was creased in thunder. "I could and would keep you safe. The worlds be damned."

Judging by the amused looks on everyone's faces, I was almost certain they'd had this argument before. "We would all let the worlds burn for our mates," Lucien said, tone light and chipper, like he was discussing his favorite hobby. "But maybe we should attempt to save them first, just for ease of where to live when there's only darkness left in the abyss."

Shadow let out a growl and released his hold on the cord, disappearing in shadows before he reappeared near Mera. Those shadows wrapped around them both, before they vanished once more.

"Hope he knows where he's going," Angel said with a low laugh. "The path through this deep is not without many dangers."

Len shrugged. "There's a reason none dare to tread here, except those too stupid to heed the warnings. But Shadow is his own special entity, and he wouldn't risk Mera. He'll probably just follow your energy trail."

"You're right," she agreed, before her wings flapped harder again and she moved toward Simone. In seconds, she'd lifted the shifter, hauling her off into the distance.

Reece and Lucien were taken by Galleli. *We'll be back for you soon*, the transcendent called as he vanished with the pair gripped at the forearms, as if that was as much assistance as the other two would allow. Luckily, Galleli was a bulked-up angel dude, easily handling their equal amount of bulk.

When it was just Len and me, I drew up more light and shifter energy, reinforcing the barrier once more. The darkness was surging behind it, chipping away, and if we didn't repair the cord to the Great Line soon, it would succeed in breaking through.

"Do you need my energy?" Len asked, and I pulled my focus back externally. "Is the barrier holding?"

"You could feel me repairing it?" I asked.

He swung closer, reaching out to grab at a spot above my cord, holding himself just inches from me. "The bond is there," he confirmed. "Even if it is weakened by everything you're going through, I'm still feeling flickers of your energy. I want you to tell me if you need help."

"I will," I promised. "I'm learning how to ask for help. I'm determined that we get our future together."

He relaxed but didn't move away. We remained so close that I could see every facet of his stormy winter eyes. Being alone, I decided to take advantage of some pressing questions. "What happened to the layers of land Angel used to control?" I asked. "She feels as strong and capable as ever to me."

Len let out a low breath. "She's always going to be a power-house, but those layers she controlled, which represented the power passed down through her family line, had to be used to save their lives in the Desert Lands. We almost lost them both..." His voice broke. "We did lose Alistair."

I wanted to release my hold on the cord and wrap my arms around Len. But considering my shaky limbs were barely managing to hold on, I settled for leaning in and pressing my lips to his. A simple, gentle kiss. "I'm so sorry about your broth-er," I said as I pulled back. "It breaks my heart that you lost him like that."

His throat visibly moved as he swallowed. "Thank you. It's a scar that will never heal, but we will meet again. Which is only slightly comforting from this side of the veil."

"Now that I have a true family," I told him, "I can finally

understand what they mean when they say pain is the price we pay for love. Fuck, it's so true."

It was Len's turn to kiss me. "I'd never trade a second of time with you and Tabitha, even if there is pain waiting for us in the end."

I felt the same way. "I miss Tabby," I admitted. "It's hard being away from her, especially when she's hurt."

"She'll be fighting, just like her mom," Len said quickly. "I'm so proud of our little girl."

"I am too," I said, a small smile breaking through our sad conversation. "Our shifter side helps us fight as well. It's part of what's allowing me to remain out of the death realm."

Len's eyes darkened. "No more talk of the death realm. You're staying right here, mate, at my side. I don't care who I must kill to ensure that happens."

Mate. The way he said it slayed me right in the damn chest. A good hurt this time, the sort of pain you wanted to feel again and again.

"What do you remember from our time together?" I asked, still caught in the snare of his stormy gaze. "What happened between us?"

He shook his head suddenly, as if to release darker thoughts. "We were together for at least two months," he said softly. "We traveled around America in an old van that you bought for five hundred dollars. It was a bomb, and I never felt more human as I attempted to fix its multitude of issues without using magic."

"Did I know what you were? Did you suspect I was anything other than a shifter?"

He shook his head. "I never told you I was fae, deciding instead to live out a human type of existence for a few months. I never saw any fae in you, and I never cared."

Truth rang in his tone, and his actions thus far only backed this truth. Len had never cared that I was a shifter. He'd have chosen me as his mate over every fae he'd met in his long life.

"The Great Walk usually lasts a night," he continued. "But I chose to remain with you for sixty, unable to tear myself away as we built a friendship and then a romance together. You painted naked in the moonlight, falling into bed at 5 A.M., only to stumble up at lunchtime, starving as you fixed us food." Mischief danced across his face. "Love, I hate to tell you, but you can't cook to save your life." A laugh escaped me. "But I ate every one of your meals and it felt like the finest dining of Faerie because it was with you. It was so much *more* than a simple magical connection."

"I have some memories," I admitted. "These frozen moments in time." I lowered my gaze to my side. "Like, when you gave me my tattoo. I should have known then that you weren't human. There was no way my shifter side wouldn't have healed and rejected the mark. I mean, I told the others I got the tatt before I shifted, which was clearly a lie, and I just ignored the fact that it stuck."

Len nodded. "The glamour you were under would have helped you to dismiss anything that didn't really make sense. It doesn't want you to think about or explore your differences. It wants you to be accepting of them and write them off without much consideration."

That was how I'd been fooled for so long. "Why did you leave?" I asked, a bite of pain pushing the darkness inside higher before I calmed once more.

His loosened one hand around the cord, reaching out to wrap it across mine. "Because I wanted more. I wanted the true bond to be triggered, so I returned to Faerie hoping to initiate the next step." Sorrow darkened his features. "I got greedy to have it all, and it cost me everything."

"It wasn't your fault," I said fiercely. "You had no idea that two spells were at work, or that when the magic from your walk kicked in, it would clash with that from the Great Queen. You certainly wouldn't have expected a child from our love. No one could have expected that."

"I will spend forever making it up to you," Len said just as fiercely. "This is our second chance, and I refuse to waste one moment of it."

"That makes two of us," I replied, the light in me burning brighter than it had since the line was severed.

Before anything else was said, two transcendents appeared in the distance. Angel and Galleli were back to ferry us across, and I had the feeling that shit was only going to get harder from here.

But at least this time I wouldn't face it alone.

CHAPTER THIRTY-SEVEN

SAMANTHA

Angel took me, since Galleli was an unmated male and my bond with Len wasn't complete yet. When Len said as much, Galleli just smiled. *Ten steps ahead of you, friend. Hence why Angel has returned.*

"How are you feeling about all of this?" Angel asked as she flapped, ferrying us to our next destination. "Your bond with Len and the knowledge of your ancestry as a descendant of a powerful Faerie queen? It's a lot to absorb all at once."

Until she asked me in such a point-blank way, I hadn't really given it much thought. I'd been too busy trying to survive and save the worlds. "It's confusing," I admitted, a little surprised by the realization. "Don't get me wrong, I'm freaking blessed to be Len's mate. The Fates couldn't have chosen better for me. But I'm also very aware that I'm not a full shifter or a full fae. I don't really fit into either world."

Angel and I had never spoken so openly, but it didn't feel odd to chat with her the same way I would Mera or Simone. "You change the world to fit you," she told me. "Not the other way around." Her voice gentled. "You've found your pack now, and you fit in as if you were always here. All of our genetics are mixed. That just makes us more powerful. You'll figure that out when we restore the fae side of your energy."

My chest and throat were tight as I said, "Thank you. I think I needed the reminder that this is just the beginning of my journey."

My eyes found Len, who was about ten feet away, Galleli gripping his forearm. He was watching me, and I didn't know if he'd heard the conversation, but the look on his eyes had my body burning in all the good ways.

"We're almost back to them," Angel said, and my focus returned to the land around us. A sight less enticing than my mate.

As we got closer, a low curse escaped Angel as she picked up the pace. "Where did they come from?" she snarled.

Our friends were on a vast expanse of what looked like bright blue sand, mostly flat with just small sections of undulation. They weren't alone, though, as we caught sight of multiple large creatures scurrying across the sand.

"Do you know what they are?" I asked, pulse racing as I mentally urged her to get there faster.

"I have no idea," she said, sending a chill down my spine.

These ancient supernaturals generally knew everything. "They look like mutated crabs," I noted, examining them from their spindly legs and two huge pincers out the front. Their black shells were dotted with purple, red, and green stones. Knowing Faerie, those stones would no doubt make them extra strong.

Len and Galleli moved closer in the air as we rushed

toward our pack. "Do you know what those creatures are?" I called out.

Both faces were set in grim lines. "I've never seen one before," Len replied. "They're referred to as guardians. Beasts of the Deep. They're strong, lethal, and near unbeatable, or so the myth says."

"Should we attempt to just fly to the next land?" I asked. "I know you both need to rest, but if you have the energy, it's got to be better than ending up as crab chow."

We dropped lower, preparing to land next to our pack, who had backed up together. "I'm not sure they'll let us leave this area until we defeat the guardian," Angel told me. "It's all part of the securities."

"It's the Faerie way," Len said shortly. "There are no short-cuts in the journey of life. Every step is a learning tool. All equally as important."

I didn't disagree. It was one of the reasons I never skipped ahead to the last page of a story, even if my anxiety was at a thousand percent because I had no idea what was going to happen next. Skipping to the end would have taken away expe-riencing each step as it happened, so I always pushed through. We just had to hope that in this story, all of us made it to the end alive.

We landed behind a giant Shadow, who was half shifted into a demonic Anubis figure. Mera was also shifted, standing heads above me now, her skin covered in flames as a phoenix danced across her body. No one had attacked, but the guardian crabs were closing in, their movements in sync as they raised both pincers, clacking them together in a near deafening sound.

Up close they were terrifying, standing twice the size of Shadow in his current form. Could the beast go even larger to counter the size difference? I had no idea.

"We can't beat them in a direct attack," Len warned, close

enough on my right side that I could feel wisps of his energy. "Faerie lore states that they're true immortals, born of Origin energy."

"Then what's our option?" Shadow snarled, his voice more animalistic than I'd ever heard, deeper than any wolf's, rumbling as the beast.

"Maybe we try and run," Mera said, a lesser rumble in her voice. "Just keep going until the blue sands end."

As soon as she said run, I knew it was a bad idea. "Predators love to chase," I reminded them. "Maybe we should submit?" No doubt that suggestion would not go over well with the powerful beings here. Each was used to being a god. Top dog, so to speak. It would go against their very nature to submit, but they had to understand, if these guardians were the top dogs here, then submitting was our only chance.

"No!" Shadow raged, as predicted. Sand flew up around Reece as he grew larger and more aggressive. Angel and Galleli had their wings out, flapping hard, even though they were on the ground. Simone was in her Lycan form, and Lucien had his fangs out as he waited for the next command. Every single one of them displayed signs of aggression, except for Len and me.

"I've been the weaker one before," I added louder. The guardians were close enough now that the clacking boom of the pincers had my ears aching. "To survive, I had to play the game. I had to give the alpha what he wanted. Submit and survive long enough to fight another day."

"I vote we give battle a go first?" Shadow rumbled. "I'm sure we can take them."

Mera let out a laugh as she transformed back into her human self. "Mate," she said, placing a hand on her beast's arm. "I know you want to test yourself against the best, but you have nothing to prove. Don't forget we have a baby girl to return to."

A huff of smoke and flames escaped the beast, but he didn't

argue with her. The vast expanse of his energy faded as he also returned to his *slightly less terrifying* humanoid version. Not that any of them could ever be mistaken for human.

One by one the others followed suit, until there was barely a whisper of our power to be felt in the area. Knowing what had to happen now, I led by example, lowering myself to my knees.

A spark of energy from the closest guardian ran over my skin, but it was more uncomfortable than painful. Grinning and bearing it, I forced my power to stay calm.

The others did the same, until only Shadow was left standing. It wasn't a stretch to assume he'd knelt to no one before this day, but as the pincers picked up the pace near him, I hoped he could find the strength to give these guardians what they needed.

After leveling all four crabs with a fire-filled glare, the beast lowered to his knees. He never dropped his head though, eyeballing the fuck out of all of them, but his power didn't follow suit. It remained low and calm.

The guardians slowed, and despite the dim light, somehow, we were cast farther into shadows. As the darkness grew more pronounced, Len reached out and grasped my hand.

At least if this was our last moments, I wasn't alone.

Together as a pack we stood, and together we would fall.

End of story.

CHAPTER THIRTY-EIGHT

SAMANTHA

There was a moment where I thought I'd killed my friends.

More than friends: my pack and true mate.

A moment where I had to wonder if maybe, once again, I'd rolled over and showed my belly when we should have fought and taken our chances. Shadow had made a decent point before; it was better to die fighting on our feet than live weak on our knees.

The crabs started to move again, this time to circle around us. The blue sand lifted with their movement, smashing across my face to the point I had to close my eyes. My skin burned from the rough texture, while the clacking filled the space like raging thunder.

Please let me be right. Please let me be right.

All of us needed to live and see our children again.

My hand still clutched Len's, even as the sand blasted our skin away. They'd have to cut my damn arm off if they wanted me to release my mate.

The march of the guardians went on for so long. An eternity where we didn't know what way it was going to go, and then... the clacking faded, and the sand slowed its assault on us.

As I opened my eyes, I checked on my internal barrier first, relieved that it was still pulsing away brightly inside, even if it did feel like the darkness was pulsing stronger too. My wolf energy wrapped around me, helping to heal the torn and broken skin, and by the time I was on my feet, all pain was gone.

We perused the area thoroughly, but there were no guardians in sight. They'd faded into the sands from whence they came, and we were once again alone.

"Holy shit!" Mera cried, shaking her ass as she danced around the place. "We're alive. We're fucking alive."

Shadow's arms were around her in the next beat as he hauled her up and into his body, his kiss aggressive as he captured her attention. Mera's excited words morphed into a moan as she wrapped her legs around his waist. They stumbled away, the odd darkness of this land shadowing them in seconds, before they completely disappeared.

After almost dying, no one questioned why they would need a second of alone time.

The rest of us focused on dusting ourselves off and looking around for more dangers. Galleli approached me, his wings tucked in against his back once more. *You did good.* I didn't jump this time, which was a huge step. *Your hybrid nature and the lessons you've learned in your relatively short life saved us today. We wouldn't have thought the way you did, and for that, we would have perished.* His hand landed on my right shoulder and he gave a gentle squeeze, before releasing me quickly, no doubt thanks to the silver fae beside me. *Thank you.*

"No thanks needed," I replied breathlessly. "I'm just so fucking happy it worked. For a second there I thought I'd gotten you all killed, and then Shadow was going to drag himself from the underworld to tear my soul to pieces." I shook my head. "It would have gotten messy."

Galleli smirked, and strangely it made him look younger and less like an ancient warrior god carved from stone.

You are exactly who our pack needed.

With those words that had my emotions all flaring and messy, he left. The barrier inside swelled with the love I felt for all of my pack. Especially the love I felt for Len.

Sure, we'd known each other for five minutes in the great scheme of things, but I'd felt this love from the first time we were together. The scattered memories showed me the playful way he'd cherished and cared for me, and the attention he paid to everything that made me who I was. It also reminded me of the ache in my soul that I'd carried every day after that, even when I had no idea why it was there.

That ache was Len.

My head swung toward him. He was watching me, and waiting patiently as he always did for me to reach the obvious conclusion.

True mate. True love.

We moved at the same time, his hands landing under my ass as he lifted me effortlessly into his body. Just like Mera, I was already wrapping my legs around his waist, needing the closeness and the feel of our powers colliding.

His mouth was on mine as I took my next breath, strong hands biting into my skin. He pulled me as hard against him as was possible. The kiss deepened, and everything else faded away, until I was forced to lift my head and suck some air into my lungs.

We were parted enough to see our pack had vanished to give us some privacy, which was nice of them. Returning to Len, I noticed the stormy color of his eyes, and it made me smile. Words of love almost left my lips, but he got in first.

"I don't ever want you to think that you're not an important and valued member of this pack," he told me, his expression serious. "I didn't even understand what I was missing until you returned in my life. Fuck, I've searched a lifetime for you, Storm. I'll never let you go now."

Gah. How was it even possible to feel so many emotions and not die from the actual ache in my chest? It was a good ache, but also powerful.

"I love you, Winter," I whispered, having no idea if the timing was right, but *who really gave a fuck about timing?* We didn't have a damn clue what was waiting for us around the corner in this land of monsters, so I would take the opportunity now to tell him how I felt. "I loved you before we were torn apart, and it's only grown over the years. You and Tabitha are the best part of my existence, and I... just need you to know."

The intensity of his gaze was unraveling me. Those silver storm eyes darkened. Soon they were a swirling mass of power, and I wondered if I'd broken him with my declaration.

He moved lightning-fast, taking me by surprise when he kissed me, his tongue pushing forward to stroke against mine so we could taste each other. *"Le tunia, formia, letina, maforta."*

He chanted that phrase between strokes of his tongue, and I wished for the knowledge to understand what he was saying.

Thankfully, he followed them with English. "You are the light, the energy, the creation, the wonder," he told me. "There's no true English word, but in Faerie we say that you're the *all*. The sum of *all* that makes us whole. *All* who complete us. My love."

He kissed me again, whispering words of love between each brush of our lips, and by the time he was done worshipping me, I was an aching mess of need and emotions. "Len, I don't think I can wait until we're done here to feel you again," I said, voice rasping. Part of me was terrified that we would fail today and I'd never know his touch again. I had to be loved by him one last time.

His groan against my mouth added to the arousal dancing through my center. "I have an idea," he said softly. "Give me a second."

He gently dropped me to the ground, and it took a moment for my balance to return. The way my body reacted to him felt like it should be illegal.

Destructive and beautiful.

Part of my *all*.

"Stay right here," he commanded, dropping another orgasm-inducing kiss on my lips.

He disappeared into the darkness, but I could still feel the pulse of his energy, which was comforting. He returned a few minutes later, shooting me a soft smile. "I spoke to the others, and we all agree that a few hours rest is on the cards. Angel and Galleli especially are drained from ferrying us across."

"Aren't we being drained here though?" I asked. "As badly as I need a few hours with you, I also know we're in a life and death situation." Sadly, that had to be the priority.

Len shook his head. "Now that the guardians have faded, there's no drain on our energy. Shadow and the others confirmed this. We conquered this part of the labyrinth, and the drain will ease until we encounter the next obstacle."

Okay, cool. That made sense. I no longer had to feel guilty that I was asking our pack to lose their energy while I got a good thorough fucking. No matter how okay with the idea my lower half was.

"A little alone time between mated couples is a good energy booster anyway," Len said with a slow smile. "Proven and fact."

Crossing my arms, I shook my head at him. "Is that right? Proven and everything? Who did this study and where do we sign up?"

He stepped into me. "Research starts today," he whispered, hands tracing along my face and down my sides. Heat and power followed, bolstering my barrier inside. "Are you ready?"

Was I ready? Apparently, I needed to state it in clear and precise terms. "Len, I'm going to need you to fuck me," I breathed. "Right. Now."

Low, deep laughter spilled from his lips, then he moved faster than I could track. From his jacket he pulled five grey crystals, and with a flick of his wrist tossed the small spheres out in a perfect circle around us. The moment they touched the sand, there was a flash of light, and a barrier rose to form around us.

"These crystals will give us all the privacy we need," Len murmured, his laughter fading under deeper emotions. "No one can see or hear us."

Done waiting, I launched myself at the fae, all but climbing him like a damn tree to kiss the fuck out of him. Hands under my ass, he pushed me back against the invisible crystal "wall," and I cried out as his hard body pressed firmly against me.

The throb in my pussy increased as our kiss grew more heated, Len dominating my mouth as his tongue lazily brushed mine. All the while my hips rocked against him, the need driving me out of my mind. Tension coiled in my gut, and I had no doubt if I kept this movement up I was going to come without even losing my clothes.

"You almost died on me today, Storm," he rasped against

my lips, emotions dragging his tone down. "When you collapsed and started to fade, my entire fucking world went dark. I lost reason. I lost every sense of who I was, and I didn't care what destruction my actions wrought. If destroying a billion fae brought you back to me, I'd have sacrificed them in an instant."

A terrifying and exhilarating thought. "I'd do the same for you and Tabby," I told him, meaning every word of it. "Guess we're no heroes."

He pushed into me harder, lips caressing my neck, sending tingling sensations down my spine. "Heroes are overrated. Too many rules. Too many people to care about. We have our pack and the rest of the world be damned. Those outside the pack only benefit when saving the world saves them too. Otherwise, they're not my responsibility."

My hips flexed harder, and I dropped my head back with a groan. "It really shouldn't be sexy to hear you talk of slaughtering a billion people for me, and yet here we are."

Did I need therapy? *Probably.*

But apparently so did everyone else in this pack, so I was in good company.

"I'm going to fuck you until you scream my name," Len warned me. Or was it a promise?

Either way, he'd get no complaints from me.

"Less talking and more fucking then, Winter," I drawled with a low chuckle. "Actions, not words."

His grin was feral, and no lie, there was a flutter in my pussy at the anticipation of what was coming next. Len didn't say another word as he lowered me to my feet, before he slowly brushed his hands down my body, ending up on his knees while I ended up naked.

Whatever that magic was, we would be using it a lot.

"I can't expend too much energy," he said, words muffled

since his mouth was already against my skin. "But we are also on limited time, so sacrifices must be made."

I was too far gone to worry or care at this point.

As long as his mouth remained on my body, Len could do whatever he wanted.

CHAPTER THIRTY-NINE

SAMANTHA

Len's hands wrapped around my thighs, pulling them apart slowly, the icy brush of his breath against my heated skin had me squirming. My hips flexed against his hold, and I was panting. Fucking panting.

"No time for slow today, love," he warned me.

"Could have fooled me," I taunted back, and as he laughed his tongue swiped through the arousal seeping from my pulsing pussy, shutting me right the hell up.

After that, he made good on his word for *no time for slow*, devouring me like I was his last meal. His strong hands held me as wide-open as he wanted, and he alternated between licking and sucking, rolling my clit around his tongue. The hard bundle of nerves pulsed, my legs growing weaker with each swipe.

I pushed back against the invisible wall behind, hands braced on either side of me, nails scraping as I fought for something to hold on to. As his fingers slipped inside me, one by one, sliding and pumping in time to his tongue on my clit, I screamed and gripped his head, coming so hard that there was a moment I wondered if I'd died again.

Everything went kind of dark, with only bursts of starlight across my vision as I rode his face shamelessly, uncaring if I was suffocating him. He was a big fae; he could handle it.

When the last of that orgasm had me slumping and groaning, I expected him to lift his head and move on to fucking me like our lives depended on it, only he didn't.

He adjusted his angle, licking from the bottom of my slit to the top, taking in every last drop of my orgasm. His fingers slid inside me once more, curling until they hit my g-spot, and even though he was "cleaning me up," all he was really doing was driving me out of my mind.

My clit spasmed, so sensitive now that even as he gently sucked it between his teeth, I was halfway to an orgasm. The flicking of his tongue increased against my sensitive flesh, moving at a pace that was definitely *extra* in nature. "Holy fucking fuck," I cried as his pace picked up even further.

Len was the best vibrator in the world, and I should know, having smuggled in more than my fair share to the Clarity pack. Had to get off somehow, since I sure as shit wasn't going near the "mate" I was assigned. Not until I had no choice.

When I was cursing, crying, and jerking my hips into Len with absolutely no shame, the sharp spiraling of pleasure grew and I almost came again, only he slowed just before I fell over the edge. My growl was impressive as my wolf raged forward. We might enjoy his dominating as he edged us during sex, but that didn't mean there wasn't frustration too.

"I can taste when you're about to come," Len rasped against

my burning skin. "Your scent grows stronger, as does your taste." He groaned. "You taste so fucking sweet."

Swallowing roughly, I tried to find moisture, but apparently there wasn't enough in my body to fill my mouth too. Which made sense; arousal dripped down my thighs, even with Len devouring most of it.

"We are made for each other. You taste like my perfect mate," I whispered back, hands threading into his hair as I jerked my hips against him. His groan filled our little crystal dome, and he was soon face fucking me again. I was so close, my legs trembling as the sparks lit up my skin, while Len continued to keep me on the edge.

Until he was ready for me to fall.

This time as I cried out, he didn't slow his pace. Nope, he moved to that super speed, building and building me. My legs shook as I clawed at the *walls*. It seemed I was beyond sound now, opening and closing my mouth as silent screams pushed up from my chest.

"Come," Len commanded. The moment that one word escaped his lips, my center exploded. Fire burned through my veins as my senses elevated to new heights, the pleasure almost too much to bear. I lost track of all reality once more, and when I came back to myself I realized I'd all but collapsed on top of Len, who was holding me up.

"Dead," I choked out in a breathless whisper. "I'm actually dead."

His response was a low growl and as he rose, hands still on my waist, I let out a low gasp. His shirt under the duster jacket was soaked, and I could smell myself on him. That dusky scent of arousal somehow... turned me on.

"Did I do that?" I whispered, knowing the truth but needing to say it out loud. "Fuck."

Len pressed against me, my shaky legs barely holding us up. "You will come like that every. Damn. Time."

When he kissed me, I groaned at how good I tasted on his tongue… and lips… and apparently half his damn shirt. Who knew there was so much explosive pleasure to be released if one just had enough build-up.

When Len was finished kissing me, I was desperate to taste him the same way he'd just tasted me. Moving my lips along his jaw, I kissed the curves and bends of his body, enjoying the smooth skin. Fae had less body hair than shifters, and surprisingly I liked that. When I reached the soaked shirt, I stripped it from him, along with his silver duster that had not one speck of cum on it.

It was as magical as the fae himself.

When he was shirtless, I let my tongue dance across all of those impressive muscles. So many grooves and divots to explore, each cut line the perfect tracing path. Len remained still, allowing me as much free run as I needed to explore him as he'd done for me.

When I reached his pants, I got the buttons undone easily. Pushing them down, the thick tip of his cock came into view, followed by an equally impressive shaft as it jutted up above his balls, which rested before firm, muscled thighs. Len stepped out of his pants, and I leaned and swiped across a bead of moisture forming in the slit of his cock. A sweet taste hit me, sugary with a hint of rain and lavender. It swept across my tongue, that single drop coating it, sending hunger roaring to life within me.

Swirling my tongue around the tip, I relaxed my jaw and took Len as deep into my mouth as I could. Which unfortunately wasn't that deep. With his size, I clearly needed some practice, and to work on my gag reflex.

If we survived this, I had the feeling I'd get all the practice needed.

As more of his sugary taste invaded my mouth, I managed to take a little more of him without choking. His fingers threaded through my hair as he groaned. "Storm, you're driving me crazy. This feels... so fucking good."

Considering more than a little pre-cum filled my mouth, I had no doubt that he meant every word. He was into whatever I did, which lit a feeling of confidence and power deep in my soul. Bringing my mate pleasure brought me pleasure, so it was a win fucking win in my books.

Using my hand to wrap around the shaft and base of his cock, I pumped as I bobbed my head on his cock. The sweetness of his pre-cum was adding life and energy to my body, as if it were truly nourishing for me, and despite my two orgasms, my body was already tight and throbbing.

He cupped a hand under my cheek, drawing me slowly up his body.

I rose, his commanding hold guiding me. "I don't want to stop you," he breathed, "but we're running out of time. If I come now, it'll take me a lot longer during sex. We can save that for next time when we're safe and back in Faerie."

The fact that he could come and then be up for round two immediately after, told me I was never going to bored with our sex life. "I'm ready for my third orgasm anyway," I said with a low laugh. "I'll be as quick as you need."

His responding rumble sent shivers coursing through me. "You know that now I have to pay tribute to Shadow for his part in creating such a perfect mate for me."

To Shadow. My shifter side was just as important to him as the Faerie side, and if that didn't slay me the hardest...

We met in the middle of the kiss this time, and as I wrapped my arms around his neck, he lifted me up into his body. He pushed me higher than usual, just so he could lower me down onto his cock. Despite his claim about *time running out*, he entered me slowly, inch by delicious inch, until I was panting, tearing my mouth from his to suck in some air.

The second he lifted me again, before slamming me back down onto his cock, a third orgasm shattered through me. I cried and rocked against him, this release different to before. The pleasure was as great but I didn't black out. I got to ride out the entire explosive experience.

Arching myself back, Len moved his hands higher to the curve of my spine. As I moved faster against him, his breaths became heavier, his head descending to suck my right nipple into his mouth. *Gods.* As he sucked and laved at the peak, in time to the thrust of his cock, I was panting and on the edge of my fourth orgasm.

This cock was a miracle worker.

Or more accurately, it was the fae wielding it who had worked a miracle.

"Come," Len ordered as his teeth closed around my nipple, a flash of pleasure pain sending me right over the edge.

His cock swelled inside, and I could feel every ridge against my pulsing walls as I screamed his name. He groaned mine, spilling into me in short, jagged thrusts.

It took a long time for us both to ride out our pleasure, and when we were done, I knew that there was nothing in any worlds that could compare to what I'd just experienced here with Len.

More than sex, there had been a bonding between us. An acceptance.

Love.

The full scope of our true mate bond might still be lost in what remained of the glamour, but it didn't hurt this connection we had.

In truth, it felt like we'd just moved one step closer to finding out the truth.

To finding everything.

CHAPTER FORTY

SAMANTHA

Len used more crystals from his jacket to clean us and create some clothes. "I could use my own energy, but it's best to conserve it," he said, when we were dressed and ready to start this journey again.

"Can you feel any drain from the Deep yet?" I asked. "I don't really know what losing power feels like, since I've clearly been cut off from a large source of mine all of my life."

Len, now in black fatigues, a plain black shirt, and his silver trench coat, stepped into a pair of black combat boots as he answered. Subtly, I attempted to wipe at my mouth in case I was drooling—he was rocking badass special-ops, and it was a good look on him.

"The drain is slight," he admitted, lips thinning. I wasn't surprised he was annoyed, since it was a theft of power without his permission, and he was too old and princely to be cool about that. Not to mention we needed everyone at full power to make it through.

Not all tests would be about submission like the last one. Some would undoubtedly require strength.

"Our time of rest did help though," he added, and I couldn't help the burst of laughter that escaped.

"Rest," I chuckled. "Right."

He crowded me against the crystal wall. "Yes, mate. *Rest.* And just so you know, I plan on resting with you many more times over our life, and each will only add to our energy and strength."

My laughter faded as my hips jerked toward him. Dammit, my body was already trained to obey his command, and what he was promising we wanted.

As his lips brushed mine, he flicked his hand out and recalled the stones. The land of blue sand reappeared around us again, and the sexual tension faded enough that I could focus on the task at hand. The reality of our situation was more apparent outside the sphere of stones, and I knew we'd done all the *resting* we had time for.

Len took my hand, and my new black boots—very similar in style to his—crunched on the blue sand as we crossed it. This time he'd dressed me in dark jeans, a plain black shirt, and a less elaborate silver jacket that ended just below my ass. *Silver for a silver princess*, he had said. He always thought of everything, right down to a brush and hair tie, so I could quickly braid my long hair down my back.

The sensation of being cared for, of having someone in my corner, would never get old.

"Do you have any guesses of how far we still have to travel to reach the Origin and Great Queen's line?" I asked as our pace picked up.

The darkness around us didn't cease, and I had zero idea of

what direction to even head in. Thankfully, Len appeared to be following a source of power.

"There's no way to tell in a land surrounded by energy such as this," he said. "From the little I've discovered, we'll face at least two more major obstacles."

Great, if they were anything like the guardians and the red lava floor, it should be a piece of cake. A cake poisoned and laced with explosives.

After walking for a few minutes, we ran into Simone and Lucien. They looked relaxed, and I thought I caught a flash of blood on Lucien's lips. "Time to move forward?" the vampire asked.

Len nodded. "Yep. If we rest any longer, we run the risk of the land trying to drain us to get us moving."

Lucien didn't argue, gathering Simone under his arm, a heated and possessive look on his face as he pulled her close. Simone all but melted beneath his touch, and when she caught sight of me gawking like a creeper, she shot me a slow smile and a wink.

It was clear she was happy, and I couldn't ask for anything more for my pack sisters. They'd found the sort of happiness romance books were built on, and now that I also had a possessive supernatural who growled and shot me heated looks, I understood those happily-ever-afters much better.

The thought of losing it all before it even begun actually took my breath away. Unable to consider the possibility, I pushed the dark thoughts down and focused on the now. We just had to get through two more obstacles and restore my line. We could totally handle that.

The four of us continued, following Len's lead as he moved us toward the next task. Along the way we picked up Reece and Angel. The transcendent had her wings away again, the exhaustion that had been dragging along her features was also gone. Whatever she'd done to rest and restore had worked. There were no visible changes to Reece, who always looked like a scary desert god, but he did show relief when he looked upon Angel.

Next was Galleli, who found us, soaring down and landing heavily upon the blue sand. Unlike Angel, he didn't look like he'd rested at all, his skin clammy. "Recon?" Reece asked.

Galleli released a weary sigh. *Yes, and I know where we must journey next. It will require all of us to work together to make it across.*

Great. That didn't sound ominous or worrisome at all.

Len must have been heading in the right direction, since Galleli didn't change our path. I was just wondering where Shadow and Mera were when their forms grew visible in the dull light. Flames surrounded them as they stood on the edge of a precipice in their huge beast forms. Clearly, they knew where the next path was as well.

"What are we up against?" Len asked as he stopped beside Shadow. Lucien fell in on the other side of him, then Reece, and finally Galleli.

The five males stood in a line of power and beauty, and I knew I wasn't the only one slightly mesmerized as we watched them assess our next move. Mera, her phoenix shifter side fading again, moved in closer to me. She wore a green army jacket now, which turned the green flecks in her hazel eyes brighter than ever. "Ladies," she breathed, "they're trying to kill us. Or at minimum impregnate us through overwhelming alpha-ness."

"It's a lot," Simone agreed hoarsely. "I mean, Lucien regularly takes my breath away, but this is extra. They don't need to be so extra."

"Over-fucking achievers," Mera growled. "Always with the overachieving." Her voice lowered into a growl. "*Sunshine, you can take my twenty-inch cock.*" She shook her head. "Like, ten would have been great, fifteen amazing, but this motherfucker can actually change the size of hi—"

Shadow laughed, and damn... I had no idea that growly, snarly, powerful bastard could laugh like that. He all but threw his head back as this deep rumble of mirth escaped him. "Sunshine," he said, "you have such a way with words, mate, but as long as it's only my cock in your mouth, I'll never complain."

Mera fanned her face, pink spots appearing on her cheeks. "You mean *as long as it's only ever your cock* that I talk about?" she replied breathlessly.

Shadow's grin was slow and predatory. "Yeah, that too."

Holy gods. "I'm not mentally prepared for this today," I admitted, feeling hot under the collar.

"It's all the testosterone," Simone agreed. "I'm drowning in it."

She wasn't wrong. I pulled my shirt away from my neck, needing to cool down.

"Chill, boys," Angel said with her own wicked laugh. "You five together is too much for us. At least dial it back until we've survived the bridge of death."

The bridge of death. That was a very accurate representation of what the guys had been staring at a moment ago. Like a switch was flicked, the sexy banter and low hum of arousal dried up and they were all business again.

"Okay, so what's the plan?" I asked. "How would someone from the Great Queen's line get through this next task?"

We leaned forward to see down the side of the small incline we stood on. The blue sand tapered off here, and on the other side was the suspension rope bridge that led across a flaming pit.

"Their power would connect straight to the Origin," Len reminded me. "It would take them over and through all of this without being touched. This is basically designed so no other could make it through. To protect the original energy of Faerie from those who would use it for their own gain."

"What's around the Origin?" Shadow asked. "I'm assuming the most powerful gems and crystals."

Len nodded. "Yes. It's where the sunburst stone came from, along with a few of Faerie's strongest gems. When the Great Queen was in Faerie, she'd travel into the Deep every decade or so and retrieve new power gems for each royal houses. This kept our energy fresh and new. Since her disappearance, we've grown weak and stagnant. No new gems and less young being born."

What he said bothered me, since it was my grandmother or great-great grandmother or whatever relative she was, who had ditched her job in Faerie. She'd spelled me to forget everything to do with Faerie and our heritage, but it was still my family's responsibility. When we were done with our task here, I had to ensure I helped strengthen Faerie once more.

"We should move," Reece said. "The power drain has begun again, and once we step onto that bridge, it'll kick in hard and fast."

I still didn't feel anything, but I had less power to begin with, so there wasn't much to lose. The barrier inside was holding at least. For now that was my only concern.

The nine of us stepped over the edge of the sand, sliding a little until our boots found traction on the rocks that jutted out beyond the blue. We hurried toward the suspension bridge, blasts of intense heat slapping us in the face as we closed in. I wasn't surprised when Shadow and Mera were the first to approach it. Fire was their dominion after all.

"I can protect you from the fires," Shadow said, sounding confident. Not that he ever didn't. "If I weren't here, you'd all be cooked before you made it halfway."

A cough escaped me. "A graphic image that's now freely floating in my brain. Thank you."

He shrugged, uncaring. "An image in your brain is better than real life." He turned then to Angel, who was standing on his right. "Hop on my back," he told her. "Take advantage of my natural immunity to fire."

Angel wasted no time, leaping onto his back, and he ran like he was in a race. Across the swaying bridge, he dropped her off and was back in record time. A few beads of sweat dotted his forehead, which was all we needed to know about how hot it was to cross above the swirling lava.

"If it's not designed for anyone to make it across, why have the bridge at all?" I wondered.

Len's expression was grim. "It's a trap. This land wants you to believe you can cross safely. By the time you realize your mistake..."

"You're toast," Simone finished grimly.

Thankfully, we had Shadow, and he made quick work of ferrying all the ladies across first. As we stood on the other side, where the heat was a little less intense, we peered over the cavernous pit together.

"I can't wait to see him giving those godlike males a piggyback," Simone said with a snort of laughter. "I wish I had a camera to capture this moment."

Mera groaned. "There must be a way to convert our memories into images. I know I will *never* forget it."

First across was Reece, and the look on his and Shadow's faces implied that if *anyone ever mentioned this again, they would destroy them*. If only that shit worked on their mates. Even Angel was smiling, her eyes brighter than usually, the pinkish sheen glowing. "I love when they play together so nicely," she said with a chuckle.

Shadow dropped Reece as soon as they were safe, the

desert warrior landing gracefully on his feet. He straightened to his full height of giant, and Shadow was already gone to get the others. Reece spent his next few minutes tickling Angel, who kept smirking at him. "Don't make me punish you later," he groaned when she burst into laughter once more.

"Just the look on your face," she choked out. "I've seen you tortured and happier than that."

The banter continued as one by one Shadow brought the others across. Most of them wore a similar expression to Reece, but Lucien did make a *giddyap horse* joke which almost got him dumped into the lava.

"Safe," Mera breathed. "Now on to the next part of this run."

If Len was right, then that was one down and one more to go. We were so close. I just had to hope that together we would be enough to make it through.

CHAPTER FORTY-ONE

SAMANTHA

Beyond the flaming bridge, there was another long plain. This one was dark, appearing to be made from fine pebbles of coal, and we paused on the edge to determine the dangers. "It feels the way the sand rivers do back home," Reece said, leaning down and running his hands over it. "This is not a stable surface. If you step one foot on here, you'll be yanked under faster than it takes to move your other foot."

Angel leaned down with him, placing her hands on the coal too. "Yep, calm on the surface," she said, "but there's power running under these depths. Possibly some creatures down there as well. More guardians."

Great, so if we were lost in the depths, we would be lost forever. Or at least long enough to get eaten.

"Can you manipulate a path for us?" Shadow asked Reece.

"I know it's not the sands of the Desert Lands, but often you can work with other crushed, earthy material."

Reece slid more of his hand into the black pebbles. "I'm not sure this could be classified as an earthy material at all, but I can give it a shot."

Galleli's wings extended in wide arcs beside him and he flapped and lifted into the air, attempting to fly out across the black grains. He made it two feet before he was knocked back.

They won't allow us to fly this path.

This time I jumped because I hadn't been expecting it. The deep rumble of his voice was filled with so much power that it caused a visceral reaction within me.

"Whatever we do," Angel said shortly. "We need to do it now. There's a building of energy deep in this land. They're becoming more aware of intruders being here, and I fear our time is running out." She placed a hand on Reece's shoulder. "I'll help in whatever way you need. But let's get it done."

Len leaned down to place his hands on top of the black expanse. "Angel is right," he said. "We're working on borrowed time. Soon, not even our strengths will be enough." He looked up at Reece. "You cannot manipulate this river of power. It's all Faerie magic."

Disappointment and worry barely had time to set in before Len straightened, multiple gems already in his hands. I only caught a glimpse, but they looked red and white, along with a few of those grey ones he'd used to give us privacy earlier. Len flicked his hand out in that familiar way and the stones arced in a beautiful rainbow across the darkness, lighting up the sky, before they settled against the black ground. As the final one dropped so far into the distance that it was barely visible, a light bridge formed between them.

"I'm going to see if this connection holds," Len said. "These stones are not the most stable against power like this, but we're out of time and options. It's this or we're dead."

My stomach sank as my chest clenched. "I'll go," I said quickly. "I'm lighter and have the Great Queen's energy. Her line might be severed, but the remnants are there, and that has to help."

"Not a chance in hell," Len bit out shortly. "You're too fucking important to risk. I have ancient Faerie power beyond any here. Even yours, Storm. This is my risk to take."

"You're fucking important too," I shot back, my voice wavering. Fear and anger were taking me over, and I wasn't always the most reasonable when that happened. I knew Len was right—I had zero fucking skills or idea how to fight in Faerie. But I needed him alive. It was a fundamental part of my existence.

"Tabby needs you," he reminded me.

"She needs us both," I countered, like a petulant teenager.

He reached out and brushed the tip of his finger down my cheek. "I don't die easily," he whispered. As he leaned in, his lips pressed against mine, and when I was suitably distracted he shoved me into nearby arms. "Hold her," he said. "If I don't fall, follow as soon as possible."

The *hold her* made sense a beat later when strong arms banded across my chest and I was lifted about seventy billion feet from the ground. I didn't even try to fight. It was Shadow holding me after all, the spark of his power painful as it zapped my skin. I wouldn't waste my energy fighting against a god when I'd need that strength to *kick a motherfucking fae prince's ass.*

Mera appeared in my line of sight, her narrowed eyed gaze shifting above my head. "Put her down, Shadow," she said shortly. "Just because we're smaller doesn't mean you get to manhandle us."

His reply was a grunt, and zero loosening of his hold.

She said something else snarky, but I was too busy watching Len step out onto the first stone before he set off, fleet of foot, following the path of light he'd set across the coal land. He moved like a being unbeholden to the same gravitational pull as the rest of us.

"I realllyyy hope he doesn't expect me to run across a skinny beam of light like that," Simone said with a snort-laugh, which dried up into a nervous cough. "I mean, I'm a shifter, reborn into a badass Lycan who will probably live forever—if the worlds don't end of course—but that level of grace is not in my repertoire."

Girl, same. Shifters might be stealthy, but we couldn't move like that. Len looked as if he was floating above the light, almost completely out of sight now. "Put me down," I said shortly. "He's already gone. I can't do anything but follow when it's our turn."

Shadow's chest expanded and he took a moment—probably so there was no way this could be misconstrued as the beast taking an order from me—until he set me on my feet. As I shook off the pain of being in contact with the shifter god, I focused on my next step. In a flash, I was naked, stripping my clothes faster than most of them could blink.

My thoughts before about being stealthy had given me an idea.

The shift came over me quickly.

Outside of a few exceptions, I'd always been able to call my wolf with ease. She just waited patiently inside, a comfort and friend. When she was free, the dark strands of her coat drifted around us and my heart soared. It was only when I shifted that the true energy of my beast filled me, and with it my love of her wilder soul.

The darkness faded even further as I pranced around, getting used to four legs once more.

"Great idea to shift," Angel said as she bent and gathered my clothes and boots, disappearing them into what I hoped was a magical pocket since I'd need them later.

In my wolf form, the world was still as dark, but I had better vision of the gem bridge across the black expanse. There was no signal from Len yet, but he also hadn't fallen, so I felt it was somewhat safe to move. Unsure if Shadow was going to stop me, I stepped toward the edge and closest red gem, waiting a beat to see if he'd move forward too.

He didn't.

With a howl to the air, I leapt across to the first gem, and then I was racing along the thin line of power almost as fast as Len had. I didn't look back, but I felt the others behind me. Everything was smooth sailing and calm on the surface, and I wondered if there was anything lurking deep in this black coal. The energy of this section of the Deep was milder than I'd expected.

The farther we crossed, the colder the air grew, which didn't bother me in my wolf form. My beast was near frolicking as we raced across the gems. There was no end in sight, but I wasn't worried. Len was clearly extending the path as he moved, and so far this was the easiest of trials.

Or so I thought.

From the moment I jinxed myself by addressing how easy it was, there was a ripple in the sand a short distance away. My wolf sight allowed me to see clearer in the darkness, and I was certain that a shadowy shape had just broken the seamless surface.

Pausing, four paws balanced precariously on the shimmery line beneath my feet, I watched to see if it would appear again.

Could it have been a current? Maybe there were some small waves out here in the middle of the coal field. Or was it something more sinister, such as another guardian? It might not be the crabs this time... it could be something way worse.

"Sam, is everything okay?" Mera's low musical voice reached me just as the dark shape broke the surface again.

I couldn't say anything in my wolf form, but I hoped the others were seeing it too.

"Why has she paused?" Shadow rumbled.

He was at her back, and as they slowed behind me, it appeared that I was still the only one to have noticed the disturbance. Was it due to my connection to this land? Or a benefit of being in my shifted form?

"She's looking out into the distance," Mera said, sounding unsure. "As if she saw something."

"I haven't noticed anything," Shadow rumbled. "Normally I'd try and connect to her thoughts, but I won't while she's working to keep the darkness from taking her. And shifting back while balanced is not a great idea either."

Despite that, I was contemplating a brief shift because that shadow was a worry. I knew it, deep in the parts of me that were connected to this land.

Just as I was drawing on the energy to change, Mera let out a low cry. "I saw it. It was a dark pointed shape, moving across the line of sand."

"Move," Shadow said with a rumble. "Don't stop and don't look back."

I was first in line, and accepting what he'd said without question, my beast leapt into action, flying across the stones like our ass was on fire. When the Shadow Beast was worried about shadows, we all needed to be fucking worried.

We were making great pace when I felt a surge of energy

below. Before I could bark or howl, the sand rippled around like a storm and darkness burst to life before me. A harsh howl escaped my jaws as those shadows crashed into me, and I managed to suck in one deep breath before I was knocked off the stones and dragged below the surface.

CHAPTER
FORTY-TWO

LEN

The entire time I crossed the dark plain, I knew that we were being led into a sense of false safety. The air was light and there was almost no drain on my energy. My stones didn't even falter, despite the unstable energy of the Deep.

Nothing ever went this smoothly in a place of power, and as I'd decided to double back and tell the others we needed a different plan, a huge crash of shadowy darkness launched up from the surface before me. It took a moment to figure out the dark form was another guardian, this one more akin to a water beast, with an elongated body, four fins, and a narrow jaw filled with a multitude of sharp teeth.

I'd never seen anything like it, and I reacted on instinct, flipping backwards along the line of power. The creature just missed crashing into me, clearly intending to take me down into the depths. It was a close call, and I didn't stick around to see what it did next, racing back along the line, using more crystals for speed.

I didn't have many stones left in my possession, but I had enough to keep boosting for now. My speed picked up and, in the distance, I caught sight of my family. They were perched on the line of power staring out into the sands. Had they seen the shadow guardian too?

A small black wolf caught my eye, and despite having never seen her shifted form, I knew it was Sam. My mate. Her beast was regal, head slightly elevated as she stared into the darkness.

Mate.

The instinct was strong. The call even stronger. A desperate need to save her drove me to levels of speed I'd never reached before. Not even when I was testing myself against vampires in Valdor. There was nothing I wouldn't do for Sam, even if it cost me every fucking sliver of energy inside.

Just when I thought I was going to reach them in time, another guardian launched from the dark stones. A shout roared from me, a warning to watch out, but it was too late. Time slowed as I watched it hit my mate, sending her off the side of the line.

I launched into the air, my energy crashing against the side of the guardian as I sought to find Sam in the midst of the creature's hold.

Only I was a second too late.

They disappeared into the depths, and as I followed my body smashed against solid ground. My rage exploded, the entire land lighting up in frost, sending whatever shadows that remained away from us. I'd been unaware that so many creatures lurked out there, waiting to pounce.

Not that I cared. Bring them on.

I'd fight every single one until I figured out which one had taken my mate.

More of my power exploded from me into the ground as I tried to shatter the barrier keeping me from Sam, but it didn't move an inch.

"Len!" Shadow's roar cut through the frost in my brain, and I focused long enough to see that I'd coated everything in ice and snow. Ice that was sparking and zapping my pack.

Shadow was on his knees, unable to move closer to me, and as I saw the others in the same position, a flake of sanity returned. My raging instinct to destroy still pushed at me, but I found that I couldn't destroy them. My family. And Sam's.

Withdrawing my power from their forms, Shadow was up and on his feet in the same instant.

"Why is the ground solid now?" he snapped, showing no anger over my attack. "That guardian took Sam below and now I can't feel any power. Why?"

I knew. I'd known the fucking truth since we'd landed down here but I'd ignored my instinct. "Her energy originated in this land," I rasped. "And they want it back. They want her back. No one has ever confirmed this, but I believed that the Great Queen was created here. Her energy, and that of her offspring, belongs to the Deep."

If Sam was the last of the line—well, Sam and Tabitha—then it stood to reason that this land recognized her as their own. Which allowed another rational thought to crash through my pain and fury. "If the Deep recognized her as its own," I managed to say without letting my rage spill further, "there's a chance it's taking her to the source of original power. It has sealed this path so that we cannot follow. But there's still the path we were on."

As fucked up as it was, now that the ground was hardened,

and there was no more draw on our power, we could cross from here easily.

"We should continue on," Shadow agreed. We all knew it was a long shot, our last hope. But that iota of hope was the single factor allowing me to continue through the darkness.

Shadow approached me, recognizing that I was slightly more reasonable. His hand landed heavily on my shoulder. "We will find her, brother. I refuse to let this be the last of Samantha and our pack."

I nodded, lowering my voice. "If we reach the end and she's not there, make sure I don't hurt the others. Get them the fuck out of here before I bring it all down around us."

"You have my word."

He understood—better than most, thanks to the reason for his existence standing a few paces away from us.

My power returned to me as I withdrew the ice. The stones embedded in the hard ground returned as well. They were drained and in need of recharge, and I hoped I had enough power to do what was needed for Sam. For my little Storm, who'd blown into my world and leveled that fucker to the ground.

Shadow remained between me and the others as we started back across the black expanse, the rest of our pack shooting me worried stares, but no one said anything directly.

"Is he okay?" I heard Mera ask her mate.

His reply was immediate. "Not even remotely. Stay on the other side of me. I'm the only one who'll survive the fallout."

At least Shadow was aware of my capabilities, and how close I was teetering to the edge. This fucking universe had to stop attempting to take my mate from me. That was the simple truth.

When we reached the end of the black plain, we were once again facing the edge of a cliff, and on the other side was a garden. Usually, flora calmed me, but this time there was no easing the raging swirls of ice in my chest.

Leaping across the final twenty-foot gap, I landed on the edge of the garden. From here, a chill attempted to encase me, but it was nothing compared to the chill raging inside.

"I'm guessing none of these plants are the friendly types?" Lucien said, his tone forcibly light. The loss of one in our pack was a raw wound that hadn't healed from the last time. Alistair had been a death that almost broke us, but Samantha... hers would shatter me.

I wasn't just fighting for her life now, but for both of ours.

"We should approach with caution," I replied flatly. "Everything is a threat."

Actually... before the others got close to the first tree, I sent out my rage, knowing it was better to ice the garden than my family. A thin sheet settled over everything, slowing their attack.

"He's killing plants," Mera said in an urgent whisper. "This is really bad."

"Not yet," I replied. "I hold a small hope that she's waiting for us at the end. If that hope fades, so will my control."

The silence was heavy, and I pushed on, needing to finish this task to know whether Faerie was about to fall. Truth be told, even if the balance wasn't out of line, I'd level this world and all the rest until I found my mate.

End of story.

CHAPTER FORTY-THREE

SAMANTHA

The moment the shadows closed over me and took me down into the depths, my ability to breathe was gone. There was no air below, and I struggled against the beast, which was plummeting like it wanted to slam into the floor of his black stone ocean.

Had that been its plan all along? Just take me down to drown?

There was no light under here, and yet somehow my wolf could still make out some shadowy creatures in the distance. More of them than I would ever be able to fight, obviously, since I couldn't even fight the one holding me.

Sending more feral power into my wolf, we clawed and bit at whatever we could reach, but the shadow didn't even react. I had a strange feeling that it had been hit by energy as it took us down, and now it was injured... maybe dead. Not that it mattered. Dead or not, it was still trapping me with its bulk, sending us both to the depths.

Deciding to shift out of my wolf form before a lack of oxygen stole my ability to fight, I drew on my change, allowing it to wash over me until I was back in my two-legged form. The change did free me from the shadow, and as it fell away I attempted to kick my heavy legs in the hope of slowing my descent. Even better if I actually headed back for the surface.

Only nothing changed. It was so dense under here that there was no way to travel up, only left or right, if I kicked in that direction. And all the while, I continued to drop.

Panic flashed in the corners of my oxygen-deprived brain. *Think, Sam. Fucking think.*

I had a daughter and a mate to get back to. I couldn't just roll over and let this land take me. There had to be a way to best this trap.

Which was, of course, easier thought than done, because no matter what I tried, down was the only direction I'd go.

After struggling for too many precious seconds, I finally gave up fighting and decided to go with the flow. Down is where they wanted me, and I was probably closer to the bottom than the top at this point. Maybe the exit was down there... somehow.

Once I stopped fighting, I plunged like there was no resistance at all. It was odd to be surrounded like this, as if underwater without air, only it was dry and cold. A sliver of light caught my eye as I descended, and I hoped that meant I'd made the right decision to drop.

Light could be an exit, right?

The hope gave me seconds of air as my lungs dredged it up from some stored part of my body. Or maybe it was my focus on the light that had me forgetting I was dying second by second.

When the glow was strong enough to nearly blind me, I

realized my mistake. This was no exit or way out... it was a line of power, similar to the ones we'd used to get from the Capital down into the Deep.

This one was four times the size, and a bright relentless gold, a shade that hadn't been in the other ones. *Original power.* Was this the Great Queen's line? A part that hadn't been severed.

My descent slowed, and as darkness crept into my shaky vision, I slumped across the glowing strand. With the last of my strength, I reached out and wrapped my hand around it. *Help me.* The words were in my mind, the last of my power fading, and it was like before when the darkness tried to take me from this world. *I'm from your line.*

The last stores of my air were gone, and I sent out a final goodbye to my loved ones, tears dripping along my cheeks, soaked up by the sandy coal that would form my final resting place. Tabitha's sweet little face flashed in my mind, and I could only pray they found a way to save her. If they couldn't, I'd wait for her in the next life.

I'd never leave my baby again.

Or Len.

His powerful features filled my mind, and his energy mingled deep inside where our bond existed. It was tempered by the glamour that held us apart, but we both knew it was there now.

My fae prince held every part of my heart, as did his daughter, and this was no wasted life to have known and loved them both.

When I released my hold on the mortal realm, my soul slipped free from the vessel it had been encased in, following the golden path of light. No longer in the depths, I was moving freely without an ache in my lungs or fear in my heart. The weight of mortality was gone, and as I drifted along, a sharp spike hooked me in my center, yanking me sideways.

Even in spirit form, the sudden movement hurt, and I gasped when I landed on a burning surface. Pushing up, confusion clouded some of the lighter energy as I tried to figure out where I was. My spirit form was standing—not floating, standing—on the surface of a land that burned in flames, as if we'd landed on the sun.

There was no heat as I took a step forward, following the curve of the land, like a cartoon character walking on the top of a small planet. It was too bright to see anything beyond where I stood, outside of the flames that tossed and turned before me.

There was no pain, heat, or cold, almost as if I couldn't quite interact with the world itself.

My steps continued on until I came upon a golden beam of light, floating a few feet above the ground. It took me a moment to remember that I'd been clutching that same beam when I died.

My pace picked up as I reached the golden line, wanting to touch it, only I didn't really have hands any longer. Deciding to follow it, I set off once more, the gold growing brighter and brighter as we crossed the curvature of this land. There were no other changes until the strand grew larger, thicker, and so bright that I almost couldn't look upon it.

It had turned the flaming surface of the sun world into a dull backdrop.

Eventually the cord was as large as a huge water pipe, with a diameter so big that if it had an opening, I'd have been able to walk right into it and not hit my head.

My ghostly head. Or whatever I was now.

This was the point the ground levelled out, and when it did the cord suddenly shrank, as if its size had all been to ensure I didn't lose it. The gold joined other cords, all of which were attached to... Uh, I actually had no actual idea what they were attached to.

It looked like a giant sphere hovering on the horizon, and weirdly, despite it being the size of a skyscraper, I hadn't noticed it until right this moment. The dozens of other cords spanned from its surface in a multitude of different colors.

Moving away from the gold line, I drifted between the other lines, heading for the sphere.

As I got closer, I could feel a pulse of energy, one of the first sensory changes since I'd been yanked here. That pulse had me wondering if the giant sphere was a hub of power, feeding or being fed. It was difficult to tell the direction of power.

Maybe it went both ways.

Balance generally required an equal flow.

Not having a clue what I was supposed to do next, I kept pushing forward, losing my gold strand as I closed in on the sphere. The giant structure, floating a few feet above the ground, was not a color I'd ever seen. It appeared to be a wash of every color and every shade that existed in the worlds, moving and ever changing.

When I was close enough to truly *see* the minute details of the surface, a hoarse sound escaped me, and it was kind of terrifying to know I could make sounds here. This land was so quiet, *and I was dead,* so sound just felt out of place. But the reason for the sound remained. The sphere was not a mix of colors as I'd thought, but its surface was made up of a trillion tiny images, small and lined up next to each other so that the individual was hidden in the whole, hard to detect until you were all but pressed against the surface.

The images were moving too, akin to a television tuned into a trillion different channels.

"What in the worlds...?" I murmured in a voice that sounded like tinkly bells.

Deciding I had nothing left to lose, I urged my ghostly form closer to the sphere, wanting to touch the power.

When my energy brushed against it, I was blasted backwards, a boom filling the air that was so loud it was almost painful despite my lack of physical ears.

It felt like a warning, and I wondered what I was supposed to do with that.

Backtracking, I returned to the place where I'd lost the golden strand. This was the cord that brought me here, and I wondered if it had something to do with my next steps.

I just had to figure out how to utilize this particular cord.

This time, when I moved toward the sphere, I kept the gold strand in my energy, as if holding on to its essence. It twisted and turned, and I almost lost it a couple of times, having to backtrack to find it again, but eventually I reached the spot where it touched the sphere. It was on the opposite side of the giant power structure.

Bracing myself for the rejection once more, I pressed right where the gold connected, only to find my essence flowing forward until I was on the inside of the sphere. The bright fiery world outside faded, the inside of the sphere just a shimmery gold.

Maybe because of my line of power.

There was nothing inside that I could see, and it was not much larger than my old bedroom back in Clarity. The outside did not in any way reflect what existed inside.

Instinct told me that now I would have to wait. Wait and see where the next path took me.

Maybe that would be for an eternity, or maybe it would happen instantly.

Either way, I'd been led here for a reason, and until that reason was presented to me, there was nothing to do but wait.

Luckily, the dead didn't fear time.

CHAPTER FORTY-FOUR

LEN

She wasn't there.

We'd made it through the garden, which only sprang to life as we neared the end. By the time we were done, we sported a few injuries, but nothing of worry. The next section brought us to a golden sphere. It was hovering in the middle of a land of crystals, this entire area containing more power than I'd ever felt anywhere else in the worlds.

"The Origin," Angel breathed. "This is the source of Faerie creation. The original power."

Every world had a place of birth, where the original power still connected to the great Origin of all worlds. Origins were not accessible to most inhabitants, or survivable if stumbled upon.

If we all hadn't been as strong as we were, the sheer energy here would have blown us to pieces.

"There's something wrong with it," Reece said, pressing as close as he could without bursting into flames. "Why is there darkness threaded through the gold?"

"Have you ever seen an original power source like this before to know?" Simone asked.

"It's tainted," I managed to growl, backing Reece's theory. "The gold should be pure."

"Maybe this is what happened to the Great Queen," Shadow rumbled. "It could explain her disappearance and the weakening in Faerie."

Maybe it was what had happened to Samantha too.

"Wait, if the severing of the line is what took Samantha's life, why does it still look whole and complete there?" Simone asked. "Was there another line?"

She was referring to the golden cord that spanned up from the top of the sphere. "That's the line to the world of creation," I managed to say, all while my rage grew. "Fredrick only severed the part that connected Samantha's family line to the main land of Faerie."

Shadow nodded. "Yes, if that other line was severed, Faerie would have ceased to exist in the same second."

My chest grew tighter. "No one can sever this line. It would take the sort of power beyond all there is. Not even our group would have a chance. Not even a million of our groups."

"Do you think Samantha is inside the sphere?" Mera choked out, her voice hoarse, eyes red as she rubbed at them.

Unable to speak again, I released my beast and drew on every source of magic here. If Samantha was inside that sphere, I was going to figure out how to get to her.

The ground we stood upon shook, and the billions of crystals littering the surface shook with it. There were many crystals that I had not seen before, and I had to assume that since they'd never been brought to the surface by the queen before, their power was beyond what Faerie could handle. Guess I was about to test that theory.

"Len!" Shadow called.

My voice boomed as the power filled me. "I have to find her. I will follow her into the sphere, and if she's not there, into the next life. With this power, I can bring her back."

The others shouted and raced toward me, but it was too late. The gems and crystals completely covered me, their power fusing to my essence and turning me into what was, without a doubt, one of the strongest beings in the entire multiverse of worlds.

A god of gods.

A force that could not be stopped.

As the power swelled within me, I rose into the air. The knowledge that I was stepping beyond what I could control was swept away in the strength that coursed through me.

Not just strength, but knowledge.

My new power told me that if I wanted to move between worlds, or even between planes of existence, then I could use the golden sphere. That was the portal... the conduit. This was also the only entity that could handle my current power load, so there was a chance to go after Samantha without destroying my friends and millions of other innocents.

Soaring forward, more crystals swirled around me, connecting to my form, until my skin was completely hidden from sight. Only my eyes remained visible; this sight allowed me to follow my path.

When I touched the golden strand connected to the sphere, power slammed against me, attempting to destroy my form. The crystals protected me, but I wasn't sure for how long.

"Len!" Shadow called after me once more. "Find your mate and return to us. That's a fucking order."

He understood that Samantha was my true mate and she

needed me. There was no existence here without her. I might have survived thousands of years alone, but now that I knew what it felt like to have a soul connection, I could never go back to that loneliness.

Where my mate went, I would also go.

The gold closed around me, burning into my soul, and since this was not the place a physical form should trespass, the pain was beyond anything I'd experienced in my long life.

Except for losing Sam.

There was no pain comparable to that, and I accepted this burn, even as it felt like my skin was being charred from muscles and bones. The light around me grew brighter as my essence finally entered the cord, and I barreled along a tunnel. The golden light was broken in places by dark intersecting beams of what looked like sludge, and it was clear that Faerie's Origin was tainted.

Whatever had happened to the Great Queen continued to impact Faerie, and eventually it would be our destruction. As frustrating as it was, Fredrick severing the line awoke us to the reasons for our weakness.

Not that it would save his life. He'd hurt my mate, and I would destroy him for it.

As soon as I got Samantha back.

And figured out why the Great Queen went to such lengths to ensure her offspring were removed from Faerie, casting a glamour across them and the rest of Faerie, until almost no one remembered her existence.

All because of that tainted power... Which made no sense because she'd condemned us all to die in doing so. The truth was out there, and once I found my mate, nothing in the worlds would stop me from uncovering the rest of the story.

Great Queen be damned.

CHAPTER
FORTY-FIVE

SAMANTHA

After some time drifting in a meditative state, my thoughts returned to Len and Tabitha. In spite of my death, I hadn't distanced myself from them. I never could, even if I were forced into the deathly plane. How could one let go of two fae so fundamental to their being? To their all.

It was fucking unfair.

Why did I have to be sacrificed on the mantle of another world I didn't even remember? Why did the Great Queen choose to have offspring, spell us, and then abandon us into the worlds?

I kind of wished she were here right now so I could yell at her a little.

As if thoughts could become reality here, there was a burst of power, and before me stood a ghostly image, almost like a projection of a person, hovering before me.

At first I thought it was the Great Queen, until I looked closer and realized *it was my reflection.*

"Sammia," the visage said in a voice the same as mine. "You have made it to the World of Creation and the Great Origin. What I most feared has come to pass."

Excuse me, what? "Who the hell is Sammia?"

The visage smiled, and it was creepy to see myself like this. It wasn't really a reflection since there was no reversal of image. This was how everyone else saw me, right down to my long flowing hair, large emerald eyes, and skin that hovered between golden brown and bronze. In the image, I looked strong and sure, filled with the sort of confidence and power I'd never demonstrated in real life.

This version of me had not been abandoned as a child, shuffled between packs, always different and alone. This version of me didn't know the pain I'd experience, and for that, I was a little resentful.

"You are Sammia," she replied. "I am Sammia. We are one and the same, only I'm a memory that has been stored for you to learn when needed."

I was dead, but this conversation was still weirder.

"A memory," I shot back derisively. "Of what?"

"Of your life before."

Simple statement, not so simple meaning.

"What question do I ask to get the most straightforward answer?" I finally said, done with the cryptic bullshit.

"I have only the answers that were left in this memory," the other me said. "And we are running out of time, so let us hurry."

Fine by me. "Okay, so I was Sammia before my memories were taken by the Great Queen?"

I was smart enough to try and assemble the pieces of the puzzle, but the whole was still missing.

An extended pause. "I hated removing our memories," she finally whispered.

The sorrow in her tone almost broke me.

Wait! Seriously...

"*You* hated removing our memories?" I said slowly, as more pieces of the puzzle fell into place. "The queen didn't spell us?"

She drifted closer until I could make out the deeper green flecks in her... our eyes.

"You are the Great Queen," she said.

The words made sense, but my brain rejected it immediately. "No," I snorted, laughter spilling from me. "I mean, come on... the Great Queen is like thousands or more years old. She's the most powerful fae that ever lived. I'm a damn shifter who's not quite three decades old."

You've got the wrong person, sister.

Why was my *other freakier self* messing with me like this? Like, come on.

"I know it doesn't make sense to you yet," the dumber Sam said, "but you don't have all the pieces." It annoyed me that she somehow knew I'd been thinking in puzzle analogies. "There's a reason that we made the decision to hide on Earth, and everything was going along just fine until our mate showed up."

Len's face flashed across my mind. "What did Len have to do with any of this?" I asked.

The ache whenever I thought about him was growing stronger, the longing enough to destroy me if I wasn't already dead.

"He showed up. He finally found us and ruined everything."

"Stop it," I snapped back. Was there anything more ridiculous than arguing with yourself like this? "Len has ruined nothing. He's been a victim in this entire shit show. Thanks to your stupid spell, we both missed out on time with our daughter, with Tabby."

The memory version of me faltered. Shorted out for a beat. "We have no daughter," it said, when it reappeared again. "That does not compute with our memories."

That had me pausing. "You don't know about Tabitha?"

That meant, if her story were true, I'd spelled myself before becoming aware of my pregnancy. Tabitha had not been the catalyst for our memory loss, for the glamour that I'd created.

HOW DID ANY OF THIS MAKE SENSE?

"Explain to me how I'm the Great Queen?" I said, still trying to wrap my brain around it. "I was hiding on Earth the entire time?"

The other me nodded. "Yes, and this is going to be a difficult story for me to tell you, but we must return to the worlds and set the right path in motion once more."

Great, more ominous and cryptic talk.

"We left Faerie to save the worlds. We spelled the fae to forget who we were, since we knew we'd never set foot on our world again. But now that you've returned to Faerie, what I was attempting to stop will have returned in full force. We're lucky that you remembered enough to return to this Origin Sphere, which was the only place safe enough to store the memories."

"I didn't remember," I said drily. "It was just an unfortunate series of events that led me here. A fae cut the Great Queen's line, which almost killed me. We had to venture into the Deep to try and restore it, only for a shadow guardian to drag me down to die. I landed on the golden cord, and it brought me here."

She blinked. "They cut the line? Why?"

"To appoint a new queen," I said. "Faerie has been weakening for years, and they're done with it."

The projected me laughed. "Appoint a queen? Are they

kidding themselves? We were not born, but created from the energy of the Origin. We cannot be replaced, and we cannot truly die."

Great, that wasn't freaky or anything.

She paused as if rerouting the information and deciding how to proceed from here. "Firstly, you need to restore the line between the Deep and Faerie above. That will give you back all of your power and memories. I can't do that from here, but I can explain enough to help you on your way."

Okay, well get the fuck to it.

Was I always this long-winded?

There was a degree of self-hatred hovering within, now that I knew I was the one to blame for everything that had happened. Especially since I still had no idea why I'd made the choices I did.

"We were created as a conduit between this Origin and Faerie," the other me said. "We are, for all intents and purposes, an Origin god." She paused heavily, and I knew those last words would probably mean something to a being *with fucking memories.*

When I didn't comment, other me continued: "There are fifty of us, one for each of the worlds. Some in the Solaris System, and some in other systems."

If a dead mind could be blown, mine would be in pieces. "I'm barely capable of being a basic-ass shifter and now you tell me I'm a god."

What in all the fuckery...?

Other me nodded. "You are, and not just any god. I have used my limited energy to investigate your memories, and I see you are friends with some other godlike creatures. They're what we would refer to as tier two gods, the level below the Origins."

Great, I was going to win Shadow's annual dick-measuring contest. *Perfect.*

"If I'm so powerful, why did I run away and hide on Earth like a little bitch?"

Her expression grew darker, and the energy inside the sphere was colder too. "A very long time ago, one of the Origins lost sight of their place. Dalmia, from the world of Traylor. He wanted the Origin of more than just his world, he wanted the Origin of all the worlds. During one of our annual meetings of power, we tried to reason with him, to stop him from carving out more than his slice of the energy grid." She sighed. "We thought he was listening, only it turned out each of us were deceived. While we were there, Dalmia placed a spell on all Origin gods. A dark energy that we took back with us to our worlds."

She shook her head, as if this hurt, even though she was just a memory.

"Darkness and light exist together. Origin gods are testament to that, but he threw us all off balance."

She paused again, and I was desperate to know what happened next. "The darkness hurt Faerie?" I pushed.

I got a slow nod in return. "It did. It tainted the source of our original power. Our energy. As soon as I saw the darkness seeping into the gold, I hurried back to the Origin. One by one, the other gods also returned, each with the same story. It didn't take us long to figure out that this was Dalmia's darkness seeping into each of our worlds.

"It was a spell, that if completed, would give him total control over every ounce of original energy. He would have no equal, no balance, no blockade against destroying it all."

Each sentence hit me like a blow, and even without memories I could no longer deny the truth of these events. "What happened after that?" I asked her.

I still couldn't quite figure out why I'd left Faerie and rejected our mate. Because clearly this time I'd done the rejecting by sending out a glamour strong enough to erase anything to do with Len and our bond, including our daughter.

"Knowing there was limited time before his spell was complete, we decided the only option was to remove the source. The majority of us left our worlds, since his spell would slow without our energy bulking it up. Once we were gone, the strongest ten gods would hunt Dalmia down."

"They never hunted him down?" I burst out. "We've never been able to return to our world?"

She shook her head. "No, they destroyed him. But it took the combined power of all ten to end his existence. An Origin can be killed by another Origin god if they have enough power behind them. They bonded their energy together and wiped him, *and themselves*, from existence."

I was vibrating, this memory creating a visceral reaction in my body. "Did that kill their worlds?" I whispered.

"Yes." Sorrow creased her face. "Ten worlds sacrificed to save the many. It was a choice we all would have made."

I was not capable of understanding what she was saying. My current brain was young, and we thought like a young being. "I couldn't sacrifice my people."

"Then all would have fallen," she said simply.

True, but what a choice to make. "If Dalmia is dead, why did you never return to Faerie? All of this had to have happened long before the memory spell."

"I was eleventh in the power scale," she said simply. "One being from going after him. Upon their deaths, I became the most powerful Origin god. I ordered everyone to leave their worlds and hide on Earth, the one planet that had no real power grid. Here we hid and waited, until such a day came that Dalmia's tainted energy was destroyed."

It was starting to make sense, all in a super fucked-up way. "Killing him didn't stop the spell?" I said with a shake of my head.

Other me shrugged. Fucking shrugged. "No, it didn't, but it allowed us to halt the spread, providing we stayed away and didn't add our power to the Origin any longer."

She shrugged again, and I had the sense that other me was a real cunt at times. "It might have weakened our worlds, but they still survived."

"Barely," I bit out. "I'm sure there's been a ripple effect from this weakening through all the worlds. I mean, is this the reason the Solaris System has had so many issues lately?" My pack had spent the last few years saving the worlds on a regular basis. "Did your abandonment of the worlds allow new darker energies to emerge? New gods?"

"Yes. The Origin gods not returning to their worlds has led to gaps in their protective shields. It's allowed other gods to step forward in power. Your friends are the prime example of that. It allowed a beast to create new life on Earth and be the catalyst for the strongest pack of supernaturals that we've seen in a long time."

Other me might believe she only had memories, and information that she'd lifted from my mind, but I sensed word was spreading about Shadow and his pack. About our strength. Which created the worry that we'd soon be fending off attacks on the regular, as others sought to test their strength against ours. Not that we couldn't handle it.

But first... I had to figure out how to fix this situation and get back to my family.

Before it was too late.

CHAPTER
FORTY-SIX

SAMANTHA

Other me looked like she was thinking hard thoughts, so I pushed for more information. "How could a being of light and darkness tilt so far into the dark that they'd be willing to destroy worlds and their family?"

"We still don't know why," she said, "but the assumption was that the balance faltered for a moment, which happens at times, but in this instance Dalmia's world was at the end of the sliding scale. And once the darkness took hold, it refused to give up."

"How do we stop it from happening again?"

Other me shook her head. "The Origins are lost now. Most of them have been gone so long, and are so weakened, they could never return to what once was. Proof of this is how your line was cut on Faerie. At our peak of power, it would be impossible to destroy us in that way. Any who tried would explode the second they touched our cord to the Orig—"

She was cut off as a low humming energy washed over us. I was shot back against the wall of the sphere. Power zipped around the space, akin to a thousand dazzling crystals.

It took almost a minute for the kinetic energy to die down, and when it did, a familiar set of silver eyes came into view. The rest of him was covered in crystals, but I'd know my mate anywhere.

"Len!" I gasped.

He headed straight for me, his ghostly energy wrapping around me. Pain welled in my spirit, and I wanted to cry at the knowledge that he must have died to make it here.

Died and followed the golden line too.

He came for me.

"Storm," he breathed, and maybe it was that we were both dead-ish, but I could feel him as solidly as I had when we were alive. The crystals cut against me in hard lines, and I relished in the sensation of feeling.

"Winter," I sobbed back, no tears falling due to a lack of physical body. "What have you done?"

"You're my life," he said simply. "Where you go, I go. No exceptions."

A hysterical laugh escaped me. "You are too fucking good to me, but everything is not as we thought. I'm not the descendent of the Great Queen."

He paused, confusion tinting the small slivers of skin I could see around his eyes.

"She is the Great Queen."

He finally turned to the other me, showing no visible reaction to the fact that I was hardcore twinning. "Explain," he shot back.

"How did you know that version wasn't me?" I asked before she could answer him.

"We're bonded," he said, without removing his shrewd gaze from her. "That's a memory, with slivers of your power but none of your soul."

I sank against him, my body molding to the crystals surrounding him.

"She is a memory," I confirmed. Len's arms wrapped around me, so tightly that if I'd been alive I'd be bleeding over his stone suit. "A memory I sent here, to the origin of magic and worlds, in case I returned to Faerie without my memories."

"Explain," Len bit out once more, and this time there was less patience in his voice. Even in soul form, his power filled the space, swelling in its intensity.

"Young god," she said, "you have elevated in the power vacuum I created within Faerie. It makes sense that you would be chosen as a mate for us. It was my weakening and your burgeoning strength that allowed us to meet. For you to finally find me on your Great Walk. Earth could only hide my energy for so long when one is as strong as you."

Len looked down at me, his eyebrows drawn together, and I nodded. "Yeah, it's a fucking weird story, but I believe what she's saying. I was the Great Queen, an Origin god of Faerie, until I had to walk away to save it."

This got a reaction. *Origin god* meant more to Len than it had to me. "There's a lot of backstory," I continued, "but we don't have time. We have to return to Faerie and attempt once more to save it."

I didn't care what it took, *we* would be returning. They made a mistake in allowing an Origin god to find a true mate, because damn the fucking worlds if I lost him. I was no hero when it came to my family. I'd save my daughter and pack and

Faerie, but the rest of the worlds were on their own. This god thought like a shifter now too.

"We do need to hurry," other me said, even though she was apparently fond of monologuing. "Here's the basic points of it all. I removed myself to Earth to ensure the darkness didn't have the power to keep spreading. All the remaining Origin gods hid on Earth too, and in doing so we created a space in the power balance. That is how new gods were born. It was all working until you found me." Her voice broke. "We were together for two incredible months, and I told myself to walk away every single day, but I couldn't. I'd been alone for so long, having no idea that there was such a perfect love out there. A love only possible due to my weaker state, but weirdly, when I was with you, I felt as strong as ever."

"As if I contained the power you'd lost?" he mused.

The memory paused, before nodding. "Yes, that's a possibility."

Len's voice grew harder. "What happened when I decided to complete the true mate bond, by heading home and calling you to me?"

Her voice shook. "It was the chance I'd been waiting for, so I encouraged you to return, knowing I'd have to do the hardest thing in my long life."

My chest hurt so badly I wondered if I was dying again. Could a soul die multiple times?

"Wouldn't it have been safer to keep your memories at least, so you knew not to return?" I choked out.

"Safer, yes," she said with a sad laugh, "but it turned out I wasn't strong enough to stay away. When the call came for me to return, I was mere seconds from letting myself fade into the abyss to find Faerie. It kept almost happening, and I knew that the only chance I had was to block off my Faerie side."

She waved her ghostly hand between us. "The glamour I

created was designed as a rebirth. We shed our Great Queen energy—and her memories—and turned ourselves into a shifter. A fascinating supernatural race I'd spent a little time with. I figured being with other magical beings would hide whatever quirks the glamour released."

"Two things didn't work though," Len replied gruffly, his super brain putting it together faster than I had. "You couldn't remove the mark I gave her, and you couldn't completely remove the memories of our time together."

She shook her head. "With the power I had, I should have been able to do both, but... maybe I didn't want to remove everything. Maybe I needed to keep some of you. So, I decided it was *easier* to create *a* story to explain away most of the memories Samantha was left with."

"You didn't know I was pregnant," I choked out, as pain and regret rippled through me.

Her face crumpled, and the fact that this "memory" kept exhibiting emotions told me I'd placed more than just memories here. I'd placed a small part of myself. "A child was an impossibility I never considered," other me said. "But clearly that was another quirk of the imbalance we created. Had I known about Tabitha, there's a chance my choices would have been different. Something we'll never know now. What is done is done, and we must repair the worlds to save our daughter."

The absolute fucking insanity of this conversation wasn't lost on me, but when shit like this happened, you had to roll with the punches. At this point I was pretty much a fight champion, taking shots like a boss.

"What do we need to do to come back to life and repair Faerie?" Len asked.

He must have so many questions, having missed much of the first conversation, but in true warrior fashion, was already focused on the most pressing issue at hand: how to save our daughter and the worlds.

Neither of you are dead," she said. "You can't be dead and be here in the Origin. Which means you can use the golden line of power to return to your bodies, stronger than ever." She focused directly on me. "Samantha, you will never be Sammia again. We are gone now, and you are shaped by the life you have experienced since the loss of power. Even if all of your memories return, they'll be fuzzy, as if they happened to someone else."

"Will I be able to truly bond with Len?" I asked, unsure what this meant for us.

A single nod. "Absolutely. If you can figure out how to restore your line and stop the darkness seeping into Faerie, you'll have the chance at something I never did."

She paused briefly, as if composing herself, before she said, "Happiness."

Gods, it was all I'd ever wanted. This elusive "happiness."

I tilted my head to find Len's eyes on me. "Together we'll find peace and happiness," I told him. "I'll accept nothing less."

"Agreed," he rumbled.

Turning back to the memory, I said, "First thing is to restore the Great Queen's line, and then my power and memories will return. After that, I believe the way to destroy the darkness is together as a pack. There's a reason the new gods and the old gods are coming together once more."

"Stronger together," Len agreed. "We will do what the Origin gods could not."

The memory nodded and flickered briefly. "Wait," I called. "How do we return?"

She flickered again. "The same way you got here. Through a rebirth, along the golden line of Faerie."

It was painful to watch her flicker strongly, until she started to fade before my eyes. This was a goodbye to the me who was also not me. As she'd said, I was no longer Sammia, no longer the Great Queen of Faerie.

"Wait, how did you have a shifter mate?" Len asked suddenly when she was almost gone.

Her laughter echoed around us. "We didn't. I created the false bond as part of the spell. I wanted to have a strong mate and blend in with the shifters. But that was never to be. A true mate will always best any magic. Even from an Origin. Now take our world back."

When she was gone for good, I felt lighter and sadder at the same time. The memory version of me had finished her task and was released into the great energy of the Origin.

Gone forever.

"Winter," I said softly, since he was still staring at the spot she'd been. "You okay?"

Despite the crystals covering his face, hiding most of his expression, I saw his lips twitch. "Never been better. Got my girl back, she's an Origin god, and we need to save the worlds again. Just an average day for our pack."

"*Was* an Origin god," I told him. "You heard the memory. One, we're weaker now. Two, I'm no longer Sammia."

His lips definitely twitched before he smiled. "Once you break the final glamour, you'll understand that even weakened you're still one of the most powerful being in the worlds. If anyone says otherwise, we can fry their asses."

A snort of laughter escaped me. "Great, we've already gone mad with power, and we've only had it for three minutes."

He surprised the shit out of me when he leaned forward and pressed his lips to mine. There was a rough texture of crystals, and while I couldn't taste him, I could feel the slide of our mouths together, and the surge of our energy that followed. "I lost you," he whispered against my mouth. "*Again.* I almost brought Faerie down in my rage, *again,* but thankfully I was reminded that we don't die easily. The hope that you were waiting for me somewhere kept me moving forward, and saved the damn worlds."

"I'd end the worlds for you too," I told him, having already figured out who I was now. "And since I might eventually have the power to do just that, we better hope nothing ever happens to you or Tabby." Or our other friends.

Speaking of, it was time to figure out how to leave our little bubble of *almost dead* and head back into the real world.

We had some shit to deal with.

CHAPTER FORTY-SEVEN

SAMANTHA

"It should be easier to return," Len said as we moved toward the edge of the sphere. "Since we're not technically dead, our souls will want to find their vessels."

"Mine is at the bottom of a coal pit," I said with a grimace. "And I don't have my powers unlocked yet to bust out of there."

Len rubbed a hand over his crystal covered hair. "Even worse, the surface hardened the moment you went under. Not even the full force of my power could break it."

I hadn't known that. There'd been other things on my mind as I fought a shadowy beast dragging me into the depths.

"The Faerie line was at the bottom," I said. "Fate wanted me to land down there so I would find my memories. I don't think anything could have stopped it."

Len was nodding. "I believe you're right, and I also believe that your body will have been freed the moment that task was complete. But if not, I'll find you, I promise."

"I know you will," I replied. "Even better, we'll find each other."

Another of those weird but perfect kisses, and then we pushed our souls from the sphere back to the fire planet. Len took a moment to examine the massive outer structure of the Origin, eyes wide as he shook his head. "I never thought I'd see a source of creation. Look at the worlds."

That was what all the images were. The worlds. And the other lines were connected to other worlds, all of which were missing their Origin gods, just as Faerie had been.

It was nearly impossible to believe, but after everything I'd learned being here, there was no other explanation.

We left after that, willing our essence along the golden line, and just as Len said, it was almost effortless. We were heading home.

The line grew brighter and brighter as we moved along it, and then when it was completely blinding, everything started to burn. When the pain was too much, a whimpering scream escaped me, and Len let out some curses, so I knew he was feeling it too.

I must have blacked out at some point during the somewhat painful rebirth, and when I came to I was not at the bottom of a coal quicksand pit, or naked as I'd been after my shift. Clothes had formed around me, black pants and a shirt, and I was hovering in the air beside a similar but much smaller sphere to the one on the fire world. This one was completely golden though, and I knew this was Faerie's Origin of power.

My sphere.

Before I could think it through, I reached out and grasped the beaming golden cord at the top of the sphere, and through it I reconnected myself to Faerie. My severed line was restored, and the glamour fell away, like I was shedding clothes instead of power.

The darkness I'd been keeping at bay was gone. In its place: a shimmering power that connected right to Faerie. I could feel the world. The ebbs and flow of its energy. Energy I could tap into if needed.

"Holy gods," I cried, my skin glowing so golden it was almost blinding.

Along with the cord to Faerie, I could also feel my mate as if he was right at my side, even though he was standing on a crystal-covered ground with our pack, skin illuminated like those crystals he'd worn in the fire world were now embedded in the surface.

Energy expanded between us. *Mate.*

He heard me, and I felt his amusement. *Someone found her power.*

The power and memories had returned. Now I truly understood how painful my decision had been to cast the glamour. It had almost destroyed me at the time.

Thankfully, that memory was fuzzy, just as Sammia had advised.

"Yo!" The shout had my gaze returning to the crowd gathered below. Mera was the one who'd called out. "Anyone going to explain what the hell is happening?" she said, hand on her hips. "And why my sister is shedding light like a glowstick?"

As I decided to move closer, my newly released power kicked into gear, and I vanished to reappear right in the midst of them. *Whoa, that was going to take some getting used to.*

None of them jumped, but I didn't miss Shadow angling himself in front of Mera. He wasn't the only one, with the other males edging in front of their mates.

All the while, Len just smiled with this stupidly proud

smile, and I felt like I was a fucking goddess for real under his gaze.

"She's not dangerous," he told them as he moved closer and wrapped his arms around me. His skin was smooth and silvery-gold once more, but there was definitely a glow of crystal on the surface. Neither of us had returned from the Great Origin unchanged, and it was exciting to know that we were moving up in the power scale.

Len lifted me against his body, hands under my ass as he held me like I was still Samantha, a mere shifter from Clarity. "It's a long story, but she's an Origin god, and we need to help her save Faerie."

His lips crashed into mine, a kiss that we'd almost died and come back to experience. This time, our mate bond was strong and thrumming between us, a mix of gold and silver, shimmering in our energy. I could also taste him, that minty freshness, with the hint of sweet that was all Len.

This fae prince was the savior I never saw coming, bringing me out of my dark and lonely existence, and gifting me the most precious little girl. All we had to do now was ensure that Dalmia's spell was destroyed so we had a chance for true happiness.

Our kiss lasted longer than we probably had time for, but what could I do—my mate was sexy as fuck.

A throat cleared nearby. "Did you all say that we needed to save the world?" Reece sounded both amused and exasperated.

"Not that we don't understand," Angel added. "The almost dying and rebirth thing definitely takes a toll, and mates need a moment to embrace their second chance, but first things first..."

"Should we smite them all?" Len whispered against my lips, mostly joking I was sure.

"If she's an Origin god, she should have no trouble with that," Angel replied, amused rather than defensive.

We will need an explanation of the how and whys soon, Galleli started in my head, and I didn't even flinch this time. Go me and my rebirth. *But for now the darkness is spreading. We must cut it off before it takes over the main source of energy here.*

He was right, and with that Len lowered me back to the ground and I took a second to examine this part of the Deep. It was a vast flat space, covered in millions of crystals, the power of them all quite breathtaking. In the center was a drop-off, where the Origin of Faerie hovered, golden and spherical.

As I stepped closer, I could clearly see the dark tendrils winding through the golden energy.

"Before my rebirth, I was Sammia," I said, still moving closer to the sphere. "An Origin god created through Faerie's energy. Another Origin god spelled us all so we would take this dark entity back to the source. He was defeated, but the spell remained, and since we had no clue how to destroy it, we only managed to slow its assault by leaving our worlds, effectively weakening them and the spell."

The others were spread out around me now, and no one said a word, clearly not wanting to interrupt the story. "Now that I've returned and reconnected to the source of energy, the boost is going to spread this darkness like it's on steroids."

"Did you learn how to stop it?" Simone asked. "When you went... wherever you went?"

I shook my head. "No, we went to the Great Origin. The hub for all the worlds of the Origin gods. But it was only so I could find the memory I'd planted there before I recreated myself as Samantha."

I felt their confusion, but no judgment at all. Most of them had been reborn in the last couple of years, so they understood in a way no other could. Not even other Origin gods.

"Samantha has something Sammia did not," Len said as he

stepped in behind me, wrapping his arms around my waist, pulling me back into his strength.

"Us," Mera chimed in. "We're the strongest pack you could hope for, and with that in mind, maybe we need to, like, *Captain Planet* this shit."

Now it was her turn for everyone to stare at her. "Who is Captain Planet?" Shadow asked. "And should I kill him for knowing my mate?"

Mera burst into laughter. "The fact that I find your possessive alpha bullshit sexy as fuck probably says more about my mental state than yours. It's an old human cartoon that I used to like. They would join all their powers together to form the strongest entity. Their strength was in their group and friendship. I believe it's the same for us."

"I believe that too," I said suddenly. "This group exists because the Origin gods departed from their worlds and left a power vacuum for you all to grow in. You filled the balance by becoming the new gods." I shrugged. "Apparently I'm the strongest of the Origins left, so it makes sense that I'm part of this story too."

"It makes all the sense," Mera agreed, shaking her head. "Fuck, it's like a giant puzzle we didn't know we were building, but I can see the final product now. It's kind of flawless."

It was. More than kind of.

"Okay, so, how do we join our powers?" Lucien asked.

The knowledge of how appeared in my mind, as if it had been buried there all along. "I can do it," I told them. "I can connect us all to the Faerie Origin, and from there we'll be able to act as one. But we will need to move quickly, or the darkness could affect us all."

A final warning, not that most of them needed it.

I had no idea if this would work, but it was really the best and only option. Maybe if the Origin gods had joined our powers together instead of splitting our energy and moving off our worlds, we'd have been able to best Dalmia when he cast the spell. We screwed up in thinking we were all working alone, and by leaving we only weakened ourselves and our worlds anyway.

At least that choice had paved the path for the new gods, and since they were already learning from our mistakes, I had a feeling they'd do what the Origins couldn't.

Save the worlds.

With reluctance, I stepped away from Len, and my body lifted into the air so I could touch the golden strand at the top of the sphere. From deep in my essence, I released eight similar but smaller golden strands, which burst out of my chest, hovering in front of me like snakes mid attack. I then sent those strands scooting away, ensuring each one reached the chest of my pack members, connecting us in an instant.

The moment we joined, I felt all of their unique and individual strengths.

Mera was bright, her energy strong and burning, like a new flame being constantly fueled through the power of her mate bond. She was fire that drew you in, warm and giving, but get too close and you'd be burned.

Then there was Shadow, her mate.

He burned as well, but an older, deeper, and more intense flame. There wasn't much that could change that flame, but it also wasn't one many could get close to. It warned you to stay away—warned with its depth and the deep flare of strength. There were also intermingling threads of darkness through the deep red of his fire.

The only light in this beast came from the bond he had with his Sunshine.

Next was Angel, and her energy was like a spring day, the most perfect and pure moment of creation. Strong, clear, and without any shadows, Angel didn't burn, but she was almost too perfect to get too close to. As if she were the literal embodiment of the human lore of angels and God. Her mate's energy felt ancient. Reece had the original sands of time drifting through his veins, and I was sure he could create and destroy the land. Very natural, very earthy, powerful like nature itself.

Lucien had a newer energy, but no less strong. Blood power filled his veins, and blood was life. It made sense that he would be drawn to this group. He was a powerful master, and as he grew older there'd be very few who could stand against his compulsion, or his speed and strength in attack. His mate, Simone, was animalistic in her energy, but so much more than a regular shifter. Like me, she was a unique mix of two energies: shifter and vampire. She could walk in multiple worlds, and while her power was young, she showed signs of being the strongest of all beasts—one day.

Galleli's energy was cagey, the only being not to completely open himself up to me, but there wasn't a way to truly hide when we were connected like this. Galleli, the mysterious one, was a veritable well of power, but he kept it all locked down, hidden away, as if he were afraid of what might happen if he opened himself up and became who he was always meant to be. I wanted to assure him that this world was ready for him now. If anyone knew, it was the being who'd been hiding for thousands of years herself.

"Holy fuck."

The low groan from Reece pulled my attention before I could examine Len, but I already knew every part of my mate's energy. From his silvery, light power, to the force of nature that was a budding beat of his heart, he could give Father Nature a run for his money when it came to pure and earthy creation. There were threads of gold in his silver, which was how he'd been able to find me in the Great Origin. It was our bond, the one that not even Sammia's powerful glamour could annihilate completely.

For which I was very grateful.

"She's so powerful," Simone said in response to Reece.

"I am," I said, finally owning it. "As are all of you. Our powers have been learning each other, and now that we're connected in this way, I can assure you... each of you are a special piece of the puzzle. We are parts of a whole, and I know exactly how to repair the darkness."

Individually we never could have fixed this, but together we had everything we needed.

Time to get cleaning.

CHAPTER FORTY-EIGHT

SAMANTHA

The darkness pulsed with new life, feeding off the energy we'd brought to Faerie's Origin. We really had to hurry. Each second allowed it to tangle further into the whole. Soon it would be nearly impossible to unravel the complex web it was weaving.

Thankfully, I had no doubt we were powerful enough to do what was necessary.

"We made a mistake," I told the others. "The Origin gods chose to run instead of fight. Our unity would have defeated Dalmia. Not just killed his vessel and sent his power back into creation, but also destroyed these dark spells he'd left across the worlds. This is the last of his legacy, which has lived on for far too long."

Shadow stepped forward, the golden beam between us shortening as he moved closer to where I hovered. "I finally understand..." he said, his voice deeper as I drew more of his power to the surface, his beast hovering as a flaming image above his head. "...why this pack has been forming."

"I do as well," Mera said suddenly. "This is the reason all of us have been drawn together, over and over, with so many complicated bonds emerging between us. If we are, as Sam says, the newer gods stepping into the power void left by the old, it makes sense that we'd ensure the mistakes of the past weren't repeated."

Shadow's chest rumbled as he nodded, and I felt ripples of his intense power along the cord. "Exactly," he said, "we're not like the Origins. They were solitary, living in their worlds, and only venturing forth for their meetings. The Fates have decided that it will be different this time around. With that in mind, we need to test the theory and cleanse the darkness."

He was right, and we had reached the limit of time. If everything went to plan, then we'd have the rest of eternity to discuss the deeper meaning for all our existences. Delve into the reasons that Shadow was the beating heart at the center, his Solaris System and shifters drawing so many of us. But for now, we had darkness to destroy.

Reaching out to touch the main cord of the Origin once more, a massive surge of power filled the well in my center. It overflowed nearly immediately, and had I not had other wells to feed it into—aka, all my powerful pack mates—there was a chance that I'd have had to release my hold, unable to handle the power. Check another point for this being a group project.

"Well, fuck," I heard Lucien groan and laugh. "Now I know what it feels like to be Shadow. No wonder he's an arrogant asshole."

Shadow snorted, even as the flames around him grew higher. I had a good view of them all from my vantage point, and their energy was brighter and stronger than I'd ever seen.

"You couldn't handle one minute in my fur," he rumbled at his friend, his tone lighthearted. "This is but a fraction of my power."

He was full of shit, because this was way beyond any of our powers. Even mine.

"Len," I called, my voice deeper, "I need your help."

It was his light that would guide me through the darkness— the reason a being like me, who was essentially a vessel and not designed for mateship and motherhood, would have been reborn and evolved to need both.

He was my light. *My all.*

Len rose into the air, and it wasn't from me, so he'd figured out a way to use this new burst of energy. The dark tendrils surged suddenly and I urged him to hurry. "I'm going to try and gather all of Dalmia's spell into a ball," I said in a rush. "Len's light will allow me to see the intricate strands, and when I have it all as one, we'll use our combined strength to blast it into oblivion."

Their agreement traveled through our connections, and I focused completely on the task.

Delving deep into the core of where the dark spell had started, I felt Dalmia's oily presence so strongly. Part of him was dead, but a much worse part lived on in the power of my world.

"Mine," I snarled, as the oil tried to creep over me. "Faerie is mine, and this pack is mine."

"Mine," Shadow countered, but didn't fight me any other way.

"Ours," I continued, amusement warring with my determination to destroy the darkness.

Len wrapped a hand around mine, and his light burned so brightly that it had the dark tendrils bunching together to avoid it.

Whatever you need, Storm. His voice was in all our minds since we'd formed nine parts of a whole. *You're never fighting alone.*

The light soared, and so did my power, burning through the darkness. For a moment I thought we'd won, as the strands retreated, curling up into a ball, releasing their hold on the essence of Faerie. Only, I'd underestimated how oily this spell truly was, so insidious, designed to infiltrate with nothing more than a drop. You couldn't miss a single spot or it would return and spread even faster.

No matter how many times we gathered it together, a spot always managed to avoid the light, and it would be back to square one.

Understanding what needed to happen now, I called on the others, tugging on their energy until they all rose into the air with no need for wings. The nine of us encircled the Faerie Origin. "We have to use all of our skill and strength," I said, eyes burning from how bright the cords connecting us and Faerie were. "Shadow and Mera need their fire. Reece and Angel will cleanse with their sand. Galleli's light will join with Len's to chase the final drops. And Simone and Lucien's new blood should help renew the power left behind, so it's strong enough to repair the damage."

I would be the conduit bringing it all together.

No one argued with their assignment, each understanding and recognizing their various strengths, and how they would come together to form a stronger and more resilient being. I hoped it would be enough.

Despite having gathered the darkness into a bundle a moment ago, it was already back, pulsing and infiltrating the golden energy. We got straight to work, Len and Galleli's light blinding in its intensity, and I was easily able to unravel the strands. With double the energy and power, I could move through the darkness faster.

At each section we cleared, Shadow and Mera burned through strands of darkness, after which Angel and Reece sent their sands out, scouring the charred flesh, but before we could make it to Simone and Lucien's new blood, the magic in Faerie pulsed.

Pulsed and then let out a shriek, almost like it was in pain.

"Stop!" I shouted, drawing all of the power back as I examined the area we'd been working in.

The power there was fading as it rejected our form of help, the strand starting to brown.

"It's dying," I cried, my throat thick with emotion as I observed the damage. "What did we do wrong? Was it too much power?"

But without all the power, the spell continued to evade me.

"We're missing a step," Len said hoarsely. "What are we missing?"

Missing.

We were missing...

The cords I'd sent into my friends came from inside of me, and as I searched through those strands I noticed that there were some unused. Some I hadn't thought anything of, too focused on the eight I needed.

"There's three cords of power within me that are not connected," I whispered. *Holy fuck.* "We're missing three pieces of our puzzle." Three pieces vital to completing this task.

Len grasped my hands firmly, pulling me into his arms, his warmth wrapping around me along with our bond of power.

"Do you know who they belong to?" he asked me.

"No," I replied immediately. "Clearly they're members of this pack we haven't met."

Shadow soared a little closer. "You don't have to have met

them," he said suddenly. "Time and distance will not shape this power grid. You just need to send the cords out. They will find their connection."

"We can boost you," Len added. "Connected like this, it's easy to feel the energy and know where to send it."

Pulling back to see his face, I marveled at the streaks of purple in his irises now, as if some of the reven gems which had dusted his skin also filled his eyes. Like our little girl.

Our little girl we had to save, no matter the cost.

"I just send the cords out into the universes?" I confirmed one last time.

"Yes," Shadow and Len said.

"We're clearly twelve parts of a whole," Angel added. "Twelve is the complete circle of our power. Without it, we won't succeed here today."

We had to succeed. This was our last shot before Dalmia's spell was too strong to ever destroy. Faerie would be lost, and that could have a serious ripple effect to the rest of the worlds.

Trusting in my pack, I closed my eyes and let their powers fill up my well. When our essences were sufficiently mingled, I drew on as much Faerie magic as I could, needing the boost to send those three unmatched strands out into the world.

At first I attempted to direct them, but it soon became clear that they knew what they were doing. They understood the assignment and went off in three different directions.

No, wait. Two directions.

"Earth," Shadow said softly. "Two are on Earth."

There wasn't a lot of information coming from the connection, but the other beings felt familiar. As if I'd known them. Or maybe Mera had known them.

Either way, these two were part of our connection, the cords locking on to them, no doubt confusing the fuck out of them.

"Where's the third?" Reece rumbled, the air growing thicker and dustier around us as his power soared. "It's moving between the worlds."

It was Angel who put it together first. "Alistair," she said with a mournful sob. "He's part of our family. Our pack. We should have known he'd be one of the bonds."

Panic flooded my veins, bitter and coppery in my mouth. "It's his water," I said with a shake of my head. "His water is the life needed to cool the fire and burn of our other powers."

Alistair was the key to keeping the magic alive after it was cleansed.

A key who was no longer in this world.

CHAPTER FORTY-NINE

SAMANTHA

The dark, panic-filled cloud that was threatening to pull me down faded when Len brushed his hand across my face. His lighter energy could wash away dark thoughts with ease. "You can reach him," he told me, always so confident in my abilities. "You're an Origin god, designed to walk through realms and planes of existence. You can step into the afterlife."

Our eyes locked, and I wished that we were alone and without worries so I could lose myself in him for a few hours. Or days. Years and lifetimes.

"We *will* have lifetimes," he whispered close to my lips. "We just have to do this one little thing first."

When the brush of his mouth ignited a million fires inside my veins, I let out a soft sigh. "You're right. I can do this." I *had* to do this.

The final cord was far from us now, but it would never penetrate the veil between worlds without an extra boost. There was only one boost I could think of: Origin power.

This power was the reason I could travel between realms.

Drawing from deeper in the golden cord, I managed to take without hitting any of the dark spell, knowing the last thing I wanted was to spread that taint between worlds.

I got what I needed, thankfully, and as soon as I sent a potent shot of that power along the last cord, it pierced through the veil of the living and landed on the other side.

I gasped at how warm it felt there, how calm, how perfect.

With no extra effort, that cord found the spirit of their brother, and as the cool flow of his energy finished our twelve, the others grew quiet.

Sorrow hummed in the air around us; they lowered their heads, one by one. A moment for their fallen family. My heart hurt for them, but we had no more time to waste.

As they mourned, I drew all the power into me once more. The eleven other cords, along with my connection to the Origin, hummed to life.

"We will proceed the same as before," I called, voice booming into the abyss, "except this time water will cool the strands after fire and earth, and it will allow the blood to rejuvenate."

And the light, Galleli added in our minds. *Len's light is for you, but ours is for life. We need to help restore what will be lost.*

He said *ours* as if he knew that one of the other strands out there was connected to him. Another light bringer.

"You are right," I said quickly. "Let's get it done."

Exactly as we did before, Len and I found the strands, and the fire and sand burned through the darkness. Only this time, the water and life-light from the others ensured that when we were done, the Faerie magic was whole and glowing.

The spell was thicker already, and took us more time, but we were also stronger in the complete bond of twelve. Once we found our groove, we were able to untangle the darkness. Piece by piece. Strand by strand. It took almost all our energy, and by the time we were done, not a single iota of Dalmia's spell or power was left in the brilliant gold of Faerie's original magic.

Exhausted, we drifted down to the gem-strewn land and collapsed. As I fell, I knew it was time to release the cords, though it hurt to know I'd be letting Alistair go. He might not have been someone I knew or loved, but he was part of our pack. A brother to my mate.

For them, I felt broken.

"His energy is happy and content," Shadow rumbled, picking up on my thoughts through our connection. "We must release him into the afterlife until such a time he chooses to leave it. He is not ready yet."

It was a truth we could all feel. There was lightness in the cool spray of his water magic. I sensed that he wasn't quite done with the mortal realm yet, but for now he didn't want to give up his afterlife.

Len held my hand as I released the eleven cords, the shiny strands fading back into my chest, waiting for the moment they'd be called again. The nine of us continued to rest against the gems, a sense of mourning among the group. Len pulled me closer so that I was completely wrapped in his arms. "I love you," he whispered, burying his face in my neck, breathing me in deeply, his lips brushing my skin.

The love I had for him was as strong as my connection to Faerie. Powerful and golden.

"I love you too."

We snuggled together, letting our bodies heal, and our powers renew. Luckily, we were all on beds of literal energy, even if they were rather uncomfortable.

When we eventually made it to our feet, Mera looked around. "So, what do we do now?" she asked. "Did we save the worlds again?"

"Faerie has been saved and restored," I told her, feeling the clean and steady beat of energy from the Origin.

"The other worlds weren't as lucky," Shadow said, staring out into the golden globe of Faerie. "Do you think we need to deal with the dark energy in them as well?"

"I don't think so." I shook my head. "Not unless their gods return and set the spell in motion once more. I guess we just keep an ear out for word of that."

Those worlds might be weaker, but they were still functioning. Their new normal didn't really have space for the old ways, not any longer. The fact I was *Samantha* now stood testament to that.

"We can let the worlds rest for now," Len said, backing me completely. "They've existed with the darkness and weakness for centuries already. The compensation to fill the power void has begun. We might be doing more harm than good by stepping in and fixing what we haven't been asked to fix. From what I can see, none of the other worlds have encountered a dumbass local who cuts their main cord of power and thinks he can just take it over."

A snort escaped from me. "If I'd been a normal shifter and royal it would have worked," I said. "It would have killed me instantly, no matter what you did to try and stop it. But thankfully I'm a god, and even weakened, I could hold on when needed. Which is going to really come back to bite Fredrick on the ass."

Might even shift into my beast form and literally give that a go.

The illumination under Len's skin grew stronger, a sign of his new power, and our bond hummed strongly. "We will ferret out everyone involved," he said in that low, scary tone. "Ferret and destroy. They hurt my mate, and for that there's no punishment strong enough."

All the mushy feelings inside me soared up, and he released some of that fury to turn and capture my face, leaning in to press his lips to mine. "No one will ever take you from me again. I don't care who must die to warn the others. It's all a sacrifice I'm willing to make." He kissed me again. "You and Tabitha are my home. Not Faerie or any other world. You."

Tabitha, our precious perfect miracle. "I've been lost for so long," I said, dropping my head against his chest as emotions overwhelmed me. "Lost without memory, identity, or purpose. You gave me everything back, and I'm so fucking grateful for you." I lifted my head to be captured by blazing grey-purple eyes. "Thank you. Thank you for being my home too."

The small sigh of happiness burst up from my chest.

"Such a great ending," Mera clapped. "Now, let's get our kids."

"Fuck yes," Reece whooped. "Damon's probably a foot taller by now."

No kidding. Our exceptional children made a lot of sense now that we had all the pieces to the puzzle. The babies of gods. And just like with our pack, we'd only just began to see what they were capable of.

CHAPTER FIFTY

SAMANTHA

"Mama!"

The voice, small but so clear, had me sprinting across the Silver Lands' courtyard.

As predicted, Tabitha looked older, sitting in Queen Glendriel's arms, waving as she called my name. Her skin was darker, bronze and glowing, with light curls falling around her face to rest above her shoulders. She looked happy and full of life, her eyes so purple they were piercing.

"Baby," I cried, wrapping my hands around her to gently lift her from the queen. "You got bigger."

She looked almost a year old now, and when she snuggled into me she felt solid and healthy, nothing like the frail child we'd grabbed in Clarity mere days ago.

"Mama," she said again, seemingly proud of herself. "Papa."

His power hit a moment before he wrapped arms around us both. "I'm here, little one," he said, voice rumblier. Tabitha let out a happy chuckle, before she settled into the family hug.

Shadow and the others had already left Faerie for the library. They'd offered to return and help us deal with Fredrick and any others involved, but Len assured them that we would be more than fine. None of them argued, having felt our power, and instead we were told that we'd be at dinner in the next day or so. Non-negotiable.

"Family dinners are a must," Mera said as she pressed a kiss to my cheek. She then dragged her mate away in a rush to get back to Aurora. She was an amazing friend and mom, and I was blessed to have this pack. The others had hugged us and left too, and it was nice to know we'd see them all again soon. The new connection had added another level to our bond.

Len and I spent the next few hours existing with Tabitha, letting the rest of the world and our worries fade from mind. With the glamour removed, we learned that her energy was felt by all, and it held strong princess-of-the-Silver Lands essence, just as we'd always felt.

After giving us privacy and time to connect, Queen Glendriel reappeared with food and drinks, preparing for us to eat family style. She used her own energy to arrange the plates on a small table, and then gestured for us to join her.

A silver fae dropped off a white chair that looked like a huge marshmallow, and Len showed me how to sit Tabitha in it, safe and protected as all that padding rose around her sides and held her in place. Not that it would be too long before she was sitting in a regular chair.

"Tell me everything," Glendriel said when we were all seated.

It was just the four of us, cozy and comforting. A first for me. Even with the glamour broken and my fuzzy memories returned, there were none that included a family moment like this. The closest were the meetings with the Origin gods, and that had been more about business, not love.

Len changed everything.

"Samantha is my true mate," he said, pride in his voice. That tone stirred up my energy, and I barely managed to not wiggle against the ache low in my body. "She's also the Great Que—"

Glendriel gasped so loudly she cut him off. "Yes, I remember her now," she choked out, before turning to me. "You look a little different, but... why couldn't we remember you before?"

Len and I both took turns explaining the somewhat complicated series of events that led to me being here today and the multiple glamours I'd used to leave Faerie. First when the spell was set by Dalmia, and the second time with Len. As we talked, we ate and drank, my energy growing with each bite of Faerie food. I might not need food now my connection to the Origin was restored, but the shifter side of me would be lost without it.

Tabitha appeared to feel the same, sampling everything put in front of her as she happily babbled and spoke, each of us acknowledging her throughout the conversation.

When our bellies were full, the story told in its entirety, right up until we destroyed the darkness, Queen Glendriel sank back in her chair, a contemplative look on her face.

"I'm ancient," she finally said. "I've lived through wars, the death of my mate, all the while watching my son struggle to find his place in this world..."

Reaching out, I grasped Len's hand, our fingers linking together so seamlessly it was as if we'd been doing this for years, rather than days.

"It all makes sense now," she said with a smile. "The struggles and the darkness existed so you'd know how to recognize the light when it showed up."

The light she spoke of was all but spilling from Len and me, our bond so new and bursting with energy that it occasionally escaped our hold. Tabitha kept running her hands along Len's arm, giggling at the play of the gem-infused light in his body.

"I'm stronger and surer than I've ever been," Len said, his eyes briefly devouring me before he returned his gaze to his mother. "And I'm ready to use this energy to clean up the last of the mess in Faerie. New royals will emerge before I am done. Two lands need their dead wood pruned."

That was my mate, always a gardener.

"Wait for me to call everyone together," Glendriel said, pushing herself to stand. "We need to make this official, with witnesses so that their line doesn't suffer for the actions of their leader."

The innocents had to be spared, but the rest... they would know our wrath.

"Tell them they have twelve hours," Len said shortly, his eyes darker grey. "They tried to destroy my mate, broke the rules of Faerie, and almost released an ancient spell on the world. There's no escaping this punishment."

Queen Glendriel didn't argue with him, merely crossing around the table, her silver robes trailing behind her as she moved gracefully. When she reached Len, she touched him gently on the cheek. "You shall avenge your mate," she promised, and I recognized the fae ritual of what they were doing here. A mother sending her warrior off to battle.

To my surprise, when she was finished she did the exact same to me. "I'm honored to have such a strong, capable, and powerful female as my new daughter," she told me, brushing her energy across my face, leaving a trail of burning power that faded after a few seconds. "We will build from this, and the Silver Lands and Faerie will be stronger than ever. A superpower once more."

It was inevitable now that the dark spell of Dalmia was destroyed. Only time would tell if the other worlds would need the same protection. As scary as it was to have a child in an unstable set of worlds, it was reassuring to know that she'd been born into the strongest family possible. The next generation, judging on what I'd seen so far, would surpass us ten to one.

The queen left us then, and for a quiet moment the three of us existed in a bubble of contentment. It was hard to believe I'd died, been reborn, discovered all the truths, and saved the worlds since I saw Tabitha last, but being here with Len and her made all the rest worthwhile.

When our daughter yawned, so big it took over half her face, we finally got to our feet and left the cozy tranquility of the courtyard. Shifters had restless animalistic energy and rarely sat without trying to do ten other things at the same time. Fae were not like that. Their longevity had them stopping to smell the roses, or whatever exotic plants Len created, and I enjoyed that just as much as the bustle of a shifter world.

"Let's get this little one to bed," Len said, lifting Tabitha from her marshmallow chair. "We all need to rest, and when we wake, Mother will have the meeting called."

"Rest sounds amazing," I said softly, falling in beside him, my heart fluttering happily as his free arm wrapped around me. He held us both close, and we moved together as if we'd been doing this for years.

"Yes, it does," he replied. My heart fluttered again, harder this time, and Len's chest rumbled as he leaned over and pressed his lips to mine as if he couldn't help himself.

"Here's hoping our baby girl sleeps through the night," he growled as he pulled away, very shifter like.

"Or at least for a few hours," I replied breathlessly.

Len's smile was feral. "A few hours... ah, little Storm. That's a decent start, but I'm going to need much longer than that."

Did my pussy flutter? Yep, that greedy bitch was about to take flight she was so excited. As Sammia, I never had sexual desire, but this new version of me wanted everything. Every part of Len, and our new matebond.

My pace picked up, and a laugh burst from him as I dragged them across the bridge toward home. "Come on, buddy," I joked, "you're only a few thousand years old. Can't you move a little faster."

I let out a low shriek when his chest rumbled and hauled me over his shoulder, Tabitha secure in his other arm. He moved at super speed then, and I spent the time running my hands down his back, digging my nails into hard muscles as I traced the contours of his shoulders.

"Sam," he said warningly. The heat pouring off him told me he was more than affected by this little prelude to our night tonight.

First though, we had to get Tabitha, who was yawning again, off to bed for a decent few hours' sleep. The truth was, even if she didn't sleep tonight, we would be happy to spend the time with her. Len and I had an eternity together for nights like this, and that meant, that when she needed it, Tabby had all our attention.

One day she would leave the nest and find her own destiny.

A bittersweet truth, but at least there was a future to plan for now.

A proper second chance.

Home and happiness.

CHAPTER FIFTY-ONE

SAMANTHA

The house was lit up, as if it waited to welcome us home.

"You are my home," Len said, keeping me firmly over his shoulder.

Jerking my head toward him, I blinked. "You read my thoughts?"

We were connected as true mates, but without the direct link we'd had earlier, his mind was closed off to mine.

"No, not directly," he said, "but I can sense some of your stronger emotions. When we entered the house, your energy grew soft and warm."

He was smart and observant. The first to ever truly pay attention to me. Before Len, I'd been an Origin god—a tool to be used and forgotten when not needed.

"And now your energy is sadder and cold," Len said softly,

pausing in the entrance as he dropped me back to my feet so we could face each other. "What are you thinking? I don't want to guess at this, I want to fix it."

Warmth returned to me as my lips tilted up. "Origin gods were always on the outside looking in. We didn't get the mate or the family or the pack-like connection that most others crave. We were tools, created and designed to keep the worlds turning and powered. My memories of that time are clouded now, so I feel some distance, but it's painful to truly understand the difference now."

I shook my head to dispel the memories. "I really didn't comprehend it until Tabitha and you came into my life. Funny to be so grateful to Dalmia, since he almost destroyed our world, but I kind of am." His actions had changed everything, including the power balance in the worlds, which allowed me to weaken enough to find a mate and have a child.

"Baby, I need you to look at me." The command in Len's voice had my head jerking up, my gaze locking on his. "You will never be alone again," he said. "Not for one second from this moment on. If the magic allows, we will have a dozen babies, travel every world with them, and I will love you and our babies through each and every moment. My life began the day we met."

"Yay!" Tabitha yelled suddenly, breaking the spell he had me locked in. "Love. Together."

Her words were clearer each time, and as she hugged her daddy closer, my heart swelled painfully. "A dozen babies," I rasped, filled with so much light. "I'm ready to practice."

The purple in his gaze pierced into my horny soul.

Yep, the vagina had spoken. She was ready.

Len grabbed my hand and all but swept me upstairs, leading us down the hall. "Where will Tabitha sleep?" I asked, needing her close but also hoping we'd have some privacy while she slept.

"My room," Len said when we reached the largest door at the end. "There's a small nook inside that will be perfect until she's old enough for her own room and space."

The relief to know I could have both made my knees a little weak. "That sounds amazing."

Inside, his room was done in neutral colors of white and silver, with a massive bed in the center. It was dressed in dark bedding, a storm in the middle of a cloud land. It reminded me of his eyes when they darkened, amidst the silver of his being. Off to the right was a small sitting area with what looked like a bar lining the wall behind. Crystal bottles and decanters filled silver shelves, all set up for a nightcap.

"There's a bathroom in here too," he told me. "You have everything you need."

"Oh, am I sleeping in here?" I laughed. "I thought I'd still have my own room."

His eyes darkened to match his bedding, though he also looked amused. "You sleep with me, Storm. No exceptions."

He didn't have to worry. I wanted to be by his side and in his bed. "No more time wasted," I agreed.

He relaxed and gestured for me to follow him. "The nook has no furniture, but I can conjure up a mattress for her, and tomorrow we'll find the rest."

The nook turned out to be a small room, as he led me toward a door. "I never imagined designing a room for my daughter," I said with a happy sigh. "Thank you."

Len shook his head as he reached for the door and pushed it open. "Thank you, Sam. You've given me everything."

We stepped inside then, and I ground to a halt, blinking at what I saw.

"What the hell?" he rumbled, and it was odd to see him taken by surprise.

Tabitha waved her hands at the beautiful room, furnished within an inch of its life. "Gran-mama," she cooed, wiggling against Len until he set her on the floor.

Underfoot was a soft carpet-like material, purple to match Tabby's eyes. The walls were silver though, since she was a Silver Lands' princess.

"Your mom did this?" I said softly, pressing a hand to my chest.

"You can redo it," Len said quickly, maybe misunderstanding my tone. "She would have just wanted to keep busy while we were in mortal danger, but she'd understand you wanting to design Tabitha's first room."

Shaking my head, I finally managed to say, "No. Oh my gods, no. This is wonderful, and it goes to show the true family unit we're part of now. Tabitha clearly loves it already."

She had crawled her way across the floor toward the gorgeous bed in one corner. It had no visible base, and instead looked like a larger version of her chair at dinner, a silver cloud. It appeared so soft that I wanted to crawl in there and have a little nap.

Tabby reached out to grasp a small stuffed animal wolf perched on the edge of the bed.

"Mama, mama!" she called, waving it at me.

She remembered our pack, and Glendriel had thought to give her a piece of our new history.

I hurried forward, reaching down to wrap my hands around Tabitha and the stuffed animal. "You're so clever, little one," I said in a ragged voice. "Momma can turn into a wolf."

Len was crossing to join us when a shiver of energy raced over my skin, and I jolted as if being shocked. A second later, I was holding a tiny bundle of fur in my arms.

Len's laughter broke through my shock, as I stared down at a silver wolf pup with flaming purple eyes. "What in the worlds?" I choked out. "How did she...?"

If I ever needed extra evidence that the new version of myself I'd created was more than a "glamour," it had just landed in my lap. My shifter side was a part of me now, and clearly part of Tabitha's story too. "Apparently she's not held to Shadow's rules of shifters either," Len said with a laugh, as he reached down to cuddle our wolf. She was so damn cute as she bounced around on the bed, growling and barking, before Len captured her cheeky butt and hauled her up into his arms. "Okay, littlest love," he crooned softly, "time to shift back so you can get some sleep."

His commands worked on both the females in his life—in completely different ways of course. Tabitha returned to her fae form, and unlike with normal shifters her clothes returned with her. Len moved her over to a small table that matched the bed, finding sleep clothes there that he quickly changed her into.

When she was clean, wearing a purple onesie with crowns across it—I see what you did there, Queen Glendriel—Len placed her in the center of the bed. He reached around her and molded a barrier in the material to ensure she wouldn't roll off.

"Clever," I said with a smile. "She looks so cozy."

Her blinks were already slowing as she clutched the soft wolf. Leaning over next to my mate, we both pressed kisses to her cheeks and told her we loved her.

As we pulled away, watching her fall into slumber, Len started to hum. Soft words followed soon after. "*Little fae, dream of night in the silver streams.*

The world is yours to claim.

The light burns in your lifeforce,

warrior of our hearts.

Burn brightly, and honor the lands, for you will
Be honored."

There were more verses of the journey young fae take to be warriors, poets, and energy wielders. Len's deep rumbling tone had her drifting off in seconds, and as tears burned in my eyes, I knew that this would be one of my favorite moments for eternity.

No matter what happened, I'd treat each magical moment like it might be my last.

Soaking it all in.

Forever.

CHAPTER FIFTY-TWO

SAMANTHA

Even when Tabitha was clearly sound asleep, her gorgeous face relaxed and her breathing even, we remained in her room. Staring. Like the stalkers we were.

"We did good," Len said softly, drawing me into his side.

"She's everything I could have dreamed of," I murmured against his skin. "You both are. It was worth the centuries of isolation to know you were waiting for me at the end. I'd do it all over again just for this moment."

Rumbles filled his chest. "No more talk of being alone." His voice was deep. Hypnotic. It had the animalistic part of my soul rising—she liked when he went alpha.

All of me liked it. A lot.

More rumbles. I barely managed to swallow my moans as he moved lightning-fast and hauled me up into his arms. When we left Tabitha's nook, the door closed silently behind us without the fae even touching it. I wasn't worried about the closed door—I could hear her breathing even as we moved away.

Instead of taking me to the bed as expected, Len walked into the bathroom, two small sconces on either side of the mirror flaring to life. "Tabitha has hearing as strong as ours," he said, keeping his voice low. "So, you're going to have to be quiet. Can you do that for me, mate?"

No. No fucking way. Not a chance.

Just the way he said mate had me wanting to groan out loud, my clit already throbbing, nipples pebbling hard against my shirt so each time he moved the material sent sparks of pleasure into my gut.

"Samantha," he rumbled since I hadn't answered him. He placed my ass on the edge of the sink, his hand sliding down my front, across the sensitive peak of my nipples, before slipping inside the band of my pants. He brushed over my clit, sending sparks through my heated body, before curving his fingers into my pussy. "You will stay quiet, baby girl. For me."

"Fuck, yes. Okay," I sobbed, ready to agree to anything if he just eased the need inside me.

"Good girl," he crooned, and then he used the wetness seeping from my pussy to lubricate his fingers as he pumped them twice inside of me. "Come."

The force of my orgasms had me jerking in his arms, my body exploding as I barely managed to cut the scream off. All that emerged was an almost audible gush of air.

Len's palm pressed against my clit as his fingers fucked me hard, and I scraped at the smooth marble on either side of me. A second orgasm followed before the first was even finished, and I never knew silent screaming could push the pleasure higher and higher, until I was genuinely worried I was about to pass out. Or explode the house with my newfound power.

When I was completely done, he slowly removed the hand from my body, swiping his tongue across the moisture coating his fingers and palm. "Fucking hell," he groaned. "You're going to be the death of me, and I'll go a happy fae."

His mouth was on mine straight after, and the taste of my arousal between us was enough to have my hips jerking toward him. He stripped my clothes off with a wash of prickly energy, and I decided to do the same to him, finally in touch with my own power.

It was near effortless to direct gathered energy now.

His clothes unraveled from his body, leaving all of that toned, bronzed skin on display.

Not to mention an impressive cock jutting up and ready to bring pleasure.

I wanted to taste him, my tongue sliding across my lips, and considering my dominating mate had fulfilled his need for my pleasure first, I decided to make my move. Before I could, though, Len lifted me off the sink, our mouths meeting as heat exploded in my gut once more. Just the taste of him... it fucked with my equilibrium.

He moved us again and water hit me seconds later as Len continued to destroy me, one kiss at a time, worshipping me as the shower beat down on us. His hands moved across my skin, caressing and stroking, and by the time he was done, small gasps escaped my lips as I gripped the wall. His touch slowed over my thighs, the feather-light caresses turned into firm strokes, and I was out of my mind, feeling everything.

All the pleasure. All the love.

Emotions zipped between our bond, until the shower stall was filled with a golden glow. His grip tightened, holding me in place against the wall as he lowered his head, tongue sliding up my pussy. He circled my clit, and my teeth clenched so hard that I'd not have been surprised if I'd broken them.

His tongue slowed, a consistent stroke against all that sensitive flesh, which allowed me to build and build, holding onto the pleasure until it was pulsing at the seams of my skin. I was growing slightly addicted to the sensation when he edged me to explosion.

Of course my best intentions to hold out were shattered as the need inside took over and I started to rock against his mouth, chasing the high and pleasure while torturing myself and refusing to fall over the edge.

We both knew what I was waiting for, and a sob escaped before I silenced it immediately.

"Good girl," Len purred, and my dripping, needy pussy did the same. Swear to fuck, that was where the name came from.

Light burned through Len's hands on my thighs, locking me against the wall of his shower. The water heated until steam surrounded us, but in the next instant it was icy cold against my over-stimulated body. The switch between temperatures had the tremble in my limbs increasing and I was gasping for air silently, still obeying his command.

I'd given myself to this dominant fae, assured that whatever path he chose would be a good fucking one.

As the water grew colder, the heat under his palms felt near burning, contrasting dramatically to the chill of the shower. Len's hands moved until one was cupping my pussy, fingers slipping inside. The heat under his touch continued, and I moved against him, the burn sinking deeper inside me. With that one touch and his power, he pushed me a few inches up the wall so I was no longer standing on my own.

His power pinned my arms and legs on either side of me, thigh parted so I was exposed to him in every way.

"Are you ready, Storm?" he purred. "You're about to come until those pretty eyes close in exhaustion."

His fingers inside me weren't even moving yet, and I was dripping down his hand. Just the thought of orgasming until I passed out was enough to have my energy thrumming.

So much pleasure.

All the time with my mate.

What more could a shifter god ask for?

CHAPTER FIFTY-THREE

LEN

Her breaths came out faster, the tip of her pretty pink tongue poking out from full lips, as she tried to rock against me.

Samantha. My true mate. The one I'd searched a lifetime for.

Now that I had her, I would never let her go.

Needing to taste her, I pushed myself up to reach her mouth, tasting the sweetness of her lips. She opened for me immediately and I was hit with that citrusy burn of her power, filled with fire and life.

Her near-silent groans echoed as my cock bucked between us. The tip ached, a desperate need to thrust inside her almost knocking me down, but I was determined that all the pleasure would be hers first.

My perfect mate. My fucking home.

My all.

Our kiss deepened, and I deliberately left her head free from my control, so she could kiss me back as she desired. Desperately, she sucked against my lips, small mewls escaping her, and I curled the middle finger that was buried deep in her pussy, caressing the spot that sent her crazy.

She was dripping down my hand, and as frustrating as it was not to be devouring her arousal, her lips were almost as tasty. When I couldn't hold off any longer, I released her mouth and lowered myself down her body, finger remaining deep inside.

Stroking slowly, I flicked my tongue out and tasted her. Just like her mouth, only stronger, and I groaned, my fingers stroking harder. "Fuck. You taste like citrus and spice, two of my favorite flavors."

Shifting to adjust my cock, which was so damn hard it was painful, I fought the instinct to slide inside and fuck her until we both forgot our names.

Sam had her mouth open in a silent scream, out of her mind, trying to move against my hold but accepting it at the same time. My tongue moved faster, my fingers did the same, and I had to tilt my head back to watch every minute change in expression as she near her next release. She was a goddess, my mate, with her green eyes, dusky skin, and nipples a slightly rosier version of her skin. The package was enough to bring a fucking fae to his knees.

I'd get on my damn knees for her all day, every day.

Feeling the walls of her pussy clench around my hand, I increased the pace and she released a moaning scream that she cut off a beat later. Her orgasm exploded in my mouth, her release filling my senses, and I ate every drop like it was my last meal.

The nectar I needed to survive.

My addiction was real, and I had zero regrets over my desire for Samantha.

When the pulse in her pussy eased, I used my energy to heat the water once more.

My mouth went back to work, my tongue moving as fast as was possible for me.

Generally, it would have required crystals in hand to reach this speed, but now I had them lining my skin, no additional boost was needed. Through our mate bond, I felt her pleasure building as I pushed her hard and fast, her silent screams visible as she exploded once more.

And we were just getting started.

Some hours later, when the taste of her filled my fucking veins, I finally released my hold on her body—and her pussy— and she slid down the wall to collapse in my arms. Her eyes were closed, her breathing ragged, and she felt near boneless when I lifted her closer.

"Dead," she rasped. "You've fucked me within an inch of my life."

Her mumbles continued until she let out a soft sigh, and no joke, my heart backflipped in my chest at having her close like this. Standing, I lifted her against my body, drying us as I walked into the bedroom. Tabitha's light breathing hadn't changed, and I mentally thanked our baby for giving us some time to bond. Time to heal.

When we reached the bed, I crawled up with her still cradled in my arms. She felt small and frail against me, even though I knew she was a powerhouse on the inside.

My dick complained loudly as I shifted her under the covers. *Simmer down, fucker,* I mentally shot back at it. *We have an eternity. This is about our mate's pleasure.*

There'd be time for my release later, after she rested.

Or so I thought.

As I got in beside her, Samantha surprised me by rolling to her side, fingers wrapping around my shaft, stroking against it before I'd even settled against the soft cushions. "Len," she whispered, prying an eye open a slit as if too exhausted for more. "My turn."

"Little Storm," I started, knowing I'd already pushed her to her limit. But before I could finish my sentence, she'd leaned over and was dragging her tongue and lips across my shaft, opening wider to take the head of my cock as deep inside as she could.

My groan was low, determined not to wake Tabitha, but fuck... if she kept this up...

Deciding to obey her for a change, I tilted my hips to the angle I wanted, and when she was in the right position, thrust as deep as I could. Her gag reflex engaged briefly before she shut it down. Knowing her limit now, I thrust just past it, tingles already pulsing through my balls as I fought not to come yet.

Not that it would matter. With Samantha, I was ready to go right after I blew my load, but the sensation of her tongue and mouth on my cock had me wanting to drag it out. She flicked her tongue and scraped her teeth as her hand continued to stroke in time to her sucking.

"Sam, fucking hell."

She adjusted her gaze to watch me, and I knew there was no way I could hold out any longer. Just the sight of her pink lips wrapped around my cock had me losing control, the tingles rising into the shaft. "I'm going to come," I warned her.

Instead of pulling away, her pace increased, and I grasped the back of her head so I could keep her steady as I thrust once and then again, the buildup an explosion at the end of my cock.

"Samantha," I groaned, coming. She gasped as the first load hit the back of her throat, which only spurred my greedy cock on harder. The second shot was just as strong, and my good girl swallowed the entire lot down.

She sucked me near dry, and when she was done, she licked her lips and smiled. "You taste like caramel," she told me, her grin growing larger. "Like fucking candy. What are the odds?"

Interesting. "Appears our gods knew what they were doing."

She licked her lips again, and I was a little surprised to see her energy renewed... from the taking of my essence it seemed. I wondered if that was part of a normal mate bond, or if it was unique to us, with our unique power combination.

Rolling over, I pinned her down under me, and she was already wiggling against my cock, which remained rock hard and ready. "Home," I rumbled.

"Home," she shot back as I thrust once, pushing past the tight muscles at the entrance of her pussy, until she relaxed, allowing me to slide fully inside.

"Ready, Storm?"

"More than fucking ready, Winter."

Whenever she said my nickname, it was like a shot to my heart. And my cock. She was the only one to ever call me that, and I was already addicted to hearing it.

Losing control, I started to thrust into her, the buildup slow and steady after our previous release. Of course, my mate was a goddess—literally—and all too soon that tingling was back in my cock. Leaning down, I kissed her hard, our essence mingling together, and as she cried out my name, her pussy tightened around me, milking me as hard as her mouth had.

"Fuck," I groaned, before she spasmed intensely, and I came strong enough that I forgot my fucking self. Forcing myself not to collapse on her, my limbs were jelly as I rolled to my back, taking her with me.

"I want this forever," she said softly once she'd caught her breath.

Since we were still joined, I thrust again, dragging another moan from her. "Forever is only the beginning."

Next time I was around the Fates, I was sending those assholes some flowers.

I could finally forgive them for the past, and for the first time the future was brighter than all the jewels in Faerie.

CHAPTER FIFTY-FOUR

SAMANTHA

Len loved me into a coma. I lost track of the number of orgasms I had long before we were even out of the shower stall, and then through the rest of the hours our child slept, we fucked so many times that it had to break some sort of record.

When pure exhaustion dragged us under, I went to sleep thinking about the fact that I'd never been happier or more content, and... how in the heck did Len's cum taste like a candy bar? Not only that, but it had given me a boost of energy, that had me ready to run a marathon. A sex marathon apparently. Sexathon.

Tabitha woke me the next morning. Opening my eyes to her coos was one of the nicest alarms I'd ever had. She sat on Len's chest while he chatted quietly with her.

"Good morning, little one," he murmured, bouncing her as

she waved her hands. Her face was bright, eyes shining purple in the low light of the bedroom, curls springing up everywhere. The picture of health and beauty and power; our baby was going to be one powerful fae when she grew into herself.

"Daddy," she chanted back, repeating it over and over. "Daddy, Daddy, Daddy."

Len's smile was the sweetest damn thing I'd ever seen. Since they were both so wrapped up in each other, I remained quiet and just watched, breathing in this flawless moment. A moment that was almost stolen from me through my own damn choices.

Mera and Shadow had arrived at Clarity right when I'd needed them to, circumventing the fate I'd been trying to create. Their actions sent me down a new path, and now I had the sort of happiness I didn't know existed.

My power thrummed, and when my skin started to glow, golden and mellow, I alerted Len and Tabitha to my state of being awake.

No need for a nightlight when I was around.

Len rolled toward me, depositing Tabby between us, so we were both touching her. As she lay on my chest, giving me a hug, he leaned across and kissed me thoroughly, the faint hint of sugar caressing my tongue.

"Morning, love," he said when we pulled apart. "Waking up to this little one calling out for her mommy was the second-best part of my morning." He leaned in closer and whispered, "The first was waking next to you."

I love you, I mouthed to him, before turning to focus on Tabitha. "You called for Mommy," I said, my teary vision blurring as I reached out and hugged her tiny body.

"Mommy, Mommy, Mommy," she said, as if I'd reminded her.

She babbled and hugged me, and I held her until she

wiggled for me to let go. "I can't believe it," I admitted hoarsely. "That this is the day and life I'm waking up to. I don't know what I did to deserve this, but I'm thankful. So fu—freaking thankful."

Curbing the cursing was never going to happen, and I wondered if Tabitha, Aurora, or Damon would be the first to drop the f-bomb.

"This is our life for eternity," Len told me, leaning back against the cushions.

"Eternity sounds like a plan," I said with my own happy sigh. "And day one starts with a visit to the Capital. Time to deal with Fredrick and company. Then we head to the Library of Knowledge."

No way would we forget our promise to see Mera and have that family dinner. That pack was the second most important part of my world, after Len and Tabby.

Len tensed as his brow furrowed. "Mother has called a meeting of the royal houses. It's time for those fuckers to be punished."

"Will Fredrick have been held in lockup, or whatever you use here?"

He nodded. "Yes, they'll be holding him in power bands so he can't use energy to escape. I suspect that Petre of the Ochre Sands had something to do with this as well. I'm curious if he shows his face today. If he doesn't, the Silver Lands will be knocking on his door."

I wasn't worried. Not now that my power was unlocked. Even if they fought us, we had more than enough strength to take them on. It wasn't just me either, with Len a stronger, jewel infused prince now.

We stayed in bed for another half an hour, the three of us cuddled together like we'd been a family for years. It was a natural bond, and I had no doubt that it would only grow with time.

Queen Glendriel broke the moment when she sent a message to Len, via a small butterfly-shaped piece of blue paper. It zipped under the door and flapped into the room to land on his lap. He opened it quickly and read out loud. "Meeting is soon at the Capital. Will we see you there?"

His energy caressed my skin as he replied on the same paper. *Yes. Give us a few minutes to get Tabby ready.*

The little butterfly zipped off again, and we all hauled ass out of bed. "You shower and get ready first," Len said to me. "I'll get Tabby changed and dressed, and we can feed her as we walk."

"Okay, sounds like a plan," I replied, nodding rapidly. "Let's do this."

After kissing them both on the cheek, I raced toward the bathroom and was done with my shower, teeth, and other morning necessities in about ten minutes. This new version of me was part shifter, with the normal needs of my kind.

The air dried me in the room, so I padded naked to the mirror and applied light makeup—all the items that had been in the guest room were now here in Len's. I had no idea if it was Glendriel or my mate who had moved it all, but either way I already felt like this was my home.

Once my hair was pulled up in a high ponytail, I raced out naked, and found Len and Tabitha already dressed. He'd used magic to clean himself up, but I preferred the "shifter way."

"Be dressed in a second," I said brightly as I hurried past.

Len shot me a broad smile. "Don't hurry on my behalf," he called after me. "This is my new favorite look of yours."

Shaking my head, I couldn't help but laugh. "Right, but are you cool if it's everyone else's favorite look of mine?"

His rumbling growl followed me into the closet. All the answer I needed.

My unlocked Fae energy allowed me to move much quicker and turn lights on without touching them. It was nice to feel like I could blend the two worlds seamlessly. I could be a fae Origin god and also a shifter who preferred the old-fashioned way.

Pulling on a bra, underwear, and jeans, I found a white shirt hanging among dozens of other shirts, which I slipped on, followed by a black leather jacket. The jacket matched the black leather boots I pulled on over my socks a second later. When I entered the bedroom, Len was by the door with Tabby, and she was munching away on some fae fruit.

"She was too hungry to wait," he explained. I loved that she already had Daddy wrapped around her little finger. He catered to her wants and needs, spoiling her whenever he could. After living in stasis for ten years, she deserved every second of his time and attention.

"She's still building her strength," I said, pressing my hand to her back when I was closer. "And growing so quickly. I swear she's bigger and has more teeth than when we put her to bed last night."

Tomorrow when she woke, she'd probably be a full toddler.

"Fae do age quickly in the first few months," Len said, watching her closely too. "But it'll slow as she reaches her full development. We live for near eternity, so the emotional and mental maturity will take longer, even if physically she appears older."

"It doesn't matter," I told him. "Whatever speed she wants to move at is fine by me. I spent too many years terrified she was dying. As long as she's alive, she can grow and mature at whatever speed works for her."

He kissed me, a swift press of lips, and I rose on instinct, ready to be closer to him. There was no time for anything more than a brief touch before we had to leave. When we were outside of the silver palace, across the bridge, and off to the start of the Silver Lands, Len used his power to transport us to the Capital.

Tabitha didn't even blink, or make any sound as we traveled, focused on eating her piece of fruit. I'd thought I was adapting well, but she made it look literally effortless.

When we landed, the crowded platform went silent. The sort of silence that felt almost magical in its completeness. The fae all turned to us, and then, in the sort of synchronicity that I'd never experienced, they bowed. This low, deep bow that had them bent almost in half, their arms and hands remaining at their sides.

Turning to Len, I blinked rapidly as confusion filled me. "What's happening?" I breathed, feeling weirdly frantic but also content.

"The Great Queen has returned," he said simply, and then he placed Tabitha in my arms and took a step back.

Still staring at him with what was no doubt an expression of complete shock, he then bowed to me as well, and I had no fucking idea how I was supposed to react. It wasn't like this used to happen to me before I fled from Faerie. Back then, they'd all mostly taken my role for granted, and I'd never had much reason to interact with the regular fae. I'd just hand out the stones and disperse energy, and they went about their business.

This was different. As they'd bowed, I saw their expressions: grief, happiness, relief, terror. The fair folk were *feeling a lot of feelings* about my return, and it seemed that maybe for the first time they truly understood what they'd lost when I disappeared.

"We already feel the new strength," Queen Glendriel said, as she walked toward me through the silent, bowing fae. I hadn't noticed her until now, the other fae stealing my attention, but when I turned her way I noted how regal she looked today, her silver cloak longer and adorned in jewels, the silver and reven crown across her brow even grander.

Glendriel meant business, and I was here for this kind of queen energy.

Len was the only one who rose from the bow when his mother approached, shooting me that *proud as hell* smile that had butterflies dancing in my stomach. "We realize how much we took you for granted before," Glendriel continued. "Now that you, and the power of this world, has returned, we remember how it was. We won't make the same mistakes again."

I appreciated the gesture, but I wasn't here to be worshipped. "Rise," I called, since they appeared to be ready to stay bowed all day. "Thank you for that greeting."

I switched to Faerie after that, the knowledge of our language mine once more. "We have much to do to rebuild Faerie to its previous strength, but rest assured, we have already taken the right steps. The energy is pure that fills our land, and I will be distributing more power to the royal houses. As soon as we deal with those in our midst who do not want to play by the rules. Power is not to be hoarded or corrupted for personal gain. It's to be shared for the greater good."

During my speech, most had risen, their gazes locked on me. Not just me, but also Tabitha, who was an obvious miracle since my kind couldn't normally have offspring.

"Together," I continued, "Faerie will be stronger than ever."

A cheer rang out, and I sighed as Len's strength and energy settled in behind me. Falling back against him, I released another long breath. We stayed like that until the cheers died off, and then it was time to enter the building.

CHAPTER FIFTY-FIVE

SAMANTHA

When we attempted to enter Parliament House, the stones that scanned us malfunctioned, until Len neutralized their alarm. "They're not sure what to do with your power, Storm." He shot a slow smile my way. "Faerie will never be the same, and I, for one, couldn't be more grateful."

"Me either," his mother said. She was holding Tabitha, cuddling her close, and it was clear the two had bonded during the time we were in the Deep. "I'm one blessed fae this day."

We were all counting our gifts. Me more than any.

"Why are you smiling?" Len asked, watching me closely as we walked through the building.

With a shrug, my smile grew. "I'm happy," I said simply. "Happy in a way that's hard to explain. It's almost beyond words."

His eyes brightened. "I ask for nothing more than your happiness." He leaned in closer and lowered his voice. "Well, that and a few more hours to contain you in my shower."

Gods. I swallowed roughly, pressing a cheek to my heated skin. "I can agree to that," I replied in as low a voice.

The look he shot me was wicked, and I had to work extra hard to not pant as we made our way into the courtroom. The last time I'd been in here, I had been in a comatose state, but today I saw it all. My stage looked the same, along with the seats spanning out around it in an ascending stadium style setup.

All of the royal houses fanned off into their sections, most filling quickly as hundreds piled through the door. The other kings and queens took their spots on the stage, one of the bigger changes since I vanished from this world.

It was fine by me. I didn't want to be their Great Queen any longer.

Everyone had moved on from that role.

Len led me to the silver section, where we were given two seats in the front row. His mother handed Tabitha to us before she made her way onto the stage. There were eight royal houses up there, and they remained silent as they waited for the final two to arrive—the two who had taken it upon themselves to cut the Great Queen's line, to cut off Faerie from their energy.

The two who'd near destroyed this world and possibly others if it had been left to go on.

Fredrick was led into the courtroom a few minutes later, looking disheveled. Four guards were on either side of him, even with him wearing magical bands that bound his powers.

He bore no expression, the blankness of his face unnerving, though his eyes were filled with icy disdain. The guards brought him right to the stage, where he faced the eight royals.

"King Fredrick of the Metallic Meadows, you have been

charged with treason of the highest order," one of the kings said, anger filtering into those words. I didn't know all the leaders now, some of them different to when I'd walked in Faerie. A reminder of how long I'd been gone. "We are here to determine the punishment befitting a fae who almost destroyed the Great Queen and sent Faerie into darkness."

All eyes turned my way and I pretended not to notice, focusing on the stage like it was the only interesting part of this room. Len leaned in close to my ear. "That old bastard, Fernando, would have voted to cut the line no matter what, but will now act as if it was his idea all along to reject Fredrick's proposal."

Len had told me that there had been more than one house who'd argued in favor of cutting the line back during the initial meeting. This king was obviously one of the ones who'd believed that by cutting the line, they'd open up the power grid, and allow another to step in to restrengthen Faerie.

It was my fault that none of them had remembered me, or how my power and role here worked. I'd ensured that when I had to flee, so they'd just made their own assumptions in the many years I was missing. But in truth, no other could ever take the role I was created for. Not even now, with the power dispersed more freely across other gods. I chose to share my gifts with Len, as we were bonded, and Tabitha inherited it through birth—both technically Origin gods—but there was no other who could claim the same.

"She was gone for centuries," Fredrick shouted. "No one in existence could even remember her. Faerie was weakened, which left no other option."

Fernando sneered. "Be that as it may, it was not your choice to make. The vote was not accepted the first time, and we were due back for a second conference on it. You took matters into your own hands." He looked around. "Well, you and Petre. Where is he?"

As if summoned, the doors opened once more and in marched another royal house. Or two, judging by the apparel and mix of colors. They filed into the final two spots, and it was clear that one belonged to Metallic Meadows, and the other was Ochre Sands, Petre's house. But there was no sign of their leader.

"He's fled," a male fae at the head of the group said. "Took off through the night, and we believe has left Faerie."

Len leaned into me again. "He would have had to use the library, and if I know my brothers they'll have taken care of him in a flash."

Of that, I had no doubt. Shadow and the merry band of assholes would not have let any fae prince walk through without question. They also knew that Petre was under Len's suspicions.

"And then there was one," I whispered, eyes locked on Fredrick.

He was watching me just as closely, even with Len's rumbling predatory possessiveness rearing its head. Neither of us looked away, and I wondered if I had the power to strike him down from where I sat. I wouldn't, not yet at least. I'd give the fae a chance to make the right decision, but if they didn't, then I would make it for them.

I was a shifter with a family now, and if you threatened their existence, I would destroy yours.

"Petre will be dealt with in due course," Glendriel said, taking over from Fernando. "For now, we focus on Fredrick and the Metallic Meadows. He's here, and his royal line needs a conclusion."

"We all need one," Queen Gemma of Copper Straits said. "It's time for Faerie to heal and come back stronger than ever."

Agreement rang out around the room, along with small cheers and some clapping. And all the while, Fredrick stared me down like he wanted to rip my face off and suck the life from my body. *Bring it on, fucker.* I was mentally taunting him, because the new me was reborn with attitude, and I had zero fucks to give.

Len got to his feet and interrupted our stare-off by putting himself between me and the fae on the stage. "He broke our rules. He sent Faerie into a spiral of destruction that would have ended all of our lives," my mate said, a rumble in his tone. "He almost killed my mate and daughter. I demand retribution." He let out a low laugh, but there was no humor in that tone at all. "I will allow him to choose if he deals with me or Samantha, but he will face one of us."

What a romantic mate I had. Nothing like a little murder to get the bond flowing between us. But seriously, I was very much into Len giving me the chance to fight my own battle, even knowing he'd be at my back no matter what happened.

"I could deal with both of you," Fredrick shot back, his lips curling in a sneer. The disgust in his eyes, finally dripped across his expression, until he was sneering. "I don't even believe you're the Great Queen. You're so fucking weak."

"It's decided, then," Glendriel said suddenly, not that Fredrick looked away from me. "His punishment will be handled by the ones who he wronged the most. Any fae disagree?"

None on the stage said a word, and I felt the power of the Origin swell in my gut, until flickers of gold escaped my skin. On my feet, I handed Tabitha to Len. "I'll take this one, Winter," I said with a smile, my voice deeper as power filled me.

He took her and dropped a kiss on my cheek, and I moved toward the stage. With each step the power swelled, and it was soon so bright in this room that I doubted most could look upon me. I made sure Fredrick could, though.

That bastard deserved to see what was coming for him.

The sneer faded from his face as his eyes grew wider, and I took a moment to rifle through the many life forces of Faerie until I found his.

When I tugged on it, he gasped, swallowing hard. "You almost killed my daughter," I said conversationally. "You almost took me away from my mate and pack. All through greed and the desire for more power. But why? You were a king, with all the power you'd ever need."

"Were?" he rasped, visibly trembling now.

Ignoring him, I raised my voice. "Do any object? For I am not without mercy. Will any speak up for him."

Not a single voice sounded in the silent room, and Fredrick finally tore his gaze from me to look toward the section of the room where his council and other members of his royal house sat. "How fucking dare you?" he snarled, struggling to get free from his bands.

Still, no one moved or spoke up, and I was done with this bullshit.

This motherfucker was keeping me from the rest of my life.

The cord in my mind snapped. A simple flick of power and his shouts died off mid-sentence. He slumped forward into the guard's hold. They released him a moment later, letting the body fall against the grounds. "May the gods offer you mercy in the next life," I said coldly, before releasing the energy I'd gathered, the golden light fading into my skin, as a calmer vibe returned to the room.

The silence extended for many seconds as the fae focused on the dead king. I could taste their fear on my tongue, and it bothered me less than I'd expected. Seriously, I'd never been their friend before, and I wasn't about to start now. My role was larger in the scheme of their world, and this was a good warning to not mess with the balance.

Len's hand on my back reminded me that he didn't fear me, and Tabby was already reaching for me, either not knowing or not caring that I'd just destroyed a fae without even touching him.

Queen Glendriel cheered, breaking the awkward tension. "Here's to the Great Queen," she called. "Prune out the weak to expose the strength."

With almost no hesitation, the room exploded in cheers, my name chanted in time with the shouts. Even the Metallic Meadows cheered, looking like a weight had been lifted from them with the death of their king.

"Shadow just sent a message through," Len said close to my ear, his mouth brushing my skin and sending shivers down my spine. "Petre was disposed of, so now we just have to bless the new leaders of Metallic Meadows and Ochre Sands. Then Faerie is ready for healing."

Healing sounded like the best plan ever. "Count me in," I whispered back.

Faerie was on its way back to being a superpower, and I was on my way to a bright future.

Sammia might have died the day I shed myself to form a new being, but there was no need to mourn. Fuck knows, Samantha was exactly who I hoped to become one day, and I was embracing every second of it.

For now until eternity.

CHAPTER FIFTY-SIX

SAMANTHA

The council of royals were easily able to handle the blessing and ascension to the throne for the new kings and queens, since their line of succession was already in place.

No need to vote. The mantle was inherited by blood or battle.

"They'll vet them first, and ensure they weren't involved," Len told me as we left the room. "But by the new day, there should be two new royals."

The smaller details like that weren't my role here, so we left them to it, and Len and I spent that night at the silver palace. There was little sleep to be had again as he destroyed my body and soul until I couldn't breathe or remember my own damn name. Our sweet daughter continued to sleep through the night like a perfect angel.

The next day as we made our journey to the Library of Knowledge, my steps were light as flickers of silver and gold energy pulsed through me. Excitement and anticipation filled my soul, and I couldn't be sure if I'd ever felt this particular combination of emotions. Just seeing my pack, and the library again, had me buzzed up.

Even Tabitha noticed, patting my cheeks as we crossed from Len's garden. "Happy," she said, and I leaned over and blew a small raspberry on her cheek before kissing it.

"Very happy, baby," I told her, kissing her cheek again. "We're going to see our family. Your little baby family too."

Tabitha would grow up with the other powerful offspring of the pack. Aurora and Damon would never fear her since they were children of gods too.

"How does your wolf feel now that your other power is unlocked?" Len asked me, and I loved that while we got the sense of each other's emotions, there were still mysteries between us to be explored. It kept life interesting.

"She's the same as she ever was," I said, brushing a metaphorical hand across the dark fur of my wolf. "A true beast, but one who is tempered by the Faerie energy I used to create her. She will be part of me forever, but with my fae power unlocked again, she's more of a spirit friend. I don't have to shift, not that I ever had much urge, and she's not burdened by that because she's a created fae beast, not a true soul from the Shadow Beast." I paused. "If that makes sense."

"Perfect sense," he said.

When we entered the library, it felt a little smaller and less powerful than the last time I'd stood in here. At first, I wondered if the room had changed somehow, before I realized it was me. My new power tinted the world in different shades and reminded me of my place in the scheme of it all.

"It feels less intimidating," I told Len, breathing deeply. "More homey and comforting."

He wrapped me in his arms, holding me and Tabitha for a beat. "This has always felt like home to me. Just as Faerie does. I've never seen a downside to two homes."

There was literally not a single fucking downside.

"Home," Tabitha echoed as she waved her arms and wiggled in my hold. She was getting bigger and stronger, so I had to really hold on to her when she was excited like this.

Len looked more relaxed as he pulled away. I loved the duality of who he was. On Faerie, he was a silver prince, with all the responsibilities that came from that role. He loved his world and fae, but it was clear that here he was calmer and carefree.

I felt the same way, as if here I could simply be Samantha, and not have to worry about the role of the Great Queen. Even powerful fae with responsibilities needed some downtime.

As we wandered out of the fae shelves, there was a small pop, and I almost dropped my baby when another child appeared in my arms. Aurora had zapped herself right to us, and before I could wipe the look of absolute shock off my face—I hadn't even remotely felt her coming, and I could sense energy all around me—she was hugging Tabitha.

Len's laughter broke me free from my surprise. "You look like you're about to throw up and then cry," he told me.

"Fuck," I mumbled. "I almost dropped Shadow's child. And my own."

"Aurora!" Mera's shout rang out through the library as she raced into view. "Holy shit, I'm so sorry." Shadow was behind her, and even though he was walking at just a normal pace, he caught up to his frantic mate. "She keeps zapping herself to our pack members when they show up, and literally no one is ever ready for her."

I could finally laugh now, relaxing as the unease in my chest faded. "I'll be ready for her next time. She apparently just wanted to give Tabby a hug."

Mera clapped her hands, her face clearing of any frustration. "Holy shifter pups. They're so freaking adorable. I honestly would have ten more, but Aurora still doesn't sleep through the night. And she's a boob monster. The combination means I must tap into goddess powers just to function every day."

She didn't look tired. She looked luminous.

"We don't need more babies," Shadow said with a shrug. "Aurora is our perfect child."

Mera rolled her eyes in my direction, before turning to the beast. "Babe, all of our children would be perfect, even if they had four fingers and one eye. I know it's hard to imagine loving another as much as we love A, but it would happen naturally. I promise."

He shrugged again, and it was clear he was all *agree to disagree* on this topic.

Aurora remained where she was, arms wrapped around Tabitha, the pair very content in my hold as I cuddled them close. Shadow's eye was twitching, but it appeared that since his daughter was now choosing who to zap to, he could no longer tear the arms off anyone who touched her.

"So, what's the plans for today?" I asked, conversationally.

Shadow turned to Len first. "The traitor royals of Faerie have been taken care of on your end?"

Len nodded. "Yep. Both royal houses have new leaders, and the council was informed that you disposed of the one who attempted to escape."

Shadow nodded once, and that was the end of that conversation. A little murder chat and we were ready to move on.

Mera rolled her eyes once more before smirking at me. "Males. Simple creatures."

She let out a shriek when Shadow scooped her up in his arms. "We'll be right back," he called, already turning and sprinting away. "Keep an eye on Aurora."

Apparently, he did run if the situation warranted it.

Len and I exchanged a laugh, before we continued deeper into the library. My arms and heart felt stupidly full, a sensation that only increased when Simone and Lucien popped out of a crimson-colored door as we passed by.

"Sam!" she cried, cheeks pink, and huge smile on her face as she raced forward to hug me and the two girls. "I thought I felt your powerful, gorgeous presence here."

I couldn't hug her back, but I smacked a kiss on her cheek as she pulled away. "Here and ready for family dinner. I'm starving."

No rebirth or godlike powers would change the fact that food, and family gatherings to eat food, were my happy places.

"Shadow and Mera will be back in a few minutes," Len said drily. "The beast got a little handsy."

Lucien chuckled, stepping closer to Simone, pulling her against him. "Understandable."

The pretty pink flush in her cheeks made sense now, and since I'd spent the last twelve hours being thoroughly loved by my mate, I totally got it. True mate bonds were intense.

"Oh, we have to show you the new play area," Simone said suddenly, pulling from Lucien's hold to wave us all down a small hall until she reached another door, this one white and discreet. "Mera has been renovating and adding rooms to the library like you wouldn't believe. I haven't even seen Shadow grimace about it. What his Sunshine wants, his Sunshine gets."

I loved that for her as much as I loved Simone's glow of contentment and happiness. There was very little in this world that I enjoyed more than seeing my friends and family succeed and grow into the best versions of themselves. It heightened my own happiness to new levels.

Another version of magic, but this one built on love.

When we reached the door, Simone popped it open and we entered a gigantic space. It had soft padded floors, a dark purple in color. The walls appeared to be padded as well, in a cheery yellow. Near the back corner was a small playground, with swings, slides, a fort, and other play equipment. There was also a reading nook, surrounded by shelves and books, a sandpit—I had no idea how it remained so immaculately clean, but it had to be magic—along with baskets and bins of toys.

"Even though your children are all powerful mini-gods, this is baby proof," Simone said with a huge grin. "And will age with them as they grow and develop. Shadow's energy surrounds it so no one can enter unless they're authorized."

We'd had no trouble entering, so he'd already input our energy into the security.

Lucien was smiling too. "It's a safe space for the kids to run wild with each other, and we can all relax here and eat our meals." He pointed to the top right corner where a huge timber table sat with dozens of chairs around it, designed for large family gatherings.

"Not that we're totally giving up the table in the dining hall," Simone added. "It's the backup."

Moving farther into the room, I placed Aurora and Tabitha down on the soft floor, and they immediately crawled off toward a mat that had blocks and other little puzzles and toys.

"Aw, damn," I breathed, before sighing when strong arms came around me and I slumped back against Len.

"It's a lot," he said, minty breath hitting my senses.

I swallowed roughly. "I'm just not even sure what to do with all my emotions. It's going to take some getting used to."

"For me too," he said with a brush of his lips against my skin. "But first, we eat."

My stomach rumbled in agreement.

We turned to find Simone and Lucien at the table, watching Aurora and Tabitha, who were working together on a puzzle. I wouldn't have been remotely surprised to wander over there and find they'd solved world hunger or some shit. They were most definitely the powerful, change the world types.

We took our seats, and a second later Angel and Reece strolled into the room, looking very regal. Damon was in their arms, and the moment he caught sight of the girls he disappeared from his mother's arms and reappeared beside Aurora and Tabby. The three spent a few seconds hugging and babbling away, before they settled back into their puzzle.

"Well, that's a bit freaking cute!" Angel exclaimed as she took the seat beside me. "We're so lucky that our babies will grow up together."

"You are," Simone said with a wistful smile. "Crimson and I haven't decided if we want offspring yet. We're pretty happy in the honeymoon phase."

Breathless laughter filled the room from the doorway, and we turned to find Mera there, clothes askew and hair a tumbling mess of curls. "Trust me, friend. That phase never ends. Baby or not." She shook her head, like she was trying to clear the sex fog Shadow had her under.

Speaking of, the beast entered a moment later, his energy slamming against all four walls of the playroom.

"What do you think of the room?" Mera asked, settling in beside Simone. "Amazing, right? It's such a great and safe space for them, not that I'm particularly worried, since our kids are all but unbreakable. But it's nice to let them just go crazy and run free."

"They also shouldn't be able to zap themselves out of here," Shadow added.

Extra bonus when you had powerful god babies.

"I absolutely love this space," I told them. "And the kids appear to enjoy it too."

As I said that, there was a whoosh of energy across my skin, and Tabitha was back in her wolf form.

The table grew silent for many seconds before Shadow let out a hearty bark of laughter. "What do you know, the second generation of the pack is going to be stronger than ever."

Understatement of the year.

Another buzz of power, and Tabitha returned to her fae form, while Aurora and Damon didn't blink an eye. They were going to be well prepared for whatever this crazy universe threw at them.

We'd all be prepared.

CHAPTER
FIFTY-SEVEN

SAMANTHA

"Tell us everything that happened in Faerie after we left," Simone said after the eight of us ordered food and settled back waiting for it to arrive. The robot servers apparently knew when they were being summoned, and with special permission were able to enter the room and take our order.

Shadow had thought of everything.

"Sam destroyed Fredrick without even touching him," Len said, proudly.

Mera clapped her hands excitedly, and it was clear that all of us needed a little therapy. But, whatever. We were powerful new gods who didn't kill indiscriminately.

That was the best the worlds would get.

"The fae lifeforce is easy for me to find and sever now," I said with a shrug. "He never denied his involvement, and he wasn't repentant at all. He would try and take more power than he should again, risking Faerie's balance each and every time."

No one else appeared concerned by my actions. If anything, they joined Mera in voicing their agreement. "We've all been in tough situations like that," Lucien said with a shrug. "Sometimes the corrupt must be taken out. Forcefully."

Mera nodded. "Yep, totally agree. The older I get, the less inclined I am to even offer a second damn chance. Not for those trying to destroy the worlds and my fucking family. One strike and you're dead."

Shadow looked like he wanted to drag her out of the room again, but before he could follow through on that thought, Mera leaned forward and slapped her hands on the table. "Before we go any further, there are two very important things we have to discuss. After which, we can settle into the next phase of our lives without any more world-ending bullshit."

A spark of hope lit up around us. I prayed that she was right.

As an Origin god, who I was praying to remained to be seen. Possibly the Sphere of Origin itself since it created all the life before us. Or maybe it was to the combined energy of this pack.

Both were powerful and beyond these worlds.

Everyone waited patiently for Mera to continue. "First, we need to decide on Sam and Len's couple name?"

I blinked at her. "Couple name?"

She nodded enthusiastically. "Yep, every couple in the pack gets one. Shadowshine, DesertAngel, CrimsonBee, and now we need one for you two."

As the couple names flowed from her lips, the others around the table exchanged smiles that spoke of the deep love they all shared.

Mera regarded us carefully, tapping a finger on her chin.

"Slen is not going to work. Neither will Lamantha. That style of name has not worked for any of us. What are your nicknames for each other? I've heard you both use something."

"Winter," I said, meeting his clear, stormy eyes. "When Len feels strong emotions, his eyes turn into a winter storm, silver and grey, filled with power. It's my new favorite color."

Mera's face softened. "Aw, that's fucking adorable. I definitely know the storm you're talking about when he gets pissed off."

"And other things," I replied casually.

As laughter rang out around the table, Len's chest rumbled, and he hauled me up from my seat into his lap. "When you have a stunning and powerful mate, what do you expect?"

Gods, he was going to be the death of me. Just settling against the hard lines of his body, cock jutted against my ass as I wiggled, I almost forgot what we were even talking about.

Mera was a thankful distraction, so I didn't embarrass us both. "What do you call Sam?" she asked Len.

His lips twitched, and those purplish grey eyes caught on mine. "Storm. Like those rare natural phenomena in Faerie that change everything. They breathe in new life and energy, remaking our world, just as she has remade mine."

Mera let out another *awww* as her face softened. "There's really only one option and I'm digging the duality of it."

She paused, and I found myself strangely excited by the prospect of getting a true couple name.

"WinterStorm. Since both of you have a reason to embrace the storms in your life, and the beauty of your bond."

WinterStorm.

Emotions swelled hard in my chest, as the two sides of who we were to each other collided.

Shadow's chest rumbled but he didn't comment. It was hard to tell what he was thinking, but if I trusted my gut, I thought he was happy. This coming together of friends and family was cementing the strength of this pack.

"It's perfect," Len said as he moved his hand, thumb slowly caressing the bare skin between my jeans and shirt. "Our power and our personalities combined."

"Perfect," I agreed.

Our food arrived a moment later, and I reluctantly removed myself from Len's lap. For a second there, I almost thought he was going to refuse, but after a growled *"Later,"* I was sitting on my own chair once more.

All three babies appeared at the table then, ready to eat, just like their food loving parents. As I dished some Faerie fruit onto Tabitha's tray, I remembered that Mera had said there was a second important thing to discuss.

When I asked her about it, she just smirked. "The second thing I have to show you, so let's enjoy our food, and we'll get to that later."

Okay, then, cryptic goddess.

"Where's Galleli?" Len asked as he sipped on a glass of Faerie ale. It smelled like whiskey, but with a richer oaky taste and more of a kick.

Shadow lowered his own glass, shaking his head. "Whatever he felt when we were all bonded in the Deep has sent him off on a quest."

"He says he doesn't want or require a mate," Mera piped up. "But there's a compulsion to assure himself they're safe. Galleli won't take a mate because of his power, but this is a task he can't seem to let go. I hope he finds them and can set his soul at ease."

I hoped so too, especially since they felt as if they were on Earth, and I was curious about the mate of a powerful transcendent being on such a powerless world. Was it another shifter as I suspected? Or... an Origin god?

When we were finished eating, the babies returned to their play, and I looked up to see Mera standing at my side staring down at me with the biggest grin. "Come on," she said, reaching out to grasp my arm and haul me up. "I can't wait any longer."

Stumbling, since she was in too big a rush to let me get up from the chair gracefully, I let her tug me along. When we were almost at the door, she shouted back for Len. "Come on, Prince. The others will watch Tabitha, I need to show you both something."

At the call of her name, our daughter looked up and we both waved. "Keep playing, baby," I told her. "We'll be back in a minute."

She looked between Len and me for a beat, before resuming her puzzle with Aurora.

Len reached us then and we headed out of the playroom and into the library. Mera led us to the door just down from the playroom. It was ocher in color. "This is Angel and Reece's wing," she said with a soft smile. We walked another dozen or more steps and stopped before a silver door trimmed in gold. "And this one is yours."

I ground to a halt. "Ours?" I breathed.

She let out the happiest laugh, hugging me hard. "Yours. This library is our pack's, and I know that all of you have homes and lives on the other worlds, but you also have a home and life here. I designed this with Shadow, and I tried my best to incorporate factors that make you feel comfortable and happy." She shrugged. "It's easy enough to change any parts I got wrong."

My chest and throat were tight, so I couldn't get words out. Instead, I just returned her hug and hoped she knew how grateful I was. Len moved in, his huge frame wrapping around us both. "Thank you," he said, managing words when I couldn't. "This is our home and family, and we love knowing that there's a place here for Tabby and us."

I nodded roughly, eyes blurring. "Yeah, what he said."

Mera looked a little teary-eyed herself. "And you've only seen the front door."

As laughter burst from me, the constricting emotions eased and I could breathe again. It was overwhelming for someone who'd never really had a family to suddenly have so much.

Mera opened the door and then stepped to the side so we could enter first. The first impression was shades of silver and white, with a deep brown timber lining the floor. The entryway had built-in racks for shoes and coats in the front section, leading down the main hall.

"Entryway here," Mera said, stepping into the role of tour guide. "The first room to your right is the library." She shot me a smile so broad it had to be hurting her cheeks. "We all get libraries, because loving books is our first bonding point. And I expect it will be the same for our kiddos."

I suspected the same... wanted the same, really.

We entered the library to find ceilings twenty feet high, and white shelves that spanned all the way to the top. It was already half filled with books, and I was desperate to explore the many worlds on the shelves. "I figured you'd want to fill some of the shelves yourself," Mera said, stepping farther into the room. As she did, the fireplace along the back wall, surrounded by a silver brick hearth, sprang to life. Warmth washed over the room, and I noted the multitude of squishy couches, in silver and gold filigree-patterned material, and a thick white rug that spanned most of the wood floor in here.

"You can play in here later," Mera said with a smile when I hesitated to leave. "And the first book club is at yours, but first, let me show you the rest."

Beyond the library, the hallway opened into a huge kitchen

and dining area, and farther on from that was the living area. It was an open-plan space, and the colors remained in that silver and gold neutral palette. The kitchen was sleek and modern, with so much bench space and storage that I considered learning to cook.

It would be a nice bonding activity to share with Tabby, and even if there was a five-star restaurant here, cooking felt like a decent life skill to learn.

"I love it," I said softly, running my hands across the marble bench. "It's modern but warm, and it feels like home."

Mera's smile was huge. "It's been fun and stressful trying to figure out your individual and couple styles. Not going to lie, I was quietly shitting myself that you'd hate what I did here."

It was far from hate. I loved it. "You did an amazing job. Better than I could have done myself," I assured her.

The dining room had a long, fancy marble table, with carved silver legs. The living room held more couches, a white coffee table, and a television on the wall. "Shadow figured out how to hook on to human and shifter cable," Mera said with a shrug. "No one seems to watch much television, but it's there if you want to."

There was another hallway after that, which led to two bedrooms. The first opened to a pink, silver and gold room for Tabitha. It had a silver bed with slatted sides, and the bedding was pink and gold. Shelves adorned the walls, and there were already some soft toys. Including her very own wolf for this home. Along with some stuffed flowers, that I had to assume were a nod to her dad. "We put a bunch of clothes and toiletries in her shelves and bathroom," Mera said, pointing out the gorgeous wood shelves, in shades of the same pinks and silvers. "If she even uses a bathroom."

"She doesn't need it, but she might enjoy showers like her momma one day," I said softly, pressing my hand to my chest.

"This room is so damn pretty. You did amazing, friend, and I have no idea how to thank you. I owe you so much. So fucking much."

Mera snorted and wrapped an arm around me. "As we've told you many, *many*, times, we don't owe in this pack. We appreciate the kind gestures, but we don't owe anything. This is what family does."

I held onto her tightly. "Thank you for never giving up on me."

Mera let out a shuddering breath. "Everything worked out the way it was intended. I just had to be patient."

It was true. From the moment I'd met her back when she'd had no memory, trapped in a world and future that wasn't hers, Mera had been in a rush. A rush to escape. A rush to find Shadow. A rush into her future.

For the first time, now she appeared content. There was nowhere for her to rush because she'd found her home.

As had we all.

The final room was the main bedroom, and the timber floor continued in here, with three large white rugs to soften up the space. "Welcome home," Mera sighed. "And with that, I'm going to leave you two alone to explore." She waggled her eyebrows suggestively. "We'll be in the playroom when you're done. Tabby will be fine for a few minutes. Take your time."

She pressed a kiss to my cheek, and then Len leaned over so she could reach his. When she was gone, her warm energy fading, I found myself drifting into the room our best friends had created for us. It was huge, with a super-sized bed covered in bedding of a similar gold and silver filigree pattern to the library chairs. There was another fireplace in here, warming the space, and I could see a huge closest—filled with clothing—through one door and a bathroom through a nearby door.

"Mera's our very own fairy godmother," I said with a shake of my head. "Ironically, since we're from Faerie."

As I turned, I gasped to find Len right before me, watching me like I was the only one in the world. No more words were exchanged as powerful energy simmered between us, and both of us broke the moment at the same time, lunging forward.

By the time my lips met his, I was already in his arms, and he used energy to strip our clothes away. In the next heartbeat, he was inside me, and my body was screaming into our first climax.

"Did I say you could come, Storm?" Len rasped, thrusting up, neither of us able to make it to the bed in our need.

"Will you give me orgasms until I pass out as punishment?" I choked out, swirls of my next orgasm already brimming.

"Always, my love," he promised in a rumble, and I let out a sigh of how perfectly imperfect we were.

This was my forever and my home. This was my happily ever after.

End of story. Finally.

CHAPTER FIFTY-EIGHT

SAMANTHA

Clarity pack felt different when we returned the next day. Quieter, with less energy, but also less darkness coating the essence of the town. Len and I walked through, with Tabitha in my arms. Shadow and Mera were there as well, the beast holding his daughter as we moved forward to deal with the pack.

Their time to manage their corruption was done, and with Shadow deciding to pay a little more attention to the shifters, they better hope they'd chosen right.

"Shifters!" he bellowed when we'd reached the center of the small town. "Get your asses out here."

I wandered a few feet away from him, looking down the path toward the main forest, seeing that Alpha Lorenze remained frozen in the same spot, right where I'd almost lost my freedom to his son. Just seeing that area, with the debris of wedding decorations still tangled around his frozen legs, had dark memories attempting to rise.

I was too strong for that to take me down now though. I chose what memories to keep, and that was one I was more than happy to discard.

"That's where it almost happened?" Len asked quietly, his eyes swirling as he followed my gaze. "That's the alpha who hurt you and Tabby?"

Exhaling deepling, I turned away from that direction, facing Shadow and Mera once more. "Yep, that's the asshole." Or what was left of him. He looked very beat up, and I wondered if it wouldn't be kinder to just kill him now.

Rid his presence from the worlds.

Only a few dozen shifters emerged at this point, following the call of their god, stepping into the clearing with their heads hanging low. I knew all of them. They'd been in Clarity when I was, and I wondered what happened to the others. There were none of the stronger members here, including Grant.

"Where is everyone else?" Shadow asked, his voice lowering as he looked between them all.

Floe, who was no more than seventeen, shuffled forward. She ran a shaking hand through her white-blond hair, which was standing up in messy disarray. "They left," she whispered, more of her body trembling as Shadow faced her. "When you told them to clean this pack up, most of the strong ones bailed." Her eyes strayed toward Lorenze. "After they beat up the alpha for a while."

Jack, one of the older males, stepped up to join her. "It's just us left. Those who had no need or place to run to. We've been living like a pack, but without an alpha, and we've had no trouble at all since you left."

Shadow gestured for Jack to step forward, and maybe it was that I moved closer too, but they finally appeared to notice me in their midst. "Sam!" Floe called, eyes widening, but she at least stopped shaking like she was about to fall apart. "You're back. You're... so strong."

I stepped up to stand beside Shadow. "I am stronger. You are as well."

They were. Each of the shifters standing here had been the lower end of our pack, copping the worst of the abuse, but outside of their visible fear of Shadow, they looked stronger and healthier than ever.

Jack stopped before Shadow, and barely flinched when the beast placed a hand on his head. It took a minute for him to rifle through the older shifter's memories, but he seemed satisfied by what he learned.

"This pack is safe," he confirmed. "You can rebuild your ranks slowly, and be selective about who you add, for it seems that you've found a way to govern without an alpha. I'll deal with the shifters who left here and joined other packs as I make my rounds, you can be assured of this."

Jack moved away, relief crossing his face. All of them looked relieved, and as they returned to their homes, a few even waved at me. A final goodbye.

"So, what now?" Mera asked, glancing around. "I think our work at Clarity is done."

"Not quite," Len bit out. "I'd like to avenge my family and kill the alpha, if that's okay with the rest of you?"

Shadow cracked a smile. "Fine by me, brother. I'll absorb his soul when you do and send it to a place that there's no rebirth from."

I remained quiet, holding Tabitha, trying not to allow additional memories of this place to infiltrate my mind. Shadow and Len both turned my way, and I met their gazes, one a winter storm and the other a fiery blaze. "You both do what you need," I said, feeling contented. "I've already moved on from this place, and as long as that bastard can never hurt another, I don't care what happens to him."

I really didn't. It was growth I'd never expected.

Shadow's and Len's smiles grew, as if they'd been given permission to go and be deadly fuckers without consequence. We all knew their mates were the only ones keeping them in check, a truth that was awesome and a little worrying. The worlds had better pray nothing happened to any of us.

Shadow handed Aurora to Mera, before the two hurried off down the path, and we exchanged a knowing smile. "They're enjoying this way too much," she said with a laugh. "Murder should not be on our Sunday to-do list, but these pieces of shit keep popping up, needing to be eliminated."

Wasn't that the sad and scary truth. Just as I went to saying something else, there was a flap of wings nearby, and we both turned to see Galleli landing silently.

Where he'd come from, I had no idea, but the fact that he was on Earth didn't even feel that odd.

"Galleli," Mera said, stepping toward him. "Is everything okay?"

He bowed his head gently. *Everything is perfect. I've completed my task on Earth, and now can return to life as it was.*

I wanted to ask him so many questions. But the main was if he'd found the being with the energy that matched his own.

"Do you have any unfinished business now?" Mera asked, hedging around the same questions filling my mind.

The transcendent shook his head. *I am content. There's nothing more that needs dealing with.*

He stepped forward and pressed a brief kiss to her cheek, and when he pulled away, I could see her blinking rapidly. That had taken her by surprise.

It was even more surprising when he did the same to me.

Thank you, Sam, he said as he pulled away. *You have given me a great gift. Closure.*

With that, and I was no doubt blinking as rapidly as Mera, he disappeared in another flap of wings. It had all taken place so quickly that I wondered if Shadow and Len had even noticed their brother in our midst.

"I have so many damn questions," Mera breathed, before shaking her head at me. "Just all the questions."

A small laugh escaped me. "Yeah, same, but I get the sense that he's closed this chapter, and we need to accept that and move on."

Mera didn't argue with me, and we remained in a comfortable silence for a few seconds before I changed the subject. "What will you and Shadow do now?" I asked, leaning back against one of the towering trees in Clarity's main square. "Travel between all the packs and prune out the evil?"

She took a second to answer, watching the two maniacs below who had just finished obliterating Lorenze into a cloud of death. "We'll sort out the shifters, one way or another," she finally said. "Their unchecked reign on Earth has gone on for too long. The packs are about to change, and if they don't get on board, they'll go the same way as your former alpha."

Into a cloud of death, apparently, never to be reborn again.

"We'll help," I offered, and she shot me a grin.

"I think you'll have your hands full with Faerie and your mate. But I appreciate the offer. It won't take Shadow long to sort these shifters out. He's their god after all."

And hers too, if the look on her face as he made his way up the hill was any indication.

I understood that look, with every part of my being, as Len's brilliance filled my vision. Tabitha held her hands out for him, and as he wrapped his arms around us, I relished the new life coming for us all.

It burned through the haze of even this magicless world, hanging here like a beacon of hope.

New days, new powers, new gods.

Together, we were going to shape the new worlds.

For better or worse.

JOIN my Facebook group to let me know if you want future books in this world. It feels like a very fitting ending here, with just a few loose ends that we could use our imaginations to close ;). But, as always, I'd love to hear from the readers. So... join up below!

www.facebook.com/groups/jayminevenerdherd

STAY CONNECTED

The best way to stay up to date with the Shadow Beast Shifters world and all new releases, is to join my Facebook group here:
www.facebook.com/groups/jayminevenerdherd
We share lots of book releases, fun posts, sexy dudes, and generally it's a happy place to exist.

Next best place is www.facebook.com/JayminEve.Author
And my newsletter at www.jaymineve.com

xx

AFTERWORD

It has been almost two years to the day since I first released Rejected. Two years of living in this world that has stolen my fucking soul.

I love them, guys. I love them all so much that when I'm writing their story, I feel like I'm living in it.

It's so hard in a world like this to ever know the right time to walk away, and to be honest, I only ever planned six books in this series. Two characters were always going to die, but then one of them was just too strong, too broken, too intriguing to let go. Galleli is my silent knight, and while I feel that he has evolved beyond a mate at this point, a part of me still longs to tell his story.

Maybe one day I will, but for now, this is the end of the Shadow Beast world. A chapter closed. My heart bleeding into their lives for the last time. *sobs like a fucking baby*

Thank you all so much for being here through this journey. You'd all make brilliant additions to this pack. We could be powerful badasses together. I'd like that ending.

Thank you to my incredible cover designer, Tamara, for creating absolute masterpieces for this series. These covers are some of my favourite and take my breath away whenever I see them.

Thanks to Jane, my PA, for your support. Not just with this series, but all of them. I appreciate you so much!

Thanks to Tate James and Amo Jones, who kicked my ass into gear in the sprint room so I could get this book out. You two are goddess rock stars. Big hugs.

Thanks to my editors for shining up the old words, and ferreting out all my Australianisms. Except for the ones I like to keep in there for funsies.

Thanks to my error finding badasses. You fucking rock. I'd be lost without your valuable help.

A huge thanks to my Nerd Herd. You're the best group I know. Thanks for sticking around with me over the years. Promise, there's a lot more to come.

A final thank you, with all the love in my heart, to the readers. Yes, you. You beautiful humans, with the fire of Mera, the soul of Angel, the heart of Simone, and the strength of Samantha. Not to mention a few Shadows, Reeces, Luciens, and Lens out there. There aren't words for how I much I love you guys. It's a fucking lot. Take my lack of words for it. LOL.

Let's keep doing this together for another couple decades. Hugs!

Jaymin xx

ALSO BY JAYMIN EVE

<u>JAYMIN EVE</u>

Boys of Bellerose (Dark, RH rock star romance 18+)

Book One: Poison Roses (Release Jan 2023)

Book Two: Dirty Truths (Release Feb 2023)

Book Three: Shattered Dreams (Release March 2023)

Book Four: Beautiful Thorns (Release April 2023)

Demon Pack (PNR/Urban Fantasy 18+)

Book One: Demon Pack

Book Two: Demon Pack Elimination

Book Three: Demon Pack Eternal

Shadow Beast Shifters (PNR/Urban Fantasy 18+)

Book One: Rejected

Book Two: Reclaimed

Book Three: Reborn

Book Four: Deserted

Book Five: Compelled

Book Six: Glamoured

Supernatural Prison Trilogy (Complete UF series 17+)

Book One: Dragon Marked

Book Two: Dragon Mystics

Book Three: Dragon Mated

Book Four: Broken Compass

Book Five: Magical Compass

Book Six: Louis

Book Seven: Elemental Compass

Supernatural Academy (Complete Urban Fantasy/PNR 18+)

Year One

Year Two

Year Three

Royals of Arbon Academy (Dark, complete Contemporary Romance 18+)

Book One: Princess Ballot

Book Two: Playboy Princes

Book Three: Poison Throne

Titan's Saga (PNR/UF. Sexy and humorous 18+)

Book One: Releasing the Gods

Book Two: Wrath of the Gods

Book Three: Revenge of the Gods

Dark Legacy (Complete Dark Contemporary high school romance 18+)

Book One: Broken Wings

Book Two: Broken Trust

Book Three: Broken Legacy

Secret Keepers Series (Complete PNR/Urban Fantasy)

Book One: House of Darken

Book Two: House of Imperial

Book Three: House of Leights

Book Four: House of Royale

Storm Princess Saga (Complete High Fantasy)

Book One: The Princess Must Die

Book Two: The Princess Must Strike

Book Three: The Princess Must Reign

Curse of the Gods Series (Complete Reverse Harem Fantasy 18+)

Book One: Trickery

Book Two: Persuasion

Book Three: Seduction

Book Four: Strength

Novella: Neutral

Book Five: Pain

NYC Mecca Series (Complete - UF series)

Book One: Queen Heir

Book Two: Queen Alpha

Book Three: Queen Fae

Book Four: Queen Mecca

A Walker Saga (Complete - YA Fantasy)

Book One: First World

Book Two: Spurn

Book Three: Crais

Book Four: Regali

Book Five: Nephilius

Book Six: Dronish

Book Seven: Earth

Hive Trilogy (Complete UF/PNR series)

Book One: Ash

Book Two: Anarchy

Book Three: Annihilate

Sinclair Stories (Standalone Contemporary Romance)

Songbird